THE LOST PLOT

THE BURNING PAGE

THE MASKED CITY

THE INVISIBLE LIBRARY
№2 on the *Independent*'s (UK) Best Fantasy
Novels of 2015 List
On *Library Journal*'s Best Science Fiction/
Fantasy Books of 2016 List

"Ms. Cogman has opened a new pathway into our vast heritage of imagined wonderlands. And yet, as her story reminds us, we yearn for still more."   —Tom Shippey, *The Wall Street Journal*

"A dazzling bibliophilic debut."
                    —Charles Stross, Hugo Award–winning author of
                    The Nightmare Stacks

BY GENEVIEVE COGMAN

The Invisible Library

The Masked City

The Burning Page

The Lost Plot

The Mortal Word

The Secret Chapter

The Dark Archive

The Untold Story

THE
UNTOLD
STORY

AN INVISIBLE LIBRARY NOVEL

GENEVIEVE
COGMAN

ACE

NEW YORK

ACE

Published by Berkley

An imprint of Penguin Random House LLC

penguinrandomhouse.com

Copyright © 2021 by Genevieve Cogman

Penguin Random House supports copyright. Copyright fuels creativity, encourages diverse voices,
promotes free speech, and creates a vibrant culture. Thank you for buying an authorized edition
of this book and for complying with copyright laws by not reproducing, scanning, or distributing
any part of it in any form without permission. You are supporting writers and allowing
Penguin Random House to continue to publish books for every reader.

ACE is a registered trademark and the A colophon is a trademark of
Penguin Random House LLC.

Library of Congress Cataloging-in-Publication Data

Names: Cogman, Genevieve, author.
Title: The untold story: an invisible library novel / Genevieve Cogman.
Description: First edition. | New York: Ace, 2021. |
Series: The invisible library novel; 8
Identifiers: LCCN 2021040166 (print) | LCCN 2021040167 (ebook) |
ISBN 9781984804808 (trade paperback) | ISBN 9781984804815 (ebook)
Subjects: LCGFT: Novels.
Classification: LCC PR6103.O39 U58 2021 (print) |
LCC PR6103.O39 (ebook) | DDC 823/.92—dc23
LC record available at https://lccn.loc.gov/2021040166
LC ebook record available at https://lccn.loc.gov/2021040167

First Edition: December 2021

Printed in the United States of America

Book design by Laura K. Corless

To my old school, Christ's Hospital,
where I proudly held a position of Junior Librarian
and spent as much time as I could in the library.

THE
UNTOLD
STORY

From: Kostchei, Senior Librarian
To: Coppelia, Senior Librarian
BCC: Melusine, Library Security
Subject: Inconvenient juveniles

Coppelia,

Don't worry, I'm not going to propose killing Irene. We've been through this before, and I agreed with you. We both know how the story goes: the hapless innocent finds out that she's actually the child of someone ridiculously dangerous and evil, at which point her employers attempt to kill her "because of the danger she presents" and it all goes horribly wrong and she turns against them. I have absolutely no desire to repeat that sequence of events. I'm not going to suggest disposing of her—no matter how much I'm tempted.

Yes, I'm tempted. The girl's had a meteoric career as a Librarian and demonstrated that she's very capable, but she's also a huge flaw in our defenses. What happens if her father *does* somehow manage to use her as a weapon against us? How much is one Librarian's life worth, against the security of the entire Library?

But as you've pointed out repeatedly, we both know how that narrative ends. And here in the Library, even if our outer layer is order, we have an inner heart of chaos. We read too much for it to be anything else. Unjustly betraying a loyal servant—or at least, doing so without trying all other alternatives first—will ruin us all.

So . . . let's consider where we stand, and what our alternatives are.

She knows her father is Alberich (though hopefully, not who her mother is). *He* knows as well, now. She's in a state of mind where she might try anything—even attempting to assassinate him. The Library's been trying to kill him for several hundred years now and he's managed to escape our best attempts, but you know how these children are. They're always convinced that they're the Chosen Ones and will somehow succeed where hundreds of others have failed—even when it's something as dangerous as trying to kill the greatest traitor the Library's ever known. Honestly, when someone's committed multiple murders, theft, kidnapping, sale of Library information and has tried to destroy the Library itself, you'd think that anyone sensible would take the hint and stay well away from them.

However, refusing to tell Irene anything will just push her into overt disobedience. We need something a little more subtle. We need a distraction to keep her busy for a few weeks while we work on something longer term.

We have that treaty signatory request from the Fae underworld boss in world B-268. Irene was the one who went on that heist with his subordinate, which makes her the logical person to handle negotiations. And she *is* the treaty representative from our side. No doubt she'll suspect that we're giving her the work in order to keep her busy—she's an intelligent girl. (I'm still open to debate on whether she's a *sensible* girl.) From our reports, he'll take a month or so to make up his mind, which will have the additional benefit of keeping her somewhere safe. I'm sure you can word the introductory letter that goes with her so that her host will keep her out of the way and under wraps.

And in the meantime, you can think about what you're going to say to her when she gets back. Yes, I'm dumping this in your lap. Yes, I'm being completely unfair. Yes, you are going to be stuck with it. You are one of the few people she really trusts. Any explanation from me—or from other senior Librarians—is going to sound self-serving. You're the one with the best chance of persuading her to save her own life by staying out of trouble. Remind her that her life isn't just her own—when she made her vows to the Library and received her Library brand, she made the choice that she belonged to the Library. Getting herself killed in a futile attempt at revenge will be wasting everything else she's done. Tell the brat whatever you think will work. Just keep her within bounds, and then with luck we can all avoid unnecessary harshness.

Also, hurry up and get over that pneumonia. We don't have time for sickbed drama. The letters from the Cardinal and from Ao Guang about the missing worlds are disturbing—we're still understaffed, and there's too much to do.

Does it seem to you that we spend too much time playing politics these days?

Yours,
Kostchei

PS—You wouldn't have so many health problems if you actually went to sleep at a sensible hour.

PPS—Kindly send back that copy of Louisa Alcott's *Attack of the Zombie Brides*, I want to check a reference.

CHAPTER 1

The snow hissed against the windows, flakes visible in the harsh spotlights which ringed the building. Irene could dimly make out the well-groomed gardens outside and the faint outline of the ornamental lake—and beyond that the guard outposts, the high walls, and everything necessary to keep this manor house and estate private and undisturbed. The trail of darkness across the white lawn—fresh blood, left behind by the corpse which had been dragged across it—was rapidly being covered by the snow.

She couldn't see the Siberian dire wolves, but she'd been assured they were out there. To be honest, she wasn't even sure that dire wolves were or could be Siberian, but as the saying went, *Don't contradict an autocrat on his own territory unless you have either a very good reason or a very secure escape route.*

At this precise moment she didn't have either of those. While the mansion did have a library, it was one of the few rooms she was strictly forbidden from entering. A logical precaution—after all, they knew she was a Librarian, and she could use a smaller library in any of the alternate worlds, like this one, to enter the secret interdimensional Library that was her home. A place that was, at the moment, very far away.

Suppressing a sigh, she turned away from the window and wandered back toward the fireplace. Newspapers were available—foreign ones like the *Times* or the *Observer, Le Monde* or the *Wall Street Journal,* as well as Russian ones—and she could always do the crosswords or read about the current state of the world while she waited for the master of the house.

Irene wasn't a prisoner—but she wasn't exactly a guest, either. She was an intermediary who'd been summoned to do a job, and while that secured her a safe-conduct, it also meant that her personal wishes weren't priorities. It wasn't so much the enforced inactivity or even the dangers of the locale that were driving her up the wall: it was the constant circling of her mind around the possibility that most of her life had been a lie.

She'd found out that Alberich, oldest and most dangerous traitor to the Library, might be her father. She'd come back from her latest mission desperate to know more, with urgent questions for all the senior Librarians, who must have been covering it up. She'd sent messages to her parents—the ones who'd raised her, whom she considered her *real* parents—to ask what they knew. But she'd barely had enough time to get her most recent injuries bandaged when she'd been sent on this solo job, well before any answers could reach her. Words such as *desperately urgent* and *vitally important* had been used; she hadn't been quite ready to disregard her orders and refuse to go.

Her friends had understood that. Kai—ex-apprentice, dragon prince, friend, and lover—had promised to find out anything he could. In the meantime, she was stuck on this mission with no way of leaving, and no way to answer the questions which overshadowed her entire life.

To add insult to injury, it wasn't even a mission to collect a book—her usual sort of mission as a Librarian was acquiring a unique book (legally or not) from a particular world. The Library's collection of stories allowed it to maintain the balance between all the alternate worlds; Irene wasn't entirely clear how it worked, but it demonstrably *did*. This, on the other hand, was a matter of *politics*, something on which she'd been spending far too much time recently. Something which the Library itself seemed to be far too involved in of late . . .

The door swung open, and she hastily modified her expression to one of mild curiosity, looking up from the newspaper to see who it was.

The elderly lady who entered was almost the complete opposite of the large man who held the door for her. He was muscled and blonde, with bulk that even a well-cut suit couldn't hide; she was petite with waved white hair and wore an artfully rustic outfit which Irene identified as genuine silks and velvets. Irene suspected that the two did have one thing in common, the same thing as everyone in the house. Crime.

The man nodded to Irene as she rose politely from her chair. His name was Ernst, and while she wouldn't have said she knew him *well*, she was sure that she could trust him. He was one of the henchmen of the Fae master who owned this dacha—this Russian country estate and second home—and he was responsible for Irene's visit. "Sorry you've had to wait," he said in Russian. "The boss is busy."

"These things happen," Irene replied in the same language. "I understand he's a very busy man." After all, being an archetypal crime boss who coordinated activities across multiple worlds was the sort of thing which occupied a person's time.

Ernst shrugged. "Only two executions so far today. Traitors never put him in a good mood."

The woman's eyes narrowed as she considered Irene, taking in her neat but only modestly expensive clothing, her tidily cut short hair, and her generally sober appearance. A good trouser suit was accept-able in many parts of the twentieth or twenty-first centuries: easy to pack and very convenient for running away in. "Ah. An independent? Or are you representing an organization?" She tilted her head to look up at Ernst. "I wasn't told about her."

"Madam, you know the boss doesn't like me telling anyone about anything," Ernst said. "It's not in the job description."

"The *Observer* crossword is still available," Irene said helpfully. "Or do you prefer sudoku?" However harmless the woman looked, she must be as dangerous as everyone else in this house.

"I'd prefer conversation. But I don't think I'm going to get it."

"There will be drinks after supper for those who are still alive," Ernst rumbled cheerfully. "In the meantime, the boss has time for Miss Winters now."

"Then I won't keep him waiting," Irene said, following him out of the room.

The house itself was two things: expensive and defensible. It was as if someone had gone to an architect and said, Give me something that looks like pre-Revolution French royalty's worst excesses, but laid out strategically so my private guards can fill any intruders so full of lead that they could be used for church roofing. Ernst and Irene passed several loitering pairs of guards on their way, all of them on the alert. It made Irene rather glad she wasn't trying to steal any books from here.

"The boss is not in the best of moods," Ernst said quietly, as they approached a heavy wooden door flanked by two alert-looking guards. "Mind your manners, Librarian girl, and don't expect any decisions tonight."

"I'm touched by your concern," Irene said, only half joking.

"Concern, bah. I was the one who advised in favor of your visit. I do not want to be in trouble because of it."

"Enlightened self-interest is one of my favorite motivations. I can work with that."

"Good. I was afraid you were still sulking because you couldn't bring dragon boy with you." The invitation here had been for Irene alone, with specific instructions that no other "assistants, bodyguards, assassins, handmaids, secretaries, bedwarmers, experts, or other supernumeraries" were permitted.

"I'm not the one who's sulking," Irene said. "He was. He's sure I'll get into trouble without him."

"Bah. From what I have seen of you both, I have no doubt he will get into just as much trouble without you."

"That's not exactly reassuring, Ernst."

"Reassuring is not my job. Brutal practicality is. I would say that you should try it, but . . ." He shrugged. "Today you are a diplomat, Librarian girl. Be diplomatic."

One of the guards gave them a nod. Ernst opened the door and Irene walked in.

It was a room designed for secret discussions and interrogations. The overhead lights had been turned down, leaving the ceiling and corners in shadows, and the flames leaping up in the fireplace warmed the room but did little to illuminate it. While there were a couple of freestanding lamps by the armchairs near the fire and another over by the desk in the corner, they were arranged to light the area near them rather than to make it easy for intruders or visitors to inspect the surroundings. Irene cataloged the room with the experience of a spy and the personal interest of someone who wanted to stay alive and might have to escape in a hurry. Four people—one man at the desk, two bulky figures, gender uncertain, in the far corners, and most importantly, the elderly man in one of the armchairs by the fire. A couple of white tiger skins were spread across the dark wood of the floor, their glass eyes glittering as they caught the light.

"Come in, Librarian," her host said. "You have my permission to sit."

"Thank you, sir." Irene preferred to begin meetings politely and get ruder if the situation demanded it: it was much more awkward to start off by being rude and then try to raise the level of courtesy when you realized that you were in trouble. She approached the fire, conscious that everyone was watching her, and took a seat in the waiting armchair. "How should I address you?"

"You can call me . . ." He paused, considering. The firelight made a relief map of his wrinkles, hiding any genuine expression behind the mask of extreme age. Liver spots stained his bald scalp, and his hands were gnarled and arthritic—though still, Irene thought, quite capable of firing a gun. "'Boss' would be inappropriate, wouldn't it? After all, you're not working for me. But I've moved beyond the necessity for an actual name. Why don't you call me . . . Uncle."

Beyond the necessity for a name, you say? I don't think that's completely accurate, Irene decided. She'd met quite a few Fae by now. As they grew in power and fell more deeply into the patterns of their narrative archetype, they discarded or hid their original names. First they used pseudonyms, then they moved all the way to titles such as *the Cardinal* or *the Princess* as they reached the peak of their power. By the time they'd achieved *that* level, they were walking embodiments of whatever stereotype they'd chosen to become. The world bent itself around them to make their stories come true.

Her host wasn't quite there yet. The name she'd been told earlier, "Mr. Orlov," was a pseudonym rather than a title. Still, she didn't want to offend him. The sooner she could get this done with, the sooner she'd be out of here. "As you wish, uncle. Thank you for being kind enough to receive me here as a guest."

"It's always pleasant to have young people like yourself around the house," he said, his tone appropriately avuncular. He leaned forward. "Now, Librarian. How do I know you're not here to betray me?"

That was . . . rather more direct than Irene had expected. She answered with similar frankness. "What would I have to gain by that?"

He leveled a finger at her. "You have a reputation, Librarian. I've seen the files on you."

"What a shame that I never get to," Irene said regretfully. "Whenever I ask for them, people start talking about *burn before reading* and *over my dead body* and so on."

"Personal name, Irene. Aliases including Irene Winters and Clarice Backson. One of the Library's most efficient thieves, recently turned diplomat in line with the Library's interesting new policies, and currently the Library treaty representative on this three-member commission for the dragon–Fae peace treaty."

Irene spread her hands. "I'd have thought you'd appreciate efficiency, uncle."

"Depends on whether I can use it or not. If it's being turned against me, then that means you're my first target."

A cold thread of nervousness spread its way down Irene's back, mapping every inch of her spine. She'd thought this was a comparatively safe assignment—though negotiating with a powerful Fae was never truly safe. "I thought you asked for me personally, uncle. Why invite me to your home if you think I'm an enemy?"

He chuckled, and the sound was more resonant than his age would have suggested. "Maybe I want to see how serious the Library is about getting people to sign their 'peace treaty.' If they're prepared to send one of their best agents, then I'm prepared to give it some consideration. Assuming you're the real Irene Winters."

"Rather than an assassin traveling under her name, here to kill you and place the blame on the Library?" Out of the corner of her eye, she saw the two watching bodyguards tense. She'd hoped the joke might amuse him, but it clearly hadn't amused them.

"Are you?" He paused. "I understand the situation if you are, but in that case I need to reconsider my attitude—and whether you'll be going out of here with an employment contract, or feet first."

Irene tried to pick her way through the possible answers to the question. *Remind me not to make clever jokes with people who can snap their fingers and order me killed.* "I'm a thief and a spy," she finally said, "not an assassin. And I'm definitely Irene Winters."

"Good, good. So let's consider what you can offer me." His tone was cheerful enough, but Irene could hear the subtext beneath it. *Show me that you're not wasting my time.*

She put on a smile. She was good at smiling, especially when faced with people who could kill her. "The Library's position is that a truce is good for everyone. We're not making any judgments about previous hostilities between dragons and Fae, and we freely admit that many of them may be entirely justified. What we're trying to stop is the sort of random aggression which doesn't achieve anything and which causes needless collateral harm and destruction."

Specifically, harm and destruction to *humans*. Not to the dragons, creatures of order who could command the elements and who could simply fly off to another world if their power base was destroyed. Nor to the Fae, creatures of chaos and narrative archetype, who'd be almost as happy with a dramatic loss as with a dramatic victory, so long as it was entertaining. It was the humans in the middle, spread across the countless alternate worlds, who went about their lives without knowing that they were being used as pawns by both sides. Stabilizing the alternate worlds and protecting the humans in them was the Library's mission—previously performed via stealing unique books from those worlds, but now with a side option of diplomacy.

In fact, it felt these days as if diplomacy was the main option and stealing unique books had turned into the sideline.

Irene wasn't fond of diplomacy, whether or not she had a talent for it. She would far rather have been stealing books—and even more so reading them. But it was important to remember her job's ultimate aims, rather than just focusing on the methods. "Naturally we wouldn't ask you to refrain from hostilities against someone who had attacked you. But if they were a member of the other faction and they'd signed the treaty . . ."

"Reality-twisting interfering zmei, you mean," her host put in.

Irene recognized the term from Russian folklore—a dragon or giant serpent. She nodded. "We'd ask that under those circumstances, you submit your grievance via the treaty representatives so that their own side can punish them. You know how hierarchical the zmei are." *Use the other person's own language and terminology to convince them that you're on their side.* "Consider how you'd react if one of your own subordinates offended someone with whom you'd made a deal. I know a number of zmei who'd behave similarly."

"You mean they'd send me a few of his body parts as proof of how sorry they were?"

"Entirely possible," Irene said without blinking. "My point is, it's tidier if everyone deals with their own people's misbehavior—causing earthquakes, starting wars, assassinating monarchs, whatever—rather than having it develop into an issue that involves entire worlds, and dragging even more people into it."

"And does your list of misbehavior include stealing books?" He leaned forward. The fire chose that moment to leap up, its heat flaring like a warning.

Irene folded her hands primly. "The Library is a signatory to the treaty. Naturally we wouldn't steal from anyone who's signed it. We might ask, or offer a deal, but we wouldn't steal. Our word is our bond."

"Yes. I've been told about that too. You swear to something in your Language, you're bound to it."

"Just as a Fae who's given their word will keep that word," Irene countered.

He nodded. "We have much in common, I think, Irene Winters. Keep on talking. I'm interested."

Though not interested enough to make any commitments that day.

Irene rolled over in bed, stared up at the ceiling, and brooded. She knew that ongoing negotiations were better—*far* better—than an outright refusal, but it was still infuriating. She was stuck here for at least another day, possibly several days, until her host came to a decision. Maybe even weeks. Or a month.

She was trapped by her own sense of duty. It didn't take a great detective to realize that she'd been maneuvered into this position to keep her out of the way and stop her asking awkward questions back in the Library. *Are they afraid that I'll betray them just as my father did? Or do they think I'll find out something too dangerous to reveal?*

And if so, what secret could be so dangerous that the Library would sacrifice her to keep it hidden?

Sleep would have been the sensible thing, but her dreams were full of nightmare images. Justifiable ones—she didn't need a psychologist to tell her why Goya's *Saturn Devouring His Son* was becoming a frequent motif every time she closed her eyes—but not helpful. Even worse were the ones which had her walking through the Library amid a tide of blood that rose to her knees and kept on rising, or the ones that had Kai shouting that she was her father's daughter and always would be, and the Library itself was damned for the sins of its founders . . .

Moonlight leaked in round the edges of the curtains: the snowstorm had stopped, and now the world outside was almost as well lit as by day, full of silver light and impossibly black shadows. She'd been brought here by a Fae messenger, using their trick to travel across worlds and walk from one to another, but any normal human in this world trying to reach this dacha would have a difficult time of it.

Her train of thought was abruptly broken as something on the wall to her left *shifted*, barely visible in her peripheral vision. She lay still, keeping her breathing regular, and squinted out of the corner of her eye, trying to determine what she'd seen.

The line of shadow along one edge of a wardrobe had increased. A second later it happened again, silently, without even a betraying creak of hinges or the sound of footsteps. Someone on the other side of the wall was trying to sneak into her room.

She should have been more frightened, but honestly, the prospect of action—*violent* action—was a welcome relief. Still feigning sleep, she waited for the wardrobe to swing fully forward and let whoever it was into the room. *They* might need to keep silent, but she was going to raise the roof once she'd disabled the intruder. It would be interesting to see who was trying to kill her.

Then the fragmentary moonlight caught on the pale hair of the man who'd just stolen into the room, and she saw who it was. With a sigh she sat upright in her bed. "Hello, Lord Silver," she said. "What are you doing in my bedroom?"

CHAPTER 2

Her motion and words took the Fae entirely by surprise; he started back, flattening himself against the wall.

Irene took advantage of his confusion to turn on the bedside lamp while he was staring in her direction—anything to keep him off balance. "I'm fairly sure this isn't what my host had in mind when he promised me safe-conduct." Bad enough to have *anyone* sneaking into her bedroom at night, but when it was a Fae whose archetype was that of libertine seducer, and whose silver hair invited caresses, whose golden skin ached to be touched, whose lips silently promised unholy delights, whose every word lured listeners to his bed . . .

Unfortunately, he was good enough at it that she deliberately had to repress this type of unconscious thought. The Library brand across her back itched, resisting the force of his nature.

He raised one hand, shielding his eyes against the sudden glare of light. "Don't scream, Miss Winters. We'd both regret it."

He'd called her *Miss Winters* rather than one of his annoying pet names, like *my little mouse*. That unfortunately meant it was serious. "Don't I have enough crises on my plate right now?" she demanded. "Why are you crawling into my bedroom and bringing me more of them?"

"I object to the word 'crawling.'" He slid forward to seat himself on the side of her bed. "A gentleman doesn't crawl. Insinuates himself, maybe . . ."

He was in evening dress, though his bow tie was untied and hung loose. Irene was uneasily conscious that she was only wearing a silk nightgown. At this precise moment, she'd have preferred heavy tweeds, or even plate mail—something *solid* between his eyes and her flesh. "Lord Silver. Please explain why you've *insinuated* yourself into my bedroom."

A little of the mocking desire left his eyes. "I needed to talk to you in private. That would have been impossible in the world where I usually live, and where you're Librarian-in-Residence—too many eyes are watching both of us. When I found out you'd been sent to visit Mr. Orlov here, I decided to take advantage."

"Your next words had better not be 'of you,'" Irene said firmly.

"Shall we just say 'of the situation'? That works for both of us."

"Just explain. Please." Irene wasn't too proud to ask for a direct answer.

"Easy enough." He leaned forward, beautiful in the lamplight, a work of seductive art sitting on her bed. "I want you to keep quiet for the time being about Catherine being able to enter the Library. Tell your seniors if you have to, but don't mention it to outsiders."

Irene frowned. "I thought the whole point of apprenticing her to me was to enable her to do that." Catherine, Lord Silver's niece, was quite unlike him—Fae, but utterly uninterested in romance or sex, and passionate about the idea of becoming a librarian by archetype and a Librarian by vocation. Normally Fae couldn't enter the Library, but Irene had accepted her as an apprentice and agreed to try and get her inside—and she'd succeeded.

"There's trouble brewing." He raised a hand to cut her off before she could ask for details. "No, I don't know what's going on—it's like being at the edge of a crowded room and aware that something's happening at the center, though you can't see what it is or hear it over the noise of the crowd. Worlds have vanished. Some people aren't talking to me who should be, and others are saying things which are supposed to worry me. I'm not sure what's happening, but for now I want—no, I *would like* you to keep your sweet little lips closed when it comes to the question of where Catherine is and what she can do."

This was serious enough that Irene could put aside her distaste for his manner and his choice of words. "What do you mean, 'worlds have vanished'?"

"I mean that some worlds just aren't where they're supposed to be, and nobody knows what's going on, if it's deliberate or permanent, or anything useful. Unfortunately there's a lack of information to go with the lack of worlds. Now can we get back to the more important business of my niece?"

Some news was never good news—and worlds vanishing was definitely bad news. Irene resolved to ask for more information when she was back at the Library. "And is it Catherine who'd be in danger, or you?"

"Good question. She'd be at risk of disappearing. Too many people look for a weapon when trouble's about to start, and they'd see her as a potential weapon. One of my kind who can enter and leave the Library at will? Far too tempting."

Irene decided not to mention that it wasn't quite a case of *enter and leave at will*. Catherine had to be dragged into the Library by a Librarian who knew her true name—which at the moment was limited to Irene. But would any kidnappers necessarily believe that?

"You assigned her to me," she said through her teeth. "You gave me the job of getting her into the Library. Why did you do all that, if it was going to put her in so much danger?"

He spread his long, graceful hands. "Because she wanted so very much to be a librarian and to get inside your Library. Oh, I admit there may have been a bit of political interest here and there . . ."

"Yes, I imagine that being the uncle of the only Fae who could access the Library *would* have its political advantages," Irene muttered.

He reached out to touch her chin, turning her face directly toward him. "It was what she wanted. Have you ever been able to give someone their heart's desire, my little mouse? Do you realize how tempting it is?"

Irene ignored the urge to lean into his touch; she caught his wrist, forcing his hand away. "Well, you shouldn't ask me to do something and then complain when I do it!" Her anger was deliberate, a tool to fight the compulsion to press herself against him. "And what about Lord and Lady Guantes? When they showed up, you simply ran and left me to look after her."

"A job at which you succeeded remarkably well. Which reminds me—I owe you a favor for dealing with them, Irene Winters. You may call it in at your leisure."

That surprised Irene. She certainly *agreed* that he owed her a favor for getting rid of their mutual enemies, but she hadn't expected him to acknowledge it. "So noted," she said.

He snapped his fingers. "Which reminds me, I have something for you. A letter." He produced a small folded note from an inner pocket, sealed with plain wax. "I don't know who it's from or what it's about, but I promised to pass it on to you. Part of the deal was that it wasn't harmful."

Irene eyed the letter somewhat dubiously. "You're absolutely *sure* it's not dangerous?"

"I'd hardly have been carrying it around with me if I thought it was. Also, I want you to do me a favor—why would I give you something that might kill you?"

Irene couldn't disagree with two such strong points of self-interest. A little nervously, she took the note and broke the seal. Silver leaned over to see the contents, but she tilted it away from his gaze.

A chill touched her skin and raised the hair on the back of her neck as she saw the signature. *Alberich.* "Who gave you this?" she demanded furiously.

Silver flinched back from her; apparently her tone was sharp enough to draw a genuine reaction from him, not just a sensual affectation. "A friend of a friend," he said flatly. "No names, no details. That was part of the deal. I *can't* tell you any more than that."

"It's from Alberich. He was working with the Guantes and trying to kill us—or haven't your spies caught you up on that yet? I thought he was trapped in his own world and he couldn't leave it. How did he send me this letter? Are you *sure* you can't tell me anything?"

He chewed on his lower lip as though testing some inner boundaries. "I can't," he finally said. "Whoever drew up the deal must have expected something like this. What does it say?"

Irene glanced at the note again. It wasn't long—just a few lines.

Irene,

I realize that you won't trust anything I say. However, you should be careful who you do trust. Certain people are going to be afraid that you know too much.

Have you heard about the missing worlds? I know who's behind it. I know why. I can tell you a great deal—but you'll need to talk to me for that to happen.

There is a rot at the heart of the Library. Every web has a spider.

I'll be in touch. Don't get killed.

Alberich

He didn't sign himself "your father" or anything like that, which was good; it would have been just one provocation too many. She'd settled down for a quiet night's sleep, and now she had Lord Silver on her bed and a note from Alberich in her hand. *So much for getting away from things.*

Irene's stomach cramped with nausea. She wanted to throw up. She wanted to tear the note into a thousand pieces or throw it into a fire. She wanted to curl up and hide under the sheets. Dear gods, she wanted Kai here with her—not to have him hold her and tell her it would all go away, but because she could look at him and know she had someone she could absolutely depend on.

But she didn't have Kai—she had Lord Silver, and she couldn't afford to show weakness in front of him. He might currently be an ally, but he wasn't a friend by any stretch of the imagination. Deliberately she refolded the note without letting him see it, and tried to slow her heartbeat by will alone. "Nothing important," she finally answered his question. "Only the usual."

He snorted. "I may not be a Librarian or a great detective, my little mouse, but I'm not blind. For what it's worth, I regret causing you distress."

Irene decided to change the subject. "So tell me—*without* calling in that favor—how on earth did you get into my bedroom here in the first place? Can't Mr. Orlov be trusted?" Anyone who allowed Silver into her bedroom by night was significantly unsafe.

Silver waved a vague hand. "I know a person who knows a person who told me about this secret passage, and Mr. Orlov doesn't know that anyone knows. So let's not get anyone killed by mentioning it, hmm? I'm sure a *nice* person like you wouldn't want to be responsible for an expanding number of deaths."

"I'm not a nice person," Irene muttered. "Kindly remember that."

"Nonsense. You're an ethical person—and I find that very convenient in cases where I absolutely have to manipulate you." His smile was pure selfishness. "I came here in the first place because Mr. Orlov is making deals. He won't have told *you* this, but there's currently a vacancy at the very top for what I've heard you call his 'narrative archetype.'" He handled the words with distaste, like a translation which was technically accurate but failed to convey the true meaning. "Call it the Don, or the Boss, or the Man, or whatever you like, but the person who previously was that is gone, and now all the people who see themselves in that role are stepping up to take the position. Or in some cases, to make sure their worst enemies don't take it."

"That explains why he's chosen this moment to consider signing the treaty. He wants to avoid any serious disputes with the dragons—or the Library," she added out of loyalty, though she knew the dragons were a far more serious potential enemy for the Fae. "It'll allow him to turn his full attention to any Fae enemies." It also explained the other visitors in the mansion, and the talk of "traitors."

"See how helpful I'm being?" Silver's smile vanished. "Now do I have your word that you'll keep silent about Catherine?"

"You don't have my *word*," Irene said carefully. "I can't make any promises. But I'll try to keep the information quiet for now, and I'll get her into the Library once I'm safely back from here. She'll be safe there. You might want to speak to Kai and Vale as well. *They* both know." Kai's brother Shan Yuan also knew, but given that he was virulently anti-Fae, the odds of him telling any Fae about it were low to nonexistent—she hoped.

"The prince and the detective are far more likely to listen to you than to me," Silver complained. "The sooner you're finished here, the better. How much longer do you think you'll need to persuade—"

His voice was cut off by the chatter of a machine gun somewhere nearby in the house.

CHAPTER 3

✤

Silver bolted like a hare, heading for the secret passage, but Irene was on him like a fox, grabbing his wrist. "Where are you going?"

"Out of here!" he snapped, trying to shake her loose. "You can't come with me. If Orlov finds out that anyone else knows about these passages . . ." He paused to look fully at her. "Unless you want me to do it for you as a favor?"

Irene wasn't going to hand over that unpaid debt so easily. Favors were a currency that Fae traded with each other, metaphysical hooks sunk into their souls—if Fae had souls, which some would argue they didn't—and which they had to obey. "What I want from you as a favor is a bit more expensive than that," she said. Better to tell him here and now, rather than risk him dropping out of touch and being unavailable for the next year. Which was quite possible: avoiding being around to be *asked* a favor was an accepted Fae strategy. "I want you to put me in touch with Fae who've had dealings with Alberich. Relatively sane and trustworthy Fae. I know you have lots of contacts, Lord Silver. That should be something you can do for me."

"Fine!" he snapped. "Done and accepted!"

With a twist he broke loose from her grip and ran through the gap in the wall. The wardrobe swung closed behind him, and Irene suspected it had locked into place on the other side.

Another burst of gunfire rattled in the corridor directly outside; Irene wondered if she might have been a bit too quick in specifying her favor. She rolled off the bed, flicking off the light, and looked round for a hiding place. The bathroom? The wardrobe? Under the bed? Out of the window?

The door jolted in its frame as someone on the other side kicked it. Spurred by panic, Irene ran to flatten herself against the wall beside it.

More bullets chewed through the lock, and the door slammed open in response to another kick. A bulky man stalked into the dark room, leveled his gun in the direction of the now-vacated bed, and fired into the disarrayed sheets.

It was always nice, Irene reflected, when it was *clear* that people were going round killing indiscriminately—it made it so much simpler when choosing how to respond. Options narrowed down from *What should I do in this awkward political situation?* to *What will keep me alive here and now?* Floating on the cold iceberg raft of ruthless practicality above the churning sea of panic, she wet her lips and said in the Language, **"You perceive I'm a colleague."**

The man spun to face her as she spoke, the muzzle of his gun coming to bear, but as her final word echoed in the room, his finger relaxed on the trigger. "You shouldn't startle me like that," he said, his English American-accented.

"Sorry," Irene said with a shrug, answering in the same language.

He was tall, with buzz-cut dark hair, and in plain military gear and armored vest with various items of equipment on his belt; his boots were still wet from the snow outside. The Language would be making him see her as one of his colleagues, in spite of her tousled hair, silk negligee (blame Kai for doing the packing), and bare feet.

That was one of the side benefits of being a Librarian—being able to use the Language, something created inside the Library which could alter reality, cause things to act of their own accord, and affect people's perceptions. All three things came in very useful when people were pointing guns at you. Unfortunately, the length of time that things or perceptions *stayed* affected was variable, which meant that she shouldn't stand around too long chatting. "How's the mission progressing?" she asked.

"This wing's clear so far, but we haven't taken Orlov yet. You?"

"The same." With any luck that was imprecise enough that it wouldn't provoke any sudden realizations of *Wait a moment, my colleague wouldn't say that.* She saw something very useful on his belt. "Can I borrow this a moment?"

"Sure. Wait, what are you—"

Irene gave him a good long jolt from his own Taser until she was absolutely sure he wouldn't get up again. She briefly considered checking him for identification, but decided it would be pointless. Assassination squads didn't carry passports or ID cards. **"Sheets, bind this man securely,"** she ordered.

The sheets untucked themselves from the bed and came flowing across the floor to wind around the unconscious man, wrapping his arms and legs firmly enough that it'd take a knife to get them off.

Irene toyed with the Taser, considering what to do next. More gunfire echoed from elsewhere in the building. She didn't want to get involved in other people's private wars. She wasn't dedicated to protecting crime lords—even if her own business often involved book theft. These intruders had been going to shoot *her*, which admittedly was rather hurtful, but it might have been collateral damage of the shoot-everyone-in-the-building sort rather than personal.

It was the thought that the intruders' mission might finish up with *burn the place down to remove evidence* that got her moving. She shrugged on her dressing-gown and tiptoed out into the dimly lit corridor.

Fortunately she'd memorized the dacha's layout while she was being escorted to her bedroom. Lounge was *that* way, more bedrooms *that* way, Mr. Orlov's study was *that* way, the library that she wasn't supposed to visit was *that* way . . .

For a moment she was tempted by the idea of quietly sneaking into the building's library and using it to reach her own Library. Any library could serve as a portal—it just needed a Librarian (like her) and the Language. There was no shame in a sensible retreat from dangerous invaders with guns. But common sense cut her off before she'd managed more than a few steps along that line of thought. If Mr. Orlov weathered this raid and found her missing, everyone would assume she'd been involved. Her reputation—more particularly, the Library's reputation—would suffer.

Irene silently passed a couple of dead guards. They'd been shot from behind, by someone who'd been . . . where? She surveyed the scene, trying to imitate her friend Vale, a great detective from a Victorian-era alternate world—and an annoyingly better observer than she was, however much she tried.

A gleam of light on the window fastenings caught her attention, and she inspected it more closely. Raw metal: someone had slid some sort of tool or probe in from outside, sawed through the fastening, disconnected the well-hidden alarm, and entered this way. The snow outside showed no trace of tracks, but there was a narrow path of dark earth around the edge of the dacha, where the building's heat had melted the snow.

All right. Now she knew how they'd got in. And she knew where they must be going: to Mr. Orlov. They were confident enough to be using guns and alerting everyone who heard them, and there were enough of them that they thought they could split up and go round slaughtering random guests.

Irene really hoped that this displayed bad judgment on their part, rather than an accurate assessment of the situation.

Gunfire rattled somewhere nearby, just a couple of corridors away. She sneaked toward it, her bare feet silent on the floor, and peered carefully round each corner she came to.

Even with all her precautions, she almost walked right into the gunfight. A couple of intruders like the one who'd attacked her were firing down the corridor at some of Mr. Orlov's men at the far end. Neither side was willing to expose themselves in order to get a clear shot at their enemies, so both sides were popping off hopeful shots and keeping their own heads down. She was lucky the intruders hadn't noticed her approaching.

Mr. Orlov's men can't know how serious this is, or they'd be reacting more urgently, Irene thought. Conveniently, both the intruders were dressed and equipped exactly like her attacker—which included Tasers on their belts. **"Electrical hand weapons, discharge into your owners,"** she said quietly but clearly.

The two men went down with screams and twitching, bullets taking chunks out of the expensive walls and ceiling as their fingers spasmed on their triggers. Irene drew back fastidiously to avoid the flying lead, waiting until they'd stopped moving. Then she called out toward the far end of the corridor, in Russian, "They're down!"

"And who are you?" a voice answered.

Irene took a deep breath, raised her hands to make it clear she wasn't holding a weapon, and stepped into view, ready to dive for cover if they shot at her. "Irene Winters, visitor, on your side. One of these thugs tried to shoot me earlier—he's tied up in my room. I've disabled these two but they're still alive."

There was a brief muttered exchange, then the same voice called, "All right, come and join us. Keep your hands up."

Irene followed the instructions. She was greeted with a brisk but professional pat-down, then ignored as the three men discussed what to do next in low tones.

After a minute, she said, "Excuse me. May I make a suggestion?"

"You're not here to make suggestions," one of them said. "You're under our protection, but we're not here for you to pick up your belongings or go running errands—"

"Sergei, she *did* just dispose of two intruders," the apparent leader said wearily. He turned to Irene. "What are you suggesting?"

"You were saying that Mr. Orlov is in his bunker, which is good, but that the intruders are bunched up outside it and have explosives, which is bad, and that they're holding off anyone from getting in close to them," Irene said, recapitulating their discussion. "If you can get me close enough to them, I can jam *everyone's* guns—the way I triggered the Tasers on those two. Then it'll come down to numbers, and you'll have the advantage."

They clearly weren't convinced. "Ask Ernst," Irene added with a burst of inspiration. "He can vouch for me."

"Yes, but what is the advantage for you?" Sergei asked.

Irene advanced a step and prodded him in his security vest. This didn't do much more than bend her finger, but it made her feel better. "They tried to shoot me in my bedroom, remember? Why should I be on their side?"

"Perhaps it is a complicated plot where you use our rescue to gain our confidence, then when we bring you to Mr. Orlov's private bunker, you stab us all from behind and blow the place up with your insane Librarian magic," Sergei suggested. He shrugged. "It is how these things so often go."

"Sergei, shut up," the leader said with a sigh. "Ernst said earlier that she was useful. We will try it."

He led the way past the two unconscious intruders, pausing only to put a bullet into the head of each as he passed. Irene controlled her wince and looked away. She'd known what she was doing when she'd rendered them unconscious and helpless in the presence of guards who were willing to shoot to kill. And the intruders had been willing to shoot *her*.

It didn't make it any easier to live with cold-blooded murder, though. *The sooner I'm out of this, the better. And I wish I wasn't involved in the first place.*

The leader pressed an inconspicuous bit of molding and a concealed door slid open in the wall. He gestured to Irene to follow him inside. The other two men were right behind her. It would have been nice to think of them as bringing up the rear in case of surprise attack, but she suspected it was more to shoot her if she tried any tricks.

The passage itself was gloomy—darker than the exterior corridors, with just enough light to allow someone who knew the way to navigate. It wound between the walls which Irene had thought of earlier as overly decorated; she now realized that the decoration hid eyeholes and gun-ports.

"You weren't surprised by the secret passage," the leader said, suspicion edging into his voice as they hurried along.

Oops. "It's my business to know what other people don't know," Irene parried, paraphrasing one of her favorite authors.

"Hmm." They turned a corner, then another. In the distance, through the walls, Irene could hear occasional gunshots. "When we get there—"

He was cut off mid-sentence as a small metal object fell from above them, landing on the floor in the center of the group. It exploded into a cloud of gas, doubly effective in the confined quarters of the passage. Irene covered her mouth with her sleeve, trying to get enough clean air into her lungs to use the Language to disperse the gas, but her head was spinning and she knew she wasn't going to make it.

A strong arm closed round her waist and she felt herself being tossed over someone's shoulder. Motion was a dizzying blur—backward, forward, she wasn't sure which way she was going or even which way was up.

Then abruptly she was breathing something bitter, and her head was clear. She was propped up against the wall, and a man with a weird facial protrusion—no, her vision was clearer now, a man wearing a gas mask—had just broken a capsule under her nose. *An antidote. But why?*

He was in the same gear as the other intruders. "Are you ready to talk?" he asked in Russian.

"Who are you?" Irene gasped, not having to work very hard to feign dizziness and helplessness. She instinctively tried to twitch her dressing-gown into a less revealing position, then reconsidered and let it gape.

The man slipped his gas mask off. Beneath it, he was . . . handsome. Black hair as dark as the shadows that surrounded them, falling in a rough comma across his forehead, tanned skin, gray eyes, a mouth that curved in lines of cruel ruthlessness, broad shoulders, muscles visible even through his heavy combat gear . . .

Common sense hijacked the part of Irene's mind that was cataloging all these features, dumping an unwelcome bucket of cold water on her mental processes. *How is it that I'm noticing all these things when it's barely light enough to see him? Why am I feeling the urge to either fall into his arms or stab him in the back? What is happening to me?*

"You don't need to know my name," he said curtly. "Now be a good girl, and you'll get out of this alive. Do you work here?"

"Yes," Irene lied hopefully. He'd taken her alive and woken her up, so he wanted something from her. There had to be a way she could use this.

"Do you know the combination to your master's private quarters?"

"No, of course not!" She avoided his gaze.

"I think you do." He pushed closer to her, invading her personal space in a manner that reminded Irene unpleasantly of Lord Silver. "Don't be afraid. I'll keep you safe, but you have to trust me. I just need you to let me and my men into the bunker. Do that, and everything will be all right. I'll get you out of here safely."

It was the most blatant, obvious, charmless attempt at persuasion that Irene had witnessed in several years, but it was having a strange effect. The very brashness of the attempt inspired a certain trust. The light caught his gray eyes as he gazed into hers, and she could somehow sense that he was sincere in his promises, that he *would* get her out of here if only she'd help him, and that later he'd be grateful . . .

The Library brand across Irene's back stung, responding to the force of the narrative influence trying to drag her into this Fae's story. For he was a Fae—just like Mr. Orlov and Lord Silver. But he was following an entirely different archetypal path. He was a secret agent who went roaming into enemy strongholds for thefts or assassinations, calmly facing down countless enemy minions and seducing beautiful enemy spies. If their current situation had gone differently, he'd probably have been taken prisoner and be facing some horrifically implausible form of death. As it was, he'd entered the enemy stronghold with his loyal troops and was currently twisting a servant of the enemy—oh, the irony—around his little finger so he could persuade her to betray her master.

Irene might be a Librarian and a spy herself, but she hoped that at least she was never *this* stereotypical. Right now, though, she had to work out how to use the current situation—and without wandering onto the plot thread where the heroic spy killed the evil villainess who was trying to manipulate him. No doubt he'd make a witty quip over her dying body.

She took a deep breath, trying to simulate an inappropriate belief that he was telling the truth, and pointed in what she thought was the general direction that her group had been going. "It's down there. You promise you'll keep me safe?" she breathed.

"I'm not going to hurt an innocent person," he assured her.

Right. And your team were shooting people in their bedrooms. Irene kept the disbelief off her face and nodded.

"And just in case you're thinking of doing something stupid . . ." He drew a sleek gun from a holster at his belt. The dim light seemed to gather on it, casting the rest of the corridor into deeper darkness. "Start walking. Don't shout, don't call out, don't do anything we'll both regret."

Irene kept her mouth shut and did as she was told. On the negative side, she had a man behind her with a gun who could shoot her before she could finish saying anything in the Language. But on the positive side, she might just have gained a huge advantage—a passport into the middle of the enemy. Admittedly said passport was behind her and holding a gun, but nothing was ever perfect.

Her captor already knew the way, which was more than she did. He must have been testing her honesty earlier. He issued curt directions from behind her. As they began to hear noises from ahead, he came up next to her and caught her right wrist with his free hand, twisting it behind her back.

They turned a corner in the passage and were abruptly faced with a collection of pointing guns—which were lowered when the men there saw who her captor was. There were half a dozen of them, all heavily armed. One was kneeling next to a thick steel door in the side of the passage, assembling what looked like blocks of high explosive into a configuration Irene didn't recognize, but didn't want to be standing next to when it detonated.

"Any further attempts by our friends to interrupt us?" her captor asked.

"Nothing yet, Commander," the apparent second-in-command answered. "They're still trying to figure out how to assault us on terrain they designed to favor the defender. I love it when that happens."

"Good. Because this young lady knows the combination for the lock, and she can let us in." Her captor gave her a little shove forward, releasing her arm.

Irene rubbed her wrist and looked around the group, assessing her chances. Her real advantage was that none of them knew she was a Librarian. The moment any of them suspected her, things would probably get lethal.

Perhaps she was looking at this the wrong way. They were armed to the teeth and on a hair-trigger for violence. The slightest wrong move would have them shooting her down. *That* she could use.

The man with the explosives frowned at her. "There's a master combination?" he demanded.

"There is," Irene lied. She took a step forward, away from the gun barrel directly behind her. Time to roll the dice. "But you see, **you men perceive that you are all each other's deadly enemies.**"

She dropped to the floor with her final word in the Language, her head spinning with the effort of using the Language on so many people at once—even in a high-chaos world like this.

Above her, gunfire filled the corridor as the men reacted without hesitation or conscious thought, shooting to kill. A body landed on top of her, knocking the breath out of her. She felt blood soaking through her dressing-gown and into her peignoir, and walled off the part of her mind which dealt with perfectly normal reactions like horror or shock, focusing on the part that handled staying alive. Rolling over to get the unmoving body off her, she caught a glimpse of her surroundings. Almost everyone was down.

Wait. The *almost* was bad news.

A booted foot took her in the side and she curled up, gasping for air. Her attacker kicked her again, and she slid across the floor into another puddle of blood, her arms drawn up to shield her face. She had to get some air into her lungs, she had to breathe or she couldn't speak, and if she couldn't speak, she was helpless . . .

"It's a bit late for that." Oh, wonderful, the one survivor was her captor. She lowered her hands to see him facing her, his gun in a firm grip, clear fury written across his face. "I did *warn* you not to do anything stupid—"

But as he spoke, the door behind him was silently sliding open, and Ernst stood there. Before Irene's eyes had time to widen, he had reached out to clamp one hand round the commander's right wrist, dragging it up to point at the ceiling, and hooked his free arm round the commander's neck.

Irene dragged herself up to a sitting position, focusing on trying to breathe properly again. In the background she could hear the thuds of Ernst and the commander struggling, with others of Orlov's guards coming out to assist Ernst in subduing his prisoner.

Her clothing was soaked in blood. She was surrounded by dead men—ones whom she'd persuaded to kill each other. It didn't matter how aggressive they'd been, that they'd been enemies, that it had been a matter of life or death for her. She was a Librarian, a spy, and a book thief. *This* was not what she wanted her life to be.

And if it was her life—then what precisely had gone wrong, and what should she be doing about it?

Irene took a deep breath and pulled herself to her feet, asserting her right to be seen as an equal rather than a victim. The now-unconscious commander was being dragged away by his ankles. "What'll happen to him?" she asked Ernst.

Ernst shrugged. "The usual. Interrogation. Meaningful execution. Perhaps Mr. Orlov will feed him to the wolves."

Irene had a nasty suspicion what would happen in that case; it was a standard narrative trope for heroes to escape from that sort of situation, and Fae were slaves to narrative tropes, however much Mr. Orlov might want the commander dead.

However, it wasn't her business to point it out. In fact, none of this was her business any more. The assault was dealt with. She could go back to her room and have a shower and get rid of this blood and try to sleep—well, *try*.

Mr. Orlov emerged from the steel doorway, flanked by two more guards, and surveyed Irene. In the shadowy setting, even surrounded by bulky and heavily armored men, he was perceptibly the most dangerous person in the room.

"Effective," he complimented Irene. "Not actually *necessary*, but effective."

"It is my pleasure to be of service to you, uncle," Irene said, falling back on trained formalities in order to stop herself saying something much, much ruder. "Especially when they were trying to kill me as well."

"And would you have come to my defense if they hadn't tried to kill you first?"

Trick question. The attempted flattery of *Yes, of course* would have been exactly the wrong thing to say. "The Library doesn't get involved," she replied instead. "We are not your allies, but neither are we your enemies' allies."

"Fair answer." Something clicked over behind his eyes as he came to a decision; his face was as impassive as ever, but the atmosphere eased a little. "Very good. I will sign your treaty. You have my word. Now you will return to your bedroom and pack your bags. An escort home will be with you shortly."

Irene blinked. "You want me to leave that quickly?" It was better than she'd dared hope for—she'd be out of here and able to ask those burning questions about Alberich—but had she done something wrong?

"You're here under safe-conduct, but my enemies almost killed you. I have no wish to pay reparations to your Library." He turned to Ernst. "See her to her room. Make sure she gets there safely."

Once they were safely out of earshot—though one could never entirely ignore the possibility of cameras and hidden microphones—Irene turned to Ernst. "Did I annoy him somehow?"

"No," Ernst answered, his voice a low rumble. A bandage and dressing round his head suggested that he'd sustained injuries earlier in the attack. "It was two things. One is that you were more danger-ous than he expected. He had not thought you could work your per-ception tricks so quickly or so well, and he had thought that part of your strength was having dragon boy as an ally. The other is that the men were taking bets on what would happen. He did not like them being distracted."

"Oh."

Ernst patted her on the shoulder. "Do not worry, Librarian girl. I had already warned him you *were* that dangerous, so my reputation is intact."

"And the betting?"

"Oh, I bet on you." He tapped one pocket. "Perhaps we should do this again, some time. You are very good at looking helpless and co-operative."

"Sorry," Irene said drily. "Dragon boy wouldn't like it."

CHAPTER 4

"W hat are you doing back here?" Kai demanded, opening
the door.

"I'd expected something a bit more welcoming than
that," Irene said, a little hurt. "Do you mind if I come in? This suitcase
is heavy."

Kai stepped back to let her in. The morning light—for once, London was denuded of fog and naked to the sunshine—gave some color
to his pale cheeks and brought out the hint of dark blue in his black
hair. A dusting of toast crumbs on his sleeve suggested that he'd been
enjoying a late breakfast and a lazy morning. "That did come out the
wrong way, didn't it? Here."

He extended his arms, and Irene kicked the door shut behind her
as she dropped her suitcase and enjoyed a warm embrace. She would
have taken it further, but out of the corner of her eye she could see a
flicker of skirt at the top of the stairs. Catherine was watching.

"You smell of blood," Kai muttered, his nose in her hair. He shifted
back slightly, still holding her firmly. "What happened?"

"This relationship would be easier if you didn't interrogate me every time I get back from somewhere," Irene muttered. Of course dragon senses were keener than humans, but she *had* rather hoped to get to the breakfast-and-coffee stage before the awkward explanations. "It has to do with why I'm back early. You will notice that I'm entirely safe and unharmed. Not even a bruise or a graze."

"Is the current situation urgent?"

"Moderately. Is it just you and Catherine here?"

"Vale's here as well." Kai jerked his head toward the lounge. "We were just having coffee."

Irene wasn't *exactly* jealous, but it did seem a bit unfair that her friends had been lounging round having coffee while she'd been targeted by unreasonable men with machine pistols. "It would probably be a good idea for him to hear this too. Catherine!" she called up the stairs.

"Here." Catherine advanced a few steps down. The sunlight caught her as well, warming the brown of her skin and giving a spring tint to the dark green velvet of her dress. Her cinnamon hair was bundled back with ruthless practicality and a duster was tucked into her belt. She cradled a stack of books in her arms. "Am I needed? Because I was just getting these in order."

"I'm sorry to drag you away from that," Irene said with some sympathy. She could understand being lost in that sort of job. Then her eyes narrowed. "Wait, are those my copies of the *John Sinclair Ghosthunter* books?" A belated Christmas present from her parents, not native to this particular alternate world and highly anachronistic. It had been months, and she *still* hadn't had time to read them.

"Don't worry, I haven't done anything to them," Catherine said reassuringly. "I'm just organizing them. They've been sitting there for the past fortnight and nobody had put them in order."

Irene bit back a comment that she'd been reserving that pleasure for herself, to be indulged in slowly and pleasantly while dipping into the books for enjoyable passages. Possibly two Librarians—or one Librarian, and one would-be librarian—in the same house was too many. "Well, anyhow," she said. "Come on down. I have some news that will probably mostly please you."

"Probably and mostly?" But Catherine put down the pile of books and obeyed. "Does this mean I get to go back to the Library?" she asked hopefully.

"Let me get some coffee and I'll tell you all everything." Irene gave Kai one more hug before releasing him and heading into the lounge. Small surprise that Catherine wanted to go back to the Library. She was everything that her uncle wasn't: profoundly uninterested in other people and in any possible physicality between them, but deeply fond of books. Like any bibliophile, she lusted after access to the Library, which had been stocking fiction for time out of mind.

Vale was in one of the armchairs in the lounge. They were on good enough terms that he didn't bother to rise politely to his feet, but simply offered her a cup of coffee which he'd poured while she'd been talking. Recent acid burns marred his knuckles: he'd clearly been doing some sort of chemical analysis before coming over from his lodgings. His morning suit was irreproachable and his shoes were polished—though that was to his housekeeper's credit rather than his own. There were deep shadows beneath his eyes, and his lean face was haggard with weariness, but beneath it was smug satisfaction. "I perceive you have been successful, Winters," he said.

"You don't need deduction for that," Irene answered. "You only need to be able to hear what's being said out in the hall. And I perceive that you've been investigating something."

He waved a weary hand. "A case of poisoning. Venom was extracted from puffer fish, and the pillows in question were dosed with it prior to the application of pillowcases. The victim's body warmth and the pressure of his head during the night were enough to give him a fatal dose, though it was written off by the police as a cardiac arrest. A small matter—though I fear Miss Sally Carruthers will have to look elsewhere for a new fiancé, given that her own is now under arrest for murder."

"I'm glad you've been keeping entertained—that is, keeping London a safer place." Irene settled down with her coffee as Kai and Catherine found chairs of their own. She took a life-restoring swallow as she assessed the room's mood. Catherine was the easiest to read: impatient, wanting to get back to her books, expecting to be disappointed. Vale was more neutral, willing to judge whatever she said on its own merits and then apply his own intellect to the matter, which—given his deserved status as the greatest detective in London—might produce some implications which she herself hadn't noticed. And Kai—Kai was like a live wire at rest, calm for the moment but with an energy which burned inside him, fierce enough to challenge the heavens for her.

That thought disturbed her. She didn't *want* to get him into trouble on her behalf. Of course she appreciated his support, his confidence, his love . . . Yet so often she worried that she didn't deserve him, and that it would be better for him to be somewhere else less dangerous. Her newly discovered heritage felt like a metaphorical bloodstain on her hands when she held him.

Irene set her teeth. That was why she was going to be extremely careful about what she asked of him. She wasn't the sort of ninny who would try to keep him out of things on the sentimental grounds that *I love you too much to risk you being hurt.* Any Librarian knew how that sort of story went: the victim would be involved even deeper because they'd insist on forcing their way into events. If Irene ever tried to sneak off secretly to hunt down Alberich, she knew Kai would be only a few steps behind her. But she *could* at least be careful about what she asked of him—which meant taking control of the situation.

"All right," she said, putting her cup down. "I'll cut to the chase. I'm back early because my target, Mr. Orlov, decided to sign the Fae–dragon treaty last night. My next step has to be dropping off his signature at the Library, but after that my time will be my own again."

"Unless one of your seniors has a job for you," Kai said.

"Well, yes," Irene admitted. "But for now, let's assume that they don't." She turned to Catherine. "Your uncle caught up with me while I was at Mr. Orlov's dacha. He requested that I keep you under wraps at present, and the easiest place to do so would be the Library. Do you have any objections to me taking you back there?"

Catherine's eyes gleamed with a hungry light. "Objecting would be the *last* thing I'd do. Thank you! I mean, of course I'll miss you all . . ." she added hastily, in a vague attempt at tact.

"Why did Lord Silver ask you to keep his niece out of the public eye?" Vale asked, coming directly to the point.

"He's concerned that there's some sort of inter-Fae power struggle going on, and that Catherine might be in danger if people think that she has access to the Library," Irene replied.

"But I don't," Catherine objected, still starry-eyed from the promise to take her back to her own private heaven. "I only got in there because you pulled me in using my true name. If any other Fae want to do that, they have to find a Librarian."

Kai picked up a folded newspaper, reached across, and rapped her head with it. "You're not thinking. They don't *know* that. The only people who do know are the people in this room and Irene's superiors. As far as everyone else knows, you did it on your own. If you go round telling them what Irene did, then you're putting Librarians across the worlds in danger."

Catherine glared at him. "That's the Library's problem, not mine." The dead silence in the room made her reconsider her statement. "Um, perhaps that sounded a little harsh . . ."

"Not *sounded*, Catherine," Irene said quietly. It was easy to forget that the younger woman was only seventeen, but when she made the sort of comment that reduced the room to silence, it was a brutal reminder of her age and inexperience. "*Was*. I know that you don't have any personal loyalty to the Library in the same way that I do, but if you want to be a Librarian, then you are eventually going to have to make that choice."

"But what if I just want to borrow books from it, and visit it occasionally? We've talked about this, Irene. I'm not sure I want to be a Librarian in the way that *you* are. I want to be a genuine librarian somewhere that I can share books with people, and maybe have occasional adventures. Be honest—the Library doesn't share."

"But you still want access to the Library," Irene pointed out. She'd been carefully steering clear of the whole eventual possible conflict-of-loyalties problem. Catherine would have to argue about her future with her uncle and with the senior Librarians. Irene intended to stay well out of that discussion. "You don't have to make the sort of commitment which I have, but you do need to start thinking about your future."

"I can do that in the Library," Catherine said serenely. "And I'll be safe there. Everyone wins."

Irene bit back the words *Except me, when I'm blamed for you not wanting to be a Librarian like me*. After all, she was about to get Catherine off her hands for the foreseeable future, which would leave Irene free to research Alberich. This *was* a win-win situation. "Fair enough," she said. "I don't suppose you know anything about current Fae power politics or factions? Or about worlds vanishing?"

"How could I? I've been with you for the last couple of months now. I haven't even had the chance to go through Uncle's private correspondence." She paused. "Wait, worlds vanishing?"

"I'm curious about that myself," Kai said.

"A rumor Lord Silver passed on and that Alberich mentioned . . . I received a letter from him," she hastily explained as Kai and Vale stared at her. "The usual. Threats, insinuations that the Library's corrupted, wanting to talk to me. Nothing that came as a surprise. He mentioned worlds vanishing, but didn't go into any detail. And Lord Silver didn't know any more than that himself. I need to report it at the Library and see if it's genuine." She turned back to Catherine. "You'd better go and pack a suitcase. You may be in the Library for a while."

"But there are plenty of books there to read," Catherine protested.

"With *clothes*, Catherine. Clothes to wear while you're there."

Catherine sighed, but bounced to her feet and stampeded toward her room.

"The difference between the two of you," Kai noted, "is that you'd have had exactly the same thought about packing books to take with you, but you'd have stayed outside the door to listen while we were talking rather than go and pack."

"I had the benefit of good teaching from an early age." Irene finished her coffee, feeling better about the world.

"Rather, you had a total lack of moral upbringing from an early age," Vale said. He'd lapsed into a slouch and was surveying the two of them from under heavy eyelids. "Winters, are you still convinced that you want to investigate this matter of your possible parentage?"

"I don't see any other choice," Irene answered, suppressing a flare of annoyance. After being the one who'd deduced it, it was hardly fair for Vale to start treating it as just "a theory." "Besides, Alberich's a current danger to me—"

"To us," Kai interjected, clearly not wanting to be left out.

"To us, then, after recent events. Kidnapping, attempted possession, attempted murder . . ." Irene put down her cup and spread her hands. "He's a traitor to the Library. He's the Library's enemy."

"Those are certainly reasons for you to be glad that you weren't raised by him," Vale said. "But what are your intentions if you find out that he is indeed your father?"

His words were a painful intrusion into an area Irene had been avoiding. She'd been deliberately putting off thoughts about what she might do afterward. Especially since one of those thoughts involved killing Alberich. Before he could kill her—or worse. "I don't know," she said. It was an evasion, and both of them knew it.

Vale pulled himself upright and leaned forward, fixing her with his gaze. "Winters, I have never tried—well, not significantly—to compel you to adhere to the laws of this country, or even this world. I have accepted that you come from outside this world—and indeed, as a Librarian, from outside all worlds—and that the best I can hope for is that you are restrained by some personal morality. I have come to terms with the fact that you will lie and steal without the slightest compunction. However, if you propose to murder someone in cold blood rather than immediate self-defense, and without any orders from your theoretical superior authority, you will stain that personal morality of yours—your soul, if you like. I would rather that did not happen."

"You know I've killed before," Irene said quietly. "I stabbed Lord Guantes. And that was right in front of you." And that hadn't been the first—or the last—time she'd killed someone, either.

"In immediate self-defense, and to protect others," Vale answered. "I may not precisely applaud that, but I can accept it. But this is something else."

"It's a matter of life and death for all of us," Kai broke in angrily. Clearly he'd been thinking the matter through as well. Was that what he and Vale had been discussing over breakfast? "Alberich is alive, and he will most assuredly try to kill all of us—Irene in particular. Or for Irene, worse."

Irene felt her hands tighten on the arms of her chair. Alberich had seen her as a potential *body*. He'd tried to possess her—and if Vale hadn't distracted him by claiming that Alberich was Irene's father, he would have succeeded. It really would have been a fate worse than death. "I won't deny that the thought of being turned into a puppet and used to destroy everything I believe in affects my judgment." An understatement. The concept curdled her stomach and turned her throat dry. "This is a matter of self-defense. I told you that he sent me a letter while I was at Mr. Orlov's house—he's still taking an interest in me. I can't ignore him and hope that he'll go away."

"I'm not going to try arguing the point with you, Strongrock," Vale said to Kai, ignoring Irene's comment. "I know I have no hope of changing your mind. But since you will accept whatever choice Winters makes, I will do my best to persuade her."

"It's straightforward enough," Kai said, and all the arrogance of a dragon prince was in his face and voice. "He dared to assault me and my household. I will remove the man. It isn't a matter of crime and judgment; it's a matter of war."

"Yes, I thought you might say that." Vale turned back to Irene. "Is that what you intend to do, then? Murder him?"

"It's a state of war, as Kai said." Irene was determined not to lose her temper. She reminded herself that Vale was presenting these arguments because he was her friend. "Let's say that I'll avoid killing him—but I want him *stopped*. What would you suggest that I do? Go and find somewhere else to hide out and hope he never finds me there? Abandon this world and any other world that he knows I've been to?"

"I thought you Librarians were supposed to cultivate non-attachment."

"Oh, rubbish," Irene snapped. "We're not Buddhists of any variety. We get attached to everything—to our books, our friends, our favorite streets, the brand of coffee we like most . . ."

"Your revenge," Vale added.

"I don't bear grudges."

"Tell that to Bradamant," Kai muttered.

Irene ignored that. She'd put her animosity for her colleague Bradamant behind her *long* ago. "This is all hypothetical," she insisted. "I need answers to my questions before I can go any further. You don't normally argue on unproven suppositions like this, Vale. Why are you doing it now?"

"Because I'm concerned for you, Winters," Vale said quietly. "It is far too easy for you—for any of us here—to be preoccupied by current necessities and ignore where we are going in the long term. You may have killed—but you are not a murderer, and I don't want you to become one."

"Then what do you expect us to do?" Kai demanded. It cheered Irene to hear his use of *us*—a reminder that he was on her side, there to support her.

"If we were dealing with a normal criminal, I would suggest capture, trial, and judgment," Vale said. "He was once a Librarian. I suppose that the Library could claim rights of jurisdiction—it is a sovereign power of sorts, after all. He may be the oldest criminal in their records."

"*May* be," Kai said unhelpfully. "When I was a journeyman in the Library, I tried to research the place's history. You have absolutely no grounds for complaining about how little I know about my ancestors, Irene. The Library's just as bad."

Irene was not interested in being diverted from the subject. If she really wanted information on how many traitors had betrayed the Library, she could ask Melusine, the Library's head of Internal Security. She might not get an answer, but she could always ask. "Then what are you suggesting, Vale? That I ask my superiors for a formal warrant and try to bring Alberich in alive?"

"I don't agree with trying to bring him in alive, but formal orders would be useful," Kai put in.

"Kai, work with me here," Irene muttered. "I thought you supported me."

"I do." His voice was flat. "But I also want to keep you alive. If the Library wants you to take action about Alberich, then they're going to have to answer your questions. And if you *did* have some sort of formal warrant of pursuit, you could call in help. You've got allies— on my side, and on the Fae side. A lot of them would be *pleased* to have some way to assist you which didn't involve political issues and that was purely inter-Librarian."

Irene looked between the two men. Both of them her friends, both of them willing to help her, but both of them being so damn *inconvenient* in their personal morality or standards. "I have actually taken some steps toward that idea of using my allies. When I saw Lord Silver earlier, he said he owed me a favor, and I asked him to find someone who could give me useful information about Alberich."

"Now that's exactly the sort of thing I had in mind!" Kai said cheerfully. "Unfortunately you do have to associate with Fae to get the information, but it's a step in the right direction."

"Your prejudice is showing, Kai," Irene sighed. "Showing very dramatically. You really need to stop lamenting about how dreadful it is to work with Fae while Catherine is listening at the door."

"I'm not *listening*," Catherine said from the other side of the door. She didn't open it, but her skirt was still visible in the gap between door and frame—which was what had alerted Irene to her presence. "I'm *waiting*."

Irene was aware, from her days at a wholesome boarding school in her childhood, of the principle that nice people didn't listen at doors. She had later decided that it was a perfectly valid principle, but that she herself wasn't a nice person. "As you say." She turned back to Kai and Vale. "So are you both insisting that I get formal orders from my superiors about what to do next? Assuming I can get them to answer my questions?"

"You're not usually so petty, Winters," Vale said, and he had the nerve, the *gall*, to sound disappointed in her. "I for one am not *insisting*. I will support you—if you'll accept my assistance—but I have the right to express my concerns."

"Just as you'd do for us, if we'd put ourselves in that position," Kai chimed in.

"Clearly I have more of my father in me than any of us would like!" Irene spat. She regretted it a moment later when she saw the outright hurt in Kai's eyes, the withdrawal in Vale's face. But how was she supposed *not* to think of it?

She rose to her feet, feeling anger uncoil inside her like a serpent. "Neither of you had his thoughts in your mind. Neither of you really understands what sort of creature he is. I'm not just talking about him being a murderer. I'm talking about how he tortured people, how he used their skins to disguise himself . . . I'm not throwing myself into this out of some petty desire for vengeance. I'm doing it because if I don't, then other people are going to be hurt later. I'm not the only person at risk. *We* aren't the only people at risk. And yes, I will use my allies, and I will use my advantages, and I'll ask for formal permission, and I'll do anything which I think will increase my chances of . . ." She'd been going to say, *killing him*. Instead she finished with, ". . . surviving. But I'm not running away any longer."

All of it was true. But always in her thoughts, like a poisoned treasure in a triple-locked chest, lay the one thing that she wasn't going to say to Kai. His brother Shan Yuan wanted the two of them separated— for Kai's own good, he'd said, and he might even believe it. But *he* knew that she was Alberich's daughter. Perhaps some people might believe that sort of evil wasn't hereditary—but dragons were all about heredity and descent and legacy. Kai's father and uncles would be polite about it, they'd have good reasons for their actions, they wouldn't *blame* her for her unfortunate parentage . . . and she and Kai would lose each other.

She had to know if it was true that she was Alberich's daughter. And if she was—then she had to do *something*.

"What are you going to do, Irene?" Catherine asked quietly.

Irene was tempted to say *I don't have to answer to you*, but then she imagined the sound of the words, and she heard her father's voice in them. Not her adopted father's voice, the man she loved, but her father by blood and crime and sin. The thought made her recoil as though she'd discovered a rotting clump of pages in a favorite book. "This isn't getting anywhere," she said, with a great effort. "I'll take you to the Library, Catherine. While I'm there I'm going to demand the answers to some questions. Then I'll work out what I need to do next. Kai, Vale, do either of you want to come with me?"

Vale and Kai exchanged glances. Kai was the one who answered. "I've sent a message asking for information myself. If I stay here, I won't risk missing any replies."

"And I'm currently tracing the remains of Lady Guantes's organization here in London," Vale said. "There may be some record of her communications with Alberich."

"Very well." Irene tried to hear the common sense in their answers, rather than the immediate sting of *No, go off on your own, we don't care*. She knew that was an overly emotional, unjust, unreasonable sensation—but that didn't make it go away. "Thank you both. Come on, Catherine, we'll need to lose anyone trying to follow us first, so be ready to change carriages a few times."

Kai rose to hug her again before she left. "Be careful," he said. "There's . . . odd talk."

Irene raised her eyebrows. "Who, where, when, what, how?"

"When I wrote to Li Ming to ask for information and advice, he said that he'd do what he could—but he also suggested I should stay out of trouble. He mentioned that some of my kin are being politically difficult and that there's something going on. It's a bit of a leap, but maybe this has something to do with the vanishing worlds thing that you mentioned—if it's true."

Irene didn't like to ask him for private dragon information, which he clearly didn't want to give, but this was so non-specific a warning as to be almost useless. It wasn't even clear whether the warning referred to Kai's direct family, or to dragons in general. "I won't press you about this now, but is there anything I should be *particularly* careful about?"

Kai wobbled a hand vaguely. "I'm not sure, but ... if someone asks you for help, or a favor, you might want to be very careful about agreeing to it."

Irene almost smiled. "When am I not?"

"Well, you agreed to take me as an apprentice." He smiled a little at that. "And Catherine too."

"And I don't have any regrets about either of those decisions." She gave him a last squeeze before letting him go.

But as she donned her coat again and headed for the door, Irene remembered Kai saying, *You smell of blood.*

CHAPTER 5

"Come into the Library, Talita," Irene commanded in the Language, pulling Catherine by the hand through the doorway. It was still as difficult as it had been the time before—like dragging heavy luggage uphill, or shouldering an unconscious body—but it still worked. The Fae's true name, combined with the Language, was enough to pull her from a small suburban library in Vale's London and into the Library itself. It was a total change of scene and place: from a drab second-rate room that teased the nose with mold and shelves packed with three-volume sets of the most popular current novels, to a room that might have been from the interior of an Ice Queen's palace, all white marble and beechwood, the bookcases filled with heavy books bound in cream and ivory leather.

Irene tidily closed the door behind her while Catherine looked round in delight, crossing to run her fingers over the packed shelves. Her expression was a pure celebration of the books, a joy in their existence—and in the fact that she had access to them. Irene felt a little pang of melancholy as she watched. It had been years since she herself had been so uncomplicatedly happy.

Fortunately there was a computer in the room, which spared Irene having to search for one while dragging a Fae along behind her who'd rather be exploring. "Let me notify my superiors what's going on," she said, sitting down and turning it on. "Don't wander off."

Ignoring what she hoped was a mumble of compliance, drowned out by the sound of books being shifted around, Irene logged in, already plotting an email to her mentor Coppelia which would explain everything. She was taken aback to see an email to herself marked *Top Priority* heading her inbox.

It was from Coppelia herself, sent in the last few hours, and she hadn't bothered with niceties. *See me immediately. Use a transfer shift, code word Frustration.*

Irene skimmed down the titles of other waiting emails, but nothing else was important or relevant—and nothing from her parents—so she shut the computer down again without bothering to check them. "You're going to get an entertaining new experience today," she said to Catherine, who'd sneaked close enough to read over her shoulder.

"I could just stay here," Catherine suggested. "That way you'd know where I was."

"It's for your safety as well. Some Librarians might react badly if they found a total unknown wandering around—especially if she turned out to be a Fae."

"How did 'I'd stay here' become 'wandering around'?" Catherine muttered, dragging her suitcase along in Irene's wake.

"Personal experience." Irene looked from left to right as they headed down the corridor outside the room; more white marble, more beechwood, and an aurora borealis flickering outside the arched windows and casting strange lights across the pale walls. "Not that I don't understand—believe me, I do, I'd do it myself, which is why I'm being harsh and cruel and totally unfair to you." She finally caught sight of her target at an intersection. "There we are. A transfer shift cabinet. It's how we move very fast in here, rather than spending several hours walking until we find Coppelia's office."

"Why don't you use it all the time, then?" Catherine clearly still held a grudge from her previous experience of getting around the Library on foot.

"Because it takes a lot of power. Only senior Librarians can authorize it."

"And you're worried, because Coppelia wouldn't authorize it without a good reason?"

Irene turned to look back at Catherine. She needed to remember that, like Irene herself, the young woman was more than just an obsessive bibliomaniac. She'd had some political training from her uncle, though she lacked Irene's practical experience in the field, and she was capable of adult emotional judgment—even if she didn't always bother to exercise it. "Yes," she admitted. "If Coppelia wants me there urgently, then . . . well, I can't think of any way that it could be a good situation."

Catherine was silent as the two of them crowded into the cabinet, her suitcase squeezed in between them. Irene closed the door, leaving them in darkness. "Brace yourself," she warned, then shifted to the Language. **"Frustration."**

The cabinet jolted into motion like the world's fastest dumbwaiter, dropping fast enough to unnerve the most daredevil stuntman and turning unseen corners in the darkness. Catherine squawked in shock as the motion flung her onto Irene. Irene gritted her teeth and held her position, counting silent seconds as she waited for the trip to end.

They landed with a crash. Irene set Catherine back on her feet before opening the door. Light poured in.

The room they were in could have been a medieval solar: wide glass panels in the roof let exterior sunlight come filtering down to bathe the whitewashed stone walls and paved floor below. Threadbare tapestries on the walls depicted armored knights facing off against—or allying with—giant wolves, hags, and firebirds. The furniture was minimal, with only a battered wooden table and a chair, which had been shoved to one side. The woman using the table was sitting in a wheelchair, fingers paused on her laptop keyboard as she surveyed the new arrivals.

Irene blinked. "Melusine," she said politely. "I hadn't expected to see you here." She'd thought the Library's head of security never left the cellars where she kept her information.

"Just because I never leave the Library doesn't mean I'm always down on the security level," Melusine replied, apparently guessing Irene's thoughts. Her sandy-brown hair was cropped untidily short, and she was wearing a loose checkered shirt and jeans. Her wheelchair, however, had clearly been imported from some highly technological world and had more controls on it than Irene could easily count. Probably hidden weapons too; she was a Librarian, after all. "I take it this is your apprentice?"

"Yes. Melusine, this is Catherine, Lord Silver's niece. Catherine, this is Melusine; she's a Librarian, as no doubt you've guessed, and"— Irene caught a small negatory gesture from Melusine and rapidly adjusted her next words to something other than *head of security*—"she's one of our longest-serving members, I think. I've reported to her a few times before."

Irene could guess Melusine's motivation; the older Librarian wanted to question Catherine without Catherine knowing Melusine's rank and position. It wasn't entirely fair, but Irene could understand why. This was something Catherine would have to handle for herself if she wanted to stay in the Library. Being the first Fae to enter it had downsides as well as upsides.

"Pleased to meet you," Catherine said politely.

"Yes, one hopes so. Irene, Coppelia's in her bedroom. She's not well at all. It's a good thing you came when you did."

Irene swallowed, her throat dry. The words "not well at all" terrified her. Coppelia was old, even for a Librarian, and since the business in Paris with the unseasonably cold winter and the dragon-caused ice storm, she'd been nursing a cough, which had steadily become worse. Of *course* she'd downplayed it in Irene's presence. Nobody *ever* told Irene when they were seriously ill, or in trouble, or . . . "Thank you. May I leave Catherine out here with you?"

"Of course," Melusine said. Her tone was almost gentle. "Take as long as you need."

Irene jerked a nod, crossed the room, and knocked on the door.

"Come in . . ." Coppelia's voice was barely audible, trailing off into a thin, tearing cough.

Coppelia wasn't in her bed; she was reclining on an amber velvet couch beside the window. Her skin had an undertone of grayness to it, sallow rather than healthy, and she'd lost what flesh she'd had; her bones were far too perceptible in her face, and her human hand was thinner and more delicate than her carved wooden clockwork one. A pile of papers lay next to the couch, within easy reach, but a cheap science-fiction paperback with a gaudy cover had been propped open on top. The walls were hung with more tapestries, and the corners of the room were full of shadows. Coppelia herself was blinking as she focused on Irene, weariness showing in her movements as she coughed again.

"Let me get you something," Irene said, looking round for something, *anything*, that could help. Tea? Drugs? Coppelia was one of the elder Librarians who set policy for the rest of the Library. There should be something in one of the worlds with advanced technology or advanced magic which could help her, which would have been brought here to keep her alive and get her well again.

"There's very little that will help me now." Coppelia pressed her hand against her sternum, keeping it there until her breathing eased. She was in one of her favorite velvet robes, crimson deep as venous blood, but it hung loosely on her.

"Oh, don't be so melodramatic."

"Death, my dear child, has an unfortunate drama to it. Do you remember the old philosophical argument about how if a tree falls in the wood when there's nobody around to see it, does it really fall? Death's like that, but unfortunately by its nature there has to be at least one person present to be dramatic about it."

"If you can talk that much, then you can't be that ill," Irene said, her words more an attempt to convince herself than a serious argument. "And if you were in better condition, you'd point out that there could be a situation where the person dying was unconscious, which would cut down on the drama."

"Yes, but I try not to spoil my own propositions." Coppelia pulled herself upright, and Irene helped her adjust her cushions until she was comfortable. "We have at least two things to discuss: one is Alberich, the other is me. Is there anything else that I should know about?"

"I persuaded Mr. Orlov to sign the treaty. Lord Silver caught up with me and asked me to keep Catherine here and out of the limelight; there's some sort of inter-Fae problem, and he's worried that she'll be a target if they think she can access the Library."

"And either nobody will believe her if she says she needs a Librarian's help, or it'll just make Librarians targets too," Coppelia said, putting her finger on the problem with her usual accuracy. "I think under the circumstances we can keep her here for the time being. Though not as a hostage, of course."

"Of course not," Irene agreed hastily. "And no, before you say it, I don't think this is all a complicated plot by Lord Silver to get us to bring her here and then claim we're holding her hostage."

"It did cross my mind, but I'll trust your judgment." Coppelia paused, but didn't start coughing. After a minute, she relaxed. "So she's our guest for the moment. Any idea about what to do with her?"

"I was thinking we could put her in with the student classes. Or class. I'm hoping there are classes. I know that we're short on numbers, but we're not *that* short, are we?"

"No, we're not that short, and there are classes. That seems sensible. I'll see to it. Have you told anyone her true name?"

"Well . . ." Irene hesitated. "It's on a need-to-know basis, isn't it?"

Irene found herself very reluctant to say what she was really thinking; namely, that she had no intention of handing that level of control over Catherine to *any* other Librarian. Or possibly to any other living being. Fae could be controlled and bound by their true names, which was why they kept them so absolutely secret. Catherine herself had only given Irene her true name under the most desperate of conditions, when it had been a matter of life or probably worse than death.

It wasn't that Irene didn't trust other Librarians. She did. Mostly. But if the Library itself, as a political entity, found itself in an awkward position, someone might decide to use Catherine as a lever—and as her teacher and her guardian, Irene wasn't going to let that happen.

"I mean, why would anyone else need it?" she added, in a tone of bland innocence.

"Ten out of ten," Coppelia said approvingly, and the glint in her eye showed a full comprehension of Irene's words. "Keep it up. Now let's get back to the other points under discussion. Alberich. And me."

Irene took a deep breath. She didn't want to ask her next question, because it meant an answer one way or another—and that answer would shape the path ahead of her. But Coppelia's weakness and ill health made her own maunderings feel petty by comparison. The shadows in the room seemed to close in around them like warning omens.

"Is he my father?" she finally asked.

Coppelia reached across to touch Irene's hand with her own wooden one. "He is, child. By blood—but nothing else."

Irene let her head sag forward. She couldn't meet Coppelia's eyes. "I trusted you. I've always trusted you. How could you *do* this to me?"

"I'm confirming what you know because there's no other choice. If you hadn't found out, then I'd have happily lied to you for the rest of your life."

"And let me live with a lie?"

Coppelia sighed, and her breath rattled in her lungs. "Don't waste my time being self-indulgent."

"No, of course not," Irene muttered. There was a hot lump in her throat, and she wasn't sure if it was because Coppelia had confirmed the truth or because she'd admitted that she'd known and lied about it before. "You've never let me do that, have you?"

"People with power can't afford to be self-indulgent." Her hand tightened on Irene's until Irene looked up. "It's a bad habit to get into. And don't try claiming that you don't have power. You know you do. The question is what you're going to do with it."

"Well, what I was going to do is to ask the Library for a full explanation of the situation regarding *my father*," Irene said, emphasizing the words deliberately. If she couldn't lose her temper at Coppelia, then she could at least be sarcastic. It lowered the heat of the roiling mass of acid which seemed to have replaced her heart. "It seems the neatest and tidiest way of sorting things out."

Coppelia frowned. "That's unusually formal for you."

"I have a legalist and moralist to appease. He's concerned for my virtue."

"Ah. Yes, he would be." Coppelia had met Vale. "It won't help, you know."

"Getting answers?"

"Killing Alberich." Her gaze was very direct. "That's what you're thinking about, isn't it?"

"This had better not be something along the lines of 'If you kill him, you'll be no better than him.'"

Coppelia clicked her tongue. "Please, Irene. I know you accused me of drama earlier, but do you really think I'd be guilty of a statement like that?"

"Then what do you mean?" Irene controlled herself so that the words didn't come out in too much of a wail. She wanted answers, not philosophy. She wanted guidance which she could actually live with. She wanted *help*.

"We've all had difficult situations in our past." She patted Irene's hand again. "Things like, 'shall I forswear my oath, will I sacrifice my brother, can I abandon my arm for the wolves to eat,' that sort of thing. When you've lived as long as I have, you've had at least a few moral dilemmas. And I'm telling you the absolute truth when I say this, Irene: the fact that you *want* to kill him because he's your father shows that you do feel a bond to him, which makes it absolutely the worst thing that you could do."

Irene sat back with a snort of annoyance. "That's excessively complicated."

"Real things often are. Your parents didn't—and don't—know. That's the absolute truth, and I'll repeat it in the Language if you want me to. They were aware that your birth mother hadn't conceived you willingly and that she'd never wanted a child, but that was all they were told. I'll leave it up to you whether *you* choose to tell them or not."

Something inside Irene relaxed a little. For her parents to have lied to her about that—on top of everything else—would have been the last brick in an overloaded, overbalanced tower that would have buried her beneath its ruins.

"Who is my birth mother?" she asked experimentally, not really expecting an answer. "That story I read in the unique Brothers Grimm collection suggested that Alberich—well, his own sister . . ." She didn't really want to complete the sentence.

"That is something it won't help you to know." Coppelia's tone was as implacable as flint. "I can tell you that she wasn't his blood sibling. All of us used to call each other brother and sister back then. It was the fashion at the time, and it seems to have carried over into the story. But who she is, or was . . . It isn't just a question of your rights. She has rights, as well. Let it go. In fact, let it all go. Get on with your life."

"Oh, come *on*. He's not going to let *me* go. He sent me a letter." She flourished it by way of proof. "Warning me about the Library. Saying there's an evil spider in the web. Talking about vanishing worlds."

Coppelia sighed wearily and relaxed back into her cushions. "They never tell you this when you're younger. I was all 'ooh, ooh, I want to steal books and preserve the universe,' but did they mention having to mentor students and convince them to do the right thing? No, they did not. I should put in a formal complaint that I was given this job under false pretenses."

"Be serious," Irene demanded, torn between laughter and bitterness. "I need some help here."

"Oh, I am, I am. You'll be in the same position someday and you'll wish you'd listened more closely. Pass me a pen and some paper."

Irene obeyed, and watched as Coppelia scribbled a few sentences and signed them. "There," she finally said, and coughed again. "Orders for Catherine to be placed with the current classes of apprentices.

Standard lessons in the architecture of the Library, filing, organization, theft, forgery, that sort of thing. Her tutors will know what she is, but she doesn't have to tell the other apprentices unless she wants to. Personally, I think she'll get more peace and quiet for reading in her own time if she keeps her Fae-ness under a bushel. Up to her."

"Thank you," Irene said with genuine gratitude, taking the paper. As one of the oldest Librarians around, Coppelia had authority. Catherine would be safe.

"And now we get to the bit you aren't going to like."

Irene raised an eyebrow.

"Have you ever wondered what happens to old Librarians, Irene?"

She was right: Irene didn't like the way this was going. "The ones who don't die on the job or while out in service as Librarians-in-Residence?" she asked.

"Yes, quite obviously those. Let's cut to the chase. Ones like me, who are old and who've been living here for a long time . . . and frankly, ones who are tired. Age grows on you. Ill health makes it worse. There's only so long that reading books can keep you going." Coppelia's attention wasn't on Irene now; she was talking half to herself, her voice a whisper. "Oh, I could go out into a high-technology world and have them transplant my lungs again, or a high-magic one so they could wave a wand and repair me, but then I'd just have to do it more and more often . . . and I've had enough. I've seen a peace treaty signed which we'd never thought was possible. I've seen you grow up into an adult. The other Librarians whom I knew when I was young are almost all dead. The brand on my back is heavier every day. It's time for me to go deeper into the Library."

"Is that some sort of ridiculous euphemism for suicide?" Irene demanded. Fear was nearly choking her. She couldn't lose Coppelia like this. The woman had been her mentor—was her *friend*. "I'm not going to let you—"

Coppelia held up a wasted hand, and Irene cut herself short, schooled by habit into obedience. "Always so dramatic," the older Librarian said. "No. It's not a euphemism. Listen carefully, Irene. I'm going to tell you a secret."

"Of course I'm listening."

"Old Librarians who finish their lives are . . . preserved. The Library keeps everything that belongs to it—and all of us are marked with the Library's brand. The body ends, but something continues, whether you want to call it mind or soul or spirit. And that is what will happen to me."

Irene took a moment to think that over, careful not to let her mouth drop open in shock. "This is news to me," she finally said.

"Of course it is. Junior Librarians aren't told about it. You're encouraged not to even think about it. One day we're here and the next we're gone."

"That isn't a particularly happy thought for Librarians who died outside the Library and never even knew about it," Irene said, her logic automatically taking her to one of the less pleasant consequences.

Coppelia shrugged. "Well, if we assume that this situation demonstrates some form of after-death existence, then presumably they have a soul which goes *somewhere*. For all I know, we're condemning ourselves to eternity here rather than blissful union with the presence of God, or reincarnation, or whatever. Theology isn't my subject. Or maybe they show up here as well—or perhaps it's just a copy of us which persists here. Philosophy's a big subject, and arguing it over the dinner table always gave me indigestion."

Irene was mentally going through old Librarians whom she'd known, who had been resident in the Library and had passed away at some point when she wasn't around. "So if you'll still be here—if other Librarians are still here—does that mean I could communicate with them?"

"That doesn't seem to be part of the deal," Coppelia said regretfully. "I'm sorry. We go deeper into the Library. We help support and maintain it in some sort of metaphysical way. But as I understand it, we don't communicate with the living. Which is probably a good thing. You need to get on with your lives. We . . . well, I hope I'll have time to catch up with my reading."

The whole idea was almost too much for Irene to encompass. "This is too strange," she said, where "strange" was a placeholder word for "big, enormous, vast, impossible." At the same time, something at the back of her mind was telling her that it was not only true, it was *right*. It was how it should be. It . . . made sense. Of *course* the Library would preserve its own—Librarians just as much as books. It was one less thing for her to worry about. "I never considered anything like this was possible."

"As I said, you're encouraged not to think about it." Coppelia reached out to embrace Irene—warm, but so fragile, so delicate. "Does that make you feel better? For when you come back and I'll be gone?"

"No," Irene said, tasting grief again. "It doesn't really console me. Because even if it's true, even if you get to carry on in the heart of the Library . . . I'm still going to lose you."

"Oh, Irene." There was real pain in Coppelia's voice now. "I can't spare you that, and the Library can't spare you that. Not me, not your dragon prince, not your detective, not your apprentice, your parents, your friends . . . And if you find an answer in a story somewhere, then you're doing better than I have."

There was a brisk knock on the door.

"Can I say 'Go away'?" Irene whispered.

Coppelia sighed, then started coughing again. In between coughs, she muttered, "Tell them to come in."

Catherine poked her head nervously around the door. "I'm sorry to interrupt," she said, "but there's a summons for Irene from the working group headed by Kostchei, and Melusine said she'd like a word with Irene first."

Coppelia gave a little nod, as though she'd been expecting it. "Go on, Irene. They won't want to wait."

Irene wanted to say something more—something meaningful, something *useful*—but faced with Coppelia's resignation, there was nothing left to say or do. Anger at herself, at Coppelia, at death itself, met with the certain knowledge of coming loss and brought tears to her eyes. "Try and stay a bit longer?" she asked, struggling to keep her voice even. "Please?"

"I make no promises," Coppelia answered, bowing her head. She wouldn't meet Irene's eyes. "And you must be going. Send Catherine in; I'll talk with her."

There were no words which could change this. Not the Language, not human speech, not even the deepest confession of Irene's heart. Coppelia was her mentor, her friend, and as much family as her parents, and now she was going to lose her.

Irene drew the last rags of her pride around her and set her lips. She was not going to burst out crying. If Coppelia could do this, then so could she. "I'll see you later," she said, trying to make the words into declarative truth through sheer force of will.

"Don't get yourself killed," Coppelia said. "You still have far too much to do."

The moment Coppelia's bedroom door was shut, Catherine turned to Irene. "What did she say?" she demanded.

Irene forced herself to remember that Catherine's own concerns were just as real and valid as Irene's own. "She's agreed you're to stay."

Catherine squealed and hugged her.

"Yes, right, please remember I have ribs under here and I don't need them broken yet," Irene muttered. She patted the younger woman on the shoulder as she slackened her grip. "You're to go in and talk with her so she can assess your current abilities and assign you to classes. I may not be able to come back immediately, but I'll try to keep you informed . . ."

"Classes?" Catherine frowned. "I thought you'd just be letting me self-educate via the books."

"Sadly that sort of thing's much more practical in fiction than in fact. If you want to stay here, you're going to need tutoring."

"I will be such an excellent student that they'll be recommending me for full membership in the Library before the month's finished," Catherine said firmly. "Don't bother about me. I'll be fine here. Go do your stuff."

A needle of nostalgia and regret threaded its way through Irene's heart, as she watched the Fae's enthusiasm. *I was like that, once.* It used to be nothing but the sheer pleasure of books. Now it's diplomacy and power struggles and negotiations and vengeance. What happened?

Part of her suggested, *I grew up,* but somehow she felt the answer was more complicated than that. *You're encouraged not to think about it . . .*

Melusine waited for Catherine to close the door behind her before she gestured Irene to the lonely chair. "Sit," she said. "You and I need to discuss a couple of things."

"Kostchei can wait, I take it?" Irene said as she sat down. The sun seemed to have passed its zenith, and the room was no longer so brightly lit. Darkness clung to the corners and edged its way across the floor.

"Oh, he expects me to question you. Security, after all. I'm more interested in what you want to ask *me.*"

This had potential. "Alberich," Irene said flatly. She'd grieve for Coppelia later; she wanted answers now. "How much did you know?"

"I knew whose child you were." Melusine's eyes were distant, unapologetic. "I honestly thought you'd be happier if you knew nothing about it for the rest of your life. Was I wrong?"

Irene slumped in her chair. "No, you weren't. Everyone's going to say that, aren't they? 'It was for your own good.'"

"Something you'll learn as you get older is that truth and reconciliation may be necessary for *nations*, but it isn't necessarily best for *individuals*. My job means that I know a lot more about some Librarians than they do themselves—but telling them the full story wouldn't necessarily improve the situation."

"So basically, you consider yourself judge, jury—"

"And executioner, yes, if necessary," Melusine agreed equably. "We aren't a democracy. You agreed to follow orders when you chose to become a Librarian and take the Library brand. Sometimes that's going to mean we lie to you for your own good. If you wanted different working conditions, then you should have chosen something else."

"You really don't believe in sugarcoating the situation, do you?"

"Not since I started working in Security, no."

"So, just out of curiosity . . ." Irene tilted her head. "Who watches the watchmen?"

Melusine's expression darkened. "The Library watches me. No, I'm not going to explain that. Some day you may understand what I mean. And if you do . . ." She frowned, as though weighing up a decision.

"Yes?" Irene prompted, when it became clear that Melusine wasn't going to continue.

The older Librarian sighed. "There may come a time when you need to speak with me urgently. If you do—and trust me, you'll know when, and you'll know why—then use a transfer shift cabinet to get down to Security and my rooms there, rather than taking the regular lift. The code word will be, oh, *History*."

This additional layer of secrecy and paranoia made Irene's heart sink. "What precisely is going on?"

"It's a contingency. I like to have contingencies. I failed to have any contingencies at one point, and look at me now." She gestured at her wheelchair. "Consider this a valuable life lesson."

Irene desperately wanted to ask what incident had left Melusine in a wheelchair; the way the woman had phrased those last words suggested that it had been a traumatic injury rather than a congenital condition. But the other Librarian's demeanor suggested that any questions on that subject would mean the immediate end of the conversation, and—whatever some people might suggest—Irene *was* capable of taking a hint. "All right," she said quietly. "*History.* I'll remember. Does this have anything to do with what Kostchei wants me for?"

"It might do," Melusine answered unhelpfully. "I don't agree with what he has in mind, but I was outvoted. It happens."

"I thought you said the Library wasn't a democracy."

"Not at your level, it isn't." She leaned forward. "Be careful. There's been news that worlds have been vanishing."

Irene nodded. "Lord Silver told me that too. So did Alberich—it's in a letter he sent me."

"I'll want to see that letter." Melusine frowned. "I don't know whether or not it's true, but the Library's connections to those worlds aren't operative any more and we don't have any way to get there ourselves to check. We're having to rely on reports from dragons or Fae."

"Are there any links between the worlds that have apparently vanished?" Irene asked. "Not like the connections to the Library, but similarities in type?"

"Not as such—but they were areas notable for malcontents. That is, dragons who disagreed with their superiors, or Fae who didn't like to cooperate with the rest of their society . . ." Melusine shrugged.

"Four worlds so far. Two in high-order areas, two in high-chaos. Even Vale would agree that isn't enough for a solid theory yet."

"Not yet." A thought crossed Irene's mind, spurred by her own preoccupation. "Could it be Alberich? Some sort of sucking life out of entire worlds to keep himself alive?"

"That's a nice theory in the sense that it puts the blame on someone we all hate, but it's significantly lacking in evidence," Melusine said. "You said you had a note from him?"

Irene proffered the battered letter again.

Melusine opened it, read it, and frowned. "Nothing new. Leave it with me. You should be going down to see Kostchei. Give him my apologies for the delay. And . . . be careful. This is not the moment to make things worse. You're to use the transfer shift cabinet—the code word is *Deniable*."

"Right." Irene looked one last time at Coppelia's chamber door, then forced herself to walk across to the cabinet.

"Be seeing you," she said, and stepped inside.

CHAPTER 6

The cabinet door swung open slowly, as though it had aged between one room and the next and developed dust-clogged hinges and a decrepit, warped frame. Candles burned to light the new room, but did a poor job. It was a small room—the word "secretive" came to mind—and there was little room for furniture besides the central table, the transfer shift cabinet, and a few chairs.

"Come in and sit down, girl," Kostchei said. He was one of the senior Librarians and no doubt knew *all* about her parentage. He'd never shown any particular sign of liking her, but then he didn't show any sign of particularly liking anyone. He was bald, but his beard sprouted in thick magnificence, and he tugged at it with heavy-knuckled hands. He was swathed in heavy, pale woolen robes like some ancient Druid, and his expression suggested he was calculating a shopping list for the contents of his next Wicker Man.

The other two at the table were strangers to Irene. Both of them were elderly—unsurprising, as this was clearly a briefing by very senior Librarians. One of them, a woman, was in what Irene recognized as a Korean hanbok, a yellow wraparound blouse and red full-length skirt, which spread out around the feet of her chair. The other was in black monkish robes, with the hood drawn up to conceal both face and gender; their hands, twisted by age and arthritis, were the only part which Irene could see.

The three of them were seated around one half of the round table. Irene took the single remaining chair on the opposite side. Candlesticks had been set on either side of her place, giving the three older Librarians a rather better-lit view of her than she had of them.

This feels like an interrogation. Or an inquisition. "Is this where you ask me when I last saw my father?" she enquired, her memory flashing back briefly to old paintings and old stories.

"She has a sense of humor," the person in the monk's robes said, in a voice that was light and toneless. "That wasn't in her record."

"It was," Kostchei disagreed. "But it said *inappropriate* sense of humor."

"Let's get to the point," the woman in Korean clothing said sharply. Her hair was too vigorous and full for her age, not matching the wrinkles on her hands or the drawn thinness of her face. It must be a wig, Irene realized, unable to pause her trained habits of assessment and evaluation, even when among other Librarians—her own kind. "For this meeting, I state that present here are Kostchei, chairing; senior Librarians Honorius and Myeongwol present, also Librarian Irene."

"And the purpose of this meeting is to discuss Alberich," Kostchei said, his voice like falling tombstones. "We've all read your report, girl. No doubt you left a few things out; any agent does. We're trusting you that they weren't *important* things."

Irene had always had a good memory for exactly what she'd put in her reports, especially when contrasted with what had actually happened. It cut down on awkward self-justifications and being caught in lies during later discussions. "Nothing important," she said firmly, "though there have been a couple of recent developments."

The monk—Honorius, by default—turned their head, so that the dark oval of their hood faced her squarely like a challenge, inviting her to try to gauge their features and to fail. "What?"

"I had a threatening letter from Alberich; it's currently with Melusine. Also, Lord Silver asked me to bring his niece Catherine here to the Library to keep her safe for now. I haven't had a chance to write up a full report yet. There are reports of worlds vanishing, but Melusine says you already know about that. And there's some sort of Fae power struggle going on."

"When *isn't* there some sort of Fae power struggle going on?" Myeongwol muttered, glaring at Irene as though it was her fault.

"I haven't had time to look into it in more detail yet," Irene excused herself. She fished inside her jacket for the documents she was carrying and placed them on the table in front of her, pushing them across to Kostchei. "Here are Mr. Orlov's signature to the Fae–dragon treaty and Coppelia's clearance for Catherine to join our trainee classes."

Kostchei trapped the envelopes under one finger, not bothering to open them. "Useful. Both of them. But we're wandering off the subject. Alberich. You know he's your father? You know why you weren't told about this?"

"I know he's my father," Irene said, feeling the words harsh and sour in her mouth. "I have been *informed* why I wasn't told about this." She wasn't going to say that she *knew* or that she *understood*. It was still too raw a subject.

"Right. Point established. Now normally we wouldn't be making this sort of suggestion—"

"Because normally we don't encourage junior Librarians to waste all the training and effort we've put into them," Honorius cut in.

"Stop dancing round the subject, Kostchei. Irene, are we correct in thinking you want to deal with Alberich once and for all?"

Now who's dancing round the subject? Am I the only person who's prepared to use the specific word here? "Are you asking me if I want to kill him?"

"Yes," Myeongwol said. "Normally we don't sanction assassinations— but can you see why we're considering it in this case?"

"It's not just because he's a threat to the Library," Irene answered. "It's not just that he's murdered other Librarians, that he's tried to destroy the Library within recent history—and maybe other times that I don't know about in the past." The quick glance that Honorius and Kostchei exchanged, the way that Myeongwol tapped her fingers, suggested that her hypothesis was correct. Alberich *had* tried in the past, but for some reason the facts had been covered up. "But now *he* knows I'm his daughter too. That makes me a potential liability for you."

"You could stay in the Library," Honorius pointed out.

"Forever? Because that's what it would be. And even that would only be a delaying strategy, until he attacked the Library again." She remembered the fairy story she'd once read, a folkloric preservation of something which had genuinely happened; it had said that Alberich's sister was still alive, hiding from him somewhere in the depths of the Library. Irene didn't want to add herself to that tally.

There was another exchange of glances. "Why now?" Myeongwol said. "He's been a thorn in the Library's side for centuries. Why do you assume that we're capable of doing something about it *now*?"

"Because we've reached a current state of detente where we can call on other sides for help," Irene answered. "Or at least, we can expect them to remain neutral to some extent rather than take the opportunity to make the situation worse, or to play him against us for their own gain."

She kept her tone polite and respectful, but inwardly she'd pricked up her ears at Myeongwol's question—and indeed at the whole set of questions. This wasn't an open interview where they honestly wanted to know what she had in mind. This was the sort of session which had a very definite end game, and where they were checking that she fitted the bill for whatever they had in mind. *Was Vale asking me about my intentions because he thought I wanted to kill Alberich—or because he suspected I'd be ordered to?*

I didn't join the Library in order to become a killer, but how can I say no to this?

"Do you have any actual plans?" Kostchei asked, frowning. He yanked at his beard as though it was a bell pull. "Anything more definite than going to where you last saw him and demanding that he come out and face you?"

"Just a moment, please," Irene said hastily, feeling this was going a bit too fast. "You've been talking about Alberich being killed. How exactly did this get to discussing my *personal* plans for doing something this suicidal? Alone?"

"Treat it as an intellectual exercise—up until we give you formal orders," Honorius said coldly.

Irene's emotions were severely mixed. She'd been willing to argue about her right to try to kill Alberich with Vale, but now that an actual mandate for execution was looming on the horizon, she felt increasingly uneasy. "Give me some credit for common sense," she temporized. "I may currently be furious, but I'm not stupid or suicidal, nor do I believe I'm living in the sort of story where I can march up to his front gates and challenge him. I leave that to the Fae."

Kostchei snorted. "That's a rational response, but it's not an answer."

Irene leaned forward, resting her arms on the table. "My first step would be to research him *here* and take advantage of what information we have on him. I'd speak to Melusine—is there some reason she isn't at this meeting, by the way?" That had been nagging at Irene. *I don't agree with what he has in mind, but I was outvoted,* Melusine had said. If the Library's head of security disapproved of this mission . . .

"Classified information," Myeongwol said, and her mouth closed like a steel trap.

"I apologize for the digression." Irene suppressed her unease for now. She'd indulge in paranoia later. Melusine had told her to be careful. If she said the wrong thing, would she be allowed to leave the Library—or this room? "Right. Research Alberich in the Library. Then turn to my Fae contacts, a number of whom owe me favors, to see if they can give me any information. We know that Alberich has frequently been involved with the Fae on a freelance basis, but the last few times haven't turned out very well for the Fae involved. It's quite possible there will be someone who's interested in selling him out."

"Do you plan to turn to the dragons for information, too?" Honorius asked.

Irene picked her words carefully. "Between these four walls, I wouldn't be surprised to find that there were dragons who'd made deals with Alberich—even if they didn't necessarily know who he was, or his full background." *Or had been careful not to ask in case they found out,* she thought. "But I think it very unlikely that we'd be able to identify any of them in the near future or get any useful information out of them, short of a miracle."

"Yes, that fits with what we know," Honorius agreed.

"Kai might know who'd be helpful—or who to talk to. If we can trap Alberich in a high-order world, that would cut down on what he could do with the Language or through chaos."

Alberich could do things with the Language that were far beyond her capabilities. He knew words and structures that she'd never even touched on during all her years with the Library. It was more than irritating to be so thoroughly outclassed in what was supposed to be her particular strength; it was infuriating. But if the Library wouldn't give her access to those vocabularies, then she had no way of getting hold of them, short of going renegade herself . . .

Again her interrogators exchanged glances. Then Kostchei nodded, and the other two did the same, a moment behind him. It was almost synchronized. It reminded Irene of Venice, nearly a year ago, when the overriding power of the local Fae had controlled the will of the population and turned them into puppets. It was unnerving to see that merely normal humans—well, Librarians—could be so similar when they were united in a common purpose.

"Pay attention, granddaughter," Kostchei said grimly. He shook his head, as though bemused by his own words and the temporary suggestion of kinship. "No. Girl. *Irene.* This is going to be complicated. It's time to take Alberich out of the situation. However, if he knows we're actually going on the offensive, he'll go to cover and stay hidden for the next few decades. Based on that, tell me why you think we've brought you here."

A possible solution dawned on Irene, but the more she thought about it, the worse an idea it seemed. "He's unlikely to be particularly worried by me chasing him alone," she said. "So—you want me to be apparently doing this without Library support? But this is the sort of operation that absolutely needs backup. Competent skilled backup. Other Librarians."

"You've gone rogue before," Honorius said.

"I have not!" Irene objected.

Honorius clicked their tongue. "Let's say that you have a *public* history of acting first and getting permission later—as in the Venice incident."

It made sense. But it was still an appalling idea. There were thousands of ways it could go wrong. It was the sort of overly complex plan dreamed up by armchair manipulators who thought they could play chess with the universe and didn't realize that the universe ignored rulebooks. Also, it put Irene herself—and her friends—at horrendous risk. "What if some overly enthusiastic dragon or Fae tries to capture me and turn me in to you for future favors because they think I really *have* gone renegade?" Irene suggested, trying to come up with *practical* reasons to avoid this.

"Try to avoid that sort of interfering busybody," Myeongwol recommended. "Try very hard."

"How many Librarians are going to know about this?" Irene asked.

"Just the three of us," Kostchei said, "and Melusine, of course. Can't have her *seriously* trying to track you down. It wouldn't be pretty."

"But what about Coppelia?" Irene asked, increasingly desperate. She wanted to know there would be at least one person here who was genuinely on her side and knew the truth—and who might be able to pull her out if things went wrong. These others, Kostchei and Myeongwol and Honorius, might be her fellow Librarians and see her as a trusted agent, but they weren't her friends.

Kostchei's eyes were like empty windows, gray and blank, looking onto an endless winter. "I'll tell her the truth, girl, but let's be honest here—she'll be gone before you come back. You've been talking to her. You know that. I'll make sure she doesn't go out thinking that you were a traitor. Fair enough?"

Irene jerked a nod. She couldn't find words for this sudden knowledge of loss. *She'll be gone before you come back.*

"And your parents are out on assignment," Kostchei went on. "Your real parents, the ones who raised you. There's no reason for them to hear about this, as long as you get the job done fast. Think of it as an incentive." His mouth twitched in an attempt at a smile, but his eyes were still bleak and distant, as though facing his own personal loss.

How long has he known Coppelia? Irene thought. Even if they're not friends, they've grown old together here in the Library, which is its own sort of closeness . . .

"Understood," she said, forcing herself to speech. *Though not accepted.* "But if we're keeping this secret from all the other Librarians, does this mean you suspect Alberich has a spy inside the Library?"

"No," Myeongwol said, drawing the word out thoughtfully. "We don't think so. But information is difficult to control once it's loose, and you're not the only Librarian with friends among Fae and dragons. The fewer people who know about this, the better it will work. In fact, we have a little disinformation operation in mind."

"We'll get to that in a minute," Kostchei said quickly. "For the moment, do you understand how this will work? You will be operating on your own—or with your friends. We'll pass you what information we have on Alberich's background and history. If you need advice, enter the Library and send us a message, and we'll respond privately."

"We'll prioritize it," Honorius said smoothly. "You'll have our full attention."

"Everything will be under control," Myeongwol added.

Kostchei must have seen the growing rebellion in her face. "Of course, the other option is to keep you here in the Library until Alberich loses interest in you—effective immediately. If he's already sending you messages, he knows too much about where you are and how to reach you. Do I *really* need to draw you a map?"

The threat was clear enough. Either Irene went along with this plan, or she'd be immured here in the Library for years—or decades, or maybe even centuries. She might have the books she loved, but she wouldn't have anything else. She wouldn't have any of the worlds that she enjoyed visiting.

She wouldn't have Kai.

She tried to pinpoint why this situation was making her so uneasy—and it wasn't just Honorius's use of the word *prioritize*. Part of it was the certainty that *publicly* going rogue left her in a very dangerous position, however much they might promise that they'd support her privately. The other part was the feeling that this was all too clever for its own good. It was putting her at the end of a very long branch—with people she didn't trust holding the saw to cut her off if they considered it necessary.

The Library brand on her back prickled as though in reassurance. She was safely inside the Library—the place to which she'd sworn her obedience, the cause in which she believed—and she was working with other Librarians who shared her aims. Kostchei might be ordering her to kill someone, but he was an elder Librarian. These were people she could trust.

"All right," she said slowly. "I accept this as a plan going forward. But hopefully the whole 'going rogue' thing isn't going to be a major issue. If I need to get help from other Librarians to finish the job, it's going to be a positive hindrance if they think I'm acting outside Library approval."

"Honorius, do you have the briefcase?" Kostchei demanded.

"Here it is," Honorius said, with a suppressed sigh. They brought a glisteningly smooth black leather briefcase into view from where it had been resting against their chair, and slid it across the table to Irene. "Information on Alberich. We trimmed out some of the details where it relates to previous Library operations that are still under privacy seal, but they shouldn't be relevant."

"How am I supposed to know that until I've checked?" Irene objected to being given pre-edited research sources when the situation was this potentially lethal—and not just for her, but for everyone else who might be involved.

"Melusine reviewed it. Take the matter up with her." Honorius folded their hands again, clearly wanting to close the issue.

Irene would have liked to rip the briefcase open then and there to start going through the material, but she managed to restrain herself. "Thank you," she said.

Kostchei reached into his robe and pulled out a heavy gold watch on a chain, which he checked. "We're almost out of time. Any further questions?"

Either I go along with this, or I'm effectively a prisoner. There was no choice at all. She'd have to play along for now and look for other options later. "None for now."

"Good. Then we can get to the disinformation operation. The easiest way to make it look as if you've gone renegade and you're disobeying orders is to act as if you were. Which means that in seven minutes exactly . . ." He checked his watch again. "A couple of Librarians are going to arrive in this room and be told to apprehend you."

"What?" Irene objected. "This is ridiculously overdramatic, you only need to put out an email alert after I've left the Library or something—"

"Six minutes forty-five, girl," Kostchei interrupted. "Start running. They'll be following you."

Irene glared at him, but sadly, her eyes didn't have the power to melt reality or emit laser beams. She grabbed the briefcase and rose to her feet. "Which way is the exit to Vale's world?"

Myeongwol pointed at the door on her left. "Out that way, third right, down the stairs, second left, trapdoor, third right, take the solid rock corridor at the junction, and then it's fourth right and second door on your left. It's about twenty minutes if you run."

Irene was grateful for her years spent studying in the Library and interpreting directions like that. "I'll be in contact," she said, and ran.

She was busy squeezing through the trapdoor when she heard footsteps behind her. Silently she cursed. Of *course* they'd know she'd be making for Vale's world and they'd be following her. She briefly considered striking out in a random direction and then circling back later, but that left too many variables—and too many other Librarians who might actually believe she had gone renegade. The Library often seemed as empty as a rifled pyramid, but the moment one truly *wanted* secrecy and solitude, there would be half a dozen colleagues just around the corner. Right now, it didn't feel like home; it felt like enemy territory.

Irene dropped through the trapdoor, landing in a subterranean tunnel of shored timbers and packed earth. She hurried down the corridor, putting aside thoughts on how utterly *stupid* a plan this was in favor of trying to come up with a good diversion or blockade. The packed earth underfoot was firm enough that she wasn't leaving footprints, so there was little point trying to create a false trail. The doors she passed were heavy wood and the passageways were low-ceilinged tunnels like mineshafts. *Should I duck into a side tunnel and hide, wait for them to go past, then circle round? No, they'd just stake out the room with the exit to Vale's world and I'd have to escape into a different world and hope that Kai would come looking for me . . .*

The third passage on the right was narrow enough to give her claustrophobia. Bare lightbulbs dangled above her, swinging as she passed and making her shadow flex and contort along the floor. She couldn't hear her pursuers, but they had to be closer now. She needed a way to slow them down, one that they couldn't simply dismantle with the Language.

Ahead of her she saw a junction where multiple tunnels splayed out like the fibers of a plant root. *Right. Desperation plan go.*

Irene stopped next to the final door before the junction and laid her hand against it. "**Room door which I'm touching, open outward to block the corridor,**" she ordered.

The door shuddered as it strained against its hinges, forced by the Language to move in the opposite direction to its natural swing, then ground jerkily out into the corridor, forming a temporary blockage.

"**Floor rise up and ceiling descend between me and the door to fill the corridor,**" Irene continued, backing away as the earth began to shudder beneath her feet and fragments of soil cascaded down from the ceiling. She covered her face with her sleeve as the air filled with dust, hoping that she hadn't overdone it. She didn't want to bring down this whole section of the Library . . .

But when the earth stopped moving, the Library around her was still in one piece. Mostly. There was now a horrendous rent in the ceiling, through which a distant light flickered and a fresh flow of air brushed against Irene's face. But she'd let someone else sort that out. For the moment, there was about six feet of raw earth blockage behind the door—and, more importantly, the people on the far side *wouldn't know how much there was.* Once they managed to get the door out of the way they'd be faced with a solid mass of earth and no idea how far she'd collapsed the corridor. It'd buy her time.

A faint headache ran from temple to temple, like a gilded net of pain, but she ignored it and began running again, suppressing the pain of aching limbs with a mental promise that she could sit down and have a breather on the other side.

Finally the door of the room that led to Vale's world came into view. There were still no footsteps coming from behind her. She'd made it. Kostchei and the others had wanted her *pursued,* but they hadn't actually wanted her *stopped.* She didn't like to imagine what might have happened if those other Librarians had caught up with her and tried to apprehend her. Someone would have been hurt. Possibly her, but definitely them. And while she was reluctantly prepared to accept Kostchei's disinformation plan—for the time being—she didn't want to injure her fellow Librarians in the process.

With a sigh of relief Irene opened the door and stepped inside.

And went sprawling to the floor as she tripped over the foot extended in front of her.

CHAPTER 7

The person who'd been waiting for Irene dropped on her from behind as Irene hit the floor, leaning her full weight on her and hooking an arm around her throat. "Don't struggle," a familiar voice hissed in her ear.

Irene went limp. She knew that voice. "Bradamant?"

"No, it's all the dragon monarchs come visiting." The arm round her neck tightened for just a moment, to demonstrate the possibility of suffocation, before relaxing again. "Of course it's me. You stupid, stupid, *stupid* idiot."

"Granted," Irene wheezed. She should have been more careful when she came through the door. A clock at the back of her mind ticked down the minutes before her pursuers circumvented the blockage and caught up with her. "What are you doing here?"

"Stopping you."

"I thought we were on the same side." She and Bradamant had a tangled history, as twisted as a blackberry vine and with just as many painful thorns. Bradamant had been a full Librarian when Irene was just a journeyman, and had supervised her on multiple missions. While Irene was prepared to admit that some of it might *possibly* have been her own fault, the two of them had never got on, and a mild dislike had developed into a full-blown feud. Age, maturity, and having other people try to kill them had shaken that attitude out of them to some degree, but they definitely weren't friends.

Bradamant's arm tightened again. "Like I said, you're being stupid. I'm stopping you from making a serious mistake."

"What do you think I'm trying to do?" Irene asked, keeping her voice all sweet reason as she mentally ran through a list of ways to get out of her current position. Unfortunately they mostly defaulted to *Don't get into it in the first place.*

"You're *trying*," Bradamant emphasized the word, "to go after Alberich. Because of some ridiculous strokes of luck, you think you might have a remote chance of killing him, rather than the *far* more likely possibility that you'll end up dead, skinned, and regretting the whole idea. And because you've been officially told you can't do it, you're about to sneak out and go renegade, in the sort of self-aggrandizing, petty, teacher's pet, sure you'll get away with breaking the rules way"—her voice was rising into a snarl—"that is *so* characteristic of you."

"I thought we'd got over that," Irene said plaintively. "Believe me, I'm really *not* the object of any favoritism round here." *No, I'm the number-one experimental specimen and person who'll be blamed if things go wrong because of my father.*

Bradamant's grip tightened briefly before she could control herself. "That's easy for you to say. You, Irene, are suffering from a potentially lethal case of lifelong privilege."

"Why's it lethal?"

"Because it'll get you killed."

Irene dragged herself back from the temptation to argue. Her parents—her adoptive parents—were Librarians, and she'd grown up knowing about the Library and had been a frequent visitor. Bradamant had come as an apprentice from nowhere in particular and didn't like to discuss it, though it probably wasn't pleasant. Irene supposed that Bradamant did have a point about privilege—but it wasn't relevant right now. If the other Librarian kept her here much longer, she was going to get *caught*, and so much for Kostchei's stupid disinformation plan and everything else.

"Why were you waiting here?" she asked instead. Had Kostchei set Irene up to be captured as a renegade? The thought chilled her. She'd believed she could trust him.

"I'm Kostchei's assistant; I have access to his schedule. I knew that he and some others were going to talk to you about your plans and that he was going to warn you not to go after Alberich. I thought I'd just sit and wait here in case . . . anything happened. When I saw you come running in here, I knew you'd been stupid."

There was nothing different from normal in the way that Bradamant said *Alberich*, and Irene allowed herself a silent prayer of thanks. Bradamant didn't know about Irene being his daughter. If she *had* known, she wouldn't be so casual about it. "Does Kostchei know that you read his schedule without telling him about it?" she demanded.

"That's hardly the issue," Bradamant said a little too quickly. "Now are you going to be sensible and come quietly?"

Any attempt at using the Language would get Irene choked. She released her grip on the briefcase and shifted position slightly, trying to creep her hand up underneath her body without being too obvious about it. "Look," she said, hoping that reason would work and she wouldn't have to resort to violence. "You see that briefcase? That's information which Kostchei gave me. I'm being *allowed* to go after Alberich."

"That briefcase doesn't prove anything. And no, I'm not going to let go of you to check it."

"Would you believe me if I swore in the Language that it's true and I'm being ordered to go?"

Bradamant hesitated. Librarians couldn't lie in the Language. If Irene gave her word in *that*, then it would be confirmed. "I don't trust you to say anything in the Language," she finally said. "You'd just try to get loose from me."

Fine, Irene thought. *I've tried the truth. I've tried being reasonable.* And a selfish little part of her was glad of the chance to hit back. Tripping over Bradamant's foot had injured her pride as well as knocking the breath out of her. **"Library brand, burn!"** she ordered, cutting across the end of Bradamant's words. She slid her fingers up to protect her throat from the arm across it.

Bradamant's arm tightened round her neck, going from *restraint* to *absolute throttle* without a breath's hesitation. However, the nature of the hold meant that Bradamant's front was pressed against Irene's back.

It hurt to have her Library brand heat up. It hurt a great deal. But she'd known it was coming, and while it was extremely painful to have her back feeling somewhere between an agonizing sunburn and the application of red-hot metal, she knew that Bradamant would be getting exactly the same pain, since Irene hadn't bothered to specify *whose* Library brand in the Language—and from both sides.

Bradamant screamed, her grip loosening, and Irene broke free, frantically rolling to one side and cursing her long Victorian skirts. She grabbed a book from one of the piles along the walls and flung it in Bradamant's direction: a small missile, paperback rather than hardback, but the natural reaction to *incoming* made Bradamant duck and shield her face.

Irene's back was still screaming in agony, but at least her clothing hadn't caught fire with the heat—it just felt as if it should have. She grabbed the briefcase and staggered to her feet. The two of them glared at each other, both hunched over from the burning pain across their backs.

Bradamant looked slightly less perfect than normal. Her razor-cut black hair was ruffled from where they'd rolled around on the floor, and dust marred her business trouser suit at elbows and knees. Her eyes flicked for a fraction of a second to the room's other door—the one that would lead out of the Library, and to Vale's world—and then back to Irene again. Neither of them spoke, each knowing that a few words from them might give the other enough chance to use the Language in an effective or explosive way.

Irene sidled toward the door, one hand stretched out for the handle. The pain in her back was slowly dying away, and she was conscious again of how little time she had until her other pursuers arrived. She met Bradamant's eyes, trying to stare her down. *Don't try again. Let me go.*

"This is a bad idea," Bradamant said. "The political situation's dangerous. It doesn't need you making it worse."

"Vanishing worlds?"

"So you've heard about that. No. There's something else happening. Accusations of Librarians getting involved in politics where they shouldn't. Someone's working against us."

"If it's Alberich, all the more reason to stop him."

"But if it's not . . ." A shadow darkened Bradamant's eyes, and she shook her head. "You don't need to know about that. What I'm here for is to stop you making things *worse*."

"Give me more information, or get out of my way and let me go."

With a little sigh Bradamant straightened, and her hands dropped to her sides. She shrugged. "It's your funeral," she said.

Irene felt the door's handle against her fingers. She yanked it open and stepped through in a single motion, slamming it behind her.

The room she entered was bare, from scoured walls to empty floor, with no trace of its previous furniture. No museum cases, bookcases, or anything else—such as bloodstains or scars from broken glass. It was a small storeroom in the British Museum, and it just happened to be the Library's fixed gateway into this world. Unfortunately, it had also been the scene of several rather violent events, to the extent that the curator—with some persuasion from Vale—had decided to leave it empty and keep it that way. Irene had heard that some of the guards thought it was haunted, probably due to people appearing in it from apparently nowhere, as she'd just done. The key point now was that there wasn't anything she could use to block the doorway and stop the other Librarians from following her through. She'd have to rely on speed instead.

Irene alternately pushed and sidled through the crowds of museum visitors and was lucky enough to spot a cab as she stepped outside. With a total lack of shame or manners, she dodged past the middle-aged woman in heavy jet and furs who'd been about to climb into it and slid inside. "Triple fare if you can get me to my destination within the next ten minutes," she called up to the driver.

"And where would that be, ma'am?" he enquired, the words "triple fare" having their own kind of magic and rendering him deaf to the complaints of the other would-be passenger.

Irene gave him the address of the lodgings she shared with Kai, and settled back into the seat as the cab jolted out into traffic. She took a moment to check the briefcase—simple catches, no lock. Presumably if it fell into enemy hands, said hands would be competent enough that no lock would be of any use, so why bother? She was tempted to open it then and there, but common sense helped her resist; a cab going at high speed was no place to read historical archived information, however scandalous and informative it might be.

In eight minutes the cab came rattling to a stop outside their lodgings. "Here," Irene said, handing up the promised triple fare, "and thank you."

Kai came striding out of the lounge to meet her in the hallway, all action and decision. "I heard the cab outside, and you come running in," he said. "Is there an emergency?"

"Possibly," Irene admitted. "I may be being chased by several Librarians, including Bradamant, who have the impression that I've gone renegade from the Library in order to hunt down Alberich."

"And have you?"

"No, I'm just meant to look as if I have. Gone renegade, that is. The hunting down is genuine."

"That puts me in an awkward position," Kai said thoughtfully. "Would it be more in character for me to help you, however dubious your actions and motivations, or to pursue you for a breach of trust to your lawful overlord?" He saw her expression. "I mean in terms of perspective and keeping up this façade of going renegade, of course."

Irene was relieved. She should never have doubted him. "I think you should help me, however dubious my actions. After all, I would logically have lied to you about it all, wouldn't I? You wouldn't *know* that I was an untrustworthy renegade."

"Perfect." He smiled, and it was like sunlight on the ocean, a sudden flash of light across the cool perfection of his face, a note of warmth and humanity that turned him from polished marble to flesh that one could dream of touching. "So do we run for it, or bunker down here and deny all callers?"

Irene frowned, thinking it through. The pursuers Kostchei had sent after her might stop chasing her once she'd left the Library, but

Bradamant would be more persistent, and was carrying a grudge now as well. "Where's Vale gone?"

Kai shrugged. "Out on business."

Irene mentally tossed a coin. "Let's go to his lodgings. Even if he's not there, we can start going through the research material I have. Bradamant knows where he lives, but she'll check here first, which will buy us some time."

"And you can tell me what's been happening while we're on the way there," Kai said, in tones that made it clear he wanted the full details.

"I will. Though I'm afraid there's some bad news." Irene felt the brush of sorrow again, and knew that having to talk about it would be worse—yet Kai deserved to know. Coppelia might not be as close to him as she was to Irene, but he considered her a friend. Everyone should have the right to mourn their friends.

Vale's housekeeper knew and trusted them by now, after their frequent visits, the criminal investigations, the murder attempts—and the fact that Irene had taken care to find out her favorite area of cooking (scones) and pass on several recipes from alternate worlds. She was happy to wave them up to Vale's rooms and to promise that if anyone except Vale asked, she'd claim she knew nothing about Irene's presence.

Vale's sitting room was as crowded as always: scrapbooks with details of past criminality and curious facts filled the shelves, while stacks of reference books spread outward from the corners of the room and toward the center like infectious diseases. The mantelpiece was crowded with curious items—a black-and-white puzzle-box, a mysterious pouch of red leather embroidered in silver, two matching teak-handled switchblades, an incomprehensible piece of machinery which sparked regularly and silently, a piece of paper with *Six weeks were allowed* scrawled across it—but the lack of dust indicated that the housemaids were used to its contents. Pipettes and test tubes from Vale's most recent piece of chemical analysis glowed where they stood in the shadow with an eerie luminosity, a crawling green light that suggested something fungal and abhorrent. Next to them was a half-eaten sandwich.

"Time to see how much information they've given me," Irene said with relief. She set down her briefcase on a relatively clean area of table, and was about to open it when they both heard the sound of carriage wheels coming to a stop outside.

Kai crossed to the window, and his expression abruptly darkened. He gestured for Irene to join him.

Irene's heart sank as she recognized the tall, brusque figure who was climbing out of the carriage and heading for the front door. It was Kai's elder brother, Shan Yuan. A sensation of impending trouble crawled its way up her spine. While Shan Yuan cared about Kai's welfare, he'd made it clear that he wanted his little brother away from Irene and back safe in dragon-controlled worlds. And he knew about Irene's parentage—he'd been there in the shadowy archive when Vale had announced it to everyone who was listening. This did not bode well.

They could both hear the sound of knocking on the door and Shan Yuan's voice as the housekeeper answered. "I am looking for my brother, who goes by the name of Strongrock. Is he present?"

Kai and Irene exchanged glances. "I can't just leave him standing there," Kai murmured. "I have to go down."

"I'll go into Vale's bedroom and hide there," Irene suggested. "He's looking for you, not me."

She could see the clear indecision on Kai's face. On the one hand, he'd appreciate her moral support. On the other hand, if she, as an outsider, was present, then Kai would have to behave *properly* by dragon standards when in the presence of an older relative, which would be a severe cramp on the conversation. "Thank you," he said quietly, and headed for the door.

Irene concealed herself in Vale's bedroom, leaving the door open a crack and giving herself a good angle of the room. This might well be a very private conversation, but she hadn't actually made any promises about not listening. Kai might be relying on her good taste and proper instincts, which was a mistake on his part. If some Librarians were playing politics, then they might be doing it with dragons. And if that was why Shan Yuan was here and looking for Kai . . . then Irene *had* to know about it.

Two pairs of footsteps rang on the stairs, and then the door opened and the two dragons walked in. Shan Yuan was in the lead, looking no worse for the injury he'd taken recently while fighting Alberich. There was something in the way he carried himself which suggested he felt fully in control of the situation—and that worried Irene.

"Well, Kai," he said. "I've had to go to some trouble to find you, but here you are at last. We have matters to discuss."

CHAPTER 8

The two dragons were clearly brothers, but it was easy to see which of the two held the balance of power. Shan Yuan had black hair and dark blue eyes, like Kai, but there was an added note of arrogance to his posture, while Kai's was shaded with the deference of a junior to a senior. He waited for Kai to close the door, looking around the room with the air of a man judging and condemning the contents.

"I'm glad to see you well, elder brother," Kai began. "May I offer you refreshments?"

"The offer is welcome, but I don't expect to be here long. I trust that you are in good health yourself?"

"As you can see." There was a brief pause, then with the demands of courtesy met, Kai said bluntly, "Why are you here?"

Shan Yuan raised an eyebrow as elegant as a stroke of calligraphy. "To offer you an opportunity. I'm glad that the Librarian isn't here; she'd only be a complication. And since you didn't respond to my earlier letters..."

Irene's thoughts were somewhere between *Ha ha, fooled you!* and *Please go on, you have my full attention.* But she kept herself absolutely quiet and still. If she was discovered doing a "rat in the arras" impersonation for a conversation she specifically *wasn't* supposed to be listening to, the consequences would be unpleasant. Stabbing might well be involved.

Also . . . *what* earlier letters? Kai hadn't mentioned those.

"Does this have something to do with Lord Shang Yi?" Kai asked. His tone was diffident, but at the same time . . . intrigued. Irene felt a pang of concern but suppressed it. It wasn't her job to police his choices.

"Not immediately," Shan Yuan said. "That will hopefully be the long-term result, but for the moment there is a post vacant in our lord uncle Ao Ji's administration. You would fit there well."

Kai seemed at a loss for words. "Our lord uncle Ao Ji—elder brother, you do *know* what happened in Paris?"

"Yes," Shan Yuan said flatly. "That's why there is a post vacant in his administration. Due to our uncle's illness and his decision to take a temporary rest from affairs, his administration is under stress. You would be useful there."

Well, that was certainly one way of putting it. Ao Ji, one of the four dragon kings, had decided that peace with the Fae was unacceptable and had done his best to sabotage the treaty negotiations in Paris, including killing one of his own servants to frame the Fae for the murder and nearly wiping out Paris in a blizzard as the endgame. Both Irene and Kai had been among the potential victims. The whole matter had been diplomatically hushed up, and Ao Ji declared a victim of temporary insanity due to the influence of malign Fae. (As opposed to the good Fae who were signing the treaty.)

Still, Irene couldn't imagine why Shan Yuan thought this offer of employment would be remotely welcome to Kai. In fact, she could already see Kai's face settling into a look of polite negation. "I'm very flattered that you think I could be of service there, elder brother, but—"

Shan Yuan raised an admonitory hand. "Before you say something unwise, let me be clear; it would be temporary. A few years at most. You would resume your technological studies later."

"If it's for a few years, then I might as well continue serving our father here," Kai countered. "He placed me in this position, after all."

"Let's be honest with ourselves, Kai," Shan Yuan said, a statement which to Irene's ear sounded very much like *I'm going to suggest something which you'll find credible purely through its nastiness and unpleasant implications and your own desire to seem mature.* "Our father placed you as treaty representative because he felt you were best suited to manipulate the Librarian Irene Winters."

"And if he did?"

Irene was fairly sure that wasn't *exactly* what Ao Guang had had in mind. He must know that Kai wasn't the manipulative type. Now if Shan Yuan had accused him of doing it in order to prejudice Irene a crucial one percent in favor of the dragons because of her fondness for Kai, that would have been nearer the mark.

"We've received reports that the Library is considering recalling her due to her obsessive pursuit of their traitor Alberich," Shan Yuan said, his tone distinctly smug. "When that happens, your influence will no longer be necessary. It would be . . . cruel . . . for you to break with her at that point. Better to sever relations now rather than have it appear you only tolerated her because of your influence over her."

Irene could see the flush of anger on Kai's cheeks, the fern-patterns of scales that briefly washed across his skin as his dragon temper raged. When he spoke, his tone was surprisingly mild. "Are you certain of the veracity of these reports? A Librarian who's prepared to sell information to contacts outside the Library cannot be trusted."

"You're the one spending time with her," Shan Yuan replied. "Is it true that she's hunting for Alberich? That she's disobeyed orders in her search for him?"

Very curious, Irene thought. This had only just happened. How did Shan Yuan already know about it? Either he had a highly placed agent inside the Library, or Kostchei had already been spreading rumors before he made Irene "escape."

"Alberich *did* try to kill us both," Kai pointed out. "And you as well, elder brother. It seems to me that disposing of him serves us just as much as it serves the Library."

There was a pause. Then Shan Yuan said, "You're going to be difficult about this, aren't you."

"I appreciate the honor you've done me in coming to make this offer—" Kai started.

"Stop right there." Shan Yuan moved in closer, prodding Kai with a finger in the center of his chest. Irene saw a muscle twitch in Kai's cheek as he controlled himself. "I'm making allowances for you, Kai, because I realize that you have feelings for this human, even in spite of her abominable parentage. But I'm *not* going to let her drag you down with her."

Kai looked down at the finger as though it were a maggot which had crawled out of a once-respectable apple. "If you truly believe I have feelings for her," he said softly, dangerously, "then your words are ill-advised."

"Where is your loyalty?"

"Where it should be. I stand where our lord father has placed me."

"True loyalty involves doing what you know your lord genuinely wants, rather than blind obedience to his spoken orders."

Kai folded his arms. "If you have come from him to give me updated orders, elder brother, then I await them with interest."

The temperature in the room had risen. Even in Vale's bedroom,

Irene could feel sweat crawling down her forehead. Shan Yuan's personal element was fire—and he wasn't taking this refusal well.

"I'm here to make a suggestion which would serve everyone!" Shan Yuan snapped.

Especially you? Irene wondered. When she'd met him previously, she'd developed strong suspicions about his ultimate aims in trying to pry Kai out of his position as treaty representative—namely, that Shan Yuan wanted that position for himself. He couldn't outright contradict their father or order Kai to step down, but if Kai apparently did so of his own free will, or asked to be removed . . .

"I appreciate your generosity in coming to make this offer—" Kai began again.

Shan Yuan raised one hand. "Don't even finish that sentence. I've tried to be reasonable about this. Since you lack the perception and the common sense to see what a good idea this would be, I'll have to resort to stronger measures."

The atmosphere in the room changed. "Oh?" Kai said, his tone as flat and level as a sword blade.

"Bear in mind that I've done my best to be fair about this," Shan Yuan said. "I've been perfectly reasonable to your human favorites. But lines must be drawn. There are limits to tolerance—and I think our lord father will agree."

"I fail to understand you," Kai said, in tones that made it quite clear he did understand.

"I believe our lord father would say that you should not be consorting with someone who's a traitor's daughter and a threat to his ally the Library." Shan Yuan paused. "Of course, should you *choose* to leave her now and take up suitable duties elsewhere, it won't be necessary for me to raise the matter with him—*publicly.*"

Irene silently cursed. She'd hoped that Shan Yuan might keep his mouth shut about her heritage, for Kai's sake. Wishful thinking, but . . . he'd been silent until now. He'd just saved the information to use it at the worst possible time for her.

"You think he doesn't already know?" Kai parried.

That made Shan Yuan pause. "You've told him?"

"Have you?"

"It was clearly your duty to make him aware, if you suspected such a thing," Shan Yuan said firmly.

"Elder brother, was it not your duty as well?" Kai's brows drew together and his eyes glinted dragon-red with rising anger. "It might seem almost as though you personally didn't care about this, until it came to a point when it was convenient for you to use this information."

"I was allowing you to inform him first, as the most closely involved," Shan Yuan snapped. It wasn't much of an argument, and he clearly knew it. "Since you haven't told him—"

"How do you know that I haven't?" Kai demanded. He took a step forward, actively confronting his brother. "Does our lord father tell you everything that I tell him? Are you privy to all his secrets? Don't you think that perhaps he might have a *reason* to keep me here?"

"Your insolence only demonstrates how ill-fitted you are for your current position," Shan Yuan said softly. "Don't provoke me further."

Kai took a deep breath. The ruby glow in his eyes dimmed. "Elder brother. I regret if my words have given you offense. But surely you must have considered that if *you* would keep such information for when it's useful, so would our lord father? If you make it public, then you will place him in a position where he must take action—one way or another. Are you sure that you want to force this situation?"

Oh, nicely done, Irene thought.

For the first time, there was uncertainty in Shan Yuan's voice. "You *have* told him, then? Even though you're fond of her?"

"I've reported what took place," Kai said coldly. "Are you accusing me of keeping silence in order to protect her?"

"I'm . . . surprised," Shan Yuan admitted. "And what if our lord father did tell you to leave her? Would you do it?"

The question hung in the air like an open wound. Finally Kai said, "I would obey my lord father's command."

Irene felt something twist in her chest. She knew—she'd always known—that Kai wasn't going to throw away his family and his entire life for her sake. In her better moments, she hoped that if it ever happened, she'd tell him to go and to be happy without her, that the two of them had duties and responsibilities which went beyond the fact that they loved each other.

But it was amazing how much it hurt to hear those words from him.

On the other hand, they seemed to embolden Shan Yuan. "Then you'd do better to leave her now," he said. "Whether it's sooner or later, that information *will* come out. Even if you and she keep silent, there's the detective, and her Fae apprentice . . . Make a clean break of it. Leave your current position to someone else and go to a task which better suits your talents."

"I am treaty representative," Kai said, his voice strengthening with each word, "and I do not think that I have done too badly in the role. You are not the only family member who has written to me, elder brother. Some of them have been quite *pleased* by my efforts."

Shan Yuan jerked his chin. "Some of our family have no discrimination or judgment."

"You are our lord father's eldest son and I am his youngest. Who am I to contradict you?" Kai's shoulders stiffened. "But at the same time, I'm not going to leave this position without direct orders to do so."

"Then I promise you that I shall *get* those orders," Shan Yuan snarled. Fire glinted in his eyes, and faint scale patterns flashed red on his hands and cheeks. "I'm not going to let your juvenile obstinacy stand in the way of what's best for you—and for all of us."

"Elder brother . . ." Kai's voice trailed off. "Why are you doing this?"

"For your sake!" The coals burning in the fire jumped and shattered. "This position's too important for you to hold it any longer, Kai. I can't tolerate it. I *won't* tolerate it. Someone else will handle these matters with greater discretion. And *you* will be out of danger."

Irene wished she could believe him. It would be much nicer—much more wholesome—if Shan Yuan was *honestly* acting out of concern for Kai's safety. Granted, it would still be horrendously inconvenient and misplaced, but at least it would be due to good intentions—albeit the sort which could pave the road to hell.

Unfortunately, she suspected that Shan Yuan's motivations were twofold and ran in parallel, and even if the first might be *Keep my little brother safe*, the second was *Advance myself by usurping his job*.

"If this position is dangerous, then whoever takes it will be in just as much danger as I am," Kai objected. "How could I place someone else in that position?"

"Whoever takes it will be older and stronger than you," Shan Yuan said wearily. "They will be more *capable* than you."

"I don't think so." There was a new note to Kai's voice, an increased firmness to his stance. "Elder brother, I've learned through experience. I've faced down Fae in their own territory and grown stronger from it. I was present at the peace conference and I . . . provided aid when it was needed. I *helped*. I stood in the way of our lord uncle when he suffered from madness and I held him off for long enough that others could bring him down. I'm not incapable. I'm not helpless. And I will *not* resign this position without orders from our lord father who placed me in it. Whatever threats or temptations you may offer."

Shan Yuan's hand tightened, and Irene thought he was about to strike Kai. But he took a breath, and the moment passed. "You're making a mistake," he said, fury rising in his voice like bubbles in lava.

"I'm following what I believe is the correct course of conduct," Kai answered. "I have no regrets."

"You will do."

"Do you have any other business with me, elder brother?"

Kai's phrasing and manner reduced his elder brother to a mere petitioner, rather than a respected guest who had the right to control the conversation. It was an open insult. Shan Yuan's head jerked back as though Kai had actually hit him. "No," he said through gritted teeth. "I have no other business with you. I have no greetings for your friends. I will be returning, soon enough, and then we will resume this discussion."

He slammed the door behind him.

Irene hesitated briefly before opening the bedroom door. Raw fury still showed in the lines of Kai's posture and burned in his eyes, and in his place she would rather have been left alone. Yet it would have been a sort of lie to stay hidden and act as if she hadn't heard every word. She entered the room quietly, and the two of them listened to the sound of Shan Yuan's departing cab outside.

Finally she asked, "*Did* you tell your father about me?"

He didn't meet her eyes. "I told my father that Vale confused Alberich at a crucial juncture by claiming you were his long-lost daughter."

"That's actually rather brilliant," Irene said thoughtfully.

Kai blinked, looking her in the face at last. "You approve of that? You understand . . ."

"Kai." She moved closer, folding her arms around him, feeling the knotted tension of his muscles. "I understand that this wasn't something you could keep secret from your father." Maybe there were some branches of history, some alternate realities, where Kai would choose her over his family—but she knew deep in her heart that this wasn't one of them. For better or worse, his loyalty was part of who he was—and she loved him for that. "I appreciate the way that you chose to put it."

After all, Ao Guang wasn't stupid. One couldn't be stupid and also be the eldest of the four dragon kings. He'd ruled the more orderly end of reality together with the four dragon queens for millennia—or at least, as far back as dragon recorded history went. He could put two and two together, and probably add another two from sources which Irene didn't know about, and get a total which added up to Irene *being* Alberich's daughter. But plausible deniability was a wonderful, wonderful thing.

He relaxed a little in her embrace. "Thank you for understanding," he said softly.

"It's what we do." But cold calculation was overriding her emotions. "Shan Yuan took a cab. That means either he wanted to get away from here before he took dragon form, or he's staying somewhere local."

"He probably wouldn't care about the implications of taking his true form on Vale's doorstep." Kai frowned. "But why stay locally?"

"If he'd thought that you were going to say yes to him . . . he might have wanted you to leave immediately, and he'd have stayed here to take over."

Kai nodded. "Yes. There would have to be *someone* here until a new dragon representative was assigned in my place. He'd know I'd never just walk away and desert my post."

Irene weighed the possible results of sharing her suspicions with Kai. The flip side of absolute family loyalty was, unfortunately, absolute family loyalty. "I have to wonder what he truly wants out of this," she said carefully.

"He's said it himself—he's worried about me."

"Yes, but . . . none of your other siblings have been beating a path to our door to demand that you resign." There had to be some way to get Kai to see what she meant, to make him aware of the danger they were in. If Shan Yuan really wanted Kai's position, then he wasn't going to take no for an answer.

Kai hesitated. "It's possible that my other siblings don't know how dangerous things are here. I don't think my elder brother realized it himself until he was dragged into things. But to be fair, he's always been concerned about my upbringing." His mouth twisted a little, as though recalling something unpleasant.

"Oh?"

"It's not important. It's what any older brother would do for his younger brother. The younger brother doesn't necessarily appreciate it at the time."

Irene decided to let sleeping dragons lie for now. "Vale can probably find out where Shan Yuan's staying in London. That'll give us some leeway."

"What do you mean?"

"If your brother does decide to go to your father and suggest that you resign your position, then he has to leave London to do it. If we keep tabs on Shan Yuan and what he's up to here, then we'll know that we're on a deadline the moment he leaves." She released Kai. "But right now, we need to be working on our first line of defense."

He tilted an eyebrow.

"No Alberich," Irene explained, "no problem. Or at least, very much reduced problem."

"Having me keep my position is not a good reason to kill Alberich!"

"We're planning to remove him as a threat. Somehow." Even if the details were still up in the air. "Shan Yuan's pushing the notion that I'm compromised because I'm Alberich's daughter. If Alberich's not an issue any more, then that invalidates half his argument. And if you've helped the Library dispose of a long-running problem who's actively hostile to the peace process . . . well, your father can't possibly disapprove of that."

He caught her wrist, his long fingers closing round her fragile human flesh. "I'm not letting you put yourself at risk by rushing your plans."

"Kai," Irene said reprovingly. "I'm not going to *rush* anything. I'm just thinking out loud that it would be useful if we could show some concrete planning." And, the thought crossed her mind, if they were both off hunting for Alberich, then it became significantly harder for Shan Yuan to deliver any writs for Kai to leave his position. The good old *We would have obeyed the order if only we'd known about it* defense.

Though would it be better for Kai—safer for Kai—if he wasn't involved with her? Alberich was a millstone round her neck that might drag him down as well. If she really loved Kai, should she consider doing what was best for him rather than what she wanted?

She forced herself back to the immediate situation. "Let's finally take a look at these." She snapped her briefcase open. The sheaf of papers inside came spilling out, drifting across the table, and she had to grab them before they could waft onto the floor. They were onion-skin thin and very lightweight, written in script rather than printed, in multiple languages. Fortunately the pages were numbered.

"I'm going to need something to take notes with," Irene muttered, appropriating some of Vale's spare notepaper and a pen. "Kai, will you help? We're going to need a rough index of what's in here, and then we can start looking for useful information."

Kai tilted his head. "Are you allowed to show me this classified material?" It was a pro forma question rather than a serious one.

"I haven't been told otherwise."

"Did you *ask*?"

"No, which is possibly why I haven't been told otherwise. Then again, they must have known I'd show it to you and Vale." *And if they didn't know that,* Irene reassured herself, *then they clearly don't have a full grasp of the current position and I don't need to worry about their opinion.* "Pull up a chair and—"

Someone banged on the front door. "Where is Peregrine Vale!" a voice demanded, loudly enough that they could hear it upstairs, drowning out the housekeeper's remonstrations.

"I'll get it," Kai said with a sigh.

Irene nodded absently and went back to the papers, ignoring the screams and crashes from outside. Kai could handle that.

Each page seemed to be a copy of a different record from the Library's archives, with the first ones referring to the days when Alberich had been loyal to the Library and the missions he'd been sent on.

There was one thing Irene particularly wanted to know, but she suspected she wasn't going to find here. *What was the crucial thing that made Alberich betray the Library?* In an earlier mission to locate a unique copy of a Grimm Brothers fairytale she'd read a version of his betrayal, but that had been clouded by its presentation as fiction. Though, given that Alberich himself had been trying to steal the Grimm volume, there must have been some truth to it . . .

Her memory wasn't perfect—but this was one story she wouldn't forget.

Once upon a time, there lived a brother and a sister who both belonged to the same Library. Now this was a strange library, for it held books from a thousand worlds, but lay outside all of them. And the brother and sister loved each other and worked together to find new books for their Library.

One day, the brother said to his sister, "Since this Library contains all books, does it contain the story of its own founding?"

"I suppose so," the sister said. "But it would be unwise to seek it."

"Why?" the brother asked.

"Because of the nature of the Library's secret," the sister answered, "that we both wear branded upon our backs."

Irene noted the page numbers as she skimmed through the documents, with references to when and where each mission was, and which book had been the objective, but the words of the fairy story still echoed in her head.

Now the brother had never troubled to look at the mark upon his back. But that night he sought a mirror and read the writing on his skin, and what he read there sent him mad. He left the Library then and he colluded with its enemies against it. But most of all he swore vengeance against his sister, for she had spoken the words that set him on this path. A hundred years later, his sister returned to the Library following a quest that she had been set, and she was with child.

"Is something the matter?" Kai asked. He'd come back in, followed by drifts of chlorine-scented steam, dusting off his hands and adjusting his cuffs. "You're frowning."

"The more I read about the man who sired me, the more I worry about myself," Irene confessed.

"Don't."

She looked up and met his eyes, and saw his uncertainty. His response had been a little too hasty. This wasn't a conversation where either of them knew the right answers or would believe easy reassurances.

Irene gestured at the papers. "There's far too much evidence that I should."

"I'll get some tea," he said firmly, taking the convenient route out of the discussion before it became more awkward. The door closed behind him as he went downstairs to the kitchen, leaving Irene alone with the records of Alberich's crimes.

She stared at the page in front of her, an account of Alberich's trip to an alternate Kyoto under that world's Tokugawa Shogunate to collect a complete copy of *The Tale of the Matsura Palace,* and tried to concentrate on her notes. It didn't work; the fairytale ran through her head:

And this caused great trouble, for there could be no birth nor death within the Library. Yet she feared to set foot outside it lest her brother should find her. So in pain she begged them to cut open her belly and take the child out and they did so, and she was delivered of a child. They sewed up her belly with silver thread and hid her among the deepest vaults for fear that her brother should seek her again.

And then Irene—that baby—had been given to her parents, with a convenient story about a female Librarian who didn't want to raise an unwelcome child. Her parents—yes, she still considered them *her parents*—hadn't asked questions. Irene wished *she'd* never needed to ask questions.

It wasn't the heritage she would have chosen. It wasn't the heritage she'd even have dreamed possible, a year ago. *So how do I live with this?*

Another thought, even less welcome—might Alberich's madness be something that she'd inherit from him? It would be a relief to find that there had been something that drove him over the edge, some shock or misunderstanding or trauma. It'd be one less thing to trouble her sleep.

She focused on the papers and sorted them into three categories: reports of Alberich's earlier career, the incident where he'd broken with the Library, and reports of his activities afterward. She singled out the pages concerning his betrayal, rather surprised that a couple of pages was all there was. Surely there should be more? If she'd been there at the time and investigating, she'd have expected to produce a book's worth of information. Or was this part of the "edited" section?

Feet came trampling up the stairs again—not Kai or Vale. While

Irene didn't have Vale's specialized ear for such things, she could identify the heavy-booted tread of multiple policemen. She hoped Inspector Singh might be with them. He was one of Vale's closest acquaintances among the police—a friend, even—and he knew about the Library.

But she didn't recognize the policeman who thrust the door open. He was a sergeant, by his uniform, and a total stranger to her, as were the others behind him. She rose from her seat at the table, considering what to say, but just as she opened her mouth to speak a cold thread of caution restrained her.

Something was wrong here. These men certainly *looked* like policemen, but they weren't *acting* like the typical policemen who came here to see Vale. Those policemen didn't come stampeding up here in platoons. They came one at a time, rubbing their hands nervously, ever so apologetic for bothering him but at the same time hoping he could give them something they could use, and—with a bit of luck—leave them the credit afterward. Either they were genuine, in which case something very unusual was going on . . . or they weren't genuine.

Irene let her eyes widen in her best imitation of innocent respect. "Oh, good afternoon, officers! I hope I'm not in your way—I just came to see Mr. Vale, but he's out, and I was told I could wait . . ."

The sergeant fished a notebook from the depths of his tunic. "Not at all, miss," he said. "We're here to see Mr. Vale ourselves. Now perhaps you'd like to tell me who you are and what you're here to see him about?"

"My name's Clarice Backson," Irene lied, falling back on an alias she'd used before, but one that Vale would recognize. "My great-uncle died recently—he'd always looked after me, you see, as my parents died when I was a small child. When I was looking through his study for his will, I found these documents." She gestured at the papers on the desk, hoping that the policemen wouldn't be able to read the French that the current upturned page displayed. "There was a note with them saying that they'd give me the directions to his hidden wealth—well, I *knew* he had a bank account somewhere, but there weren't any other details, and I've tried to have these translated but they were all about history, and I was hoping that Mr. Vale could help me . . ."

"Very good, miss," the sergeant cut her off. Which was a good thing, as she was running out of breath. Portraying a feckless innocent who could talk for several minutes without stopping was hard on the lungs. "That sounds a very reasonable, er, reason for you to be here. Now I'm not going to ask you to leave, but I would like you to stay over there by the table and not interfere with our work."

"Oh, of course not," Irene murmured. "But are you—that is, so many police here to see Mr. Vale—has there been a murder or something?"

"Official Scotland Yard business," the sergeant said firmly. He looked gratified when Irene gave a little squeak and pressed her hands together in feigned excitement. "I'm afraid I can't tell you about it, miss. All very hush-hush."

As Irene nodded obediently, she watched the other men from under her eyelashes. They were casually spreading out across the room, in such a way that anyone coming through the door would see the sergeant—but wouldn't see the rest of them immediately. One of them was hovering near the door to Vale's bedroom, and she suspected that he'd have gone through to poke around there if she hadn't been present. *So either this is official trouble for Vale, or it's criminal impersonators but it needs to look official—which is why they haven't done anything to me. Yet.*

Urgent footsteps sounded on the stairs; she recognized Vale's hasty tread, coming up them two at a time. The policemen exchanged glances.

And Irene considered her options.

CHAPTER 9

When Irene saw the policeman behind the door sliding his hand into his tunic, the action placed a thumb on one side of her mental scales and dropped it all the way to *decided*. Genuine policemen—in this world and city, at least—might conceivably carry hidden weapons, but they wouldn't use them in a straightforward arrest. Ergo, these men weren't genuine policemen.

Ideally she wanted to incapacitate them while *not* incapacitating Vale, which limited her vocabulary. Using the Language to order something to happen to every man in the room would inconvenience Vale as well. Decisions, decisions.

Fortunately, these men were all wearing excellent disguises, which meant complete police uniforms . . .

The door swung open, but for a moment Vale stayed a pace outside, taking in the room with a quick sweep of his eyes. No doubt he'd noticed something askew downstairs—a smear of mud on the boot-scraper by the door, or a diatribe from the housekeeper, or some similar clue which had warned him in advance. Then his lips curled in a thin smile, and he stepped into the room with a nod to Irene. "Well, gentlemen," he said. "How may I be of assistance?"

"An urgent request from Scotland Yard, Mr. Vale," the sergeant declared earnestly. "You're needed at once, sir. Matter of the highest importance. There's a cab waiting downstairs."

"I'm sure there is." Vale wandered further into the room almost absently, but just enough to take him out of immediate reach of the man by the door. "Now I'm not going to ask you who sent you, because I'm quite certain you'd lie about it, but I can assure you that anyone who decides to turn witness will have no cause to regret it."

The sergeant didn't seem surprised. He made a quick gesture with his left hand, then strode across toward Irene as the other three men closed in on Vale.

Irene wasn't interested in being a hostage or casualty. **"Helmets, descend over your wearers' faces,"** she ordered in the Language as she darted back.

The effect was immediate. Helmets were designed to rest on the top of the head: when they chose to squeeze down over the faces below, it wasn't good for the helmet or the wearer. The coordinated attack on Vale dissolved into three men lunging at him blindly, and he neatly sidestepped them. "Need any help, Winters?" he enquired, tripping one of the stumbling men with his cane.

"Not really." Irene moved silently to the sergeant's side and delivered a solid kidney punch. When he went down, she kicked him in the stomach. It was extremely cathartic after the day she'd had.

"I didn't think so." Vale clubbed the second thug in the back of the neck with his cane, then delivered a neatly gauged pair of punches to the third, who'd just managed to rip his helmet off. "Would you mind having a word with their cab driver downstairs? Use that perception trick of yours to persuade him to come up here."

"Of course," Irene said, and hurried downstairs.

There was indeed a cab waiting downstairs, a police carriage of the local Black Maria variant, suitable for carrying a prisoner and several guards inside. The driver—another apparent policeman—looked suspiciously at Irene as she came running out of the house and up to him. "I'm afraid I'm here on duty, ma'am," he said sternly.

"Naturally," Irene agreed, "which is why **you perceive that I am someone you trust, and you need to leave the cab and come into the house with me.**"

Five minutes later, the sergeant, his men, and the driver were all in various positions of helplessness, with their own handcuffs (their disguises had been very complete) locked on their wrists.

Kai had emerged from below stairs with tea and scones, highly annoyed that he'd missed the brawl. "If only I'd known," he said to Irene, not for the first time, "but she insisted on giving me her latest baking—"

"A woman's natural maternal impulses," Vale said dismissively.

Irene raised an eyebrow.

"I find it easier to flee the house rather than admit hunger," he added, not meeting her eyes. "In any case, I see that you left your lodgings in haste. What new emergency is this? Does it have something to do with your new studies?" He gestured at the documents, which still lay on the table. "And should I expect further visitors?"

"I'm rather curious about these ones," Irene said, nodding at the prisoners. "An emergency?"

"Hardly an emergency. I am currently dealing with the detritus of last month's business, when we removed the Professor from the hidden throne of London's criminal underworld. As a result, half of the contenders wish to dispose of me for being involved, and the other half wish to dispose of me in order to prove their worthiness for the position. It has made my life a little inconvenient these last few days."

"You didn't mention this," Kai said, frowning. "Nor did your housekeeper."

Vale shrugged. "I didn't like to bother her with minor details, and it was hardly a problem on the level of the Professor. Besides, you had your own issues, and Winters has been out of London recently."

"Yes. Speaking of that . . ." Irene glanced at the men on the floor, who were doing their best to fake unconsciousness. "Can we discuss it after the police have removed these gentlemen?"

"Of course." Vale tilted his head at the sound of cab wheels outside the window. "Here they are now."

"Assuming they aren't more impostors," Irene pointed out.

"A valid point, but . . ." Vale strode over to gaze out of the window. "I recognize Sergeant Barton. Safe enough for the time being. When we are alone, you can explain a little further."

Vale was not overly surprised by the senior Librarians' stratagem, though he pointed out one flaw which Irene had not yet noticed. She liked to think that she *would* have done, if the day hadn't been quite so hectic.

"Nobody has removed your position as Librarian-in-Residence to this world," he noted, sipping his tea and crumbling a scone. "More importantly, you are still Library representative for the Fae–dragon treaty. Careless of your elders, Winters. If you were truly unreliable, they should have removed you. If they have not done so, it may be assumed they approve of your actions."

"It's only been a few hours," Irene said. "It's entirely possible that there are Librarians at our lodgings right this minute, ready to remove my authority."

Kai chewed his lip thoughtfully. "Yes, but if they were to do that, they should make a significant attempt to apprehend you and take you into custody for your own safety. That is the cover story, after all, isn't it? That they're trying to stop you from effectively committing suicide by attacking an impossible foe?"

Irene frowned. "Yes. But . . . something else is clearly going on here, and I don't know what it is, and I'm not sure who I can ask about it."

"Your parents?" Kai suggested.

"If you were a secretive mastermind in the heart of the Library and organizing a complicated plan which involved using me as a cat's paw, then wouldn't my parents be the *last* people who would be told about it?" Irene hesitated. "No. Not a cat's paw. A bait. I didn't think—they didn't allow me *time* to think—but that's what's happening, isn't it? I'm being publicly exposed as bait."

"I think you may be overly suspicious here, Winters," Vale said. "I suspect that what your superiors are doing is what my own sister would do."

This was not exactly a statement suggestive of high moral values, as Vale's sister Columbine was a major player in the British Secret Service.

"Would you explain?" Irene asked.

"You are not bait for Alberich. You are bait for whoever it is inside the Library that they fear is passing information—whether to Alberich, or to the Fae, or even to the dragons. Once the information about your presumed status is known to other Librarians, your superiors can discover who else mysteriously hears about it, and trace the resulting channels of communication."

Irene thought about that. It felt . . . right. "Well, drat," she said, hastily modifying her language from *damn* in deference to Vale's sensitivities regarding proper speech for women. "In that case, I suppose

I *don't* need to worry too much about the Library sending people here after me. What I do need to worry about is when *Alberich* hears I'm coming after him; he's going to want to take action first."

"Except that he can't enter this world," Kai said firmly. "He managed to send a projection here because his agents planted his tokens in the Language, but those agents have been dealt with."

"The ones that we know about," Irene said gloomily. "Besides, that only works until he gets new agents. I may not need to hide from the Library—but I do need to hide. But equally I need to stay somewhere local so that I can be in contact with people. And I have these documents to go through."

Vale took another scone. "I may have a solution for you."

"Oh?"

"I imagine that you have some secret hideout of your own here in London, but that your Library superiors know about it?" He waited for her nod. "So if the Library is compromised, that may no longer be a secret. However, I have a couple of rooms in this building which are not obviously connected to the main lodgings—a spare bedroom and the attic. Leave here publicly, return in disguise, and I will be glad to give you room and board, while Strongrock here acts as a public contact and deals with any Librarians who come looking for you. Put your Library wards on the place to keep yourself safe from interference. Will that answer your problem?"

Irene took a moment to turn the idea over in her head. It wouldn't need to be for long; it could work quite well. "Perfect," she said gratefully. "Thank you very much indeed, Vale. And, while this is an added imposition, I would be very grateful for your help with these documents."

"A small matter." Vale's tone was dismissive, but he couldn't repress the glint in his eye at the opportunity to read the Library's private records. "How severely do you suppose they have been edited?"

"Probably quite severely." Irene's gloom returned. She spread her hands. "We're going round in circles here. They send me out with incomplete information because of their complicated disinformation strategy, but then how am I supposed to do a good job with incomplete information? It would have been more sensible to let me stay in the Library and read any classified documents there. I might have taken the knowledge away with me, but at least I wouldn't have the physical paper record. What were they *thinking*?"

Vale frowned, his eyes hooded and distant. "This is speculation, Winters, and I abhor speculation, but either I am correct in theorizing that you are being used to find the informer inside the Library, or they lacked the time for what you suggest. Some other agenda has them on the back foot, and they are hurrying to catch up."

"For heaven's sake, haven't we had enough disasters for the current year? The current *century*?"

"Disasters, my dear Winters, are like public omnibuses," Vale said sententiously. "They come in multiples rather than singly, are inevitably overloaded when they arrive, and stay far too long in any one spot. Besides, it may not be a disaster. It may simply be a crisis. You yourself told us there was gossip about vanishing worlds—which has been confirmed from multiple sources. Next to that, your own problems might be considered comparatively minor."

"And it may be a crisis that doesn't involve *you*," Kai said helpfully. "After all, we know where you've been for the last few weeks. You have a solid alibi."

Irene looked at him sidelong. "This is where you remind me that not everything about the Library involves me personally, correct?"

"You might very well think so," Kai said. "I couldn't possibly comment."

Irene let herself relax, just a little. Kai and Vale were solid walls whom she could lean against—whom she could trust absolutely.

More than you trust the Library? a chill voice of cynicism asked at the back of her mind.

That was different. She trusted the Library to do what was best for the Library—which usually included her. She trusted Kai and Vale to do what was best for *her.*

Still that nagging murmur of doubt wriggled like a worm on a hook, fished up from her subconscious and now uncomfortably prominent. Was her first instinct correct here—that she was bait, staked out by the Library to get Alberich's attention? And if so, was the Library watching her now?

And if she was bait for Alberich to strike, what might the Library's countermove be—and how dangerous would it be to everyone around her?

CHAPTER 10

There's someone in the house," Vale remarked quietly. His casual saunter remained the same, the loose amble of a London gentleman in no particular hurry, but there was a glint in his deep-set eyes. "It seems Winters may have been correct when she feared pursuit."

"One person, or two, do you think? Or more?" Kai didn't stare at the house where he and Irene shared lodgings, but he did flick a casual glance in its direction. There were no obvious signs of intrusion. They'd left Irene at Vale's lodgings, busy with her research—as she had been for the last few days—and come to check for signs of hostilities.

"I cannot tell without further evidence."

"How can you tell at all?" Kai didn't *doubt* Vale's deduction, but he was interested in how the detective knew.

"The curtain on the study window. If it's not drawn back properly, it catches on the side of the cupboard there and hangs at an angle. You and Winters draw it properly; your housekeeper does not. But since you've given the lady this week off, we know she hasn't been in there. The inference is clear."

"Right." Kai resolved to have a word with the housekeeper later. They strolled past the house together, making no immediate attempt to enter. "This may be a request for contact—or an ambush."

"An ambush for Winters, perhaps, but I think it unlikely that a Librarian would attack you," Vale noted. "Quite apart from the physical difficulties and the political implications, they would have no actual reason to do so."

"Yes, but that assumes it's Librarians in there, rather than Alberich or his minions." Kai would quite welcome an attack by Alberich's minions. The possibility of presenting them to Irene for interrogation, tied up and with a bow on top, was one of the best things about the day so far. "But I agree the Library's more likely."

"I believe you are about to suggest that you go in publicly through the front door while I enter by stealth through the rear door from the backyard," Vale said, his tone rather dry.

Kai eyed him sidelong. "How did you deduce that?"

"Prior experience of your tactics, my dear Strongrock. In this case I agree with you. Give me five minutes to reach my position, and you may begin."

"I'm perfectly capable of a subtle and strategic approach," Kai said firmly. "Besides, if Irene were here, she'd be insisting that *she* go in through the front door while we go round the back."

"Indeed," Vale agreed. "We must both be grateful that Winters is safely elsewhere and not jeopardizing herself as usual. I hope you have some ideas about how to convince her to continue her current research."

He didn't actually say it, but his message was clear. *Irene has to be persuaded to keep herself safe.*

Kai nodded curtly and checked his watch as Vale walked away,

Kai's thoughts still circling like a whirlpool around that central fact. Irene was *not* going to keep herself safe. She had all the courage of one of his own kin, but as a human she was desperately vulnerable. He sympathized with her desire to kill Alberich, but . . . there had to be some way to do it that didn't place her in such personal danger.

If they could locate the world where Alberich was hiding, then Kai could appeal to his father to devastate it until the man exposed himself—and then utterly destroy him. Of course, there *would* be some incidental casualties, which ran counter to Kai's own responsibilities toward lesser beings such as humans. Also, such a hideout would probably be a world on the more chaotic end of the spectrum. Given the peace treaty, there might be political implications if the dragons made inroads into chaos. Perhaps a specific Fae could be found who'd be prepared to give the whole political aspect his blessing, in return for some quiet private favors.

He snapped his watch shut. Five minutes had passed while he was musing, and he still had no convenient answers. Still, with luck, he was about to have some action, which would have to do for now.

The door of the house was locked, just as it should be. Kai opened it nonchalantly and walked in, closing it behind him. He glanced around—a certain amount of caution was only natural, after all, even if he was being observed—but there were no signs of any intruder. He shrugged off his hat and coat, tossing them on the hatstand, and headed upstairs to the study. Should he whistle? Probably not. It was so difficult to remember what "normal" was when trying to act normally while under observation.

The Librarian Bradamant was sitting behind the desk in Irene's chair, an expression of sweet reason and amiability pasted on her face. "Good afternoon," she said. She was in proper clothing for this world—her coat and dress were deep gray velvet trimmed with black, matching the gloves which lay on the desk. Her hair was a raven-wing black, razor-cut to pristine neatness, and her wide eyes were mirrors rather than windows, giving nothing away.

A swell of anger rose in Kai like the dragging of a tide, pulling him toward an unexpected fury at seeing this woman attempt to *steal* Irene's place. "How interesting," he said, his tone sharp as a sword's edge. "I leave this place alone for just two minutes and I find that you've crawled in and are attempting to establish yourself."

"I'm just a visitor," Bradamant protested, drawing back a little. "A representative of the Library, like Irene."

"And yet you whisper our locks open and sneak into our private rooms, rather than waiting on the doorstep as a regular visitor would have done." Kai stalked toward her. "Why do you present yourself before me?"

A muscle jerked in Bradamant's cheek as she held herself steady, preventing herself from what might have been a flinch away. "Why are you treating me like this? I'm not your enemy."

With a great effort Kai forced himself into composure—not the icy precision of cold fury which was surging within him, but the sensible practicality which he knew Irene would have preferred. He deliberately made himself speak in a more casual fashion, avoiding the language of royalty and court. "I'm disturbed whenever I have unexpected visitors. So many of them have been trying to kill me that it's difficult to be casual about it."

"And you think I'm here to kill you?" Bradamant demanded, sounding a little hysterical. "What's Irene been *telling* you?"

Kai shrugged. "Nothing but the truth, I'm sure."

Bradamant set her jaw mulishly. "Well, I'm here for your good, and Irene's too. Particularly Irene's."

"Explain yourself, then," Kai ordered. He thought about adding *and get out of Irene's chair*, but decided it would give away too much of his own feelings.

Bradamant must have realized that her choice of seating was irritating him, and she rose without having to be commanded to do so. "I don't know what Irene's told you. It's possible that she's misinterpreted the current situation, in which case it's nobody's actual *fault*, but something needs to be done about it."

"Maybe so," Vale said from behind Kai, "but you have yet to define the matter under discussion." He would have heard the conversation; with the study door open, it would be difficult for anyone in the house *not* to hear the conversation.

"The fact that Irene's trying to do something suicidal," Bradamant answered, not looking particularly surprised by Vale's appearance. "Let's get to the point. I know she'll have asked you both to help. I know you'll both know all about it. Why haven't *you* tried to stop her?"

"I understand that she's doing this with the support of your Library," Vale replied. "Do you have that support in trying to prevent her?"

Bradamant snorted, suppressing a bitter choke of laughter. "That's what she told you?"

A little twitch of unease crawled its way down Kai's spine. Of course he trusted Irene absolutely and without hesitation. But if someone had asked him, *Would Irene lie to you if she thought she had a sufficiently good reason?* he would have been forced to admit that yes, there was at least a theoretical possibility that she would.

His hesitation must have been visible, for Bradamant's expression changed to a smile. "I *knew* you wouldn't just buy into whatever she said. After all, you've both met Alberich. You know how dangerous he is. How likely is it that the Library would send her off on her own to try to kill him?"

"You make a good case for your argument," Vale said neutrally. "However, physical evidence exists which counters it—which I have personally seen and validated."

"What evidence?" Bradamant demanded, focusing on him like a hawk.

Vale simply raised an eyebrow, turning to stroll around the room, gaze flicking from object to object as though expecting to find Bradamant's fingerprints on them.

Kai folded his arms, enjoying the expression of frustrated bafflement on Bradamant's face. "It seems, madam, that you aren't high-clearance enough to have been told what's *really* going on."

"Either I've been lied to by my direct superior or Irene's off on a suicidal crusade to get herself killed," Bradamant retorted. "Based on past evidence, which do you think is more likely?"

Kai pulled out a coin, tossed it, caught it on the back of his hand, and inspected the result. "The first," he decided.

Bradamant made a noise of muffled fury, something like a steam engine suppressing an explosion, and her hands tightened into fists. "You need to take this seriously!"

"I'm taking it extremely seriously," Kai said. "I'm quite aware that Irene can be very careless with her personal safety. The thing is . . ." He glanced at Vale a moment, and the man returned a nod. "She's far more careful with the safety of other people. Are you saying that she'd have brought us into this and put us at risk if she thought it was suicidal?"

Bradamant stomped toward him, her grace diminishing as her temper slipped. "You're evading the point. She doesn't realize how suicidal it is. That evidence"—she turned to Vale—"was it in that briefcase she had earlier?"

"That corroborates her statement about you assaulting her in the Library," Vale noted.

"Because if it is, then someone in the Library is backing her for their own reasons, and that makes the situation even worse." Bradamant visibly reined in her desperation, stilling her face to calm. "I really don't want to be unreasonable about this. **You perceive that it would be for Irene's own good if you tell me where she is and what's going on.**"

Kai was prepared to admit that she had a point there. While naturally he supported Irene in every way—and would, in contrast, take pleasure in extending a foot for Bradamant to trip over—it was true that it would be wise to tell her everything about the current situation. "She's in Vale's private attic, researching," he explained.

Vale nodded. "She could hardly stay here if the Library intended to hunt her down."

"I see," Bradamant said carefully. She strolled toward the door. "And is this private attic very hard to find?"

"For an intruder, yes," Vale said. "Having it be easy to locate would rather defeat its purpose."

"Of course," Bradamant agreed soothingly. Kai could almost read the thoughts behind her frown. *But the Language can open doors and reveal staircases . . .*

A stray prickle of thought jabbed at him. Exactly *why* had they just told Bradamant that? Naturally it was for Irene's safety, which made perfect sense, but why did he feel there was a contradiction here somewhere?

Bradamant touched the door handle. "Incidentally," she started, keeping her tone casual, "**you perceive that—**"

Kai moved across the room faster than he'd ever managed before. Bradamant wasn't expecting his punch. She folded gracefully to the ground with a look of surprise on her face.

He didn't bother catching her.

Vale raised an eyebrow. "Is there some reason why you've taken such drastic action, Strongrock?"

"The perception trick," Kai spat. "She used it on us. She was probably going to use it again to keep us here while she went to find Irene."

Vale frowned. "Technically I believe you're correct, though I still have the feeling that she was absolutely in the right. A curious duality of perception. I should get Winters to experiment on me one of these days."

Kai rolled Bradamant over with his toe, just to check whether she was faking unconsciousness. She didn't seem to be. "We may be being slightly unfair to her," he said, feeling more generous now that they had the advantage. "She does seem to be under the perception that she's here to *save* Irene."

"We are supposed to think she came here in a hurry, I believe, and yet . . ." Vale knelt down beside the unconscious Bradamant and checked her pockets. "Local currency, and a surprising amount, more than one would expect she could scrape together from previous visits. A hotel room key, though I would need more information to identify the hotel. An open return ticket for the Underground. Sugar packets from the Lucifer's Long Spoon chain of restaurants. And observe her shoes—freshly polished this morning, but showing traces of the rain earlier today."

"There's a Lucifer's Long Spoon just down the road from here," Kai said uneasily.

"Precisely. She arrived yesterday, possibly earlier, and established herself in a local hotel. She has been watching your lodgings from a distance, and after ascertaining that they were empty, staged this intrusion. Madame Bradamant may consider she is rescuing Irene from her own folly, but she's being cautious in doing so." He gave Kai a sidelong look. "Possibly she was trying to avoid us."

"Do you think we can persuade her to help us?" Kai was prepared to admit that Bradamant was competent, even if her past attitude toward Irene had left him with a definite bias against her.

"We can try," Vale said. "But I would suggest a few precautions first..."

K ai was reading the newspaper when he heard the change in Bradamant's breathing pattern. She was doing a good job of feigning unconsciousness, but his dragon senses were superior to those of common humanity and could tell the difference. "I know you're awake," he said. "Nod your head if you understand me."

Bradamant made several indistinct noises as her eyes came open. The cloth wadded in her mouth prevented her from forming any distinct words or using the Language. Kai knew from personal experience how difficult it was to keep a Librarian restrained if they were allowed to talk.

He and Vale had tied Bradamant into a chair and gagged her, only leaving her right hand free. After all, Bradamant *had* tried to use the Language on them first. "There's a pen and paper on the desk in front of you," he said. "You can write your part of the conversation there."

Bradamant's eyes blazed in fury above the gag. She grabbed the pen, paused—probably suppressing some primal impulse—and wrote in fine copperplate, *This is not a good idea.*

"It's also a rather slow means of communication," Vale said from behind her. "If you give your word not to use the Language to affect us, we are willing to remove that gag."

Kai found Bradamant's hesitation rather telling. Clearly she didn't want to give that pledge—which meant that she wanted to keep the option of using the Language on him and Vale. He could sympathize with her feelings, while at the same time being willing to throw her out of the window if she tried it again.

Finally she scribbled, *All right. I give my word not to use the Language on Kai or Vale for the remainder of the day.*

"I find your inclusion of a specified time disturbing," Kai said as he carefully removed her gag.

"It's what Irene would do," Bradamant said, her voice dry. "She's very good at making sure she won't be bound by inconvenient commitments if circumstances change."

"Your judgment of her says a great deal about your own priorities," Vale noted. "Now let us attempt to put this discussion on a more civilized footing. We accept your intentions are good and you wish to help Irene. However, we have concrete evidence that she *is* supported by the Library, and that the current claims that she is acting alone are to protect the Library and draw Alberich out from hiding. Your superior is Kostchei, correct?" He waited for her nod. "If you haven't been fully informed about what is taking place, then it may be for your own safety."

Bradamant didn't try to swivel round in her bindings to face Vale. Instead she watched Kai—probably, and accurately, rating him as the most dangerous threat in the room. "I accept that you think you're doing the right thing in helping Irene," she said. "I . . . apologize for my hasty actions in trying to force you to assist me. But I think Irene's not *fully informed* about what's going on either." She laid an ironic stress on the repetition. "There's more going on than she knows about."

"Such as?" Kai asked curtly.

"Have either of you ever worked in an organization for a long time?"

"Well, my father's court, and then my uncle's . . ." Kai said. "If you would call that working."

"Then do you know what I mean when I say that an insider picks up on things being off-key? An outsider or an infrequent visitor wouldn't notice, but an insider picks up on the flows and currents of current affairs."

Kai had to nod—somewhat reluctant to agree with her but conscious that she had a point. "You feel that you have noticed something which Irene wouldn't?"

"Irene's never in the Library long enough," Bradamant said flatly. "Even when she is, she's either studying, reading, or hanging out with a very small group of people. I spend a *sensible* amount of time in the Library and I'm aware of what's going on. I keep Kostchei's appointments diary. I talk to people. Please believe me when I say that something's *wrong*."

"What?" Kai demanded.

"I don't know." Bradamant had used her free hand to untie her bound one. "Leaving aside the talk of worlds disappearing, which is worrying enough . . . there are odd missions going on—and no, I can't give you details, they're secret, but some of them are outside our usual area. We may need to play politics to stay afloat, since we have dragons and Fae to cope with, but we don't need to play them *this* much. I was worried that Irene was caught up in this and was being used somehow. But if she's operating under Kostchei's sanction"— she frowned—"then I don't know what's going on."

"Irene should know about any strange operations as treaty representative," Kai protested—though the nagging feeling that *of course* the Library wouldn't tell her if it was a deniable operation meant that his words lacked weight.

"Yes. She should. And if she honestly doesn't know, perhaps you should ask why."

"And what have you heard about worlds disappearing?" Vale asked.

Bradamant hesitated. It wasn't, in Kai's judgment, an act—it was genuine. "I think that if you want me to talk about that, it's time for you gentlemen to give me *your* word that this stays between us."

Kai and Vale exchanged a glance, and Vale nodded. "Between us and Winters," he said.

Kai was the one who paused. "If this is something which would endanger my family..."

Bradamant sighed. "Your family probably knows far more about it than we do. You dragons can travel anywhere, after all—we can only go where there's a library. Look, I'll be reasonable. You can share this if they discuss it with you or if knowledge about this becomes more widespread. I'm not going to insist you keep a secret when there's clearly a problem."

"Acceptable," Kai said. "You have my word."

"It's like this, then. It's not just rumors. We—the Library—have fairly definite *proof* that some worlds just aren't *there* any more. Attempts to reach those worlds via the Library aren't working. The doors to them won't open. Private Fae and dragon contacts have made it clear those worlds are gone, as if they've simply been erased—somehow wiped out of existence. But nobody's willing to make it public. At least, not yet. They're afraid there'll be a panic."

"Surely the treaty is the ideal instrument to investigate this situation," Vale suggested. "If both sides have found that worlds have, ah, gone missing..."

"All of the worlds harbored notorious malcontents," Bradamant said. "People who'd spoken out against the treaty—or who were known to be hostile to it, even if they hadn't admitted it publicly. I think certain people are rather *pleased* to have possible dangers off the table."

"And the cost in human lives is"—Vale spread his hands. His tone was dry as old sand—"regrettable, but doubtless a minor factor."

"If you want anyone to care about the humans on those worlds or others, then you'd better support the Library," Bradamant fired back. "Because we're the only ones who would see them as anything other than collateral damage."

Kai had been distracted for a moment. His lord uncle Ao Ji could well be described as a malcontent who'd done his best to sabotage the treaty. Was he safe? Common sense reassured him that if one of the dragon monarchs had gone missing, all his family would be in a state of turmoil. (His lord uncle's current location—in a state of guarded seclusion for the next few decades—had been explained to the family as a health issue after an attempted assassination, which was publicly accepted, if not totally believed.)

"So this is a real problem," he said slowly, "not just a rumor."

"Yes—but it's a completely inexplicable one. No ransom demands or warning letters. No evidence. No obvious motives. Nothing. Everyone's on the alert, but nobody knows what to do about it. I think most people are quietly hoping it'll just go away. Because what can they actually do? Wish for more worlds to disappear to give them a trail to follow?" Bradamant shook off the remainder of her bindings and stood up. "If you *gentlemen* will excuse me, I'll be on my way now."

"We would appreciate your given word that you won't tell anyone where Winters is," Vale said.

"I swear not to reveal that I know she's hidden in your private attic—but let's be honest, it's blatantly obvious that you're the logical person to be hiding her, and any other Librarian will check you out before trying elsewhere." Bradamant shrugged. "I'll be back. With more information. But I'm asking you, *for her sake*, please don't let her do anything . . . stupid."

Kai looked down his nose at her. "Kindly refrain from doing anything *stupid* yourself. I'm sure that Irene would regret the loss of a capable Librarian such as you."

Bradamant's steps were audible all the way down the stairs and out of the house.

"You did a good job of irritating her, Strongrock," Vale noted. "I believe that she was rattled enough to tell us the truth—as she perceives it."

"I can't say that makes me any more comfortable," Kai said. "My faith in the Library's leadership has not increased."

"But who directs the Library?" Vale frowned. "We hear talk of the Library's elders, but even they take direction from somewhere else, Winters said. But who? And where? And if someone inside the Library is betraying it, what then?"

"This supports your theory as to why Irene was given her mission," Kai said. "Kostchei and Melusine and the others want to smoke out this loose cannon. If they know something about these worlds vanishing, or these ongoing politics . . ."

"Possibly," Vale allowed, "but our information is highly incomplete. We need more data, Strongrock."

Kai nodded in agreement. "Still," he said, cheerfully, "at least we know where Irene is."

CHAPTER 11

Vale's attic was full to the walls with the tools of his trade—disguises, a mirror and makeup kits, mysterious crates, dusty bottles of out-of-date chemicals, and stacks of newspaper cuttings awaiting filing. Fortunately it also had the two important things which Irene needed—a desk to work on, and a camp bed to sleep on. There was a carefully concealed overhead skylight, but it was so small that it didn't give enough light to work by, only enough to stop the place from being pitch dark when the ether-lamp was turned off.

If she hadn't had work to do, Irene would have felt claustrophobic. As she *did* have research to pursue, she felt comfortable. She was nestled in here like a rat in the walls of an old house, snug and unobtrusive. While the housekeeper knew she was there, none of the other servants did. She'd had three days of peace and quiet, with occasional interludes when Kai or Vale dropped in, and for the first time she was beginning to feel that she was making progress.

For light relief she read some of Vale's saved newspaper clippings, most of which dealt with crime and punishment. It took her mind off what had happened to some of the *other* Librarians who'd encountered Alberich in the past. The gossip which had been passed round among students and apprentice Librarians had been . . . lacking in detail. Like all good urban legends, it had included sufficient levels of gore and horror to keep it being told and retold, but it was not so unpleasant that people would have outright refused to pass the stories on. These reports were clinical, presumably accurate, and the sort of thing which Irene had to think about in terms of black-and-white illustrations rather than letting her imagination stray into oozing color.

There was a clear pattern of what she termed *degeneration*. First other Librarians reported Alberich approaching them and trying to negotiate with them, or claiming that he'd been misinterpreted and they should just hear him out. Some of these events ended with the Librarian surviving; others, where they attacked Alberich or tried to trick him, usually didn't. A couple of cases did have Alberich fleeing the area, but the report suggested that he'd usually obtained whatever he was there for in the first place—a book, or contact with powerful Fae.

As the years went by, he became more brutal. The cases where the Librarian survived were ones where the Librarian had done the sensible thing and fled the area or taken cover at the first hint of danger. More of the reports were from follow-up Librarians investigating the disappearance of forerunners and finding their dead bodies, sometimes with an explanatory note from Alberich that they'd *interfered*.

And then there was the first report of a Librarian's body found skinned and mutilated. Irene had to pause for a drink of water after that one. *Black-and-white illustrations. Dotted lines. An anatomy diagram.*

Once again, Irene felt a familiar chill at the thought that she'd somehow survived Alberich when so many others had died at his hands. She would have liked to believe it was skill, or talent. But honestly, it was probably sheer luck, combined with Alberich underestimating a junior Librarian after years of disposing of them and Irene having a dragon on her side.

Was the degeneration, the worsening in his behavior over time, because the victims were people he didn't know? The older Librarians would have been acquaintances of his—perhaps even friends. The newer ones, the younger ones, were strangers, people he'd never met before. Would it have been easier to kill them?

She also found herself unable to explain the time factor. Irene herself was in her early thirties (it was difficult to keep track when one kept traveling between worlds), but Alberich's betrayal and his sister's escape had occurred far more than a few decades ago. Of course, the logical explanation was the fact that people didn't age in the Library—the pregnancy didn't come to term, or a baby wouldn't grow. Yet in that case, how long had Irene herself spent in her birth mother's womb, or as an unknowing baby in a cradle somewhere in the depths of the Library?

As for the motives behind his betrayal . . . The pages dealing with that were useless: A flat account that a certain Librarian returned in an unfortunate condition after an absence of several months and gave warning that Alberich had lost his sanity—it didn't even give her mother's name, for pity's sake. It was obvious that part had been edited. At first there was no reason to believe her story, but later acts by Alberich made it clear that she was speaking the truth, and due precautions were taken. There was hardly anything on those sheets at all.

What precautions? *Which* later acts? *What don't they want me to know?* The thought was inescapable. The total lack of information was a confession in itself that the information was dangerous. Had Melusine agreed to this redaction, or had she been against it, just as she'd been against the whole stupid plan of sending Irene alone against Alberich?

Irene ran a finger over the blank expanse of the lower part of the page, wishing that she had Melusine there to ask her—and then paused, frozen in her seat, as she felt a slight imperfection in the page.

She lifted it up to the light to see if there was anything odd about it. Nothing she could *see*—but there were ways of writing that were invisible to the naked eye. And if one Librarian had done it, another one could undo it . . .

"Writing on the page which I'm holding, become visible," she ordered.

Handwritten paragraphs bloomed into visibility on the unused part of the page. Irene didn't know what Melusine's handwriting looked like, but she would have staked good money that the older Librarian was the one who'd written it—and hidden it from the eyes of Kostchei and the others. At last. *Facts.*

She read eagerly. This text was more modern in style than the earlier ones—and much blunter. It felt as if it had been written in pain. Irene might not be as good an analyst of handwriting as Vale, but she could tell where the pen had dug into the paper angrily enough to leave the mark which she'd felt.

Alberich claimed to this woman that the Library was controlled and infested by a foul intelligence which could influence other Librarians, and that he could no longer trust any of his brothers and sisters. He said that this went all the way back to the Library's founding, and that we were no more than slaves and tools, and the Library itself—for he talked of it as a living thing—was the most helpless of us all. He thought that the child of two Librarians could be raised "innocent" of the Library's influence and be able to work against it.

His captive had already been in a relationship with him, but had no intention of having a child. He somehow took steps to ensure that a child would be conceived—she was unclear on this part—and imprisoned her in a pre-literate world where there were no libraries, so that she couldn't escape. He had already made bargains with chaos to ensure his own ways of traveling. She freed herself by writing down enough stories to create a small sort of library and fled to the Library before he knew.

Her story made it clear that he was paranoid and deluded. While his beliefs were obviously incorrect, he was quite sincere about them. "We cannot tell what caused his insanity; we can only take action to stop him and prevent anything like it from happening again.

Irene bit her lip. Did it make it any better to think that it had been a consensual relationship which turned sour? Or that Irene had been conceived as a way to destroy the Library?

It didn't. Not really. But at least now she knew a little more. She checked the other pages, but that had been the only one with a hidden message.

Maybe she could distract herself with research while looking at facts and details, but the inescapable question lay ahead of her: what was she actually going to *do* next? She had a concordance—well, a partial concordance, depending on how much the Library had removed from her data—of Alberich's actions. She had a list of worlds which he'd visited and Fae whom he'd been known to work with. What she didn't have was a convenient clue which led her directly to his hidden base, or a useful weak point that she could attack—or any knowledge of what had ultimately sent him mad.

Contacting some of the Fae he'd worked with was shaping up to be the best option, but it was still very far from being a *good* option. They didn't generally sound like nice people. They'd probably sell *her* to *him* if they thought it'd get them favors. The only one of them whom she knew personally (and who was still alive) was the Blood Countess, and really, that lady's name said all that one wanted to know about her character. Besides, she had a serious grudge against Irene for foiling some of her plans during the dragon–Fae peace treaty negotiations. While she would *love* (in the Fae sense of the word) further interaction, Irene herself preferred to avoid it, in the interests of keeping her blood in her veins, her skin on her back, and her head on her shoulders.

Then a prickle ran across her back, a tightness gathered at her forehead; it was like the sensation of approaching thunder, but worse, far worse. She could taste raw chaos in the air, gathering as though it was condensing into this world, focusing on her like the center of a hurricane.

This had happened before. With the speed of a panicked rabbit, Irene ran for the staircase. She might not be able to stop it happening again, but she couldn't afford to have it hit while she was surrounded by her vital research papers. Alberich was trying to send her a message, which would overwrite any script around her in the process, and it seemed the wards she'd set up weren't enough to stop him. Gasping for breath, feeling the pressure intensify to the point of actual *presence*, she thrust back the panel and stumbled into the narrow staircase leading downward, away from all the papers she couldn't risk losing.

The stairs were poorly lit, and she blundered against the walls on the way down, the darkness seeming to close around her like a physical presence. She felt her way with one hand against the paneling. The attempt—the attack—wasn't going away now that she was separated from any convenient paper. It was still trying to get through, and it had a fix on her. She'd thought that Library wards would be enough to keep it out. She'd been wrong.

The door to Vale's room was a lit rectangular outline in the wall. He was out—Irene had heard him leave—but his papers were there. If she went too close to them, they might serve as a vector for the attack and overwrite them. She'd never forgive herself if that happened. She needed something else, something to discharge this buzzing overload of chaos which was gathering around her like a lightning strike.

A dozen more stairs. Stumbling, nearly blind, her Library brand burning as though she'd been whipped, she staggered through the concealed door and into the basement kitchen.

Thank any and all deities, only the housekeeper was there; the maids must have been elsewhere or gone out. "Get back," Irene gasped, as the woman jumped to her feet. "Stay away . . ." She didn't know if the message—or attack—would hurt anyone who came near, but she couldn't risk it.

Through a haze of tears she saw a newspaper open on the kitchen table. That'd do. That would *have* to do. Setting her teeth, Irene forced herself over to the table and slapped one hand down on the newspaper.

Force imploded around her and slammed into the copy of the *Times*. The close type of headlines and densely printed articles ran into puddles of black ink, then reassembled into letters on the suddenly blank paper. (Even in her most charitable moments, Irene wouldn't have described it as white.) **Talk to me**, it read.

Irene found her lips curling into a snarl. Alberich seemed to think he was in some sort of intergenerational family drama which could be sorted out by a bit of heart-baring conversation. As far as she was concerned, it wasn't that sort of story at all. But perhaps she could use this. She glanced around for something to write with—good, there was a pencil, the housekeeper had been making shopping lists. She grabbed it and scrawled, **You'll only try to kill me.**

A halo of force buzzed around her: she could feel her hair prickling on her scalp and her brand itching on her back as though it meant to rip itself off her skin and crawl away. The letters on the paper wriggled and reformed, tortured into a new position by Alberich's command of chaotic power and the Language. **Mistakes were made.**

"You lying—hypocritical—*politician*," Irene growled. The link wouldn't last; it was peaking, like a wave cresting toward the beach, and in a few seconds it would be gone. **What do you want to say to me?** she wrote.

I want to tell you the truth about the Library, came the answer.

And I want you to fall off a cliff and die. Inspiration came. If you were negotiating, you were supposed to start off with unfeasibly high goals for your side and work down to a middle ground, weren't you? **Swear peace with the Library and I'll talk with you. Otherwise not.**

No answer appeared.

Then the paper twisted and jerked on the table, curling in on itself as though it was on fire. Irene moved back quickly, afraid that she'd put too much energy into it during the communication, and looked round for something to hide behind or under.

Ink scrawled across the paper in a stranger's handwriting, a sweep of movement that somehow held its own power.

Cease This Communication.

For a moment Irene could read it, harsh black on drained white—and then the paper crumpled, falling into ash without the intermediary of flame, leaving only a gray smear on the table.

Irene sagged to lean against a chair. She could taste chaos in her mouth; it was somewhere between blood, mint, and fireworks, but when it ebbed away she couldn't even recall it properly. Power drained from around her like blood from the head of a woman about to faint, leaving the world in sepia tones to her dazzled eyes. She dropped the pencil and swayed as the floor seemed to rock beneath her feet. There was a high thin whistling in her ears, like a distant train or a departing boat, signaling something to her . . .

Oh, wait, that was the housekeeper, Mrs. Wilson. "Miss Winters! Miss Winters, are you all right? What was that?"

"I think I'm all right," Irene said, surreptitiously counting housekeepers in lieu of fingers and relieved to find that there was only one. "I'm sorry. There was—that is, something happened, a sort of attack . . ." And who precisely was it who had intervened mid-conversation? The Library, protecting her somehow? It must have been. The more she thought about it, the more it made sense.

The older woman snorted. "And in my kitchen, too! At least Mr. Vale never normally brings this sort of thing into my kitchen!"

"I'm terribly sorry," Irene said hastily. She didn't want to get herself thrown out of her safe house. Whatever Vale might say, if his landlady genuinely objected, there would be problems. "I do apologize. Someone wanted to send me an urgent message. I'll take this pencil with me, if you don't mind." An unpleasant thought struck her. "Ah, your cookbooks—are they all right?"

Rather than narrowing her eyes and demanding, *Is there some reason they wouldn't be?* Mrs. Wilson plucked the nearest from the shelf and checked it. "Still the same as always. Blessed Delia of Norwich protected it," she added with smug satisfaction, nodding to a small saint's statue on the shelf amid cookery and account books.

"Good." Extremely good, in fact. If this happened again, Irene might be able to restrict the effects to a single document. She pushed away from the chair and didn't wobble too much. "Sorry again for disturbing you. I'll go back upstairs . . ."

"You'll sit down here first and have a nice cup of tea," Mrs. Wilson said firmly. Clearly her maternal instincts weren't just confined to handsome young men. "It's bad enough Mr. Vale shutting himself away all day to work on chemical experiments and turn the walls green with the fumes, but when he invites his friends to do it too . . ."

She was bustling with a kettle when the doorbell rang, and she tutted to herself. "And me without Jane or Euphemia here, because they're out doing the shopping—just stay there a moment, miss, I'll be back in two shakes of a mare's tail."

Irene did as she was told, rather enjoying being fussed over. She'd got as far as warming the pot and measuring out the tea when it struck her that Mrs. Wilson was taking rather a long time to answer the door. Silently she glided over to the kitchen door, easing it quietly open so that she could hear what was going on.

"I'm afraid nobody's in, sir," Mrs. Wilson was saying, clearly not for the first time. Her voice had all the hauteur of a housekeeper who, while talking to a member of the gentry, knew her social position as representative of her lodgers and was certain that it was rock solid. "Mr. Vale's out, and I'm not sure when he'll be back."

"And you're quite sure that nobody else is present?" Irene didn't recognize the second speaker. She peered round the bend in the stairs and up into the hall, keeping to the shadows. Two men, one positioned slightly behind the other in standard backup position. Nicely dressed, from their highly polished shoes, to their well-pressed trouser creases, to their perfectly tied cravats. Not dragons—a dragon in human form was unmistakable—but possibly Fae. "In that case, you won't object if we wait upstairs."

"Excuse *me*!" Mrs. Wilson put her fists on her hips. "When I tell you gentlemen that Mr. Vale is out, that does not mean that you have leave or permission to go and sit in his private study unless he's told you so. I'll be glad to take your card and let him know that you called when he's back."

"Please don't be so disobliging. I'm sure you'd be glad to help us." With the words there came a wave of charm which Irene could feel from several meters away. It wasn't Lord Silver's insinuating sort of desire, which one might believe was purely internal; it was external, offensive, and as subtle as a blast of perfume in the face. "We won't be any trouble at all."

Mrs. Wilson rocked back on her heels, but she hadn't been Vale's housekeeper for years without developing an immunity to unreasonable requests—Fae-backed or otherwise. "Get out of here at once!"

The man's face twisted into a mask of fury, and he took a step forward, reaching out to catch her arm and kicking the front door shut behind him, cutting off the view from the street. "Jones," he said to his companion, "secure the place."

"I don't think so." Irene stepped out of the shadows, walking up the stairs toward them. "Who are you? What are you doing here?"

Both men turned to look at her in shock. "None of your business," the first man snapped. Then a thought visibly crossed his mind. "Wait. Are you Irene Winters?"

"I am," Irene said with dignity. She came to a stop out of their reach. "But you still haven't told me who you are."

"Never you mind," the spokesman said, his accent slipping slightly from *genteel and refined* to *not wanted in polite society*. "You're coming with us right now."

Irene smiled sweetly. **"You perceive that it'd be much easier to get me to come with you if you explain who you are and what's going on and where you're taking me,"** she suggested.

She could almost see the light going on behind their eyes as the Language adjusted their perceptions. "Ah, beg pardon," the man said, touching his hat politely. "My name's Corder, and I've been sent by a lady you know, Madame Sterrington, who'd like to see you urgently. She'd like to see your friend Prince Kai as well, and she wouldn't mind Mr. Vale if he happens to be in, but it was you in particular she was asking for."

It would be prudent to wait for Kai and Vale to return. However, three days of isolated research screamed at Irene to get out of the house and do something *productive*. She reassured herself with the knowledge that the Fae was speaking the truth as he knew it, which meant the situation was safe. Well, reasonably safe. Not an active ambush, at least. "Did Sterrington say what the situation was?" she asked.

"No, madam, I'm afraid she didn't. She's still not very well, you know, after she was shot recently. I'm doing everything I can to assist, of course."

Irene knew Sterrington fairly well. The woman was the Fae representative for the dragon–Fae treaty, and she and Irene had a reasonable working relationship. Past issues of kidnapping and injury had been mostly smoothed over, or at least weren't mentioned too frequently. She was sure that while Sterrington might have sent this man to request Irene's presence, she wouldn't have told him to force his way into Vale's lodgings in the process.

Either he's over-enthusiastic, or he's trying to build his own power base while she's ill. I definitely need to speak to Sterrington.

"Very well, I'll come," Irene said. "What's her current address? Prince Kai will want to come as well when he returns here." Or, to be more precise, Kai would storm in to fetch Irene if she wasn't back by then.

"Thirty-five Grosvenor Square, madam."

"Good. Just let me fetch my coat and hat and veil, and I'll be right with you."

"You didn't need to come out of hiding for me, miss," Mrs. Wilson said reproachfully. "I've got my pistol in my pocket, same as always, and I'd have shot him right in the belly. They don't like it when you do that to them."

Out of the corner of her eye, Irene saw both men twitch at the thought. "I apologize for their manners, Mrs. Wilson, but I think that I do need to speak with Madame Sterrington. I'm sure that you can pass on the details as needed."

Mrs. Wilson gave a nod. "Oh, trust me, miss, I know what to do." The grim smirk on her face told Irene that Kai and Vale would be getting a full description of events.

"Excellent. In that case . . ." Irene plucked her outer coat from the coat cupboard and shrugged it on, donning hat and fashionable veil. "Let's be off."

She hoped she wasn't making a serious mistake.

CHAPTER 12

The house in Grosvenor Square was gleamingly cheerful, spotlessly clean, and furnished in expensive (if not good) taste. It would have been suitable for anyone, from an ambassador to a foreign banker or a member of the minor nobility. It was definitely nicer than the Liechtenstein Embassy where Lord Silver spent his time and hosted his parties. Of course there might be dubious things in the cellar or monstrosities hidden behind the walls, but you could say that of any house in London, not just the ones where Fae lived.

Yet the first thing Irene was conscious of when she entered the house was a very faint smell. It was like opening a fridge door when something inside has started to go off, but not being sure which of the many items of food was the culprit: an undertone of fetor and physical decay.

The carriage ride had been without incident. No murder attempts, no seductions, no kidnappings, no bribes. It had been *interesting*, however. Corder wasn't as subtle as he liked to think he was. He'd spent the ride trying to find out more about Irene's past history with Sterrington and suggesting that he might be a more useful contact for her than the Fae woman. He'd hinted that Sterrington was currently unstable in some way.

I suppose it's not entirely surprising that political Fae are constantly intriguing against each other, Irene thought, *but I don't want to join their games.* She didn't particularly like Sterrington but she knew the Fae well enough to deal with her.

Which made this talk of instability rather disturbing.

They were met inside the house by an impassive butler and a couple of fluttering maids who tried to take Irene's coat and gloves. Irene held onto her belongings—she didn't expect to be here long, after all. "I'm here to see Madame Sterrington," she said. "Where is she?"

"Is that Irene Winters?" a weak voice called from a room to the left.

"Here," Irene answered.

"Let her in." A pause. "Alone."

Irene smiled at Corder and walked in, closing the door behind her. She wondered if he'd have his ear pressed to it to listen to the conversation.

Sterrington was propped up on one of the chaises longues, cushions wedged in place to keep her upright. She was as neatly dressed as usual, to the extent that she looked somewhere between a child's doll and a fashion plate—dark sleek hair up in coils, cool gray dress, gloves to hide the fact that her right hand was mechanical, her face symmetrical, perfect and anonymous. Yet she was like a doll which had been broken and mended rather than in brand-new condition. That faint echo of a smell was present in this room as well, just perceptible beneath the scent of the black coffee Sterrington was drinking.

"You sent for me," Irene said, "and I've come. But I hope you'll forgive my saying that you don't look well."

Sterrington gestured toward the chair that faced her chaise longue. "Take a seat. You're in a hurry, I deduce—as our mutual acquaintance would say."

"I was in the middle of some research," Irene admitted. "But your—colleague? Assistant? Minion? He said that you wanted to see me urgently. He also mentioned that you were still recovering from being shot. I didn't want to be another source of stress."

Sterrington pursed her lips. "Unfortunately, I'm afraid that you are. Or rather, not you, but the Library. And for reference, Corder is definitely a minion."

"Would you be surprised to know that he has his eyes on your job?"

"Well, of course he does." Sterrington shrugged. "Who doesn't?"

"I've always preferred to be on the specialist side of the job, as opposed to management," Irene said.

"That only ever lasts until something comes along which you don't agree with." Sterrington's hand shook as she took a sip of coffee—a barely perceptible shiver. "Once that happens, everyone wants just a little bit of leverage."

"That's true," Irene admitted. "So what's the issue with the Library?"

Sterrington hesitated. "Can I trust you to speak the truth?"

"Are you *sure* you're feeling well?" Irene's question was entirely serious. While Sterrington wasn't one of the great Fae—at least, not yet—she was a competent negotiator, politician, and manager. She'd never ask a question that naive under normal circumstances. "We both know the answer to that one. There are certain circumstances where I'd lie to you and never admit that I'd lied, but I'm hardly going to warn you about it in advance."

Sterrington shook her head jerkily. "No, that won't do. I—" She broke off, put down her coffee, and removed a small silver case from her sleeve, opening it to show the fine white powder inside. "Care for some cocaine?"

"Absolutely not," Irene said, her concern growing by the second.

"Well, I'm sorry, because I need some." She tipped a little onto the back of her hand and sniffed it. "There. That's better."

"Sterrington, this isn't like you." Irene kept her tone even, not wanting to escalate the situation, but inwardly she felt as though she was sitting across from a primed explosive. "You shouldn't be taking something that'll affect your judgment—"

"I need to focus." Sterrington's pupils were huge. She breathed deeply, settling herself as she put the box away. "I'll make a deal with you, Irene. You give me your word that you'll speak the truth, and I'll tell you why I'm so worried. Trust me, you won't be the loser."

Irene weighed the situation mentally. She was used to dealing with a Sterrington who was businesslike and highly corporate, a woman who'd judge any situation coldly and clearly. This wasn't normal. It was very likely not safe. But on the other hand, promising to speak the truth wasn't the same thing as promising to answer all questions. Silence was always an option. **I give you my word to speak the truth to you for the remainder of this conversation,**" she finally said, her words hanging in the air as the Language sealed her promise. "But I want a look at your wound. Is it being properly cared for?"

"Forget the wound," Sterrington said, the words tumbling out in a quick, jerky flow. "Tell me, is the Library up to something? Are *you* up to something?"

"I'm hunting Alberich," Irene said, choosing to answer the second question first. "The Library's aware of it. You wouldn't object to that, would you?"

"Him? No, I wouldn't object at all. My master the Cardinal won't mind, either. Alberich's always been dangerous to deal with, and now that we have an open truce with the dragons and the Library, it's safer and easier to do deals with Librarians who *aren't* traitors."

That was a weight off Irene's mind. The Cardinal, Sterrington's patron, was the sort of Fae who spent his whole life in intrigue and manipulation. Once he found out that Irene wanted Alberich dead, he'd be looking for a way to profit from it. Irene found it comforting to think the Cardinal would find it more profitable to help *her* than Alberich. "Well, I'm delighted to be clearing annoying chess pieces off the board for you," she said drily.

"You didn't answer my first question." Sterrington leaned forward. "Is the Library up to something?"

"If it is, then I don't know what," Irene said honestly. "I'm sure individual Librarians have their own projects on the go right now. If the Library itself has any greater schemes, then I haven't been told about them." True enough. She'd only heard rumors and suspicions. "But if you mean, does the Library have some huge anti-Fae plan in progress, then I don't know anything about it—and I don't believe the Library *would*. After all this work for peace?"

"After all the work by *you and a few others* for peace," Sterrington snapped. "It'd be naive to assume that everyone in your Library feels the same way."

For a moment Irene thought of Coppelia in Paris, coughing and drawn as she tried to get the treaty drawn up—and then of her most recent meeting in the Library with her friend and mentor, possibly her last. Anger twisted inside her like hot iron. "I've answered your extremely open-ended question. If you want better answers, you're going to need to tell me what the problem is. Without any further cocaine."

"I need to focus. You don't *understand*."

"Then explain." Irene was about to say, *Make me understand,* but she knew better than to give any Fae such an invitation. Even an ally. "I'm guessing that something's come up?"

Sterrington laughed, then cut herself off, pressing her left hand against her chest where she'd been shot last month. "Yes. Something has happened, and I'm in a bad position to deal with it. You're quite right, Corder sees himself as upwardly mobile and me as a blockage in his career trajectory. Sadly, I'm not well-placed to crack down as hard as I'd like. You remember the fire?"

"The one the Guantes set?" It had taken out most of an office block, which had held Sterrington's previous base—and her records. She and Irene had been forced to escape via the rooftops and some zeppelin cables.

"Right. I lost a lot of assets in that. Now technically that wasn't my fault, and to some extent the fact that you disposed of the Guantes counts in my favor, given that you were acting on my behalf . . ."

Irene raised her eyebrows very pointedly.

"Look, this is about cost–benefit analysis and reporting to my superior in such a way that I don't get censured for carelessness and risk losing his favor and my position. Being shot is a fifty-fifty thing—it's not as good as someone *else* being shot, but it does show I was really giving the project one hundred percent of my time and attention. But overall, my position isn't as good as it could be. I'm restricted in what I can threaten to do."

"Aren't you worried I could tell Lord Silver this?" Irene asked curiously. The two Fae had been on opposite sides in the past, when Sterrington had been working for Lord Guantes, Silver's enemy. While they seemed to be on reasonable working terms now, Irene suspected it was the sort of relationship where neither would bother to pull the other out of a tank full of piranhas unless there was something useful in it for them.

"No. He's in too deep as well, with the Catherine investment. And I'm not his type, anyhow. When he's playing seduction games, he wants people who say yes yes yes or no no no, not the sort who say they're not interested and does he have any coffee."

Her words spilled out like water. Kai would have drawn unflattering comparisons to chattering streams or babbling brooks. Irene wondered how much cocaine the Fae had already taken today—and on top of an infected wound.

Sterrington shook her head. "I'm getting off the topic. The issue is that I have a *problem*, and that I don't currently have the support or the tools to sort it out. I can take it all up to the Cardinal and ask for help, but if I do, I'll lose my current position and responsibilities. This is not good. This is very not good. I need . . ." She broke off before she could say *your help*, before she could admit her weakness, but Irene saw how much the restraint cost her.

I don't need this, Irene thought desperately. *I have a mission. This is not my problem. This woman is not my friend. The best thing for me to do would be to report back to the Library that there are unfortunate rumors going around that we're up to something, and leave Sterrington to contact the Cardinal, and stay well out of this . . .*

"Let's make a deal," Irene said firmly. "You're going to tell me about this problem—and I'll do my best to help you as your Library colleague in the treaty. And in the meantime, you'll let me take a look at your wound. When was the last time you trusted someone else to take care of it?"

Sterrington avoided Irene's eyes. "A couple of days ago. Maybe three. The doctor told me to keep it clean and let it heal."

Irene leaned a little closer. Very quietly, in case Corder was listening at the door, she said, "You really don't trust anyone here, do you?"

"I can't." There was a note of desperation to Sterrington's voice, a hectic paranoid glint in her eyes. "I've come all this way, reached this position, and I'm still young for our kind. There are people who want to bring me down, disgrace me, and take my position—the Cardinal won't have any choice in the matter if I fail, he'd be obliged to remove me himself. You must understand. Isn't it the same for you?"

"A lot of my colleagues would rather be stealing books than talking politics. I don't think any of them would deliberately go out of their way to push me over the edge." Irene suspected there were probably a few Librarians who wouldn't run too fast to get her out of trouble, though. A slow saunter would be more like it, while taking photos to document her failure. "But I know what you mean about a patron not having any choice if you mess up too publicly."

She touched Sterrington's gloved hand—the genuine one, not the artificial one. She could feel the other woman's temperature even through her glove. "So since we have interests in common—keeping the treaty stable, working with colleagues we know are sensible—it's in your interest to let me make sure that wound's healing properly, and for you to tell me what the issue is that has you suspecting the Library."

"You're manipulating me," Sterrington accused her.

"Of course I am," Irene snapped, her temper breaking through for a moment. Alberich was trying to contact her, she'd been ordered to kill Alberich—she didn't have *time* for other people's problems. "I'm manipulating you because you won't accept anything else. You won't take gifts from me without a prior reason, you won't trust honesty from me unless I swear it in the Language, you won't believe that I'd ever try to help you unless I got something out of it. Naturally I'm manipulating you, Sterrington. You'll never cooperate with me unless I do!"

"Hush," Sterrington hissed. Her eyes flicked to the door. "He'll hear us."

"So tell him that you *manipulated* me into it," Irene muttered savagely. "Twisting the poor little Librarian around your little finger. Now do we have a deal or don't we?"

Sterrington chewed on her lip for a moment, her uncertainty clearly showing on her face for once, and then nodded. "All right. We have a deal."

Outside in the hall the doorbell pealed loudly enough that someone had to be leaning on it. The front door slammed open. Kai's voice was audible through door and walls—not loud, but carrying, directed, and with a leashed anger that threatened tidal waves. "Where is Irene Winters?"

Sterrington rolled her eyes wearily. "Can't you do something about him?"

"I rather like him the way he is," Irene said cheerfully. "Without manipulation." She raised her voice. "I'm fine, Kai! In here!"

The door didn't actually slam open, but it was wrenched open with a great deal of controlled force. "So you're here," Kai said, in tones that suggested he'd expected to find her chained up in the basement, engaging in nameless orgies, or both. "What precisely is going on?"

Perhaps Irene could live with a *small* modification of his behavior when it came to him always assuming the worst. "Madame Sterrington's ill," she said calmly. "I was about to check her wound from a few weeks ago. Is Vale with you—ah, good. Vale, can you recommend a good doctor who makes house calls? Someone reliable?"

"I already have a highly qualified and very highly paid doctor," Sterrington muttered.

Irene leaned closer. "Yes," she said softly, "but this one that Vale's about to get for me will be absolutely definitely not connected to Corder or any other Fae who'd benefit from your staying ill or getting worse. Do you take my point?"

Sterrington twitched a nod.

Half an hour later, the doctor whom Vale had located was busy dressing Sterrington's wound. Kai had risen above the worst of his temper and was treating Irene with saintly forbearance, making her wonder what he'd been up to that he felt the need for the moral high ground. He had murmured something about Bradamant but wasn't prepared to discuss it in what he considered to be enemy territory—truce and treaty or not.

Vale had left the room. While he was very broad-minded for this time and place, he still felt it inappropriate to be present while Sterrington was in the state of undress necessary to treat her wound. He'd made some excuse about finding the kitchen and asking for a cup of tea—which meant that he was subtly interrogating the cook and servants for details about the household.

The doctor had kept up a constant stream of muttering as she cleaned the wound and redressed it. She was prim and proper, with iron-gray hair brutally pinned back and a sober black dress and coat, but her persistent limp and the gun in her medical bag suggested hidden depths. She'd also taken away Sterrington's cocaine.

"What do you think, doctor?" Irene asked, daring to approach.

The doctor drew down her brows as she turned to face Irene, glowering like an owl. "Are you this woman's keeper?"

"Well, no . . ."

"Because apparently she needs one. Sitting around with a fever and an infected wound, not bothering to go and get proper treatment . . ."

"It wasn't looking that bad earlier," Sterrington muttered. Her perfect composure was frayed at the edges. She'd refused any sort of anesthetic while the wound was being cleaned; the handkerchief she'd been gripping was in rags. "I must thank you for your attention, doctor, and your bill will be in the post . . ."

"I will present you with my bill when the treatment's over," the doctor said, turning to level a finger at Sterrington's nose. Sterrington blinked. "I'll be visiting you daily to check on that wound. I don't lose patients—however reckless, careless, or self-indulgent they may be. I didn't lose Peregrine Vale when he came to me with—well, let's not go into that. I won't lose you. Ten o'clock tomorrow morning. And stay off any other drugs except for the sedative I'm about to give you."

"Can I speak to Miss Winters first?" Sterrington asked weakly.

The doctor checked her watch. "Five minutes."

Sterrington beckoned Irene closer. Kai trailed along with her, as inconspicuous as a dragon in human form could be. Sadly the lounge offered no convenient camouflage for him to hide behind and be more surreptitious about his eavesdropping.

"I'm not sure whether to thank you or to spend the rest of my life avoiding you," Sterrington murmured.

"Think about how efficient that doctor is," Irene said briskly. "Think about how you don't need to depend on Corder for a doctor any more." She went down on one knee next to the sofa, the better to keep their conversation quiet. "And now tell me why you think the Library's up to something?"

Sterrington's eyes flicked to Kai, an obvious invitation for Irene to tell him to step back and keep things private. When Irene didn't react, she sighed. "The issue is that a number of powerful Fae are currently in conflict or heading that way, or retreating behind heavy defenses of the sort that are practically offensive in themselves. And the one thing which they all have in common is that they recently received messages or messengers from the Library."

"I could ask how you know this, but you'd just smirk and remind me that your patron's the Cardinal, correct?"

"Absolutely correct." Sterrington managed a thin smile. "Let's say that the evidence isn't conclusive yet, but it's been suggested that I have a quiet word with you and you have a quiet word with . . . other people. Just in case. I have a list here of the names and titles of the Fae involved, and the aliases the Librarians were using. Take it away and do some analysis." She fumbled with a skirt pocket, producing an envelope which she handed to Irene.

"Thank you," Irene said, tucking the envelope away. She'd look at it later.

"Let me be clear about this. My patron entirely understands that an organization may have a rebel here or there who's out for their own objectives. That's part of life. It's only natural. It's how things work. But in that case, if the organization is *effective*, it takes care that any entrepreneurs stay within limits—and cracks down on them if they don't. That's part of the social contract."

"For some definitions of it," Irene agreed. Every Fae saw things through the perspective of their chosen archetype, and the more powerful they were, the less capable they were of seeing things in any other way. Naturally the Cardinal saw the world in terms of factions, agents, and traitors—and Sterrington was his servant and his pupil.

She could also hear the implied threat in Sterrington's words. If an organization *wasn't* effective, then the Cardinal would reconsider co-operating with it. People and groups who weren't peers . . . were tools.

"I'll look into this," she said. "If I consider it appropriate, I'll pass it up to someone whom I trust inside the Library. I hope that these are just unfortunate coincidences, of course."

"Of course," Sterrington said, her words banal and clearly just for the sake of politeness.

"While I'm here, do you know anything about worlds vanishing?"

Sterrington's eyes widened. "What have *you* heard about that?"

Irene was about to answer *Only rumors*, but Kai spoke first. "Word has it that some worlds at both ends of creation have vanished—both in order and in chaos. We've also heard that people who were strongly against the treaty and who lived on those worlds have vanished with them."

"Don't blame the Cardinal," Sterrington said firmly. "It's not as if he could affect worlds somewhere in the realms of order."

No, Irene thought. *You'd need a dragon for that.* "Is there anything you *can* tell us?" she asked, phrasing her question carefully.

"At the moment, no. If I can share anything in the future, I will." Her eyes flicked between Irene and Kai. "Let's not cause any widespread panics, shall we? That would be a very bad idea. I'd hate to be the person who leaked information about worlds *definitely* vanishing beyond anyone's ability to reach them and caused a widespread panic."

"Let's not, indeed. Will you be all right?" It wasn't that Irene *liked* the woman, but it would be a waste of her time and effort if the Fae died or suffered a "tragic accident" the second Irene left the house.

"I think so. My perspective . . . may have been a little tarnished of late." Sterrington actually looked disgusted at herself. "I should have done better and relied on someone useful in the first place."

"I'm touched by your good opinion of me."

"I know you're reliable," Sterrington said simply. "Rather predictable, not very good at horizon-scanning, prone to seeing the trees rather than the forest—but reliable."

"Thank you." Irene rose to her feet, dusting off her dress.

"Now if you want a *full* personal alliance with no holds barred, all you'd have to do is tell me exactly how you managed to get a Fae into the Library . . ."

"And you were doing so well," Irene sighed. "Still, you're sounding better. I'll send the doctor over with a sedative."

"Take care of yourself," Sterrington said, her tone serious again. "I'd rather not have to deal with a new treaty representative."

"Oh, I'm sure that they'd be more sensible and easier to deal with than me," Irene replied. "They'd probably even have a secretary and organize business lunches."

And then the doctor moved in with the promised sedative, and Irene and Kai had to leave.

The cab that Kai and Vale had arrived in was still waiting outside. "Don't bother waiting for Vale," Kai said as he helped Irene in. "He said he'd be coming back in his own time."

"Well, Sterrington knew what to expect when she invited us into her house," Irene said philosophically. If Sterrington didn't want her staff questioned, then she shouldn't have asked Vale across her threshold.

"Invited *you*," Kai corrected her.

Irene shrugged. "We're more of a collective these days, I think, and anyone who knows us knows it. Now . . . I have a couple of things to tell you. Do you want to give me the Bradamant details, or shall I go first? And did you know that Vale's housekeeper carries a gun?"

"No, but it doesn't surprise me." Kai settled himself comfortably as the cab jolted into traffic. "You first, I think."

Irene didn't mention what she'd found out about her own conception. She'd tell Kai that . . . later. When she'd come to terms with it herself. Instead she ran through the details of Alberich's message, and her response—and Corder's invitation.

Kai frowned, but didn't look too concerned. "We know Alberich can send messages that way. I suppose it's no great surprise that he's being aggressive about the situation. You're sure that interruption was from the Library?"

"It makes sense," Irene said. "Who else could interfere with the Language?"

"But who at the Library would have done such a thing? Or be able to?"

"Kostchei? Or Melusine? I have a long way to go before I know everything which can be done with the Language. What Alberich was saying is the more important thing here. I'd like to hope we could use this to lure him into a trap, but he's not stupid."

"We can't risk underestimating him," Kai agreed, but he was frowning. "Now, about Bradamant—Vale and I encountered her in our lodgings. We subdued and questioned her. She tried to convince us that there was a secret Library conspiracy manipulating you in some way."

"I'd like to scoff at the whole secret Library conspiracy thing, but when we put it together with what Sterrington's just told us . . . Did Bradamant give you any specific details?"

"She talked about odd missions, and Librarians playing politics, and worlds vanishing—she confirmed that's definite, by the way, not just rumors—and having a general feeling that something was *wrong*. She assumed your mission was part of this."

"And we theorized earlier that part of the secrecy surrounding my mission was to smoke out anybody who's been leaking information . . . Kai, I'm worried. We've got information from three different sources now that something's wrong in connection with the Library. Me, Bradamant, and Sterrington. Once is happenstance, twice is coincidence, but three times is enemy action."

"So what should we do about it?" Kai asked, apparently expecting her to have an answer.

"Panic? No, more seriously . . . I suppose I pass this on to Kostchei and Melusine. Melusine is Library Internal Security, so this is something she should definitely hear about. I can give her the list of names from Sterrington. It might be exactly what she's looking for." A pang of grief touched her. She'd almost said *Coppelia* as well, but now she might never be able to do that again. "Then I get on with my particular job—but keep my eyes open."

Kai sat back in what looked rather like relief. Had he been expecting her to try to sort out the whole mess herself? She wasn't the Library in person—she was just one Librarian. "That sounds very sensible," he said firmly. "Perhaps you can drop in a report to the Library this evening."

The cab jolted to a stop, and the driver pulled back the small door in the roof. "We're here, sir, madam."

"Thank you very much," Kai said, handing up the payment.

In the interests of security, Irene waited until they were back in Vale's rooms before continuing the conversation. "We should probably check Sterrington's list of names first," she suggested. "Just in case we recognize any of them."

Kai nodded, his face sober at the implications. If it did turn out to include someone they knew—or a friend, even—what then?

The whole situation was getting too complicated. The Library wanted her to hunt down Alberich while simultaneously pretending she was acting on her own. Shan Yuan wanted Kai to hand over his position and act as if it was of his own free will. Sterrington wanted Irene's support—as long as she didn't have to show any weakness. "Everyone's being hypocritical," she muttered. "Is there anyone round here who *doesn't* want something from us while acting innocent? We need to find out what's really going on before everyone does the wrong thing for the right reasons."

Just as Irene was about to open the envelope, she heard the sound of the doorbell from below. She stalked across to the window to see who it was and whether she'd need to vanish into the attic again.

To her surprise, it was Lord Silver. She flashed back to the request she'd made—she'd asked him to put her in touch with Fae who'd had dealings with Alberich. Relatively sane and trustworthy Fae, not the sort who'd try to use her to start a war or drain her of her blood in order to bathe in it. Could it be that he'd actually managed to find someone?

This might just be the break they needed. They might finally, *finally* have a lead.

It was easy to trace Silver's passage up the stairs, sight unseen, by the squawking of the housekeeper, who was trying to stop him. She might be willing to shoot casual Fae callers, but she evidently drew the line at local notables. "But Mr. Vale isn't *in*!" she protested.

"Then I'll wait for him," Silver said cheerfully, "and I'll pass the time in peaceful meditation, breathing in the atmosphere of his happy home, sniffing his tobacco, reading his scrapbooks. Of course, if it just so happened that someone *else* was up there, I'd be very pleased to see them, but I quite understand that you can't possibly confirm it . . ."

Irene and Kai exchanged a glance. Then Kai walked to the door and opened it. "It's all right," he called down to Mrs. Wilson. "I'll take care of things."

Silver positively bounced into the room, sweeping off his hat and smirking. He was in smart morning dress, his cravat knotted neatly and his shoes glossy from recent polishing. "My very favorite little mouse. I hoped I'd find you here. What a glorious day—and how pleasant to see you!" He looked around. "Even if it's under these highly depressing surroundings. Look at all these drab books, this boring scientific equipment, these miserable chairs. How is an artistic person like myself supposed to flourish in a room like this?"

Not for the first time, Irene daydreamed about pushing Lord Silver out of the window. "It's hardly *your* room to decorate," she said. "And I've seen some of your own rooms back at the Liechtenstein Embassy. I wouldn't call them models of artistic freedom—especially given how rarely they get dusted."

Silver paused. "I was about to point out that you'd never seen my bedroom, but in the interests of friendly relations and mutual good-will, I'll control myself. Let's hope that the Recording Angel remembers this moment of heroic virtue." He flung himself down into the nearest chair, sprawling in a way that would have had Renaissance painters grabbing for their brushes and telling him to take his clothes off. "I have good news for you, my dear Miss Winters. No doubt you can tell."

"I suspected as much." There were two things that made a Fae particularly happy. The first was to do something which resonated perfectly with their narrative archetype, and the second was to pay off an inconvenient debt. "Do share."

Silver sighed. "You have no idea how much of a struggle it is not to ask you to beg on your knees for the information I've got . . . but a deal's a deal, so stop looking at me like that, princeling. I have a contact for you. Someone who's communicated with Alberich, and who says she actually provided him with some information that he didn't previously know."

Irene blinked in shock. "Please don't think that I'm objecting, but that sounds almost too good to be true."

"Oh, I thought so too," Silver agreed. "But apparently it took place a few centuries ago. Still, I think it fulfills our bargain. Would you agree?"

It would have been useful if Silver could have dug up a recent contact with a list of Alberich's current hideouts—but someone who could explain Alberich's deeper motivations might be even better. If Irene could understand why he turned traitor and wanted to destroy the Library . . . She nodded. "I agree that being put in touch with this person would fulfill our deal. Where is she?"

"Elsewhere," Silver said. "Constantinople. Another world—which means I'm going to have to lead you there. And the sooner the better, as I can't promise how long she'll stay in one place." He glanced across to Kai and sighed. "Yes, princeling, I can just about manage to transport both of you at the same time, as long as you don't do anything unreasonable. I'm not going to try to tell you not to come along."

"A good thing too," Kai said, "because I wouldn't have listened."

Irene crossed to Vale's desk, finding pen and paper. "If we can't wait for Vale, then I'll leave a note to tell him where we've gone and why. We wouldn't want him thinking you'd kidnapped us." Sterrington's list would have to wait until later. She wasn't going to mention it while Silver was here.

"Oh, Lord Silver's far too sensible for that," Kai said, but there was an edge behind his words, and Irene realized that he didn't entirely trust the Fae's promises.

Silver must have picked that up as well, because his pale eyes narrowed. "Be careful what you say. I've given my word to our mutual friend Miss Winters, and I'm not going to break it. As a courtesy to her I'm bringing you along. But don't push me, Prince Kai. I realize this is a dangerous situation, and I'm not going to put myself in harm's way for *your* sake."

"As long as we all know where we stand," Kai said.

"Besides, it'd be very awkward if the dragon treaty representative met a horrible fate while on a personal expedition with you," Irene said gently. She folded the note to Vale and left it where he would see it on entering. "And you're far too prudent to risk that. Shall we leave the threats and get down to business? I'm rather curious about who this mysterious contact is."

Silver regarded his nails. "Well, as to that—I had to make a few promises myself to get this meeting set up. And one of them—to her—is that I don't tell you who or what she is until you get there. I *can* promise that she doesn't intend harm to you or yours."

"That's ridiculous!" Irene complained.

"Oh, I agree, but a promise *is* a promise." Silver rose to his feet. "So we'd better be on our way. Because one thing I *can* tell you is that she knows who you are and she's looking forward to seeing you. Again."

CHAPTER 13

By the time they reached the passageways of the Grand Bazaar, Lord Silver was sweating from more than just the temperature. He walked like a man bracing himself against a high wind, struggling with every step. Thin trails of perspiration crawled from his temples down the sides of his face, and he had long since untied his cravat and unbuttoned his collar. When they finally emerged from between two stone pillars to look out at a long corridor of brick and stone, he sagged against the wall in as unobtrusive a way as he could manage.

This had to be the part of the market that sold silks, Irene realized. She looked around assessingly, trying to get a feel for the place. Lengths of fabric hung from rails, or were draped against the walls, or peeped out enticingly from cabinets. The stalls were recessed niches in the wall, with the merchants sitting on wooden stools or divans in front of them. The air was dry and hot; she could smell tea and coffee, spices and perfumes. A constant whisper of echoing conversations drifted down the corridor and underneath its pointed arches, as the flow of customers and passersby surged and ebbed. The general language seemed to be Turkish, and fortunately she had enough of that to get by, but other languages and dialects jostled at the edge of her hearing.

"Are you all right?" she asked Silver.

"I will be in a moment." He wiped his clammy forehead. "This would have been a great deal easier if you'd come with me alone."

"Which wasn't going to happen," Kai said flatly. "You know that and we know that, so why belabor the point?"

"Allow me the chance to complain. I feel I rather deserve it after all the hard work I've done."

Fae didn't travel between worlds in the same way that dragons did. The dragons flew *outside* the worlds, then back in when they found the world or the person that they wanted, but Fae simply walked (or drove, or rode, or even flew in a plane) through a succession of different worlds, as though they were traversing the stripes of some imaginary rainbow. Irene didn't understand the metaphysics or perceptions which made it possible for either of them to *do* this, but mid-trip was not a good time to ask questions.

Powerful Fae found it easier to travel between worlds and bring other people with them, and Fae with a particular affinity for transport in their personal narrative found it easier still. Lord Silver was quite powerful, but his archetype of libertine and seducer had few links to narratives about transport—except perhaps when it came to midnight getaways. Bringing a dragon and a Librarian with him was hard labor.

Kai didn't look much happier. While he wasn't as physically exhausted as Silver, he was still seething with distrust and had been waiting for an ambush every step of the way. He didn't like the mode of travel, but it had no particular effect on him—for a short trip, at least—and this particular world wasn't any further into chaos than Vale's was. But Irene could feel him bristling at her back, and she knew he was watching the crowds with a suspicious eye.

"What year is it?" Irene asked softly. She could see multiple skin tones all around her and the clothing was relatively timeless; she didn't have detailed knowledge of Turkey's history and culture in any world, let alone this one. One man in the distance was wearing the uniform of an English naval officer which looked vaguely late eighteenth- or early nineteenth-century, but that wasn't very specific.

Silver shrugged. "I don't know and I care less. There are no immediate wars in the vicinity, which is the important thing." He turned to look at her. "Do you want to blend in? We can pause for a shopping expedition if you like."

Irene glanced down at her clothing. While her Victorian dress and Kai's suit were certainly out of place here, she suspected they'd merely be classified under the general label of *foreigner, dressed strangely* rather than specifically identified as dangerous. "I think speed may be more important. If someone tries to attack us, we're very exposed here." She had no idea whether Alberich could track her here, or whether he was able to leave the world where she'd last seen him, but she didn't want to find out the hard way. Her skin crawled at the thought of *how* exposed they were, now they'd left a place of comparative safety. She forced herself to be calm. "Maybe a head covering?"

"Allow me," said Kai, who'd been quietly negotiating at a nearby stall. He passed her a gauzy length of gray-and-green silk.

"Thank you," Irene said with a grateful smile, and wrapped it round her head and shoulders. Of course, the two men were still incredibly distinctive, each in their own way—Lord Silver as a walking avatar of licentious seduction, and Kai with all the inhuman handsomeness of a dragon in human form—but at least *she* was a bit less obvious.

"If we can't shop, then I suppose we must get on with things." Silver pushed himself away from the wall, seemingly much refreshed by the pause, and led the way through the crowd. People fell back before him, stunned by the sheer aura of seductiveness that he projected. A few muttered disapprovingly. Others tried to pass him notes surreptitiously or drop handkerchiefs in the hope that he'd pick them up. Irene and Kai exchanged weary glances, then followed.

Silver clearly knew the path he was taking; Irene memorized the turnings as they passed, but her general ignorance made her feel vulnerable. This walled, roofed market was a city in itself, a miniature arcology; it might be dependent on the wider Constantinople beyond its walls, but it had its own rules and customs. Half of her wanted to retreat into a corner where she could have her back to the wall and hide until she had a better feel for the place. The other half wanted to find where they sold books here. Light slanted down from rectangular windows in the roof, making the silks gleam like jewels and catching on glints of gold and steel. They passed skullcaps and leatherwork, cushions and sets of silver dishes, jewelry and saddles and shoes, and still there was no sign of an outer wall or any limit on the place.

"Where are we going?" Kai finally asked. "One of the main halls? Cevahir Bedesten or Sandal Bedesten?" He clearly knew the place better than Irene did.

"Neither," Silver said. "We're going to have a drink and a chat. And here we are."

He gestured to one of the small buildings which occasionally stood at the centers of junctions or mid-corridor. Like the rest of them, it was two stories high, disconnected from the surrounding walls; a boxy building, elegantly decorated with colored tiles, open on the ground floor and with windows on the first floor to allow observation of the passing crowds. This particular kiosk didn't sell food as some of the others did—the only smells emanating from it were tea and coffee.

Irene would have held back to scan the surrounding area for spies, assassins, or both, but Silver marched ahead cheerfully, and she had little choice but to follow. He tossed a coin to the merchant and led the way up the narrow stairs to the first floor.

The clientele there weren't spending their time staring out of the windows. Instead, they were all focused on the elderly woman who occupied what was clearly a place of honor, seated on the divan with more cushions than she really needed. The other half-dozen present, both men and women, were perched on stools or sitting on the floor, letting their cups of tea or coffee grow cold as they listened to her.

Irene felt a cold shock seize her as she recognized the woman. She was Fae—and a moderately powerful one. They'd met once before on a train to Venice, when she'd been on her way to rescue Kai from his kidnappers. Irene had been masquerading as a Fae herself at the time. The woman, Isra—or Aunt Isra, as she preferred to be called—was a storyteller by trade and by vocation, and had been traveling to Venice to witness the spectacle of Kai's auction and tell its story afterward. Things had been dramatic enough that she probably wasn't disappointed by how it had turned out, but . . .

Aunt Isra looked up and met Irene's eyes, and her thin-lipped smirk might have been generously called a welcoming smile. She was wrapped in a dark blue chador that left her wrinkled face bare. The glint in her dark eyes reminded Irene of Vale's keen eagerness when he was on a scent, and she felt an increasing nervousness. Why had Aunt Isra wanted to keep her identity secret until Irene arrived?

The Fae nodded in greeting, then turned back to her listeners, clapping her hands together. "That will be all for today," she decreed in fluid Turkish. "I have other visitors to attend to. Be here at the same time tomorrow and we shall continue."

The group of listeners—students?—looked less than happy to have their session cut short, but they bowed their heads and murmured assent.

Irene was conscious of their eyes on her, Kai, and Silver as they rose to file past and down the stairs. "What if they tell someone?" she asked Silver quietly.

Silver spread his hands in cheerful submission to the whims of fate. "Entirely possible, my little mouse, but none of them should have known you were coming here—so even if they do recognize you, it'll take a little while for them to work out where to sell the information. And now it's over to you. I've completed my part of the bargain."

Kai reached across to touch her shoulder reassuringly. "You do the talking," he suggested. "I'll back you up."

Irene pulled herself together. This *was* why she'd come here. She approached the seated Fae and bowed politely. "It's been a while since we met, Aunt Isra—I hope I may still call you that?"

"Certainly you may," Aunt Isra said gleefully. "Though last time we met, you were calling yourself Clarice Backson. Tell me what I should call *you*."

It was never comfortable being caught in one's earlier lies. Irene's old teachers from school would have delivered a virtuous lecture on the subject. Irene's own reaction wasn't so much one of *moral* guilt as it was a feeling of incompetence. Good Librarians didn't get caught out like this. "My name is Irene," she confessed, "and I'm commonly known as Irene Winters. I belong to the Library. I apologize for lying to you earlier. I hope you'll understand why I did it."

"I do indeed." Aunt Isra's expression was that of a mystic deep in trance. "My child, it's what heroes do. Some are honorable, but many are not—and all would tell me that they did what they had to do. I understand you better than you know. Your eyes were set on rescuing your lover, and you had no thought for anyone or anything else in your way."

Irene weighed pointing out that there *had* been other factors in the equation, such as potential war and her being handed over to Kai's family as responsible for his kidnapping, against the fact that Aunt Isra clearly *liked* this version of the story. And right now, she wanted Aunt Isra's goodwill. "Politics were involved as well," she hazarded.

"No doubt the politics comes under blood. Love, blood, and rhetoric . . ." Aunt Isra quoted. "But you shouldn't be standing. Sit down, sit down, child! And your prince may sit as well. As for you . . ." She glanced at Silver. "Do you want to stay? I warn you that I won't tolerate interruptions."

Silver smiled. "I'm capable of holding my tongue when I'm asked for silence. What will you give me for that, Miss Winters?"

Irene returned his smile cheerfully. She'd guessed that he might try this. "I'll keep silent about the fact that *you* now know vital secrets about Alberich and the Library."

It wasn't a difficult decision for Silver. On the positive side, he'd have information which people would kill to obtain. On the negative side . . . he'd have information which people would quite possibly kill *him* to obtain. Somewhat sourly, he said, "Deal."

"Well, now that's over, perhaps we can have our little conversation," Aunt Isra said firmly. "Would you like tea or coffee?"

Irene itched with impatience, but she knew that good manners might be paramount here. "Tea, please," she said, seating herself opposite the older woman. "But why did you order Lord Silver not to tell me who you were?"

"Asked, not ordered," Silver put in.

"An old woman's whim," Aunt Isra said airily. "I'm sure you will pardon me." *And if you don't,* the unspoken message ran, *say goodbye to this conversation.*

Irene gritted her teeth—not too obviously, she hoped. This conversation was going to be an exercise in patience. With luck, it was just Aunt Isra wanting to see how far she could push Irene, rather than keeping her here for an ambush. And if it was a trap—then Aunt Isra would regret it. "Of course," she lied. "Thank you for agreeing to meet with me. I realize that this is something of an imposition . . ."

As she went through the steps of a polite conversation, sipping her mint tea, complimenting the brew and making casual chit-chat about current matters, she attempted to gauge what Aunt Isra was getting out of this. When they'd met before, the Fae had wanted to be present at a major event in order to tell the story afterward. Did she hope that Irene would take her along to any confrontation with Alberich? Or worse, was she trying to trigger that confrontation because it would *make a good story*?

Kai was as impassive as marble. Silver had given up on listening and was staring out of the window instead. The conversation ranged over current political goings-on, the quality of the tea, and past Librarians whom Aunt Isra had met. It didn't surprise Irene that according to Aunt Isra, one just didn't get the same quality of Librarians these days. Some things were universal. She knew that she should be remembering all this to add to the Library files, but time was a factor, and minutes and seconds were dribbling away like sand through an hourglass. She felt as if she'd been sitting here, melting in the heat and drowning in the scent of mint tea, for years. How long before one of those students sold the information that Irene was here? How long before Alberich tried to locate her?

"You're a good child," Aunt Isra *finally* said, patting Irene's hand. Her own hands were wrinkled flesh over thin bone, tanned with years of sun and wind. "You've learned some manners. I think it's time to get down to business."

Irene bit back the sigh of relief which she'd have liked to vent. "I appreciate your candor. Allow me to be equally frank in return: I'm looking for information about the renegade Librarian known as Alberich. I asked Lord Silver here to put me in touch with someone who'd had dealings with him."

"Which I did," Silver said, "and which is why we're here. I just hadn't expected it to be so tedious." He quite obviously suppressed a yawn.

Aunt Isra gave him a look which suggested that if he'd been her student, whippings would have been the least of it. Her expression was still sour when she turned back to Irene. "That good-for-nothing over there is correct. I have met Alberich, and I told him a story—and I think that story caused him to make certain choices. I believe you'll find it worth the price."

If Irene had had a rabbit's ears, they would have been standing on end and twitching. "Do go on," she said, trying not to grin from ear to ear. That would just push up the price.

"Naturally something so important—and so valuable to *you*—demands a significant return," Aunt Isra said. She sipped her tea.

Irene had little room to argue. "Are you looking for access to the Library?" she asked.

"Can you do that?"

"I've brought another Fae into the Library before," Irene said. "Of course, it would depend on me getting permission from my superiors, but if you're able to offer something so important to the Library's welfare as knowledge about Alberich . . ."

Aunt Isra frowned. "You're tempting me, child."

"I do hope so." Irene lifted her teacup and found that it was empty—and so was the pot. She looked around for a waiter, but they were the only ones in the small upstairs room.

"I'll do it," Silver said, picking up the tray that the pot rested on. "Try not to make any fascinating deals until I get back."

Aunt Isra looked thoughtful, then pointed one rigid finger at Irene. "What's the catch?"

"Can you be more precise, Aunt Isra?"

"I've been in stories like this before—even if I'm usually the one telling them. There's a catch to a bargain like this, a snag, a hidden price, an unexpected condition. You're smiling at me very nicely, child, but I know, and you know, and I know you know, that there's something you're not telling me which will be to your advantage and my disadvantage if I say yes. I'm not saying that's *wrong*, child, but I'm not in the mood to walk into a trap. Not at my age."

"You don't look a day over sixty," Kai said gallantly and inaccurately.

"And there's another young person who's so well-mannered," Aunt Isra said. "I do like the way you're doing this, children. You've arrived at my command, ready to fulfill my slightest whim if it'll get you what you need to save your home. That's how it should be in a story like this."

Irene had been trying to avoid contradicting the Fae, but she couldn't let that pass. "Aunt Isra, I'm a Librarian, and—as you're doubtless aware—Kai here is a dragon. We don't live in stories the way that you Fae do."

"Ah, but you do," Aunt Isra said, unruffled. "You just don't recognize it. Nobody ever does—at the time." She put down her empty cup. "But I'm wandering from the subject. Again I ask you, what's the catch?"

Irene knew perfectly well what the "catch" was. In order to get

Catherine into the Library, she'd had to use the Fae's true name. She could presumably do the same for Aunt Isra—but knowing her true name would give her power over the Fae, which was why the Fae were prone to pseudonyms and artistic titles.

"Suppose there was a catch, and I was honest about it," Irene said carefully. "Perhaps we could conduct these negotiations in a friendly spirit of mutual goodwill, rather than being overly legalistic? I'd be open about any possible problems, and in return you'd do the same for me, rather than letting me fall into any traps."

"That's very unconventional," Aunt Isra said disapprovingly.

"A special deal, between storytellers and Librarians," Irene coaxed. "Naturally I won't tell anyone else about it. And since Lord Silver isn't here . . ."

Aunt Isra tapped one finger on her knee, then came to a decision and smiled. Her rictus grin made Irene think of adjectives like *crocodilian*—anything involving reptiles looking at a prospective dinner. *What does she want from me?* "Since I like you so much, child, I'll say yes."

Irene nodded. "In that case, I'll admit that I'd need your true name to have a chance of getting you into the Library."

There was a pause. "It's a very good thing you told me that, child," Aunt Isra said. "I'd have been exceptionally annoyed with you if I'd found that out *after* making the bargain."

A nervous prickle ran down Irene's back. Aunt Isra clearly wasn't a combatant, but she probably had a lot of other Fae who owed her favors. Irene's life might become very difficult—and very short—if Aunt Isra wanted to call in those favors. She forced a smile. "As I said, a spirit of mutual goodwill. Perhaps you'd like to return the favor by telling me what you actually *want*."

"Personal desires are long past for a woman as old as I am," Aunt

Isra intoned. "I have dedicated my life to what I am—a storyteller and a wanderer. However, there is one thing which would particularly interest me, and which you're uniquely positioned to offer."

"And what would that be?"

"Your story."

"*My* story?"

"You should be flattered, child!"

"I'm incredibly flattered," Irene said, her mouth running on automatic while she tried to work out how to respond. "Please forgive my surprise and shock. I'm just stunned. Nobody's ever asked for my story before. I mean, there are Library reports, where they always want more details, but that's entirely different . . ."

"Pah!" Aunt Isra's snort cut Irene off mid-divagation. "Why aren't you more enthusiastic? Don't you *want* to tell me all about your life? Haven't you ever wanted to unburden yourself to an eager listener?"

Irene reviewed her past history in about half a second flat. "To be honest, I've always found I was secretive, closemouthed, and unwilling to tell anyone anything at all."

"Entirely true," Kai put in, not very helpfully.

Irene shot him an irritated glance. "I'm giving your proposition my serious interest, but I'm struggling with myself on this one. I hope you understand that I'm nervous about how any information I might give you would be used."

"Oh, I can settle your anxieties," Aunt Isra reassured her. "I'll simply take out the names and exact details, and improve it a little bit here and there. You'll hardly recognize it as your own story once I'm done with it. But I have to have something to *start* with, child. All the best stories need a grain of sand to form the pearl."

"So basically, you're just after the . . . good bits?"

"I'm a storyteller, child," Aunt Isra said, "not a historian."

One of the waiters had entered the room silently as they spoke, and set down a new tray with tea and cups on the table between them. He straightened, turning to move behind Aunt Isra, back to the staircase.

Irene saw a flash of light on metal as a concealed knife slid from his sleeve into his hand.

CHAPTER 14

Kai must have seen it too. He threw himself across the table at the waiter, knocking him away from Aunt Isra. The two men went rolling and crashed into the wall, and a vase of flowers in the window teetered and toppled out into the market outside.

Irene was a couple of seconds behind Kai. She didn't have a dragon's superhuman reflexes; hers were more the desperate cornered rat variety, which were still quite useful in an emergency. She jumped to her feet and dodged round the side of the table, grabbing Aunt Isra by the shoulders and quite literally dragging the Fae away from the struggle, putting herself between the older woman and the fight. She couldn't afford to lose her without finding out what she knew.

The waiter's knife went skittering across the floor, but the waiter himself was putting up a good fight. A surprisingly good one—not many people could go hand-to-hand with Kai. They'd both sprung to their feet again and were exchanging rapid blows. Irene wasn't an expert in martial arts, but she could see that the waiter was going for short quick strikes at nerves and pressure points. Kai's own style was wider, each blow carrying more weight, but less suited for the kiosk's confined quarters.

"Out of my way, child," Aunt Isra demanded from behind Irene, tugging at her shoulder. "I need a better view."

"Absolutely not," Irene replied, holding her ground. "He's probably here to kill you."

"Nonsense! Who'd want to kill a humble storyteller? It's far more likely he wants to kill you."

There was a babbling of voices from downstairs and outside, which Irene dimly registered while watching Kai and the waiter fight. "Can we just settle for immobilizing him first, and then ask him who he's here to kill . . ."

Then some of the words from the yelling outside penetrated. *Climbing. Wall. Window.* She turned round just in time to see a figure in battered robes, a scarf wrapped concealingly round his head, pulling himself over one of the windowsills.

Irene grabbed the lightweight cane table and slung it at the new intruder's head. He was forced to duck, and the diversion gave her a moment to close with him and punch him in the face. With a yell, he lost his grip and fell back out of the room.

Irene spun, looking around for threats. There were too damn many windows. All those lovely views for watching passersby were now huge potential liabilities. Another pair of hands showed themselves at a different window. She caught up the teapot from where it lay on the floor, still full, and poured hot tea over the clutching fingers. They unclenched, and their owner screamed as he fell.

"Yes, yes!" Aunt Isra murmured, watching with delight. "Perfect! Go on, child, go on!"

Irene hoped that whatever security force patrolled the Bazaar would be on their way—but how long would they take to get here?

The kiosk windows might be wide and airy, but there had to be some way to block them—for the owners' security, if no other reason. Irene searched her memories as she swung a bolster into another climbing thug's face, making him teeter on the edge. That was it. There had been shutters on the window frames—ornamental ones, and latched back for the day's business, but a barrier was a barrier. She focused. **"Kiosk shutters, close and lock!"**

The shutters on all the windows surrounding the rooms slammed closed, rattling into place to the accompaniment of surprised cries from outside.

Abruptly the room was in near darkness, with thin strips of light showing round the cracks in the shutters and the outlines of the windows. Kai had been waiting for Irene to do something—he took advantage of the waiter's momentary surprise to drop, swing a low kick which downed his opponent, then leap on top of him and get him in a chokehold.

That left one avenue of attack from outside. **"Divan, move to block the stairway,"** Irene ordered.

The piece of furniture hauled itself across the floor, shivering in every joint and creaking with the strain, and settled itself across the gap of the stairwell. Irene could hear people clawing at the shutters outside, but the would-be intruders had to cling onto the outside of the building at the same time, which made it more difficult. They clearly weren't expert breakers and enterers.

The waiter had been quietly choking. He finally reached out and tapped the floor three times in a gesture of submission.

"Not bad, child," Aunt Isra said judiciously. "Perhaps a little lacking in drama. Next time, wait till they're right in the room and one of them has a knife at my neck."

Irene looked at her in disbelief. "But that would involve one of them having a knife at your neck!"

"Oh, they wouldn't kill me. Nobody kills a storyteller. Who'd tell their stories if they did? But it'd be much more elegant."

The words *Sod elegance* crossed Irene's mind, but were hastily buried under the need to keep Aunt Isra in a good mood. "I'll bear it in mind," she lied. "Kai, is your prisoner willing to talk?"

"Are you?" Kai asked the waiter. "As opposed to the alternative?"

"I'll give you ten minutes' worth of parole, non-hostility, and conversation in return for the chance to escape," the waiter—or pseudo-waiter—counteroffered.

"Irene?" Kai queried, not relaxing his grip.

Irene really didn't like killing people in cold blood—and they might be able to get some answers out of him this way. "Deal," she said. She could hear what sounded like the Bazaar security arriving outside—screams, crashes, thuds, yells to stop in the name of the law. "We're probably safe for a little while here. But what about Silver?" He'd gone downstairs just before this waiter came up. If he'd been the first victim . . . he wasn't a *friend* of hers, but she didn't want to see him dead.

"I knocked him out before coming up here," the waiter said. "He's unconscious but not otherwise harmed. See? I'm being cooperative."

Irene nodded. "Good."

She walked across to throw open a shutter and allow some light into the room. The sea of faces looking up, of bystanders swirling around the kiosk, made her realize she needed some sort of excuse to stop them all coming upstairs and confusing things. With a wave to the crowd, she called down in Turkish, "We're all safe up here! God has preserved us!"

That received a cheer and an ebbing of interest—after all, if everyone was safe and nobody had been horribly assassinated, that might be a good thing in general, but it was far less *interesting* than a gory murder. Hopefully it'd also mean a few more minutes before anyone came up to investigate.

The waiter sat up as Kai released him, rubbing at his throat and bruises. Irene gave him her full attention, trying to look for clues as Vale would have done—but oddly, there was a sort of shadow on his features. It was as though whatever angle she might choose to look at him, he was slightly overcast by some unseen darkness, making it hard to get a clear impression of his face.

"If you don't mind sharing it with us, which of us was your target?" she asked.

He pointed toward Aunt Isra. "Nothing personal, you understand."

"How dare you!" the Fae exclaimed. "I'm a *storyteller*!"

"All of us are equal before the hand of death," he said, with rather overdone profundity. "Even those who spend their time flapping their lips in useless conversation and frivolous tales."

"Even death himself stays his hand before taking the one who'd tell his story to others, child!" Aunt Isra had the bit firmly between her teeth now. "You dare—you have the shameless affrontery, the—"

"Forgive me, Aunt Isra," Irene interrupted. "While I entirely agree that storytellers and Librarians should be out of bounds to assassins, we've only got ten minutes to question him, and he's trying to provoke you."

Aunt Isra snorted, but allowed Irene to lead her over to the divan at the top of the stairs and seat her there. "I suppose nothing more should be expected from this shameful haunter of alleys."

"No more than from a woman who's only escaped death because he saw her in a good light and ran away before she could catch him," the waiter sniped back.

"Better that than a man who'll never show his face in public because he sold it along with his name," Aunt Isra snapped.

Irene looked between the two of them. "Do you know each other?"

"Not personally," the waiter said. "Then again, I try not to know any of my targets personally. Otherwise I'd start drinking, and that's murder on the reflexes."

"I certainly don't know this fool in person," Aunt Isra said coldly. "Of course I've heard stories about the deadly assassin known as the Shadow, though."

"The Shadow," Irene said, working very hard to keep her voice neutral. There were reasonable pseudonyms, and then there were pseudonyms that were so blatantly stereotypical that it was hard not to roll one's eyes.

"Exactly," Aunt Isra said, clearly settling into storytelling mode. "Legend has it that he sold his name to demons which crawled out of hell, so that he could murder from that day to this with no family ties to hold him back."

"That's an outright lie," the assassin muttered. "No demons were involved."

"I'd love the horrible details, but can we concentrate on why you were going to kill Aunt Isra here?" Irene asked.

"Oh, that is a long and complicated story," the assassin said cheerfully. "Much as I would enjoy telling it to you, I fear it comes under patron–client confidentiality."

"So what *can* you tell us?" Kai asked.

"I can recommend the best places to get coffee, knives, metal polish, and leather belts. You might as well do some shopping while you're here."

"We just spared your life!" Irene said in frustration. There had to be some sort of lever she could use to get information out of this man—but what?

"Yes, and I'm extremely grateful. Please notice that I'm making friendly conversation rather than answering in menacing monosyllables as I'd usually do. It's actually quite a nice change. You wouldn't believe how often I only whisper something menacing while cutting someone's throat."

"That's entirely the wrong attitude," Aunt Isra scolded him. "You ought to work harder on being what you *are*. A feared assassin doesn't spend his time recommending the best shops, young man. Why aren't you snarling in this woman's face and threatening to kill her before dawn?"

"Aunt Isra, whose side are you on here?" Irene asked plaintively.

"Naturally I want to preserve my own life, but if I must be killed by an assassin, then I want it to be done *properly*," Aunt Isra explained. "Not some sort of cheap halfhearted business, but a true act of murder by someone who really lives and breathes his trade! There are greater assassins prowling the city, but the Shadow here is not entirely unworthy."

"Why, thank you," her target said. "Can I assume that you're going to make things easy for me?"

"Of course not! The fact that you're asking that sort of question shows that you ultimately lack quality." Aunt Isra looked down her nose at him. "What sort of master assassin wants a convenient, easy kill?"

"A practical one?" Kai suggested. "One who wants to make sure that the victim ends up dead?"

"You're not going to find many victims cooperating with *that*," Aunt Isra said with a sniff.

Irene was putting two and two together during the byplay. It was *possible* that an assassin might come after Aunt Isra for a reason totally unconnected with Irene, and that the timing of the murder attempt was pure coincidence—but Irene wouldn't put money on it. And that little comment about *no demons were involved* earlier, rather than an outright denial, was suggestive. "Can we make a little bargain?" she suggested.

"Well, within reason . . . what did you have in mind?" the Shadow asked. Maybe he was considering his chances of getting away, with the crowd and the official law swarming outside.

"I'm going to make a couple of suggestions about who's behind this and why. In return you'll tell me whether or not I'm correct."

"There doesn't seem to be much in the deal for *me*," the Shadow pointed out.

"A priceless insight into my current line of thought?" Irene suggested.

"Mm . . . that's true. Very well. You have my word."

And that, from a Fae, meant he'd be bound by it. It was sourly amusing that Fae—the most prone of all beings to acting according to narrative stereotype and saying only what was appropriate to their archetype—were also the only ones who could be pinned down and forced to tell the truth. Dragons could lie, humans could lie, but Fae could be trusted—under very specific circumstances.

But there wasn't much left of the ten minutes parole. She flicked a sideways glance at Kai—*Be careful*—and Kai returned a nod of understanding.

Irene turned back to the Shadow. "Right. In that case—I'm guessing that Alberich's behind your current actions."

The Shadow's face twitched with what looked like an attempt not to answer with an immediate *yes*. "Which Alberich?" he asked, in as innocent a manner as he could manage.

Irene could recognize an attempt to weasel around the letter of a promise when she saw it. "The one who's a renegade Librarian," she specified. "He may have some minor physical issues." Such as his body being currently unusable, having to possess other people to stay alive, not being able to leave the world he was currently trapped in . . .

"Oh, *that* Alberich," the Shadow said. His face twitched again, but his words came out unwillingly. "Yes. I'm currently acting on his orders."

"And those orders are to kill Aunt Isra here—to prevent her from telling me something."

The Shadow's facial tic was more agonized this time, but he grunted out, "Yes. If you know all this, why are you bothering to ask me?"

"Base ingratitude," Aunt Isra muttered. "He should be sending young Librarians to me for instruction, not trying to have me killed for telling them stories!"

Irene felt a great surge of elation. The story must be worthwhile if Alberich was so desperate to stop her from hearing it. "I just wanted confirmation," she said sweetly. "Thank you. Oh, and I'm guessing that you're not supposed to kill *me*?"

"No. You're to be left alive." He shut his mouth with an almost audible click.

"One final thing—and this isn't so much a hypothesis as a question. Is this the sort of contract where you can turn round and tell your sponsor you didn't succeed, or are you bound to do your utmost to kill Aunt Isra, with no option of refusal?"

"As it's just a question, I don't have to answer. But since you've played fair with me, I'd point out that I've got one minute of parole left—and I've been keeping track." His eyes narrowed, and abruptly there was an air of *purpose* to him which hadn't been there a moment ago. "I think a chase would be entirely appropriate, don't you? Suitably dramatic? Finishing up with you holding her dying body in your arms as she struggles to pass on some crucial fact . . ."

Irene pulled Aunt Isra to her feet. **"Divan, pin the male Fae against the wall,"** she ordered in the Language.

The divan slid across the floor, taking the Shadow by surprise and slamming him into the wall. He bit back a cry of pain. "I'll remember this next time I deal with Librarians," he muttered, his eyes on Irene.

Irene didn't stay behind to listen to any last threats, though Aunt

Isra would clearly have liked to. Instead she and Kai hurried down the stairs, Aunt Isra between them.

The downstairs room was heaving with waiters, officers of the law, customers, and a reclining Silver having his brow bathed with rose-scented water. Most of them converged on Kai and Irene, demanding details.

Irene knew they had very little time before the Shadow came after them. She didn't want to be chased through the Bazaar—she didn't know the territory, and it wouldn't be easy to protect Aunt Isra. And if she asked Silver or Aunt Isra to lead the way to a different world from here, then the Shadow might be able to follow if he was close enough behind them. Fae could do that. There was only one convenient option.

"Kai, clear our way out into the corridor, and be ready to take us up," she ordered in English. "Silver, on your feet, we're moving out."

Silver might be a debauched libertine and an extremely annoying conversationalist, but he did have a sense for genuine danger. He staggered to his feet and lurched to join them.

Kai steamrollered his way out into the corridor with a combination of muscle, height, and deafness to requests to stop. It was nearly as packed as inside the kiosk; a crowd had gathered, and wasn't going to go away before it got bored. Irene ignored the man in an official-looking uniform who was grabbing her shoulder and demanding that she answer some questions about what was going on. Instead she looked up at the ceiling.

"Brace me," she ordered Silver. What she was about to do would take a lot out of her. There wasn't time for precision work. She gathered all her strength, and shouted, **"Roof, dismantle and open upward and outward!"**

Within the sound of her voice, the roof began peeling back and opening to the outside air. Bricks and tiles sprang from their housing, fountaining up and out and scattering onto the neighboring roofs. Rafters lurched in their setting, shuddering and jarring loose, parting to leave a huge gaping rip in the roof that ran along the length of the corridor.

Pain seized Irene's temples and weakness nearly drove her to her knees as she struggled for breath, the hot air seeming to solidify in her lungs. This was a major piece of deconstruction. She could hear screams in the background, and she spared a thought to hope that not too many people had had bits of ceiling fall on them. She'd done the best she could by directing the roof materials to go outside.

Light flashed next to her, and she was almost knocked off her feet by an accidental blow from one of Kai's wings. He had assumed his natural draconic form—beautiful but terrible, scaled in dark blue as though he'd been plated with sapphires, stretching several yards from head to tail, with horns and flame-red eyes. "Mount!" he ordered, his tail lashing.

The crowd were screaming in earnest now and fleeing in all directions. Stacks of cushions and quilts in the stalls went flying in the commotion. A few of the mob raised pistols or muskets.

Irene hastily ordered, **"Guns, jam!"** Bullets might hurt Kai, if they got really lucky. They would certainly injure the rest of them.

Her use of the Language on top of the earlier one made her sway again. She was barely conscious of Silver's hands on her waist as he pushed her up onto Kai's back, between his shoulders—even the Fae's usual attraction didn't make it through her headache and desperation. But she had enough focus to catch Aunt Isra's wrist as he passed her up in turn, a heavily robed and still-protesting parcel, and to hold her in place as Silver pulled himself up.

Once the three of them were in position, Kai leaped into motion, smoothly rising through the crack in the roof and up into the Constantinople air. As always, there was something preternatural about his flying; it wasn't just a matter of wings and wind and gravity. He moved like an illustration in a scroll painting, an image painted on the air where beauty was more important than physical possibility. He spread his wings as they rose above the Grand Bazaar and the huge city, drifting to hover and inspect the urban spread hundreds of yards below.

"Now this is more like it," Aunt Isra said approvingly. "Well done, children. That was *exactly* the sort of thing I would expect from you."

Irene leaned forward, resting her head against Kai's back. The warmth of his body helped her headache, or perhaps it was just his closeness and his presence, and the knowledge of his safety. She took several deep breaths before replying. "We can drop you off somewhere safe, Aunt Isra. I'm sure the Shadow will have trouble locating you. But in the meantime, you were offering me a deal. My story for yours. I have a counteroffer."

"Oh?" The Fae poked Irene's shoulder. "Turn round and let me see you, child. I can't talk to the back of your head."

"Should I go anywhere in particular?" Kai asked, his voice vibrating in his chest.

Irene squinted at the landscape below as she adjusted her position to face Aunt Isra. "Inland for the moment, please? If you see anywhere conveniently deserted, that'll do to land. And thank you."

"Understood." She could sense his smile, even though a dragon's face was ill-suited for expressing it. He adjusted his course, heading for the city boundaries and beyond.

Irene met Aunt Isra's gaze. The older woman showed no particular concern about flying on dragonback across country; she had the air of someone who'd seen it all before, done it, and most importantly, told the story about it. Now she watched Irene with gimlet eyes, like a cobra inspecting something small and squeaky.

"Here's my offer," Irene said. "You know that I'm looking for Alberich; we've now had proof that he's looking for *me*. I think that the end of the story would be far more interesting to you than the beginning. I can either tell you my own story, up till now—or I can give you my word, on my name and power as a Librarian, in the Language, to come back *after* it's over and tell you what happened."

Aunt Isra muttered to herself, and her fingers twisted angrily in the folds of her robe. "But if you try and fail, then I will have no story at all!"

"Yes," Irene agreed. "And I'll probably be dead—or worse. It's a gamble. But if you don't take the gamble, if I accept your first offer, then you're *never going to know what happened* after this meeting."

A pause—and then, astonishingly, Aunt Isra's face split in a grin. "There speaks someone who truly loves stories. I accept your bargain, child. Give me your word."

Irene sorted through her vocabulary carefully. **"I swear by my name and power that when my business with Alberich is finished, by his death or mine or some other factor, then I shall return to you and tell you the story of what happened."** The words in the Language hummed in her throat and echoed in the windy air around them; they didn't cause her any pain or exhaustion, but she could feel them settling into her bones.

"And I swear by my name and power that I'll tell you the truth of my meeting with Alberich; what I told him, and what I think the consequences were," Aunt Isra vowed. "Will you hear it now?"

Irene was about to agree, on the grounds that nobody else was up here to hear it—but caution made her pause. She might have no evidence that Alberich owned a flight of tamed killer eagles or other monstrosities ready to attack them in mid-air—but right now, she didn't feel like taking chances. "Let's land first," she said.

Five minutes later, they were sitting comfortably in the shade of a small grove. Silver had been deaf to all hints that he might like to go for a stroll out of hearing range. Kai was still in his dragon form, having muttered something about quick getaways.

Aunt Isra composed herself, adjusting her robes and settling her hands in her lap before beginning. "Some years ago—it may have been decades, it may have been centuries—I was approached by a Librarian who'd heard of a story that I knew. His name was Alberich, and he was young and courteous. He sought a tale from me about the first Storyteller." She gave the name the weight that Fae used when they were speaking about those of their kind who truly personified archetypes—the Princess, the Cardinal, the Blood Countess, and so on. "He offered me many rare books from your Library in return for the story, and in the end I agreed."

Irene twitched. *Giving away the Library's books?* Still, perhaps they'd just been copies. She nodded in understanding.

Aunt Isra's voice shifted to the cadence of memory, and it seemed that Kai himself slowed his breathing to listen. "Long ago, in the distant past when many of us were yet unshaped because there were no dreams to shape us, the first Storyteller looked behind him and saw unshaped chaos that would devour all things, humans and Fae and stories alike, and leave nothing that could tell tales or remember them. And he looked before him instead, and he saw the onrushing clouds of war, filled with great dragons who commanded all the forces of nature, and they in turn fled from what came behind *them*. And he said: 'Neither of these will suffice; a better solution must be found.'"

Silver was frowning. "There is no current Storyteller," he said. "Nobody dares claim that title. There hasn't been for as far back as I know."

"I will have you whipped if you dare interrupt me again," Aunt Isra said conversationally. "Be silent."

Silver didn't answer, but his frown deepened.

A cold dread began to tie knots in Irene's guts. This was a story she'd heard before—but from the other side, from a different perspective. The implications . . .

Aunt Isra touched her throat and then went on, unaware of or uninterested in Irene's qualms. "He resolved that he must make an alliance with his utmost enemies, that all things might be placed in balance, and that they be neither unmade nor utterly fixed in place. So he went to the palace of their king and said: 'Let us make a bargain. We shall bind our power together and make the worlds stable, and then we shall both rule over them.' And the king agreed."

She waited a beat to give the moment emphasis. Then she coughed, her hand going to her throat again.

"Aunt Isra?" Irene queried, her existential worries abruptly becoming more focused. "Are you all right?"

The shadows of the trees seemed to be growing longer and deepening. "He—I've been heard . . ." Aunt Isra struggled for breath, swaying forward.

Irene moved to catch and support her, looking around desperately. She couldn't feel anything unnatural—no powers of chaos, no strength of order, *nothing.* How was she supposed to ward off this attack? "Can anyone tell what's affecting her?"

"Prince Kai!" Silver was abruptly serious. "Can you strengthen order in your vicinity?"

"Of course," Kai rumbled, "but there's nothing here to fight."

"It's internal, not external. I'll explain later—just surround Aunt Isra and do it!" He stepped back. "And let me get clear first."

Kai curled his long serpentine body around Irene and the choking Aunt Isra, ignoring Silver's hasty retreat. His wings flexed, curving over the two of them, blotting out the sun to leave them in a dark blue cave of crystalline scales.

He roared. The sound was nearly shattering at close range, hammering at Irene's ears and vibrating in her bones, but its power wasn't just the sheer physical volume of the sound, it was its effect on reality. The world trembled around them, becoming that little bit more real, more concrete; less prone to being swayed by the strength of a story, more bound to physical reality and all its attendant cruelties.

Irene trembled—but Aunt Isra convulsed, her body arching in a tetanic spasm of agony in Irene's arms. "Stop," she whispered. "Please . . ."

"Hold on," Irene tried to encourage her. This must be sheer torture for a Fae—just as Kai suffered under conditions of high chaos, so Aunt Isra would be drained by this sudden impact of high order. "Please, hold on, keep breathing—I'm here, we'll protect you . . ."

"So far away . . ." Her face was barely visible in the shadows. "They put their finger on my lips and bade me be silent . . ."

"Who?"

"The Storyteller, child!" Irritation seemed to restore a little of her strength. She looked around at Kai's surrounding coils. "Tell your prince not to move. I must share the rest of this story before they bend their attention to me again."

"I hear you," Kai said. "Continue."

"This would be a fine story—such a pity that it is my own, and nobody is ever interested in the storyteller's own story." Aunt Isra took a deep breath. "Listen. The king agreed, as I said. Now many among their own kinds, both the Fae and their enemies, would have cried treason, so the two of them fled in secret to complete their work. And some say that they built a tower high enough to reach the heavens, and others that they dug a secret cellar hidden in the roots of the world, but nobody knows the full truth of it. But it is true that after they departed, the worlds became more stable, like gems in a necklace or planets in an orrery, and that while from time to time they trembled, it was never as calamitous as it had been before. And so their children and their servants set out to tame the worlds, and forgot the tale of the king and the Storyteller. But the story was preserved among the keepers of stories, to be a warning to those who came after."

She paused. "Child, are you well? Your hands are trembling."

Irene couldn't answer. She might give away too much if she did. But she'd read this story before, translated from an Egyptian manuscript thousands of years old—from the *dragon* point of view. The dragon king in the tale—maybe the father of the four dragon kings—had been fleeing uncontrollable forces of order from *his* rear, and had made a bargain with his greatest foes in response. *And my fate shall be preserved by the scribes*, that tale had finished.

The scribes. The keepers of stories. Irene looked down at her own hands. They were shaking. *What is the origin of the Library? Who founded us? And why?*

"How did Alberich react when you told him this?" she asked, her voice shaking.

Aunt Isra's gaze turned inward, as though staring back at her own memories. "He was troubled," she said slowly. "Much as you are now. Which interests me. First he said that he must tell his brothers and sisters of this."

Irene nodded, remembering Coppelia's words. *All of us used to call each other brother and sister back then.* That corroborated Aunt Isra's story.

"Then he shook his head and said no, he must have further proof before he acted, but he knew where he could find it. He was in a great rage. He said that he and the Library had been used."

"Did he say how?" Irene asked.

"No. For once I am giving you his words unedited." Aunt Isra smiled, just a little. "And then he left in great haste, as though he feared pursuit."

And then he betrayed the Library. The thought was a cold barbed hook in Irene's heart. But if the dragon king and the Storyteller were acting for the greater good, to stabilize the worlds, why was that such a bad thing?

The answer came to her in Aunt Isra's words. . . . *and then we shall both rule over them.* Was that it? Power, and nothing more?

Her lips were numb. "Thank you," she said, remembering her manners. "That's . . . extremely helpful."

"You can release me now." Aunt Isra prodded Kai's side with a wrinkled finger. "I am no longer speaking that person's name; their attention will have turned elsewhere."

"Was that the . . ." Irene bit back *the Storyteller,* conscious that using those words might bring danger back upon them. "The person whom you mentioned in the story?"

"It was," Aunt Isra said, as Kai uncoiled himself. The sunlight struck down on them, as though trying to restore normality to a world which included dragons and the Language. "You can use that name freely, child. But I—well, those of us who follow in their path are linked to them—a little. It happens to us all, when we pursue a single nature and grow in power. Storytellers, libertines, princesses, cardinals, executioners, each of us tied to the greatest of that kind . . . Has that delinquent over there never told you of this?"

"It never seemed relevant," Silver said with a careless gesture that almost—but not quite—camouflaged his caution. "Besides, I'm usually busier showing rather than telling, to borrow a phrase."

"Let me make certain I have this correct," Irene said. "The Storyteller himself—or herself?—intervened to stop you telling me the end of that story."

Aunt Isra nodded. The fact that she'd nearly died seemed to have made little impact on her.

"Did the same thing happen to you when you told Alberich that story?"

"No," Aunt Isra confirmed. "But that was the first time I'd told it, after all. This is the second. I think that I shall not risk a third."

"Will you be safe?" Irene had to ask the question. She wasn't sure what she could do to protect the old Fae, but she couldn't just abandon her to be murdered. Maybe Kai could take her to a high-order world, where the Storyteller might not be able to reach her so easily.

Aunt Isra inclined her head graciously. "You're a good child—but I'll be safe enough if I keep my mouth shut on this particular tale. Anyhow, now you've had what I promised. I look forward to your return—with the rest of the story."

Irene's guts were churning, and she felt sick. "Of course," she murmured. She had to find out what the "further proof" was that Alberich needed. She had to go back to the Library. She needed more information.

But was the Library safe? Were other Librarians safe?

This was only a story. Aunt Isra herself had said that stories weren't facts and weren't necessarily true. Still, it was important enough that the Storyteller had nearly killed her to keep her from sharing it. It was this story which had set Alberich on his path of treason and murder, and resulted in Irene's own conception. *He'd* believed it—or believed something, at least.

The question now was . . . what did Irene believe?

CHAPTER 15

It was somewhere between late afternoon and early evening by the time Irene and Kai were dropped off at Vale's lodgings. Silver had escorted them back to Vale's London and insisted on paying for their carriage. Irene attributed his unusual generosity to a nagging itch that he still *owed* them for getting him out of the Grand Bazaar and saving his life. Kai attributed it to devious and dubious Fae motivations. But they still took the carriage.

"What did he say to you in private?" Kai asked quietly as they headed up the steps to the door.

"He was worried about Catherine." That was in itself a guarantee that Silver would keep his mouth shut for the moment. If there was something . . . wrong . . . with the Library, then Catherine's ignorance was her best safeguard.

"So are you."

Irene shrugged. "I'm worried about *us*."

He caught her arm as she raised her hand to ring the bell. "Irene— I realize there's something you haven't told me. Your reaction to Aunt

Isra's story made it quite clear that you know something which corroborates it. But I trust you. Don't worry. I can wait until you're ready to tell me."

Gratitude warred with irritation. "Kai, the last time we had a conversation like this, I was the one using applied guilt on *you* because *you* wanted to keep something secret!"

"The student has learned from the master," Kai said, with a deep bow.

Irene couldn't help it. She just laughed and laughed, feeling a deep oppression lift from her spirit. Whoever she could or couldn't trust, the man standing right in front of her was utterly reliable. If they hadn't been standing in full view of the street, she'd have kissed him. "You're one of the best things that ever happened to me," she said. "Thank you."

"Thank Coppelia for assigning me to you," Kai said. More quietly, he added, "I have."

His words made Irene remember that Coppelia wouldn't be with them for very much longer, and she nodded, her cheerfulness passing. "Let's go in and face the music."

A little pang of guilt twitched inside her. It had been a joke, but ... should she share her information with him? It was part of dragon history. She'd thought that she was doing Kai a favor by keeping him ignorant. Didn't he deserve the right to make his own choices?

"Oh, come now," Kai said, following her in. "Vale will understand that we didn't have the time to find him and invite him along."

"Winters!" Vale shouted from upstairs. His tone of voice was not encouraging. "We're waiting."

Irene and Kai exchanged a glance of mutual curiosity as to the identity of the *we*; then Irene glanced at the hatstand. She recognized the gray velvet mantle hanging there; she'd seen Bradamant wear it before. With a suppressed sigh, she made her way up the stairs. This was probably going to be ... difficult.

Bradamant was sitting in Irene's favorite chair, leafing through one of Vale's scrapbooks of newspaper articles about interesting and lurid crimes. She gave Irene a cold look as the younger woman entered, clearly doing her best to evoke memories of the days when Irene was her apprentice. Vale was less blatant; he merely fiddled with a microscope slide, affecting an inability to look up and greet them.

"I'm surprised to see you in the same room together," Irene said, seating herself on the sofa. "Has something happened that I don't know about?"

Vale and Bradamant exchanged looks of exasperation. "It would hardly be surprising if it had," Bradamant retorted, "since you weren't here to be told about it."

"Be reasonable. Is there any chance of tea? It's been a long day."

"There have been a few minor disturbances here as well." Vale gave up his pretense of being absorbed by his microscope, spinning on his stool to glare at Irene and Kai instead. He was probably trying to analyze their recent doings from their clothing and behavior. While he was a great detective, it would be pretty near impossible for him to deduce *the Grand Bazaar* or even *Constantinople*—which would only annoy him more. "But with you not here to be informed, and with no information about your whereabouts except for a single brief note that you had gone off with *Lord Silver* . . ."

Standing behind Irene, Kai squeezed her shoulder supportively. "For once he was useful," he said. "He gave us a lead on Alberich—and we got to his contact only minutes before Alberich's assassin did. If we'd waited, it might have been too late."

The silence which followed was of the sort where the aggrieved party has to acknowledge the other side has a point, but doesn't want to admit it. It was broken by the arrival of the housekeeper with a fresh teapot and cups for all, and the resulting household normalities left the room feeling a bit less hostile.

"So what did you find out?" Vale asked.

Irene had taken a minute to think what to say while the tea was poured. It would have been easier if Bradamant wasn't there. "Silver arranged a meeting with a Fae called Isra, who follows the storyteller archetype. *She* was able to tell us how she once met Alberich, how she told him a particular story, and how he reacted. He was deeply troubled, he said he wanted further proof, and he said that he and the Library had been used."

"Proof seems to be in very short supply at the moment," Vale noted.

"Alberich's agents tried to kill her to stop her telling me the story," Irene said. "Then the Storyteller—the Fae archetype in person, we think—tried to kill her in the middle of telling me the story. I concede that it *could* all be subtle attempts to convince me that her story was important, when it's really a false trail—but she gave me her word that it was true." And everyone in the room knew that a Fae had to hold by their given word.

"So what was the story?" Bradamant demanded.

Irene recounted what Aunt Isra had told her, word for word. She saw Bradamant's face freeze over as she listened, the other woman mentally retreating—just as Irene herself had done—to consider the possibilities.

"You think this sent Alberich mad—or at least, it made him paranoid somehow?" Bradamant finally asked. "Whether or not the story's actually true, it sounds as if he *thought* it was, and that it was connected to the Library. The active destroy-the-Library madness probably came later."

"It's a reasonable conclusion," Irene agreed. She found herself very reluctant to tell Bradamant that she had another story from the dragon side which agreed with this one, especially with Kai present. It wasn't because she distrusted Bradamant—well, not exactly. She trusted Bradamant to do what Bradamant thought was the right thing for the Library, beyond questions of morals or ethics or personal interest. She wouldn't trust Bradamant not to shove Irene over a precipice if she thought Irene was a threat to the Library. Or perhaps the point was that she *would* trust Bradamant to do that . . .

Her mind was going round in circles. The most important thing was that if this story was true, if there *was* something at the heart of the Library which none of them had ever suspected before, then unless Irene could prove it, it was safer for Bradamant to be ignorant of any supporting evidence. Because once this threat knew that *they* knew . . .

Was this what Alberich thought? The comparison was disturbing.

"It might be useful as a way to manipulate him," Vale said thoughtfully. "Your trip wasn't wasted, it seems. And Alberich's agents—I assume they escaped?"

"They did, yes. One at least that we saw—there may have been others." There was something about Vale's expression . . . "Why do you put it that way?"

"Because a message for you from Alberich arrived about half an hour ago," Vale said, just a little smugly.

"What!" Irene's tea sloshed around in her cup. She put it down on the side table before her shaking hands could spill it. "A message from Alberich—you knew that and you didn't *tell me*?"

"You weren't here to be told," Bradamant pointed out.

"No, I mean why didn't you tell me the instant I got here?" Irene realized she was on the point of shouting. Worse, of being ungrammatical. She took a deep breath. "Where is it? And how did it arrive?"

"It was handed over to the housekeeper at the door by an anonymous street urchin," Vale said. "The letter to *you* was inside a larger one addressed to *me*, which of course I examined—black ink, fountain pen, parchment, sealed with red wax. I opened it to find the letter for you inside. There was no other enclosure. While I admit I was tempted, we decided that it might be dangerous to open it." He indicated a domed metal dish cover on the table, probably borrowed from the kitchen below. "It's under there."

"It might be dangerous to open it in any case, even if it's Irene doing the opening," Kai said.

"And it might be the information inside it that's the most dangerous thing of all," Bradamant added. "It should go to the Library. Let our superiors handle it. Getting yourself involved further in this mess isn't just dangerous, Irene—it's *stupid*."

Irene raised an eyebrow. "I'm fairly sure that in the past you've criticized me for not getting sufficiently involved in things, for not taking risks, for not being prepared to commit myself . . ."

"There are *limits*!" Bradamant looked round for support and found none. "You're biased," she said, more quietly. "I'm prepared to take your word that the Library's given you a secret mission concerning Alberich." This was clearly a huge concession from her. "But that doesn't mean you should open every possible bomb that comes your way with his name marked as sender."

Irene hesitated. Alberich was a genius at creating things using the written form of the Language, while she herself was a novice. How could she be sure that this wasn't a cunning trap to wipe them all out? "How do you know the letter to me is from him if you haven't opened it yet?" she asked.

"It says so on the front of the letter," Vale said. "To Irene Winters, also known as Ray—from Alberich."

"Well . . . looking at the envelope won't kill me. Or you'd both already be dead." Irene got up and walked across to lift the concealing dish cover. The folded piece of parchment was as Vale had described, and sealed in red wax. The dissected outer cover lay next to it.

It might as well have been a letter-bomb for the potential amount of damage it could do to Irene—and to everything she cared about. "I can't risk taking it into the Library," she said after a moment. "Seriously, Bradamant, if we're going to suggest that Alberich can use the Language to create something which would explode on being opened, then we have to consider the possibility that he could create something which would do worse if it was brought inside the Library. Either we assume it's a genuine letter and we read it, or we assume it's a possible weapon of mass destruction and we throw it in the Thames right this minute."

"Hardly fair on the Thames," Kai said. "The river already has enough problems."

"You know what I mean."

Irene picked up a pencil and carefully prodded the sealed parchment with it. Nothing happened. "If Alberich could send us letters which would kill us," she said, thinking out loud, "he'd already have done it. I'm opening it." She broke the seal before the others could come up with more reasons why this was a bad idea, or try to stop her physically.

Nothing exploded. This was a good sign. Probably.

She opened the letter. The writing inside was mostly in English, rather than some sort of *die now, reader* script in the Language. There was a short bit in the Language at the end, but that was innocent enough. "It *is* a letter," she said, unable to prevent a note of surprise from entering her voice.

"Well, that's a relief," Bradamant muttered, settling back into her chair again and trying to look as if she hadn't been about to leap up and wrest the note from Irene's hand. "So what does it say?"

Irene skimmed through it. "It's, um. Implausible." Unbelievable might have been a better word.

"Winters," Vale said, his tone a warning that Bradamant wasn't the only one considering forcible letter-removal.

Irene took a deep breath and began to read. "Ray, I'm not going to pretend that we have any reason to be on good terms with each other."

Kai's snort was very expressive.

"However," she went on reading, "we do have mutual interests. You want me to stop attacking the Library—or making any other attempts to subvert it. I want to talk to you."

"Under no circumstances whatsoever," Kai said firmly. "He's poison, and—"

Irene held up a finger to stop him before he got more descriptive. "I agree, but if I may continue?"

Kai subsided with a nod.

"You've made a suggestion. I've been considering it. I realize you'll suspect any offer I make, but I'm prepared to sign a peace treaty with the Library, *in the Language.* No future hostilities. No future deaths. Are you really prepared to turn that down? I've contacted the Fae treaty representative, asking her to suggest a place for us to meet and discuss this further. She can choose a location where hostilities should be impossible, where we can meet and you'll know you're safe from me."

"Madame Sterrington is your ally," Vale noted. "You've saved her life before. If she gives her word to find a place where both parties can meet in safety . . ."

"I can't believe you're taking this seriously," Kai objected. "This man's a traitor and a multiple murderer. He *can't* be trusted. Irene, please tell me that the reason you're looking so thoughtful is because you're planning how to use this meeting to trap him and dispose of him."

Irene looked down at the paper in her hand. She wanted to agree with Kai—but cold logic was pushing her to consider Vale's opinion. "Prior to the Fae–dragon peace treaty, both sides were saying that about each other—the treason, multiple murder, whatever. I concede that in this case every possible accusation is probably absolutely *true*. But I'm not sure I have the right to turn this offer down. It's not just the consequences for me, Kai. It's the consequences for other Librarians."

"Read the rest of the letter," Kai said flatly. "Let me know the worst."

Can't he see that I'm not any happier about this than he is?

She read on: "If you're reading this letter, Ray, then you've spoken to the Fae known as Aunt Isra about a certain topic and you're still alive. I didn't think that was possible. When I sent assassins after her, I was trying to save your life. The fact that you survived suggests that I may be in error about certain things. It's leading me to consider new approaches. But for that, I want to speak with you. I'm prepared to consider making peace with the Library. I'll pledge safe-conduct for a truce. I know I've given you no reason to trust me, Ray—and I'm not asking for trust now. I'm asking you, as I always have done, to consider new possibilities. I'll be in touch through the Fae Embassy—contact me there. Alberich."

"Totally trustworthy," Bradamant said, her tone dripping with sarcasm. "How could we possibly doubt such a sincere offer? We should be on our knees thanking heaven for the opportunity and running out to arrange it right this minute."

"There's a final bit in the Language," Irene said reluctantly. Life would be so much easier if she could just assume this was all a lie. "He writes that this letter is a sincere offer and that he's genuine about wanting peace—and that it's not a trap."

Bradamant moved to see. "Oh," she said, sounding as confused as Irene felt. One couldn't lie in the Language—spoken or written. Alberich could write all the lies he wanted in English, but if he'd tried to do it in the Language, the paper would have burned under his pen. "Okay. If you'd said something about that part *earlier* . . ."

Irene put the letter down with a feeling of relief, wiping her hands against her skirt. There wasn't any physical contamination—at least, she hoped not—but she simply didn't want the feeling of that letter on her fingers any longer than necessary. "I think we all agree that this letter is unreliable. Shall we get down to considering what to *do* about it, rather than all trying to be I'm-more-untrusting-than-you?"

Bradamant closed her eyes for a moment. Irene wondered if she was silently counting to ten. Then she said, with what was clearly an effort, "I may be overreacting. I'm not used to seeing personal letters from the equivalent of Lucifer himself to people I know."

"I'm not used to getting them, either," Irene said, trying to return the peace gesture. "And I'll say this right now—this is not my decision to make. This is not *our* decision to make. This has to go to the Library. We can send our opinions along with it and all the information we have, but if I ran off on my own to try to make peace with Alberich, then I really would be . . ." She searched through her vocabulary. Nothing quite rose to the occasion. ". . . stupid," she finished, echoing Bradamant's earlier comment.

"Nevertheless, you may be the only person he's willing to deal with," Vale said.

"Then I do it with backup and permission," Irene replied.

"What I don't get is, why *you*?" Bradamant asked. "That isn't meant dismissively: there are plenty of other Librarians out there who are more experienced than *either* of us and with more political clout in the Library. Your major qualification seems to be avoiding getting killed by him."

Irene knew the answer. *Because I'm his daughter.* But she wouldn't, *couldn't* tell Bradamant that. "Maybe because I'm the Librarian representative on the Fae–dragon peace treaty," she suggested. "Or maybe it's because he knows my address in this world. I don't know. Perhaps he views 'avoiding getting killed by him' as a positive qualification."

Bradamant finally shrugged. "I suppose that in the end the important things are whether this is possible, and if it's something we should pursue."

Irene passed the letter to Vale—who'd been staring at it with hawk-like intensity—and sat down. "Possibility. Hmm. Let's suppose that it would be possible to write a treaty in the Language such that neither the Library nor Alberich could break it. That's something which I can only theorize, but it's something that the older Librarians would know—and if it can be done, then this becomes *possible*." And if it was, then maybe she might have a future where Alberich would simply fade into the background. She'd have to talk to him, but she could live with that. Maybe certain things would become *possible* for her and Kai as well.

"Nobody suggested that the dragon–Fae treaty should be anything like that," Kai commented. "Unbreakable, I mean."

"Neither the dragons nor the Fae were after a treaty which they'd be metaphysically bound to obey for the rest of eternity," Irene pointed out. "Normal languages were quite sufficient for what was eventually signed."

"Right," Bradamant agreed. "We're looking for something which can't possibly be broken by either side here." Her mouth twisted as if she was tasting something bitter. "I see your point, Irene. I suppose I'm willing to consider letting Alberich get away with everything he's done so far—murders, torture, trying to destroy the Library—if it means the Library will be secure in the future. I really don't like it, but"—she shrugged—"keeping the Library safe is more important than punishing him."

"He'd be safe from the Library," Kai said in the most neutral and noncommital of tones. "Who knows what might come after him from other directions? Nobody's asked *me* to sign anything."

At first Irene smiled at the thought, but then common sense

waved a flag at the back of her head. "Let's remember that could go both ways. He might not be able to coordinate an attack on the Library, or on *us*, but if someone wanted to please him . . ."

"That's almost a relief," Bradamant said. "I find it easier to believe in an Alberich who's willing to sign an overt peace treaty but has ulterior thoughts about how to get round it, than an Alberich who's willing to sign a peace treaty with no subsequent plans to get vengeance on everyone. It just makes more sense." She shrugged. "I'm a cynic. You know that."

Irene did indeed know that. "On the whole, I think we can agree that having Alberich *personally* swear not to organize any more attacks on the Library is a net gain. It's not perfect, but it would be a positive step toward the safety of Librarians and the Library. And we've agreed that it might be possible." She didn't like it. But then she didn't *have* to like it.

"Well then, it's a good thing I'm here!" Bradamant said cheerfully. "I can take this proposal to the Library right away."

"Now wait just one moment—" Irene started.

Bradamant held up an admonitory finger. "You're supposed to be operating on your own in secret, remember? Your very special mission?" There was an edge to her tone. Irene's behavior might be temporarily condoned but clearly wasn't forgiven. "You can't just go walking through the Library doors. The second anyone met you, they'd want to bring you in for questioning. No, you need to send someone like me to take the information to our elders. *You* need to coordinate with Sterrington—if you think you can trust her."

"You're right," Irene said, after a moment of silent fuming. "It does make more sense for you to take the offer to our elders. Once Vale's finished examining the physical note, that is."

"Do you honestly think you can learn anything from it?" Bradamant asked Vale.

"I fear not," Vale admitted. "If he's used materials from outside this world, then I can hardly say where in London he might have acquired the paper or ink. I have opinions on his handwriting but, alas, that is not an exact science." He passed Kai the note to look over. "What puzzles me is how Alberich can leave his current world of residence to attend this meeting. I had thought he was trapped there."

"So had I," Irene admitted. *And a great relief it was to think so.* "Still . . . maybe his allies left doors in other worlds which would allow him to visit them briefly—or perhaps he simply didn't tell them the whole truth when he said he was trapped. Or perhaps he has agents and ways of contacting them. If he's making this offer and letting Sterrington choose the world, then he must have something up his sleeve. We'll find out what it is when we get there." *And put a stop to it,* she thought. Even if they might have a truce with Alberich, she'd feel a great deal happier if he was confined to a single world. And let him *rot* there.

"I don't like it," Kai finally said. "I don't like it at all. But it's your decision, Irene." She could see how much the words cost him. "If you think it's worth taking the risk . . ." He handed her the note.

Irene let herself hesitate, then gave the note to Bradamant. "Here you are. You're right—you're the best person to take this into the Library. I'll get in contact with Sterrington and find out what she knows. And here, before I forget . . ." She removed Sterrington's envelope from her pocket; she'd looked at the names, but they meant nothing to her. The Library could make better use of it than she could. "This is a list from Sterrington of powerful Fae who've been getting messages from the Library recently and have reacted very defensively, and the Librarians involved. It needs to go to Melusine for investigation."

Bradamant took the papers with a nod, and tucked them into her jacket. "I'll pass them on. You're making the right decision," she said. "It'll be good news for the Library too."

"Are there any issues currently ongoing there?"

Bradamant pursed her lips. "*Issues* might be a good word for it. Not actual problems, but . . . well, there's been some reprioritizing toward political issues, which you already know about, and as a result we have a backlog of book retrievals. I've been told that the messages about them are getting positively testy."

"Who sends those messages?" Vale asked.

"They come from deeper in the Library. Some sort of automatic detection of the books we need to keep things balanced. Of course, elders like Kostchei actively prioritize what's most important . . ." She twitched. "He called me 'granddaughter' three times when I last saw him. I hate it when he does that, it means he's really irritated. But anyhow—retrieval backlogs, a certain amount of gossip about *you*, Irene, and every single Librarian I know having nightmares. It'll be nice to share something positive."

"What sort of nightmares?" Kai asked.

"Oh, children crying, elder relatives scolding, imminent doom, someone desperately trying to tell us something—nothing really specific. Have you had anything like that, Irene?"

Irene scanned her recent memory. "No. I've been spared that, at least."

"You do," Kai said quietly. "You just don't remember them after you wake up."

"But I don't—" Irene started.

"You do," he contradicted her. "And your Library brand's always hot when you wake up from them."

Bradamant was gracious enough not to ask exactly how Kai knew that. "Maybe the vanishing worlds are causing some sort of imbalance," she suggested. "In that case, the sooner we get *this* problem sorted, the sooner we can turn our attention to other things."

"Bradamant . . ." Irene picked her words carefully. Should she share her theories? Or would it be safer to leave Bradamant in ignorance? Kai's statement about her nightmares had left her off balance and uncertain. "Be careful. I can see that this proposition could cause some very heated differences of opinion."

"I'd be surprised if it didn't," Bradamant said briskly. She leaned forward, frowning. "You're worried. Why?"

"Among the many, many reasons to be worried, I'm particularly worried about that story which sent Alberich mad," Irene admitted. "Don't tell me that you haven't thought about the implications."

"A story is a story," Bradamant said with a shrug. "I'll report that as well—but frankly, it sounds as if Alberich was paranoid and a conspiracy theorist from the word go. Of course, if we can use it against him, that's worth bearing in mind."

"Fair enough," Irene said. "In that case, I do have one more request. Could you check on Catherine while you're in the Library? I'd like to be sure she's doing okay."

"Your Fae apprentice? Not a problem. I'd rather like to meet her, anyhow."

"Assuming you can pry her away from the books." Irene was relieved that Bradamant was willing to undertake the errand. She was worried about Catherine. Of course, the Library should be the safest possible place for her, but . . .

"Thank you," she said. "It's appreciated."

"Not a problem." Bradamant rose to her feet. "I'd better see to this at once. Thank you, Irene, gentlemen. You needn't bother to see me out."

"I'm afraid I've taken you rather for granted," Irene said to Vale guiltily, once Bradamant had gone.

"Winters, I have a number of important cases on my hands. An infestation of marmots carrying bubonic plague, a plan to clone giant leaf-nosed vampire bats from fossils and unleash them on London, the spread of cocaine-addicted eels in the Thames . . ." He shrugged. "I am at your service, of course."

"So what was it that you *didn't* tell her?" Kai asked Irene.

"Corroboration." The tea in the pot had gone cold. Irene looked between Kai and Vale—both people she knew she could trust. But with something this important, and this possibly threatening to the Library?

Yes. They'd both helped her save the Library before—and more importantly, she trusted their judgment in some areas more than she trusted her own. She might have pragmatism, but Vale had logic, and Kai had an honest sincerity which could pierce through her own divagations and get to the most important point.

She took a deep breath. "I've read a second story, in an Egyptian text—the old one you and I retrieved, Kai—which appears to be the same narrative, but truncated and from the dragon point of view. Both stories end with a reference to 'keepers of stories' or 'scribes.' Vale, Kai—what if this ultimately goes back to the founding of the Library?"

Her words hung in the silence as the two men considered them.

Kai was the first to speak. "This isn't something which would be accepted among my kind," he said soberly. "The idea that my grandfather could have collaborated with the Fae would be unthinkable."

"Why do you say your *grandfather*, Strongrock?" Vale asked.

Kai's smile was very dry, no more than a thin line of self-mockery. "Because he disappeared under strange circumstances thousands of years ago. And, as I have said to Irene in the past, my family does not appear to have a history any further back than that, and we are not encouraged to look into the details."

Irene knew from the increased formality of his words and tone that he was angry. "We aren't encouraged to ask questions about the founding of the Library, either," she said gently. "Our elders don't approve."

There was a glint of red in Kai's eyes. "And yet I am considering the idea. I shame my father by the admission, but—it is not impossible."

"You're both missing a crucial point," Vale said, leaning back in his chair and steepling his fingers. "If all this was true, then why should it be a secret?"

"The Fae wouldn't accept it," Irene suggested. "The dragons wouldn't accept it, as Kai has just confirmed. And if junior Librarians knew about it, then they might talk about it too widely. Maybe the oldest Librarians do know about it, and I'm just too young to have been told."

"Perhaps." Vale frowned, his eyes hooded. "But if so, then why should the very idea have sent Alberich into insanity and caused all his regrettable actions afterward?"

And Irene didn't have an answer to that.

CHAPTER 16

No," Sterrington said, quite definitely. "I'm afraid that's not possible."

This wasn't how Irene had hoped the conversation would go. Kai was tactfully waiting outside in the cab, in the hope that having it be just a Fae–Librarian conversation would improve Sterrington's mood. It looked as if he might have to wait a while longer. "I came to ask about the basic details," she tried, "but while I'm here . . ."

"I understand completely. You want an advantage." Sterrington smiled approvingly. "Like any sensible person, you're here to take advantage of your connections to get the deal slanted in your favor."

"Well, I try to be sensible," Irene admitted. "And this is Alberich—the man who's tried to kill me and destroy the Library multiple times, *and* tried to kill you very recently."

"Technically that was Lord and Lady Guantes," Sterrington reminded her. "From Alberich's point of view, I was probably just an incidental casualty as part of the treaty committee. It wasn't personal."

Irene managed to put her finger on part of what was troubling her about this conversation. "You're taking all this very calmly."

"Well, firstly, it's ultimately not *my* problem." Sterrington was looking much better today. "Secondly, I'm a great believer in conflict resolution by whatever means it takes. Since you didn't actually manage to kill him . . ."

"I tried," Irene said ruefully.

"The Library can't blame you for that. Better Librarians have tried and failed, I'm sure." She paused. "That might not have come out quite as flatteringly as I'd intended. I honestly respect your professionalism, and I'm sure you did your very best to kill him."

Irene wasn't sure what was worse—being scolded by Vale for planning murder, or being condoled with by Sterrington for not succeeding at it. "But since I failed, you feel you have an obligation to be neutral?"

"That's not quite right," Sterrington said judiciously. "Personally I'd be only too pleased if something fatal happened to him. Regarding this meeting for negotiations, though, I need to be able to sign it off with absolute honesty and say that I haven't taken bribes from either side or influenced it in any way. You do understand?" She seemed genuinely to want Irene's approval.

Irene gritted her teeth. "I can't deny I'm a bit disappointed, but I understand. It would be counter to your archetype to cheat."

"Yes," Sterrington said, drawing out the word. "And it would be absolutely counter to what I am to be *caught cheating* and hamper the negotiations by doing so."

"Would it be counter to the current planning to ask you what the position is?" Irene had deliberately chosen her words to be imprecise.

With a bit of luck, Sterrington might answer questions which Irene hadn't thought to ask.

"I've communicated with the Cardinal," Sterrington said.

Irene blinked. "That was fast."

"Rapid channels of communication are no use if one doesn't actually *use* them when it's appropriate—and in this case it is. The Cardinal agrees it would be a good idea to help the Library finalize this. And how often do we get the chance to do the Library a favor on this scale, by arranging a suitable venue for peace talks?"

Sterrington was smiling, but there was a crocodilian edge to it, and Irene found herself remembering the tag *And welcomes little fishes in, with gently smiling jaws.* Favors were currency among the Fae, and the Cardinal certainly wouldn't forget one this big. On the other hand, it might be worth it to get rid of Alberich once and for all.

"I've notified the Library, of course, but they haven't replied yet," Irene said. "I can't make any promises about whether or not they'll agree to the negotiations—and I don't want you to have wasted your labor."

"Establishing good client relationships is never a waste of time," Sterrington said firmly. She must have noticed Irene's eyes widen in shock, for she quickly added, "Not that we're considering Alberich as a *client* in the sense of doing future business with him, of course! More in the sense of gathering information about him."

Riiiiiight. Irene reminded herself that Sterrington clung to the archetype of a businesswoman. Yesterday's would-be assassin could easily become tomorrow's respected client. "Of course," she agreed. "Naturally your interest in maintaining a good relationship with the Library would mitigate against you developing any sort of links to its worst enemy."

"Unless things change," Sterrington pointed out, "which we both hope they're going to."

Irene dropped the formality. "He's not reliable. Between the two of us—I'm not going to say 'as friends,' but at least as allies—Alberich is *not reliable*."

"He doesn't have to be *reliable*, as long as he can sign an agreement in your Language and be bound by it," Sterrington said placatingly. "I'm not quite clear on why you're so upset about it."

"I doubt his motives," Irene said. "He's been an enemy of the Library for centuries. I find it hard to believe in sudden epiphanies and changes of heart. I'd *like* this to be true, but I'm watching my back and expecting an ambush at any second."

Sterrington actually had the nerve to pat Irene's hand. "I realize the last month has been stressful, but you mustn't let yourself be unduly traumatized. Let's look at this logically. Why *should* Alberich choose this moment to make peace?"

The first thought that came to mind was the one that Irene absolutely *couldn't* share with Sterrington. *Because he's found out that he's my father.* "Diminishing resources?" she suggested. "His home's damaged, he's unable to take physical shape outside it without the use of a host body or some sort of connection, his most recent scheme failed and resulted in the loss of competent associates . . ."

"That's a valid reason," Sterrington said. "Also, from what you've said, he's not suicidal. He doesn't want to destroy the Library at the cost of his own life. You ought to be proud of yourself, Irene. You're the one who did all this damage to him."

Irene couldn't help feeling a bit dubious about that. "I'm not sure if that should make me a proud achiever, or a terrified target of dreadful vengeance."

"Call it a bit of both. But you see what I'm getting at?"

Irene was a little touched at this pep talk from a notably cold-blooded associate. Yet she couldn't help but recognize that Sterrington was coming at this from a Fae point of view, where a truce after centuries of feuding was quite reasonable—and would only last until the next excuse for drama and conflict. "I appreciate what you're saying, and what you're doing," she said. "I hope you can find a suitable site and that we can come to an agreement. Do you need to find sites like this often?"

"Oh, from time to time. Normally we keep the location secret until the actual event, to stop either side from, ah, what's a good term for it? Getting their retaliation in first." Sterrington smiled, and for once it looked genuine rather than political. "I hope this truce can be signed too, Irene. You're a useful colleague. I'd like to keep on working with you."

"The feeling's mutual," Irene agreed.

But she was aware that Alberich might make demands from the Library in return for peace. And what if one of those demands was his daughter, Irene, herself?

As they approached Vale's lodgings, Irene saw that there was a cab waiting outside. The driver in his exterior seats had settled down to enjoy the spring weather, with the cheerfulness of a man who knew that the eventual charge for waiting would be paid. "This could be awkward," she said quietly. "If Vale has a client—or clients . . ."

"Then we'll just have to wait," Kai agreed. "But we're not in an immediate rush. Sterrington can't have heard back from Alberich yet, and any communication from the Library would come to you first, wouldn't it?"

"I'd certainly hope so. Perhaps that might even be Bradamant's cab there. Let's find out."

The driver turned to them as they approached, and Kai took the initiative, putting on a cheerful man-about-town attitude. "Sorry to bother you, but did you bring my sister here? I was due to meet her. Tall woman, well dressed, short black hair . . ."

The driver's frown had deepened as he looked Kai up and down. "I'm afraid it ain't your sister, sir, though it might as well be your brother, the way he looked."

"My brother?" Kai looked as though he'd been punched in the gut.

"Yup. Same height, same eyes, same looks. Sounded a bit like you too."

Irene suppressed a curse. Ten to one it was Shan Yuan looking for Kai—either to try and apply more moral pressure or flat out deliver an order. "Kai," she said quietly, beckoning him away from the driver, "why don't you take a walk around to the back of the house and loiter there? I'll, ah, come and get you later."

She could see the indecision in his eyes. This was just postponing the problem, and both of them knew it. But if Kai wasn't actually *there* in the same room as Shan Yuan, then he couldn't be given any orders.

Finally Kai said, "If my elder brother has a command for me from my lord father, then I must obey."

"If he does have a genuine command from your father, then I'll let you know," Irene promised. The words came easily—but then, words always did for her.

As Kai diverted his path toward the end of the street and the turning that'd take him round the back of the house, Irene made her way up the front steps and quietly let herself in. With any luck Shan Yuan—if it was him—hadn't been watching the street outside and wouldn't have seen their arrival. Vale *would*, but he'd keep his mouth shut about Kai's presence.

Worry churned uneasily at the back of Irene's mind. What exactly was she going to do if Shan Yuan *did* have orders from Ao Guang for Kai to leave? Would she keep her word and tell Kai—or would she let him stay in ignorance a little longer? She'd always promised herself that she wouldn't make Kai choose between loyalty to his family and affection for her. She didn't want to lie to him—but equally she didn't want to lose him. *And would it ever be the same between us if he found out I'd lied?*

As she trod softly up the stairs, she heard voices coming from the door ahead of her. She recognized Vale's voice, Shan Yuan, and . . .

"Catherine?" she said as she opened the door.

Catherine looked up from her book, sliding a bookmark in to keep her place. "There's no need to sound so surprised," she said disapprovingly.

"I thought you were comfortably settled in at the Library," Irene excused herself. She turned to the two men, who were now staring at her rather than glaring at each other. "Your highness," she said to Shan Yuan, deciding to try a soft approach before the probably unavoidable hard line, "I hadn't expected to see you here."

Shan Yuan looked over her shoulder as though sheer force of will could make Kai materialize out of thin air. "I had thought Kai would tell you I was going to return. Where is he?"

"If he isn't here yet, then he should be on his way," Irene answered with her best imitation of innocence. "We split up after leaving Sterrington's house. He was going to call by our lodgings to check for the mail before joining me here."

"So he *is* coming here?" Shan Yuan demanded.

"He should be here any minute now." Irene turned to Vale. "Has anything happened while I've been out?"

Vale gestured vaguely at Shan Yuan, then at Catherine. "As you can see, Winters, my rooms have become a boardinghouse for visitors to London. Much more of this and I'll have to charge rent."

He and Shan Yuan were standing by the table—and not, thank goodness, next to the window where Shan Yuan might have seen Kai in the street below. Vale's gesture, almost accidentally, finished up by indicating a sealed letter which lay prominently on the table between him and Shan Yuan. Next to it was an expensive leather briefcase whose deep red hue suggested it belonged to the dragon prince. Dragons just couldn't resist their "natural" colors.

"I'm sorry that you've been put to any trouble," Irene said. She wanted a closer look at that letter, but if Vale was being indirect about it then she should probably do the same. She affected not to have noticed its existence. "May I ask what you want to discuss with Kai, your highness?"

"Only his departure." Shan Yuan's smugness was thick enough in the air that one could have cut it with a knife. The temperature was completely normal; he was comfortable in his victory, nowhere near losing his temper and manifesting any exterior signs of fire. He smiled thinly at Irene, his eyes the same blue as Kai's, his hair glossy black with just a faint undertone of red. "You see, I have received an offer which should be very much to his taste, and I made haste here to share it with him."

"I'm sure he'll be delighted to have news from home," Irene said blandly. Inwardly she was drawing up diagrams for torture devices, complete with arrows pointing at Shan Yuan in the middle of them.

Shan Yuan nodded, not taking any apparent offense. Perhaps he thought that Kai wouldn't have told her about the previous conversation. Or perhaps he simply assumed that she was giving up.

The *hell* she was.

She needed an excuse to get Shan Yuan out of the room for five minutes while she investigated that letter. She *could* use the Language perception trick on him—but then he'd remember it afterward when it wore off, and nobody liked people reading their letters, especially not dragon princes. "Have you been here long?" she asked Shan Yuan.

"I arrived less than half an hour ago," he replied. "Peregrine Vale knew me, of course, and has provided me with hospitality. Your apprentice arrived barely ten minutes ago. I am still not sure why." The note of disapproval in his voice suggested that he'd asked her—and she'd refused to tell him.

A light came on in the back of Irene's head. This might just work. "Catherine, why *are* you here?" she demanded. "Is this important Library business?"

Catherine avoided her eyes. "Can I speak to you in private?" she asked.

"Is that absolutely necessary?" Irene turned away from Shan Yuan, and on the side of her body that was hidden from him but visible to Catherine she made a small beckoning gesture with her hand, hoping Catherine would understand. *Escalate it. Make it obvious.*

Catherine hunched her shoulders stubbornly. "It's important. I wouldn't ask you if it wasn't. I can't just tell everyone about it. Please . . ."

Just right. Irene sighed—a little overdone, perhaps, but it was Shan Yuan she had to convince—and turned to him and Vale. "I beg your pardon, gentlemen, but would you mind stepping into the corridor for just five minutes? Clearly this is Library business I need to see to at once."

"Of course, Winters," Vale said. He moved to hold the door for Shan Yuan. "This way, your highness. I'm sure the ladies will be as quick as possible."

Social pressure—and probably the feeling of comfortable victory— got Shan Yuan through the door and out into the corridor. Most importantly, his briefcase and the letter were still lying on the table. No doubt he thought that nobody would *dare* open the letter, or, even if they tried, that they couldn't do so without breaking the seal.

Perfect.

"Now, Catherine," Irene said as she closed the door, "I want you to understand that I'm not angry with you, or in any way going to be unfair." The tone of her voice should be perceptible through the door, just as she'd been able to hear the others earlier. She had to keep the sound of conversation going. "So let's be responsible adults about this."

She silently pulled Catherine to her feet, and murmured in her ear, "Stand with your back to the door so that they can't come in and take us by surprise. Keep talking normally."

Catherine's eyes widened, but by now she had enough experience to follow Irene's orders without any immediate questions of *Why?* or *What's going on?* or *Are you really sure we should be doing this?* She leaned against the door and said, "All right. But I just want to make it absolutely clear from the word go that I haven't done anything wrong."

"I never thought you had." Irene crossed to the table and inspected the letter. Shan Yuan's name was on the front in Chinese characters. Excellent quality of ink and paper. The seal on the back— very interesting, it was a personal seal that she didn't recognize, which had been broken and then *resealed* in inferior wax. "Why don't you tell me what the problem is?"

"I thought my talents and skills would be more useful here," Catherine said. She'd clearly practiced the speech. "As your assistant—"

"Apprentice," Irene corrected her.

"Assistant-in-training," Catherine said firmly. "I'd be derelict in my duties if I wasn't by your side."

"You were *supposed* to be studying."

"I learn better in the field."

"You were supposed to be enjoying yourself reading!"

Catherine hesitated. Finally, like a woman confessing a mortal sin, she said, "Sometimes there are things that are more important than reading."

Irene leaned over the letter and breathed, barely audibly, **"Letter, unseal yourself while keeping the seal in one piece."**

Then she took in what Catherine had just said. Her eyes narrowed. "Catherine, while I won't go so far as to suggest you're lying, your entire *raison d'être* so far has been to get into the Library by any means possible so you could get at the books. I sympathize with that. I'm touched that you want to leave them behind and help me—but I need you to tell me why."

"Need to?" Catherine said defensively. "Isn't it enough that I'm here?"

The letter unfolded itself—and so did the second letter sealed inside it. Both of them had heard Irene's words.

Irene looked up from them to stare at Catherine. For a moment she was going to demand answers in the most sarcastic way possible— but then it crossed her mind to remember how Bradamant had treated her when she was working as a journeyman under Bradamant. In a gentler tone than she'd originally planned, she said, "The current situation is dangerous. If Vale hasn't told you—no, I see by your expression he hasn't—then I'll get round to it very shortly, but trust me, it's not safe. I appreciate having you here, but we need some fundamental honesty between the two of us. Why?"

"Because . . ." Catherine hesitated, looking for words.

Irene gave her that time, scanning the letter instead. Shan Yuan might try to come back in at any time; she only had minutes left. The outer letter was from Lord Shang Yi. She recognized the name from previous discussions—he was the leading draconic expert in computer technology. Shan Yuan worked directly for him, and Kai himself had spoken wistfully of being able to study under him at some point in the future.

Shan Yuan,

I am glad to hear that you and Kai have resolved your differences. You have spoken highly of his abilities and intelligence. If you are to take over his post as treaty representative, then I will be glad to accept him as a student. Let him present himself at my dwellings without delay.

Shang Yi

Her lips pursed in a silent whistle. *Sneaky, sneaky Shan Yuan.* He'd tried the stick—now he was dangling the carrot. No doubt he was hoping Kai would take this offer, so he could then present it to Ao Guang as a *fait accompli*. Irene herself would probably be the next to be ousted, and replaced by some other Librarian.

The inner letter was only a couple of lines.

Kai, greetings. If you still wish to become my student, then I will accept you as such. There is much work to be done; attend on me as soon as you may.

Shang Yi

"It's because I'm tired of being the freak," Catherine said. Her voice was flat, toneless. "I was the only Fae there. Everyone kept *looking* at me. I've been happy studying on my own for years now. I didn't realize they would be so . . . so *curious*. They kept on asking questions—even the older Librarians, the ones who weren't apprentices, the ones who *should* have been fair to me and treated me like any other student! And even the ones who didn't ask me questions didn't trust me. I know it's only been a few days, but I just didn't like it." She met Irene's eyes. "It wasn't what I'd thought it would be."

Irene bit back a sigh. Reading secret correspondence was difficult enough on its own. Handling a teenager's moaning—no, to be fair, it sounded like an entirely justified complaint—didn't make it any easier.

"You didn't expect it?" she asked. Honestly, what had Catherine thought it would be like to be the first Fae ever to enter the Library?

"I was just thinking about the books," Catherine admitted. "I never thought about the people. And . . . something's wrong."

Something about the Fae's tone caught Irene's attention. This *wasn't* just whining; there was something more serious here. "Go on," she said quietly. "What's wrong?"

Catherine frowned. "There are shadows everywhere," she answered, equally softly. Both of them knew that this wasn't something for Shan Yuan to overhear. "Some of the other apprentices can see them—but none of the Librarians can. It's as if the whole place is . . . overshadowed by something bigger, and nobody's figured out they can't see the sun any more. And some people were asking the wrong sort of questions. About my uncle. About Fae politics. And about *you*."

"What sort of question about me?" Irene asked. The overshadowing feeling might relate to Bradamant's talk of nightmares, or it might just be Catherine's imagination—but there was nothing she could do about that for now. She had to stay focused.

"About the sort of things you've been researching or you've done previously." Catherine jerked a shoulder in a half-shrug. "Not just the rubbish some people were saying about how you'd gone rogue—I mean, who'd believe that? They wanted to know if you'd discussed your studies with me. They mentioned several documents—a story by the Brothers Grimm, an Egyptian text . . ."

Cold fear walked up and down Irene's spine. First the meeting with Aunt Isra and the story which corroborated the Egyptian narrative, and now the Library itself trying to find out if she'd told anyone about the Egyptian version . . .

No. She was being paranoid. She was allowing herself to substitute *the Library* for *at least one person who's been asking Catherine questions*. "Who wanted to know all this?"

"I think they were fairly senior people," Catherine said doubtfully. "The one in charge was called Kostchei."

Irene reconsidered. This wasn't paranoia, this was justified concern. Something was badly wrong. But there wasn't time to get the full details right now, with Shan Yuan waiting outside. "We'll talk more about this later," she said, picking up a pen and scribbling a note to Kai. "How did you get back to this world from the Library?"

"Oh, I had permission," Catherine said hastily. "I may have sort of exaggerated a little bit about how the Library atmosphere was being bad for me and I needed to go back to a chaos-aspected world for a few days. That time I was poisoned in Guernsey turned out to be really useful—I was able to fake looking ill. So they sent me along with these three Librarians who were coming to this world too: Blaise was the one in charge, and Hypatia and Medea were with him. Medea escorted me here and left me on Vale's doorstep, and the other two went to see Sterrington."

Irene dimly remembered Blaise and Medea from the Paris incident when the Fae–dragon treaty had been signed; Blaise was among the more senior Librarians. "Well, good," she said, trying to ignore a feeling of having been unfairly sidelined from the Alberich negotiations. "That proves they're taking it seriously."

"Taking what seriously? They wouldn't tell me what was going on." Catherine frowned. "Am I missing out on something?"

"You're probably about to find out what it is you've missed out on very soon," Irene advised. "When you hear, act . . . appropriately. **Letters, close and reseal yourselves.**"

She folded her note to Kai round a pencil to weight it, and crossed to Vale's bedroom door. The window overlooked the alley behind the house, and Irene could see Kai loitering there. She opened the window and whistled.

Kai looked up and grinned to see her.

Irene wasn't sure he'd be smiling so much once he read her news. She tossed the weighted note down to him, then closed the window and hastily rejoined Catherine in the main room, checking the table. The letters looked untouched. The only difference was the absence of a pencil and paper; Shan Yuan wouldn't notice that—though Vale would.

"All right," she said firmly to Catherine. "You're back in the field. But usual rules apply—when I say jump, you jump first and ask questions later. And if I ask you to stay in a particular place, I need to be able to trust you to stay there. Understood?"

Catherine took a deep breath of relief. "Understood," she said, trying to maintain a casual attitude.

Irene waved her back to her chair. "Then let's have the gentlemen back in."

Shan Yuan was displaying signs of impatience, stalking across the room as soon as he entered. "Are you certain that my brother is safe?" he demanded of Irene. "You say that the two of you separated. It hasn't been long since London was full of the criminal agents who served Lord and Lady Guantes—and your traitor Alberich. What if they're seeking revenge?"

"Inspector Singh has been rooting out their network," Vale reassured him. "The vanishing of the Guantes pair decapitated the group; they were left without direction, and have been turning on each other in a most gratifying manner."

"This still means that your world is unsafe," Shan Yuan muttered. Irene found herself realizing, rather against her will, that he was *genuinely* concerned for Kai's safety. Oh, certainly he wanted to steal Kai's job and shunt Kai off to study computers, and he'd happily bully

Kai for what he considered to be Kai's own good—but he also wanted to keep Kai safe.

Why do we all have to be so ... human?

Heavy feet resounded on the stairs, and a moment later Kai burst through the door. "It's all under control, Irene!" he exclaimed. "Sterrington's setting up the meeting, and I think that with a bit of luck this should mean genuine security and peace for the Library— oh, I beg your pardon, elder brother." He bowed. "I hadn't realized you were here."

"What meeting?" Shan Yuan asked, sharing a frown between Kai and Irene. "What conspiracy is this?"

"Irene hasn't told you?" Kai was doing quite a good job of looking innocent and sincere. "Alberich's requested a truce with the Library, and we're helping set it up. With a bit of luck, this could mean a permanent cessation of hostilities on his part. This could be a very positive thing for the Library. I hope you understand why I'm involved in it, elder brother."

The fire in the fireplace jumped briefly, flames reaching up to scorch the brickwork. Shan Yuan took a deep breath. Irene could only guess at his thoughts, but she imagined they were political. It was never a good idea to change the person in charge in the middle of complicated negotiations. If Shan Yuan gave Kai the note from Lord Shang Yi now, he'd be forcing Kai to make an immediate choice— and things could go either way. A sensible gambler didn't put money down on a bet unless the odds were in their favor.

"You didn't tell me about this," Catherine protested, her voice covering Shan Yuan's silence.

"We've hardly had time," Irene said placatingly. "*You* were busy telling me about how you were coming back to full-time apprenticeship instead. Thank you for the update, Kai. I was hoping the situation might be going that way."

Shan Yuan strode across to the desk, and picked up his letter. He frowned, inspecting it belatedly for signs of interference, then returned it to the briefcase for later deployment. "Tell me more of this truce," he ordered Irene.

Irene shrugged. "At the moment it's still very uncertain, your highness. Alberich has requested that the Fae ambassador Sterrington arrange a neutral location so that he and the Library can formally sign a cessation of hostilities in the Language. That should be a bond which neither side can break. Naturally we're treating this with due caution and suspicion—not to mention outright disbelief—but it seems too good an opportunity to pass up."

"I can see that Alberich might have a reason to deal with *you*." His tone was very near a sneer. He knew that Alberich was Irene's father, after all—and oh, how she wished that he didn't. "I hope that you will be loyal to your Library."

Something in Irene's mind ticked over from *profound dislike* to *absolute fury*. "Your highness," she said caressingly, letting her voice linger on his title, "if you wish to question my loyalty quite so blatantly, then I am sure that a formal meeting of some sort between us can be arranged. But let us make it *after* the current emergency—I wouldn't want to be less efficient than usual because of some petty argument."

Shan Yuan's eyes flickered dragon-red, and a fragile pattern of scales briefly tracked across his skin, like the image in the heart of a fire. The room turned bitterly hot, dry enough to parch her throat. "Your words will be remembered," he said conversationally. Then he turned to Kai. "Be quick about your current affairs, Kai. Don't expect my forbearance to last much longer."

The door slammed shut behind him, and every step was audible on the stairs as he stormed out.

"Did I miss something?" Catherine asked, confused.

"Nothing of significance," Kai said. He touched Irene's shoulder supportively. "Or at least, nothing that can't wait."

But Irene saw the uncertainty in his eyes. How long could he put off this flattering offer? And ultimately, did he really want to?

She knew he was interested in that area of study. Was it fair of her to keep him tied to his current position, if he'd rather be doing something else? She'd thought that she could keep him safe—but if the most important people in the Library were using her as bait, was she putting him in even greater danger by keeping him at her side?

If she really loved him . . . should she let him go?

CHAPTER 17

W e've been through this five times so far," Irene said, not looking up from the papers in front of her. "Which part of 'absolutely out of the question' seems negotiable to you?"

"But I'm your *apprentice*," Catherine argued. "Even Kai—"

"Don't drag me into this," Kai said from his chair.

"Especially Kai?"

"That depends on the argument being put forward," Kai said.

"Kai said that it was the duty of an apprentice to go into danger with their teacher, to protect them and learn from them." She presented her argument with the enthusiasm and positivity of a puppy bringing a mangled slipper to its owner. Yet there was a certain brittleness behind her eyes; she might be trying to persuade Irene to take her along, but at root she clearly didn't really want to go.

"Kai wishes to mention that when this issue was brought up, it was in the context of regular book acquisitions," Kai noted, keeping to the third person. "Not . . . this sort of situation."

Time had not been passing quickly. Time had been *crawling*. Other Librarians were handling the discussions with Sterrington and the details of the deal with Alberich. Even though Irene and the others could now return to their own lodgings, they were out of the loop, only able to wait for their instructions—or more specifically, what *Irene* would be required to do. She'd been ordered not to leave London. They could only sit and wait. While Irene had accumulated quite a few books in her rooms, it wasn't enough to distract any of them.

"I'd have a lot fewer screaming nightmares about him if I could actually see him signing the treaty to leave us alone in future," Catherine suggested, shifting her ground.

Irene put her pen down and looked up. "No," she said. "You'll be staying with Sterrington, since your uncle's on vacation again, and you'll just have to make do with us telling you about it when we get back." *Assuming we get back*. Fear was a leaden weight in her stomach; having to sit here for the last couple of days while other Librarians carried messages to set up the meeting was approaching sheer torture. "If you like, I promise to take you on half a dozen horrendously dangerous missions afterward."

"That's not funny," Catherine muttered.

"Humor is an acknowledged way of dealing with tension—and it's probably better than me screaming, running in circles, and jumping out of the window." Irene sighed. "Catherine, let me be frank. *I'm* only at the meeting because Alberich's insisting on me being present. If I could leave it to another Librarian, then I would. Do you really *want* to be there?"

"No, but . . . You're allowed two assistants," Catherine said. "I know that Kai and Vale are going to get those places—couldn't you argue for three?"

Irene suddenly thought of something which might explain Catherine's stubborn insistence. "Speaking purely theoretically, and with no names named, might anyone be pressuring you to be there in order to provide a full in-person account of what happens?"

The tension went out of Catherine's shoulders and she relaxed back into her chair, gratitude showing in her eyes. "If anyone had told me to do something like that, they'd have told me not to tell anyone else about it."

"Right. In that case, feel free to pass on to the theoretical person in question that I've absolutely refused, for all the reasons that I've already given you."

"I don't *want* to get into politics . . ."

"Believe me, I entirely understand your position," Kai muttered. He'd been brooding over his behavior to his elder brother and the offer he'd temporarily avoided, unwilling to discuss the matter with Irene. "But the Library so rarely washes its dirty linen in public— naturally everyone wants to know what's going on. I'm not blaming you for any . . . *theoretical* pressure."

Normally Irene would have celebrated the multilateral agreement and understanding between Kai and Catherine—but as it was, she was just grateful to have one fewer headache. She'd been truthful when she told Catherine that she'd rather not be involved; on the other hand, having to sit and wait while other people sorted out the details was stressful enough to make her change her mind. She'd resorted to going through the Library records on Alberich as a distraction, in hopes of finding anything which corroborated Aunt Isra's story. She'd found nothing. *And should that in itself worry me?*

Frankly, at the moment *everything* worried her.

The doorbell dragged her out of her reverie. "I'll get it," she said, as Kai began to rise. "I've been sitting down too long."

Bradamant was at the door, dressed appropriately for the time and place but with a briefcase handcuffed to her wrist. "Seriously?" Irene said, glancing at it. Then knowledge of what it must mean sank in. "Is it go time?"

"If you want to be military about it, then yes, it is go time." Bradamant maintained her usual air of cool competence, but the tight clench of her gloved hand on the briefcase handle argued otherwise. "And it may look stupid, but just think how *very* ridiculous it'd be for me to have this stolen by a casual street thief on the way."

"Fair point," Irene agreed. "We'll need to stop at Vale's lodgings on the way to pick him up."

"You don't have him here?"

"He had another case on hand, and he objected to sitting around doing nothing."

Bradamant nodded. "Well, get a move on. Fetch Kai, get a coat, whatever. There's no point in annoying anyone by wasting time."

"Kai!" Irene called, pulling her coat and hat from the coat rack. "It would have been helpful if I'd been kept abreast of what was going on," she complained.

"You've been officially rehabilitated. Isn't that enough?" At Irene's raised eyebrows, Bradamant expanded. "You've technically been undercover on a very complicated assignment setting all this up. The 'going rogue' has been wiped off the record. Not that anyone really believed it, given the lack of effort to find you. There's probably a commendation in your future." Her tone was dry. "Nobody needs to know the truth about how you had no idea of any of this until Alberich set it up himself."

Irene had decided it was the better part of valor *not* to mention she'd suggested Alberich make peace with the Library. It'd only sully her character further by suggesting she had undue influence over him. Instead she merely nodded in agreement.

Kai had taken in the scene at a glance, and was flinging on his own coat and hat. "How are we handling this?" he asked.

"I have a cab waiting. We'll stop by Vale's lodgings to pick him up, then go on to Sterrington's place for the next stage of transport." Bradamant looked over Kai's shoulder at Catherine, who was hesitating at the end of the hall. "I'm not sure it's a good idea to leave your apprentice here alone, Irene."

"I absolutely agree it isn't," Irene said firmly. "Since her uncle isn't around, she'll be staying with Sterrington while we're away. She can come with us."

Bradamant frowned. "Are you sure?"

"I *could* stay here alone," Catherine chimed in—more to annoy Bradamant than for any other reason, Irene suspected. "There are plenty of books in the house. I won't get bored."

"Life is full of disappointments." Irene passed Catherine her hat, coat, and veil. "There's still the chance that this is all some sort of complicated trap. I want to make sure you're safe. And since you chose to leave the Library . . ."

"You're going to keep reminding me about that, aren't you?"

"I hope to keep reminding you about it for years to come," Irene said. As opposed to the alternative—that we never come back from this mission . . .

Sterrington was waiting in her lounge when they arrived, Vale in tow, and she was clearly much improved. There was a new sparkle in her eye and vigor to her step, though perhaps those were just the side effects of being involved in high-level politics. "Before we go any further, there are some questions I need the Librarians to answer for me in the Language," she said.

Irene had expected this, and she nodded. "Go ahead, please."

"Firstly, I'd like your word that you're sincere in this negotiation and you have no plans to engage in aggressive behavior unless you yourself are first betrayed."

Irene repeated Sterrington's words in the Language. Reality seemed to catch for an instant around her, like cogwheels slipping into place, as the vow took hold. Librarians adjusted reality through the Language making their words true; by the same principle in reverse, the Language forced truth on *them*. She heard Bradamant do the same.

"Very good. Now . . ." Sterrington drew a list from a folder she was holding. "I'm sorry for all the formalities, but I need to make absolutely sure about this. I want your word in the Language that you don't know of any plans or intentions by anyone *else* to betray these negotiations. Technically that includes dragons, friends, superiors, lovers, et cetera, but you don't need to go into all *that* much detail— just pick a good collective noun for the rest of existence."

"I'm assuming that Alberich has already signed up to this?" Irene checked.

"Of course." She tapped the folder. "I'm not asking you to trust me *personally*. I'm asking you to trust the Cardinal's own agent, who drew this agreement up under the Cardinal's own guidance. Seriously, do you think he'd leave holes in something like this?"

Only holes that he could exploit personally, Irene thought. But there was a moment in every plan where you had to trust the experts. "**I don't know of any plan by any person or organization—associate, neutral, or enemy—to betray this meeting or these negotiations.** Is that acceptable?"

"Absolutely," Sterrington said. "Now your turn, Bradamant."

As Bradamant repeated Irene's phrasing, Irene felt tension knot tight inside her. This was like the sort of story where someone was bargaining with a genie for a wish, and the exact wording would mean success or utter failure. But if Alberich had signed up to the same conditions . . .

At least she hadn't been asked to specify that she wasn't armed. Because she most definitely was carrying a weapon—and she was sure the others were too.

Sterrington nodded, and put the list away. "So that's the four of you, as agreed—Bradamant and Irene for the Library, Prince Kai and Peregrine Vale as Irene's two allocated bodyguards. Transport will be here any minute to take you to the location for the meeting. I understand that Prince Kai can provide transport back after everything's been signed. The world's climate will be sufficiently orderly for him to take his natural form. I'm hoping this will go quickly, for everyone's sake. And I must thank you for the chance to be involved in organizing this. One doesn't often get the opportunity to have the Library owe one a favor—especially not a favor this big."

Irene knew that Kai hadn't been asked about providing transport back. But he nodded, evidently as eager as everyone else to get this *over* with. "What's the place like?"

"Oh, post-holocaust. Practically nothing there except a table and chairs. Don't worry, it's not significantly radioactive or contaminated. It's frequently used for negotiations where both sides want to make it absolutely clear that nobody's hiding anything."

Irene could have lived without the *significantly*, but as Sterrington had said, hopefully it would all be over quickly.

"Madam," Corder said, entering the room, "the transport's here."

A black carriage stood outside the door, drawn by four black horses, huge black-dyed ostrich-feather plumes nodding on their heads. Perched in the driver's seat was a thin figure in—unsurprisingly—black, so emaciated and drawn that he was practically a living skeleton. He doffed his top hat, smiling a gap-toothed smile. "All ready to go, sirs, madams. Plenty of room inside for all those who's making the trip. Always room for one more inside."

Catherine darted forward to grab Irene's hand. "Be *careful*," she ordered her, face set sternly.

Irene returned Catherine's clasp. "I'll be careful," she assured her.

"This is rather a . . . funeral transport," Bradamant said to Sterrington. "It's practically a hearse. Are you trying to give us a hint?"

Sterrington sniffed. For some reason, she and Bradamant didn't seem to have hit it off. "This driver will get you to your destination. Consider it metaphorical; death goes everywhere."

"And the dead travel fast," Irene quoted, unable to restrain herself.

"Exactly."

As Sterrington spoke, the carriage door swung open, and a waft of cold air scented with lilies and cypresses drifted out. "Get in, get in," the driver urged. "I can't wait."

Disengaging her hand from Catherine's with some difficulty, Irene let Kai hand her up into the carriage. Bradamant followed a moment later, back stiff with annoyance that she hadn't been the first to enter, and Kai and Vale behind. They were barely settling onto the facing seats, and Sterrington was still calling advice to them, when the driver cracked his whip, the door swung shut, and they were off.

Whatever else the carriage might be, it was badly sprung. It jolted as it rattled down the London street, swaying from side to side, so that the passengers had to brace themselves against the walls and against each other. Kai had ended up on the seat next to Irene, looking forward, while Vale and Bradamant were facing them with their backs to the driver. His whip cracked again, and Irene could hear him cackling, even over the noise of the traffic outside. The sound of his laughter made her want to shudder; it spoke of airless lungs, madness, and echoing tombs.

The exterior cacophony of protesting horns and complaining traffic rose, suggesting an imminent accident—and then cut off. Outside the window the sky was abruptly darkening, and the carriage was racketing onward over cobbles rather than the smoother roads of Vale's London. Irene peered out of the window and saw high buildings that seemed to lean and leer oppressively, with pale faces showing in momentary blinks at the shadowed windows.

Kai sighed. "Well, here we go," he said. While he could tolerate the Fae mode of travel, he understandably had little fondness for it.

"It could be worse," Irene said comfortingly. "It could be a chocolate river with singing boatmen."

"That's purely literary," Bradamant said. "Or cinematic, if you like."

"And this isn't?" Irene asked, gesturing at the window, which now had an excellent view of a graveyard they were passing. Thin white streamers drifted in the trees, and clouds veiled the struggling moon so that shadows flowed around the gravestones.

Bradamant shrugged. "The esthetics don't concern me. I just want to get there, get the treaty signed, and get out."

Their driver laughed again, and the carriage speeded up, the horses galloping like madness unleashed. Outside the windows it grew darker still; the graves were no longer visible, though distant shapes seemed to stride or run through the passing shadows.

"That's all any of us want," Irene said. Her hand found Kai's, and their fingers enlaced in mutual reassurance.

"I am still somewhat perplexed by my presence," Vale said.

"Irene wanted you," Bradamant replied dismissively. "And Alberich wanted Irene. No doubt he knew she wouldn't come without you two to back her up."

"Winters isn't a romantic," Vale said imperturbably. "If Alberich had thought she was afraid of him—"

"Which, to be fair, I am," Irene put in."

"Yes, but there's a difference between sensible caution and paralyzing terror. If you had truly wanted bodyguards, you could have asked more powerful people than one London detective to accompany you."

"Perhaps he knew I'd need moral backup," Irene said quietly. "People who know . . . the current situation." *People who know I'm his daughter,* she meant.

"I still find it curious." Vale regarded his folded hands, ignoring the tense Bradamant next to him. "I believe there is something else at work here."

"You'd better hope there isn't," Bradamant said coldly. "Because if this goes wrong, then you're on his list of enemies too."

Vale snorted, as if to indicate how little the matter concerned him, and turned to gaze out of the window instead. They sat in silence for a while, with dark landscapes rippling by outside.

Finally Bradamant frowned. "Prince Kai, does it seem to you that it is growing lighter?"

Kai shook off his travel-induced malaise and leaned forward until he was nearly touching the glass. "I think so, yes. If we're approaching our destination, then that was very fast."

"We have an expert driver," Irene said, nodding to the roof where he sat. As usual, it seemed that the more in touch with their archetype a Fae was—and the *less* in touch with common humanity—the more efficient they were. She decided in this case to take it as a benefit, however creepy their driver might be. They did want to get there fast, after all.

The carriage began to slow, and the light that Bradamant and Kai had noticed gradually crept up over the horizon to expose a blasted landscape. Thin crawling bushes sprawled over piles of rubble and puddles of glass. The sky was full of dust, turning the clouds a thick orange that verged toward blood-red. It was hot—unpleasantly so—and all of them were dressed for the cold days of London's spring, rather than this postapocalyptic heat. From time to time things crunched under the carriage wheels, and Irene wondered whether they were bones.

"Here we are!" the driver called as the carriage jolted to a stop. "Out you get, ladies and gentlemen, I have more calls to make, and a lot of people aren't expecting me on their doorstep." He laughed again, his cackle echoing across the empty plain.

Kai was the first out, one hand blocking Irene's passage as he jumped down to look around. His gaze moved to directly in front of the carriage, out of the line of view of the side windows. "Ah," he said softly. "So that's how it's done."

Irene coughed meaningfully.

"Sorry." He didn't move, though; he stood there, looking all around, his shoulders braced as though expecting an imminent attack. "All right. No immediate ambushes. This is probably as safe as we can hope for." He turned and offered Irene his hand down.

"Not too high in chaos for you?" Irene's Library brand was barely registering any chaos here, but she knew that Kai's dragon perceptions were more sensitive than her own human ones—even Librarian ones.

"No, quite tolerable. I can remove us from here safely when this is done." Kai led her forward a few paces, ignoring Bradamant and Vale, and indicated what was ahead of them. "You see?"

A table was surrounded by five chairs, and a wooden door in a free-standing frame was positioned behind one of the chairs. The furniture was almost aggressively prosaic, white-painted metalwork that one might find in a nice summer garden. But the door . . . that was different. Irene had seen one like it before. It was painted with words in the Language, in a scale that ran from legible to so small that they were barely readable; some Irene knew, others she didn't, but they were about *connection, openings, portals.* It was Alberich's way of entering this world.

There were no other landmarks: no buildings, no trees, no people, *nothing.* Someone who had studied the landscape could perhaps distinguish one ruin from another, or identify a specific undulation on the horizon, but otherwise the place was a statement in itself about the desolation that war left behind.

Perhaps this is why the Fae find it a meaningful location for negotiations, Irene thought. Certainly there were no visible libraries here.

Behind them the driver cracked his whip, and all four of them turned to see him jerking into action, shaking the reins and urging his horses round and away. Between one moment and the next the doom-laden carriage blurred into invisibility and was gone, traveling to another world—and leaving them here.

"What do we do?" Bradamant sounded a little lost. Then she took a deep breath, visibly working to regain control of herself—and of the group. "We should sit down at the table, I think."

"It would make a wonderful target to be hit by a meteor," Kai agreed cheerfully.

"Look, we've both agreed to keep the peace; he can't *do* that," Bradamant argued. "And I don't appreciate your sense of humor—"

"He's arriving," Irene interrupted. She'd been watching the door while Bradamant spoke, and had seen it quiver in its frame.

Silence fell as the door swung open. Irene could see Vale's hand tightening on his sword-cane, Kai's eyes flickering dragon-red, Bradamant taking a deep breath to speak. This was when they found out whether Alberich was sincere—or if he'd found a way to lie in the Language and they were all doomed.

The figure revealed by the opening door was withered and scorched past anything Irene would have thought possible for a human. Alberich was draped in a dark robe like a monk's, probably covering even worse deformities. Bloodshot eyes stared at them from a tattered face, and his hands were scarred and knotted until they looked barely functional. His breath came in a long hiss as his gaze swept across them. "So. You did come."

Irene swallowed, trying to ease the dryness in her throat. "Under safe-conduct, which you signed."

"I did."

"I'd thought that body you're wearing was no longer functional."

"It's only mostly dead. I don't tell anyone the whole truth about my situation—neither my enemies nor my allies."

"We hope that after this, you and the Library won't be *enemies* any longer," Bradamant said boldly. "Or at least not active ones."

"Perhaps—and yet they send a junior Librarian with the treaty rather than one of their more respected brethren." His eyes fixed on Bradamant. "You do realize that you're intended as a sacrifice in case I somehow fooled them? They wouldn't want to lose someone *important*."

Bradamant's hand clenched so tightly on the briefcase handle that it must have been cutting into her flesh. "You think I don't know that?"

"So why did you come?"

"Because, if I can pull it off, I'll have their respect." Bradamant stepped forward and slapped the briefcase down on the table. "And if I don't, I'll end up with nothing but duty assignments for the rest of my career. Not all of us have Irene's luck." The edge to her voice showed just how much she resented that. "So hurry up and sign. Please."

"Ah, the magic word." Alberich shuffled to the table, the door closing behind him, and lowered himself into a seat at the table. His hands left stains on the white-painted metal. "Sit down. All of you. I'm hardly going to get the opportunity to do this a second time. Allow me a few words."

Irene pulled out the chair to Bradamant's right, sat down, and wished she could control her pulse. Every non-reasoning part of her body wanted to run for it—and the reasoning parts were mostly in agreement. "Allowing any Librarian a few words is rarely a good idea."

"As you've proved in the past." Alberich's grin was ghastly. "I'm so proud of you."

"Trying to sow discord between two Librarians will do you very little good," Kai said. He was balanced on the edge of his chair, the tension in his muscles obvious.

"Indeed. I was there the last time these ladies faced you together, after all." Vale leaned his elbows on the table, as though disdainful of Alberich's ability to threaten them. "The Library cooperates well enough when it needs to."

"The Library . . ." Alberich turned toward Bradamant. "I'll sign your treaty very shortly. But I require a few words with Irene first, and I doubt that she'll stay once your business is done."

"She could give her word in the Language to hear you out once we're done," Bradamant suggested, rather to Irene's horror. "Sign first. You've agreed to it."

Alberich hesitated, then shook his head. Something in the depths of his hood trickled down his neck. "No. I don't think so. Pay attention, Bradamant. You may learn something useful." He turned back to Irene. "You've been talking to Aunt Isra."

"Yes," Irene agreed. There seemed no point in denying it; his letter had made it clear that he knew. "The timing's interesting. Was it my talking to her which convinced you to sign this treaty?"

"It was." There was a smell of decay and ash around Alberich, an odor of corruption which hung in the dead-still apocalyptic air. "Did she tell you a certain story?"

"She told me the story which she said she'd told you."

"And you survived?"

"Demonstrably."

He frowned. "It must be because you found the traces yourself and came to the conclusion without my help. The other Librarians whom I tried to tell . . . Well, they didn't have as fortunate an ending."

"What do you mean?" Irene had a growing suspicion that she knew exactly what he meant, but the idea was so vile that she would rather hear it from his lips than fully express it in her own mind.

"I mean, Ray—no, I'll be generous and call you 'Irene.' An adult can choose her own name. What I mean is that the Library itself would have killed you if I had tried to tell you certain things."

"There is nothing in the story I heard which is necessarily *bad*," Irene said carefully. "Bradamant's heard it from me as well. You don't need to mince your words in front of her. The idea that the Library might originally have been founded by Fae–dragon cooperation—"

"Why?" Alberich broke in. "Why should they have founded it? Tell me that."

"To stabilize the worlds."

"Do you honestly think that they would have done it purely out of *altruism*? For the common good? Ask the dragon there." He pointed to Kai. "You, prince, tell me—would your grandfather have sacrificed himself and made a pact with Fae just out of some sense of *ethics*? One needs to be a brainwashed little Librarian to believe that preserving the stability of all the alternate worlds is actually worth sacrificing your life. Your grandfather was more than that."

Kai's hands clenched on the edge of the table, and a frost-pattern of scales flickered briefly across his skin. "I would like to beat you to the ground for daring to speak of my grandfather, and erase you from this world and all others," he said flatly. "But I acknowledge one thing. If my grandfather did this, then he had a reason for doing it."

Bradamant had closed her eyes and lowered her head, as though seized by a headache. Irene abandoned the conversation for a moment, turning to lay a hand on her wrist. "Are you all right?" she asked.

"This has gone far enough." It wasn't Bradamant speaking. The voice coming from her lips lacked her usual accent or tone; it was her voice, but someone else's diction. She opened her eyes, and a stranger looked out through them. "We will enforce peace—and remove everything that threatens it. This ends here, traitor."

Her briefcase flew open and a stream of paper billowed out, the pages twisting like autumn leaves in a hurricane. They spun through the air, then slapped down to the ground and vanished into it, burying themselves in the sandy earth.

The world shook. It wasn't an earthquake, or a storm, or anything physical, it was reality itself trembling around them, reordering itself to a different configuration and locking there.

The wind began to rise, and Alberich screamed, "What have you done?"

"Disposed of the last loose end," Bradamant said.

Then she coughed, and fell forward onto the table, unmoving. Across the back of her coat, the fabric smoldered from beneath as the heat of her brand finally ate through all the layers of clothing in the way and burst into flame.

CHAPTER 18

Irene had no idea what to do. She'd been expecting betrayal—but not from this direction. Oh, technically she was aware that the Library might consider the loss of Bradamant and herself as fair trade for the removal of Alberich—but an agreement had been signed *in the Language.* How could the Library break its given word?

And was her own back feeling uncomfortably warm?

Kai was on his feet. "I knew we shouldn't have trusted you," he snarled at Alberich, his nails sharpening to claws in his fury.

"We're all betrayed," Vale cut in. "Control yourself, Strongrock. Winters . . ." His tone changed. "Winters, are you all right?"

Irene knew that she should be reacting, should be *thinking*, but there was a distant drumming in her ears and her head was aching as though it was about to split in half. "Give me a moment," she whispered.

Alberich forced himself to his feet, leaning on the table. He was speaking, saying something, but the background wind was so loud that she couldn't hear him properly. She sagged forward, trying to process what was going on, aware that she should be reacting differently but unable to quite think *why*. Her back was aching across her brand, and she couldn't even be sure why this was a bad thing.

Then Kai and Vale caught her by the arms and forced her forward across the table, face down against the cold metal. The shock of this sudden attack jolted her out of her half-trance state and she struggled against their grip. Alberich had moved out of her line of vision—he must be controlling them somehow, using the Language to turn them against her. Words surged in her mouth like vomit to strike them down, strike them *all* down for this treachery . . .

Her coat and dress tore open across her back like ripped paper. Someone—it must be Alberich, she couldn't see—touched her brand, and it felt as if his finger was reaching through her to touch her naked heart. She choked on the words she'd been about to scream. It was indecent, it was *wrong* . . .

. . . and then, suddenly, it was all silent. The wind was still rising, but the drumming in her ears was gone and the pain which had been about to crack her head open had eased. She could think again. "Let me go," she said, her face still pressed to the table by the two men's grip on her. "Now."

"That should do it." Alberich's voice had an unpleasant wheeze to it, as though something in his lungs was breaking down. "You can release her now."

"Stand back first," Kai said, his voice a growl. While he might not be about to rip Alberich's throat out this very instant, it clearly wouldn't take much to make him do it. He released his grip on Irene, as did Vale. "I'm sorry, Irene. He said that you were about to die too, and the only way to save you was to let him alter your brand . . ."

"You used the *you perceive* trick on them, didn't you?" Irene said wearily. She saw Kai tensing up at the realization of how he'd been manipulated, and put a hand on his shoulder. "Don't. Not yet, at least. Let's get some answers first."

Alberich shrugged. "I did it to save you."

Irene righted herself, checking for damage. There was nothing she could *see*—but then, she could hardly look at her own back. She could feel the dry air on her naked skin, and she could only speculate at what he might have done to her Library brand. She turned to face Alberich. "Explain."

Alberich limped to a chair, sagging down into it. He'd looked bad before; now he looked worse. "I burned out the part of your brand which allows the Library to use you as a direct channel," he said. "That's why you aren't dead like your friend."

Bradamant. The other Librarian wasn't moving from where she'd collapsed. Irene touched her wrist—and knew that she would never be moving again. There was no pulse. No more disagreements, no more anger, no more collaboration, no more shared books or under-standing or attempts to save each other from their own mistakes. Fury and bitterness twisted in Irene's throat and brought tears to her eyes. *You told me in the past that a true Librarian should be prepared to sacrifice anything for the Library. Did you know this was going to happen?*

She viciously forced those thoughts away for later. There was no time for mourning or for accusations. Kai and Vale were trapped here with her and Alberich in whatever was going on, and they were *not* acceptable casualties. "What did the Library just do?" she demanded—then staggered, and Kai had to throw an arm around her waist to sup-port her.

"They locked this world out of synchronization with any others and then triggered a self-destruct. Your dragon won't be able to fly out. My door won't work." He frowned. "I thought I'd been quite careful with the fine print. Ah well—I suppose that they found a loophole somewhere."

"You don't seem very angry about it," Irene noted.

"My dear daughter, I'm furious." He raised his head to stare at her, and for all that Kai's eyes flickered red, Alberich's burned hotter and with a fiercer, more destructive hate. "I almost had everything in my grasp at last—my daughter, my revenge, my chance to stop the Library—and now it's all come crumbling down. You've managed to checkmate me, whether or not you meant to. I hope that brings you some satisfaction before your death."

Irene turned to Kai. "Do you think you can get us out of here?" She knew he'd understand that the *us* most definitely didn't include Alberich.

"I . . . don't know," Kai said reluctantly. "I'm sure I can assume my true form, but something just happened which I don't understand, and now everything feels off-kilter. Reality feels different."

This should have been a moment of triumph. Alberich was finally trapped and defeated, even if it was at the cost of Irene's own life. Yet there were too many unanswered questions. Alberich might be insane and a murderer—but could the secret at the heart of the Library be something even worse than him?

She needed information before any of them took an irrevocable step like killing Alberich—or, to be fair, inciting him to kill them—or before the world blew up.

"All right," she said slowly. "The problem is that we're trapped in this world and that Alberich says it's going to be destroyed. We have access to a dragon and to a source of chaos."

"What would that be?" Vale queried.

"Alberich himself. He's told us in the past that he's done things to himself with chaos—even if he's been vague on the details."

"I never tell anyone everything," Alberich agreed. "Much like you, my daughter."

Irene touched Kai's arm briefly in a familiar request for trust—

Let me handle this—and sat down in the chair facing Alberich, hoping that it might ease negotiations by putting them on the same level. Bradamant's corpse was an uncomfortable third at the table, sprawled as though she'd fallen asleep. Irene forced herself not to look at her fellow Librarian. "Consider this. I'm not offering to get you out of here. You've done too much, killed too many people . . ." Memories threatened to swamp her: stories of atrocities he'd committed, the Library records of other Librarians who'd died at his hands, and personal recollections of another Librarian whom he'd killed to use his skin as a disguise. "This isn't an offer of mercy."

"Then what is it?" he asked.

"Explain what's going on. Tell me why you did what you did to the other Librarian whom you once called a sister." She couldn't bring herself to say it more clearly than that. The words stuck in her throat. "If there is something wrong with the Library, then for pity's sake *tell me what it is* and maybe I can do something about it."

"If you can get out of here," he mocked her.

She met his bloodshot eyes, stared him straight in his ruined face. "There is no prison that can't be escaped. There is no puzzle that can't be solved. There is no sentence that can't be rewritten. So kindly start explaining—I don't know how much time we have left."

"You *dare* speak to me like this?"

She could have said, *I'm your daughter, I dare anything,* and tried to make a connection with him that way. But she loved her parents— her *real* parents, the ones who had raised her, who *loved* her—too much for that. Instead she said, "I'm giving you a last chance to convince me. What's more important to you? Vengeance on me, or vengeance on the Library?"

The wind whipped across the plain. It was rising now, blowing hard and hot, with the hint of something fiercer behind it.

"If I could have seen this coming . . ." His laughter rattled in his throat. "Very well. But let me start with the most important thing. I *can't* tell you the specifics because it would kill you. It's in your Library brand. Ever since I fled the Library and they found out how much I knew, they've marked new Librarians to die if I tell them the truth. I've tried talking, I've tried writing—and I've killed my brothers and sisters that way. And if I'd sent other Librarians to listen to Isra or read the original text I found, then the Library might find out where they were. That was an unacceptable risk. I wasn't going to lose my only proof."

"But you said you changed my brand," Irene said slowly.

"I changed one thing—the direct link that lets them take command of you. Other parts would take too long to adjust. I've never been able to remove all the relevant script. There are other aspects as well." He turned to Vale. "Have you ever noticed it, Peregrine Vale? The blind trust, the obedience, the absolute unwillingness to consider certain things?"

Vale tilted his head, raptorlike. He stood with his hands on his stick, silhouetted against the dusty orange sky. "I have, yes. I assumed it was due to Winters being raised in those surroundings since she was a child. Bend the growing twig, as they say."

"She should have been mine to raise," Alberich murmured. His eyes fixed on Irene again. "What a wonder you would have been."

Irene repressed a shudder at the thought. "I'm happy being who I am now," she said, her voice cold. "Why did you cause me to be born?"

This time he didn't meet her eyes. "There is a place in the heart of the Library. I thought the child of two Librarians would be able to reach it without being bound to the Library. I chose the Librarian I knew and trusted best, my closest sister, the woman I . . . loved. We'd already been having an affair. I simply took steps to ensure that she'd bear my child—and that she wouldn't be able to leave until the child was born. I failed. It was a wasted effort, as it turns out, since you took the brand anyhow . . . I meant it for the best." His words died away into the wind, and he must have known how worthless they were, how little she valued them, because his mouth twisted in self-mockery. "I did, you know. One always does."

Irene bit back her utter disgust at what he'd said and how easily he'd said it, and asked a more important question. "Who was my mother?"

"Her name was Margaret. I altered *her* Library brand, as I did yours. She may be the only person in the Library you can trust now. But I think she changed her name—no Librarian I've ever questioned knew of another Librarian called Margaret."

The name meant nothing to Irene, but she nodded, trying not to think about the implications of *no Librarian I've ever questioned*. "All right. So if you can't tell me what the problem with the Library is—what *can* you tell me? Does it have anything to do with what you once said about Fae and dragons being evolutionary dead ends?"

"That's a different matter, though it feeds into the ultimate problem. But it won't kill you if I tell you that. Do you know where dragons and Fae come from, ultimately?"

"I've seen that high-chaos worlds have an effect on normal humans," Irene said. "Either they become manipulated ciphers—or they become Fae themselves. Too far out into chaos, and the Fae themselves become uncontrollable, merging into the worlds they inhabit."

"Yes. Now take that to its logical conclusion." His eyes shifted mockingly to Kai. "Where do you think dragons originated?"

Irene had once or twice toyed with this idea, but had rejected it on the grounds of physical implausibility. Yet Alberich's manner suggested that it might actually be true. "Are you telling me that some humans in high-order worlds become dragons?"

"Rubbish," Kai said firmly.

"Of course the dragons themselves don't talk about it," Alberich said, visibly enjoying Kai's reaction. "And I have no physical proof. It's hard to get hold of a dragon to vivisect. But all the evidence suggests . . ."

"This speculation is an insult. Don't you think I have enough reasons to kill you already?" Kai had moderated his tone to softness, but there was an edge to it, and Irene could see the gleam of claws at his fingertips.

"Kai," she said. "Please. It's not important."

"Oh, it's extremely important," Alberich said. "Both Fae and dragons are forcibly evolved from humanity, healthiest when they exist at their own ends of the spectrum from order to chaos—like delicate goldfish which can only survive in water at a particular temperature." He smirked at Kai. "And then there's the question of breeding. The stronger Fae or dragons are more—speciated, I think the term is—and they can only breed with their own kind. Lesser ones can still breed with humans. I think you're proof of that yourself, Peregrine Vale, if my information is correct. And in that case, how much more can humans become?"

"A man is not responsible for the ancestral parts of his family tree," Vale said coldly. "Any more than Winters here is responsible for *you*."

Irene saw the blue tinge flickering across Kai's skin, and she rose to her feet, facing him. "Kai, control yourself."

"This is neither the time nor place to give me orders." His eyes were pure red, his attitude imperial and furious. "This man, this traitor, this *thing*, dares insult me and my family . . . and *you* have long since given up your authority over me."

"I know I have," she said softly. *Admitting weakness is a weapon in itself.* "But this is between me and . . ." The words stuck in her throat.

"And my father. I'm asking you to let me finish this with him before we all die."

"*If* we die. Do you actually believe him?"

"Oh, it's true, dragon prince," Alberich said, not bothering to rise. "Come now, take your true form and spread your wings! Try to fly out of here with Irene. Let me see you beat yourself against the sky and roar in vain as you realize just how trapped you are. I wonder— will I see the flames take you all before they take me?"

Kai snarled deep in his throat, and Irene knew why that blow had hit so accurately. Everyone was afraid of being powerless, but the more powerful you were, the worse it hurt. Kai was a dragon prince, with everything that went with that—and now he was being told that he was merely the descendant of some distant human being that had been changed by overwhelming forces of order. That there was no way he could save the human beings under his protection.

He would never have been so angry, so afraid, if he didn't on some level admit the possibility that Alberich's words were *true*.

"This man is wasting your time," he spat, raising his hand. "You don't—you *can't* understand how much of an insult this is to me and to my family."

Irene took a deep breath. "Is it any worse than the reality for me that this man is my *father*?" she asked.

Seconds ticked away. Kai lowered his hand. "Find out what else he knows," he said. "Then do us all a favor and dispose of him."

Irene nodded. She sat back down. "All right, Alberich. Can you tell me anything that's actually useful?"

A new manic focus glittered in Alberich's eyes. "I may not be able to *tell* you—but I can send you to read the story I once read. I sent the assassins to kill Isra because I thought what she told you would kill you, but you proved me wrong. Which means you should be able to read the full original story too."

"If we can get out of here," Vale commented.

"Oh, as to that, I have an idea. Give me pen and paper. And don't tell me you don't have any on you."

Irene withdrew a notebook and pen from an inner pocket, and slid them across the table. "Here you are." Part of her was nervous at handing him what were deadly weapons for any Librarian, even a traitor—but honestly, if he was going to kill her, he'd already had the chance.

He scribbled a reference number. "You know the world Alpha-3?"

Irene nodded. It was pretty much the most peaceful alternate world currently in a relatively "modern" time period. "I was there just last year with Kai—you remember, Kai, we were picking up that copy of *Monte-Cristo's Daughter* with the Rops illustrations?"

"I remember," Kai said, his tone still harsh.

"Good, he can reach it. That'll make things easier." Alberich slid the notebook back to Irene. "You want the National Library of Finland in that world, in Helsinki. The specific document is in the collection of Finnish folk poetry. You've got the reference there."

"How did you come to find it in the first place?" Vale asked. "Is it a subject which interests you?"

Alberich snorted a laugh. "Believe me, there are few things which bore me more than poetry. No, I found it because I was on a mission for the Library to locate certain texts, and I had to review the whole section to find the specific ones I needed. But when I saw that one . . ."

"That doesn't make sense," Irene said. "Why should the Library deliberately point you at it, if it's a secret so important that they'll kill anyone who knows it?" *If*, she mentally noted to herself. She still had no proof of Alberich's words.

"That is something I've been wondering for a very long time now." Alberich leaned toward her. There was a whiff of carrion and cinders in the air around him. "I have a theory, but I'm not sure I can share it.

with you any more than I could the Library's founding. But if it's true, then you have a friend on your side you don't even know about." He shrugged. "Perhaps you'll find the answer."

"But for that we need to leave here." It all seemed too easy: coming to an agreement with her worst nightmare, and having him freely volunteer information. But Bradamant was seated at the table with them, a reminder that one person had already paid with their life for this meeting.

"You still don't trust me," Alberich remarked, apparently reading her thoughts. "That's good. I'd hate to think that my daughter believed what she was told simply because I was the one telling it to her."

"I don't think Irene likes you referring to her as your daughter," Kai growled. "I don't believe I like it either."

"I expect to be dead within ten minutes," Alberich answered. "That allows me some liberty, don't you think?"

"Did you allow it to any of the Librarians you killed?" Irene asked quietly.

"Numbers have been exaggerated. I'm not quite the mass murderer you take me for. If you can accept the Library's lied to you, then why not about this?"

"Because the first time we met, you'd killed a Librarian and used his skin to disguise yourself as him." That moment of horrified realization was scarred into her memory. "Answer me honestly—why so many? Why *kill* us? Your brothers and sisters, you said earlier. *Why?*"

Silence hung in the air between them. Finally Alberich said, "At first I wanted to explain—to convince them of the truth. It killed them. So I tried to find other ways to get through to them. Restraining them, modifying their Library brands . . . nothing worked. And they were constantly coming after *me*, calling me a traitor, trying to kill me on sight. There comes a point when you attack rather than try to negotiate. Perhaps it was madness, but it felt like sanity. I decided that the simplest thing to do was to bring down the Library first and explain later."

"You have a definition of 'simplest' which I don't share," Irene said. Nothing had changed between them. He was still a monster. An explanation was not a justification.

Alberich shrugged. "Perhaps it was foolish of me to think you'd understand. Hundreds of years of life make a difference in perspective. Your dragon prince will come to realize this. My condolences, by the way. Nothing lasts."

Irene turned to look up at Kai. "Is that insulting, or just patronizing?"

"Patronizing," Kai said. "I don't feel any need to discuss my private feelings further in his presence."

Alberich snorted. "Let's get down to price. I can get you out of here—but I want your promise to destroy the Library in return."

Irene had suspected that was coming, so instead of acting surprised, she simply sat back and folded her arms. "No."

"No?"

"Just how easily persuaded do you think I *am*?"

"I just told you that we're trapped, daughter. I can understand you being prepared to sacrifice yourself to kill me, but are you really willing to let these two die?" His gesture took in Vale and Kai. "I'd admire you if I thought you were ready to sacrifice your two closest friends in order to win, but quite honestly I don't think you have it in you to do it."

"We knew the risks, Winters," Vale said coolly. "You gave us every opportunity to refuse. It has been an honor to work with you."

Kai tilted his head. "This isn't the first time you've tried to put pressure on Irene by threatening her friends," he said to Alberich. "You must feel bitter that while you may have sired her, she'll never feel the slightest bit of concern or pity for *you*."

Teeth showed in the ruin of Alberich's mouth. "You don't believe me?"

"If I believed everything you tell me, I'd have been dead a long time ago," Irene answered.

"We'll see how you feel in five minutes when this world begins to break to pieces. You might just have enough time to make it out—if you're lucky."

The immovable object meets the unstoppable force, Irene thought. *He has nothing to lose now—but nor have I.*

"There is perhaps another solution," she said. "Would you accept, as a starting proposition, that I honestly believe in the ideals of the Library and the safety of my fellow Librarians? My brothers and sisters?" She borrowed Alberich's own words.

Alberich considered. "I admit you're probably sincere about that."

"Somewhat lukewarm, but I'll take that as agreement. All right. Do you think that if I knew this truth that you found, then I'd take action?"

"I know what you're going to say," Alberich hissed. "I don't want any half measures. I want the Library destroyed."

"And I want it *saved*. I'll save it from itself if I have to." She locked eyes with him. "I'll find out what the truth is and I'll share it with other Librarians. They may not be able to hear the truth from you, but they can hear it from me. You want a promise? I'll swear to *that*. I didn't become a Librarian in order to kill people or destroy worlds. I became a Librarian to save books, to save stories, and to save the worlds that create them. Isn't that what you wanted when *you* began? Either help me, Alberich, or get out of the way and let me do my job."

The wind was still rising. It tore at their clothes—the rags of her coat and dress, Alberich's robe. It was hot and dry against her face and hands, with the suggestion of a greater heat behind it, just over the horizon.

"It's probably a good thing that I'm not going to survive this," Alberich said at last. "I thought I wanted a son—but now I see you in the fullness of your strength, I would have been satisfied with nothing less than you. You burn, my daughter, with all the fire that I could ever have asked for. I wouldn't tolerate you calling other people your parents, or being distracted by anything that might lessen you. And if one of us killed the other, it would be a rather tragic ending, wouldn't it?"

"It's not exactly one of those stories which has a happy beginning in the first place," Irene said.

"No." He levered himself to his feet, having to brace himself against the table to do so. "Help me over to the door," he ordered.

Irene hesitated, not wanting to touch his decaying flesh. It was Vale who moved, walking over and letting Alberich lean on his arm as he staggered over to where the painted door stood alone in its frame.

Alberich swallowed down a cough, placing one hand against the door. "Listen carefully, Irene—and you two others. In the past I've bound a great deal of chaotic power into this body; it's what's keeping me alive at the moment. There's also a fair amount of it worked into this door. I'm going to unbind it. It'll kill me, but the force will destabilize the world around us, which should break the transdimensional lock holding it in place and stopping the dragon from leaving. If you can't seize the opportunity, then that's your own fault."

It would have been hypocritical to express any sort of grief about his death, and all of them knew it. Irene simply said, "How long will we have?"

"Seconds, once it starts. If you're lucky. It's not as if I've experimented with this sort of thing very often."

"I find it unwholesome that you've experimented with it at all," Vale said, stepping back to join the others.

"One of the few things which I regret is that I won't see what my daughter will be experimenting with in a few centuries' time." Alberich glanced at Bradamant and her empty briefcase. "It's a pity she didn't survive. You could have used her assistance. Once the Library finds out you're still alive and what you know, well . . ."

"It's a pity she didn't survive for more reasons than that," Irene said quietly. She'd have to come to terms with Bradamant's death later—there was no time for it now. As far as she knew, Bradamant had no friends outside the Library, and she'd long since left her family behind. Other Librarians would be the only people who'd remember her.

Without looking at her, Alberich said, "Oddly enough, there's a part of me that would appreciate your forgiveness."

"I'm not going to lie to you," Irene said. "There's very little chance that I'm going to give it."

His shoulders moved in a sigh. "Understanding, then?"

"For that I need the truth."

"It's a good thing I don't believe in the existence of the soul or life after death, isn't it?" He sniffed the rising wind. "Take your true form, dragon. We're out of time."

Light shimmered and flexed around Kai, casting their shadows long and black against the sandy ground. When it cleared, he was in his draconic form, scaled in sapphires and long enough to coil around the table and the door. He lowered one vividly blue wing, allowing Irene and Vale access to his back, and they scrambled on hastily. Irene found her usual space just behind his shoulders, with Vale behind her.

Alberich closed his eyes and lowered his head—and the door and frame came apart. It was like a perverse diagram for furniture assembly, separating in all directions at once, with the paintings rippling off the wood into three dimensions, spreading out in orbiting circles. At the center of it all was a writing *hole* barely a foot across, an opening into somewhere else that made the hair rise on Irene's neck. It was a *wrongness* given physical form, something which shouldn't exist in the same universe as human beings. It was chaos manifest.

Alberich raised both hands to touch it, bringing it closer to cradle against his breastbone like a baby.

The concussion tore the world apart. Kai threw himself into the air, battling for height against the sudden outward rush of air, struggling against the tidal waves of force. Irene and Vale were plastered against his back, clinging on for dear life. Below them the remains of door and man had become a rising sphere of black light, a dark sun which melted reality wherever it touched.

"Kai, get us out of here!" Irene shouted, hoping he could hear her.

She felt his chest tense underneath her, then he roared, and the thunder of his voice cut through the wind and storm, louder than the forces of nature and chaos alike. Shaken by Alberich's detonation of his power, trembling on its foundations, reality answered. A momentary gap flickered in the sky, leading out of there and into the space between worlds.

And they were through it, and gone.

CHAPTER 19

Relief broke over Irene like a wave as they entered the space between worlds. They were out of there, they were free, Alberich was dead, and they were all alive . . .

. . . except Bradamant, her guilt prodded her.

She rubbed viciously at her eyes and stared at the drifting shades of blue around them—currents and eddies of color that maybe only an artist could fully describe. It went on forever in all directions—there was no perceptible ground beneath or horizon in the distance, no upper or lower limit. Dragons were the only beings who could find their bearings in such a place.

The fact that Alberich was dead, genuinely, definitely dead, was a huge weight off her shoulders—but he'd left too many questions behind him. She forced herself to shelve thoughts of Alberich and Bradamant and their deaths, leaving questions of grief and guilt for later, and focused on their current danger.

"The Library will assume we're all dead," she said, her voice breaking the silence of their flight through the endless blue. "And before we go any further, I want to reassure you both that I'm *not* automatically believing everything Alberich told us." In fact, the further away she was from him, the easier it was to find reasons why he'd been lying. "It's quite possible that the Library was simply prepared to sacrifice us in order to kill him. That doesn't necessarily mean that Alberich was right. It may just be that the Library is . . ."

"Cold-blooded, ruthless, and willing to sacrifice its best agent and innocent victims in order to dispose of its worst enemy," Vale filled in as Irene looked for words. "I can hardly approve of such behavior—but governments have done worse."

Irene nodded. "While I don't *like* being the pawn in a scheme like this, I could theoretically accept it for myself. I'm much less happy that you two might have been collateral damage."

"The Library would know that we wouldn't let you go alone," Kai rumbled. "Or rather, whoever it is that makes the decisions in the Library . . ."

"Yes. That's the big question, isn't it? I'd always assumed it was the older Librarians. As you said, Vale, I never really thought about it . . . though that seems to have changed." Just how much damage had Alberich done to her brand—and what other effects might it have? *And what had he done to his own brand?* she wondered. Could that have explained some of his insanity? "If there's someone behind them, then I very much want to know who it is."

"I realize you're eager to read this document which Alberich sent us to find," Vale said. "I trust you're aware that it could be a forgery which he left in order to misdirect Librarians—or simply a story."

"I acknowledge all those points," Irene agreed, "but we won't know until we get there and read it."

"Tell me something of this world, then. You two clearly know it. Is it likely to be dangerous?"

Kai laughed, the sound echoing in his chest. "Quite the opposite.

It's one of the most peaceful places I know. It hasn't had wars for the last couple of centuries. Young Librarians often get sent there for training missions."

"Kai's right. I think our own trip there was meant as a vacation for us."

"I don't recall you taking any long absences from my London," Vale noted.

"Well . . ." Irene shrugged. "Frankly, it's also rather boring . . . though they do make excellent cuckoo clocks. We ended up not staying long. We do both have bank accounts there, though, which we can use to finance local travel."

"How do you want to handle this?" Kai asked. "The Library entrance to that world was in Madrid, but we picked the book up in Paris. I remember both those locations well enough to bring us through there."

Irene summoned up a mental map of Europe. "Better make it Paris," she said. "You can take human form there, and we'll catch a plane to Helsinki."

"To avoid attention?" Vale asked.

"Yes. Precisely. The Library may think we're dead, and it may know nothing about the document in that world—but I'd rather not risk any reports of blue dragons getting back to a Librarian and having them ask questions."

"Then you *do* think there's something wrong," Kai said.

Irene mentally turned over answers in all the shades of *yes*, and finally said, "I think the time for blind trust is long over. Now I need answers."

Peace, placidity, and legality proved to have the same effect on Vale as they did on Irene and Kai. By the time they reached Helsinki, he was tapping his fingers and riffling through the newspapers in growing desperation, trying to find something of interest and utterly failing. Fortunately cocaine wasn't an option.

Irene led the way up the marble steps. The outside of the building was all white marble, main hall, dome, and two wings—a temple of sorts to the preservation of knowledge. Under normal circumstances it would have reassured her and made her feel as though she'd come home. Now, instead, she felt as if she was walking into enemy territory and that another Librarian might appear at any moment—as a threat rather than an ally.

Kai and Vale followed her as she made her way to the reception desk. "Excuse me," she said, her Finnish rusty after years of disuse but coming back to her. "I need to look at this document." She showed the reference number Alberich had given her.

"Ah," the woman behind the desk said, thoughtfully. "Let me check." She turned to her microfiche reader and hummed to herself as she found the reference. "All right. That's in the Lonnrot Collection. We have a lot of people asking for those. That first bit there, see? That's the section number." She indicated the first part of the scribbled number with her pen. "That second bit is the volume in question, and the third bit is the poem. If you go to the hall on the right, and, hmm, I think it's the second floor, and check the map there for the location, that should do it. Will you be needing any further help?"

"I don't think so, and thank you very much," Irene said.

"Fascinating," Vale murmured as they followed the directions.

"I know—it all seems so strange," Kai agreed. "No guards, no locks and keys, not having to go through dozens of formalities to get our hands on the books . . ."

"True, but I was thinking more about coincidence. I expect you can read Finnish as well as speak it, Winters? Thus sparing us the necessity for a translator?"

Irene nodded. "I'm a bit out of practice, but I should be able to work through it. There must be dictionaries here too."

"Is Finnish a common language of study among Librarians?"

Irene waved a hand in a *so-so* gesture. "If you took a hundred Librarians at random, probably somewhere between one and ten would be moderately fluent in it. It's not as common as Hindi or Mandarin or English or Russian or Arabic, but it's reasonably frequent—more so than Old Sanskrit or Ancient Egyptian hieroglyphics."

They were talking quietly so as not to disturb other scholars. The hall they'd just entered was well lit and graceful; the floor was tiled with marble in shades of ivory and beige, and white-painted columns ran the length of the room, supporting long balconies filled with book-stuffed shelves. Desks and chairs stood in carefully precise files down the center of the room, and painted frescoes filled the roof high above.

"My point, Winters, is the question of precisely why *you* happen to know the language in which this crucial document is written."

That made Irene pause just as she was setting her foot on the stairs. "Oh," she said. She thought it over. "Hmm."

"Random chance?" Kai suggested. "Odds of one in a hundred are unlikely, but not impossible. Or maybe, much as I hate to say it, we're suffering from narrative influence here. Irene just *happens* to know the language in which this vital document is written."

"This world isn't particularly chaotic, though. It's . . . fairly neutral. Pretty much midway between order and chaos." Irene forced herself to move again, ascending the stairs. "The other answer is more worrying."

"And what would that be?" Vale asked.

"When we're studying as journeymen, before we're full Librarians, we often have courses of study suggested by our seniors. Particular languages, cultures, so on. That was why I studied Finnish. It wasn't an area I was particularly interested in; I preferred the Sino-Tibetan language family, with a spread of other common languages such as Russian and Arabic, and not so much the Uralic . . ." She saw the look of incomprehension on Vale's face. "I hadn't intended to study Finnish—but I was sent a suggestion to cover the language and I became reasonably fluent. The Library likes to encourage a wide upkeep of languages. People need to be able to read what we've collected. You wouldn't believe the size of our dictionary section."

"That much is only logical. What worries you about this?"

Irene was conscious of a crawling sense of unease—the feeling of having been manipulated, of being a pawn on someone else's chessboard, a mouse crawling through a maze with some invisible observer watching from on high. "Normally the Librarian who assigns you a language or study course puts their name to it and explains why. Even if the explanation only consists of 'a vain and probably futile attempt to improve your mind.' But . . . I never found who assigned me Finnish. I assumed it had somehow got lost in the paperwork, or whoever had assigned it had forgotten about it. And now, as you have noted, here we are—with a document in Finnish that has to be read, and a Librarian who knows Finnish to read it."

"In a location where Alberich was originally sent by the Library, and just *happened* to find the document in the first place," Kai said. Irene turned to see him frowning. "Just how many players are there in this game?"

"And how long has it been going on for?" Irene suppressed a shiver.

"Focus, Winters," Vale said, not unkindly. "We have a limited amount of time until we have to reveal ourselves publicly and explain what happened—assuming that is what you want to do. If not, then your Library *will* have reason to think you've turned traitor. We should at least read this document first."

"Good point," Irene said, trying not to flush with embarrassment.

She shouldn't need to be reminded of priorities. She must still be more shaken from the previous day's events than she'd thought. "All right, this is the second floor, here's the map . . ." She checked her note against it, then headed down the row of shelves. The books were clearly all part of the same edition: large, thick, bound in red leather. "Here's the one we want." She wrestled it off the shelf and looked around for a convenient desk. "Ah, thank you, Kai."

"Just make sure you translate it out loud so we can hear it too, rather than making those *Mmm* and *Really!* noises you're so fond of," Kai said, pulling out the chair so she could sit down.

Irene's hands hesitated on the book's cover. She was afraid, dreadfully afraid, that opening it and reading might be an irreversible step in the wrong direction. Even if she didn't go mad like Alberich, it would still be an action she could never take back. It would be reckless. It would be incautious. It would be *foolish* . . .

Irene forced herself to look her crawling fears and uncertainty squarely in the face. The very thought of telling Kai and Vale, *Sorry, I've changed my mind, we're leaving this behind and forgetting all about our research*, made her suppress a snort of laughter. *So much for existential angst.*

She opened the book and flipped through it, briefly pausing at the introduction. "The Lonnrot Collection seems to be a collection of Finnish folk songs and poetry compiled by Elias Lonnrot," she informed Kai and Vale, not looking up. "He based a larger work of epic poetry on his material—the Kalevala. These are all the separate entries for poems and songs that he collected from Finland and Karelia."

"How old are they?" Vale asked curiously.

"Some of them may go back to the Iron Age. Thousands of years old. Men die and stones crumble, but the song passes from singer to singer—and I'm not trying to be overblown, I'm just quoting from the introduction."

Irene turned through the pages to the specified song. "All right. Hmm. This is poetry, but I'm not going to even *try* to translate it into English poetry or get it to scan. It's part of—hmm." She was finding the language easier now, but there was a difference between casual chitchat with the desk clerk and accurate translation of an old poem. "Okay. Väinämöinen—he's the protagonist, a powerful singer and wizard and hero—has decided to find a missing spell by questioning Antero Vipunen, an ancient monster, but he's been swallowed by the monster, so he's set up a forge inside the monster and is threatening to live there and eat the monster's internal organs for food. So Antero Vipunen has to sing him all the spells he knows and all the history he knows to get him to leave. You've probably heard similar stories elsewhere."

She ran her finger down the page. "Here's where I think it becomes interesting. There's a big interpolation marked in the whole 'sang him the Origins in depth and their spells in order' section here, noted as being different from other versions. I think this is what we're after . . ."

From above, high on the roof, there was a faint thump. A few grains of dust spun down from the ceiling. Irene broke off mid-sentence; she and the two men exchanged looks.

"It's probably nothing," Kai said. "But . . ."

"I will investigate," Vale cut in. "The primary danger here is if someone stops Winters from translating the evidence. This could be a diversion to lure us away from her."

Irene looked back down at the print in front of her as Vale strode away. "Then he sang the hidden Origins," she translated, "blah blah secret nobody knows about them."

"Blah blah?"

"I'm eliding the extra adjectives. Ah, this is more like it. 'There flew a winged serpent out of the waters, stretching from where the sun rose to where it descended; his kin had suffered from sea and tempest, fleeing the waves that had claimed their kindred.'"

Kai wasn't focusing on her; he was keeping an eye on the room in general, watching for signs of attack or ambush. Yet she could sense the sudden deepening of his interest at this description of a dragon who might be his grandfather.

"'There walked a singer across the lands, his voice sweet, a caroller, a chirper, a cuckoo-caller. He came before the storm that followed him, black clouds cloaking the mass of the winds, his family strewn like leaves in autumn.'"

"The Storyteller, perhaps," Kai murmured. "But I thought you were leaving out the extra adjectives."

"If I'm translating out loud word for word, it's easier just to read it as it is." Irene wished she had some coffee—or anything that would sharpen her memory and help her remember her Finnish better. "'They met at the house of an old woman'—that's interesting, usually when the Kalevala refers to the Old Woman of the North it means a particular character, Louhi, who's frequently an antagonist except when she isn't, but here it seems to be a specific old woman who isn't her. 'She had grown old in the seeking of songs and spent her years in the learning of secrets; the cuckoo sang, a second, a third, as the three of them met in her well-built house.'"

"A lot of cuckoos."

Irene ignored him rather than go into an explanation of the poetic style. "About twenty lines of the—dragon and Fae, I'm assuming—explaining why they hate each other and can't possibly work together. Then the old woman gives them beer—ten more lines about the beer—and speaks. 'Men will be angry when in the past they have fought battles and their kin have died; but against a storm even enemies will share a roof and hearth together. If you swear together to keep the peace, maybe the winds can be stopped and the storm be broken. Build a home at the world's own heart where all songs shall be kept and all histories remembered so that, like the knots in a fisherman's net, the foundations shall be stable and the walls solid.' It's a lot more poetic than that," she added.

"There wasn't a human brokering the peace deal in Aunt Isra's version," Kai said.

"No, nor in the Egyptian story." Irene turned the page. "'A deal was sworn; a peace was made; a vow was created; a binding was signed. All three set their names together to the pact to keep it solid for all of their children. They called new singers to find new songs; they marked their backs with their family's sigil.'" A shiver ran down her back as she thought about her own Library brand. "'The songs were bricks to build a wall, ropes to tie the net, the roofbeams of the house, the foundation stones on which it stood.'"

She looked up at Kai. "If I remember my culture correctly, there's not that much difference at this point between a song and a recited story in poetic form. Songs in this context *are* stories."

"But what is there in this to drive Alberich mad?"

"Another page." Irene turned it. "'The winged serpent and the singer grew old together, under the same roofbeams and in the same dwelling. They said to each other, "Our children have forgotten us; they left us to die while they lived happy lives.'" Their songs grew harsh and vipers drank their beer. The old woman said, "Why are you wasting time? You built the house; you can destroy it. Our singers serve us and not your children." She sang like a cuckoo but her words were poison. She went from one to the other and whispered in their ears. "Half of the world shall belong to the singer and the other half to the winged serpent. Our servants shall carry word to their children. If they don't obey, you will sing up a tempest, let the winds loose on their homes and their lands, call down the lightning from the heavens ... "'"

Irene broke off. "Another twenty lines of how they'd destroy things." She skimmed down. "'Yet here at the center of their dwelling the rock on which they had marked their charter, the child of their work, wept bitter tears at this anger and hatred. It wept tears of water at the loss of friendship; it wept tears of blood at the betrayal of kin; it wept tears of rust for the servants who were bound to obey. And still that rock stands beneath the earth deep at the heart of their stronghold; for this is the origin of the singers who carry the mark upon their shoulders. Their child holds the worlds steady and weeps for their errors.'"

"That's a significant divergence from the others."

"They've all been diverging." Irene stared balefully at the printed paper as though she could hypnotize it into making sense. "The Egyptian version just has the dragon king saying that he's going to make an alliance with his worst enemies to restore the balance. Aunt Isra's version has the Storyteller approaching the dragon king and suggesting that they bind their power together and make the worlds stable, and then both rule over them—and the king agreeing. And this one suggests that it started off as a positive thing and turned sour and that the human who was involved made it worse—"

"Irene," Kai said, the word a warning.

She looked up. At the far end of the balcony stood Shan Yuan, an unconscious Vale draped over his shoulder. He shrugged the man off, letting him fall to the floor, and began to pace toward Irene and Kai.

His footprints showed charred black on the wooden floor as he advanced, and fury blazed in his eyes.

CHAPTER 20

"hy so silent?" Shan Yuan said. Anger seethed in his every word. "Don't you have some excuse for me? Some convenient explanation of why you're here, alive and well, playing your own games while the rest of the world deals with matters of importance?"

Kai moved to stand between Shan Yuan and Irene. "Elder brother, I am not sure why you are angry with us at this precise moment—"

"I'm angry with you because you're *alive*," Shan Yuan snarled. "Don't give me that insolent doe-eyed look of incomprehension. You were announced as *dead*. Both of you. Him, too." He spurned Vale with one foot. "I was given the news so that I could announce it to our lord father. Do you have the *first* idea how he would have reacted? How he would have grieved?" He was practically spitting his words, and Irene could feel the rising temperature. "How dare you sit here and toy with your books rather than attend to your duty?"

"My duty to die?" Kai enquired flatly. "How kind of you to make your priorities clear."

"Your duty was to let the rest of us know that you were alive. To spare us concern. To stop us from grieving over having lost a brother, a son..." Shan Yuan was practically grinding his teeth. "The fact that you can misunderstand that shows just how little you understand or care. The worthless son of a worthless mother!"

People from the ground level below and the circling balconies were looking toward them, attention drawn by the upsurge in noise. A few reproachful hushes whispered in their direction.

Kai went very still. Flickers of scale patterns ran across his skin, and Irene saw his nails lengthen into claws. "You have insulted me before, elder brother, and I have accepted that, but I warn you not to insult my mother."

"And what will you do to stop me speaking the truth? We both know I can outmatch you in a fight. What power do you have here, far from rivers or the sea? One more word of discourtesy, one more attempt to defend yourself, and I will burn this place down around your ears before I drag you home for proper discipline. I don't think *that* will please your paramour."

"You won't," Irene said, rising to her feet. She tucked the book under one arm.

Shan Yuan's glance at her was full of murder. "I advise you not to cross me any further. I'll leave you to your own Library for judgment."

Irene throttled back her anger at Shan Yuan's insults to Kai. This was dangerous for all their plans, if Shan Yuan carried through with his threats. "You were misinformed," she said. "We're alive. Alberich is dead. My sister Bradamant died too, and I'll grieve for her later—but the mission was a success. I'm sorry that you had this worry, but—"

"You couldn't possibly understand," Shan Yuan said. He was nearly on them by now. "You, the unrecognized brat of a traitor? Taken in and adopted out of charity? Without brothers or sisters? No wonder *you* survived when your colleague died. Assuming that you're telling the truth in the first place . . ."

Fury blazed in her like a birthing star. "I'll say it in the Language if you like, so that you know I'm not lying," she snapped, "but you may not care for what else I'll say."

"I do believe you challenged me once before." Interlacing scales patterned his skin now, just as they did Kai's, and his eyes were dragon-red with fury. "Perhaps we should finish that."

"No!" Kai squared his shoulders. "Elder brother, this is folly."

"On the contrary," Shan Yuan said, and Irene realized that his anger was past any attempt at curbing or control, "it's something I should have done long ago. Kai, this is for your own good. You'll thank me later."

"There is one thing that I noticed—as a Librarian—which you probably didn't when you came in," Irene said conversationally.

"And what would that be?"

"This library's fire-control system. I'd like to think that normally, your highness, if you weren't quite so driven by your current temper, you wouldn't be threatening to burn books. But if you do, then I promise you you'll be getting directly acquainted with liquid nitrogen." She wasn't exactly sure *how* she'd manage it, but she was quite willing to improvise.

That made him hesitate. "You wouldn't dare."

"I would dare. But I'd rather de-escalate." Shan Yuan was a powerful dragon and a dangerous opponent. Getting into a fight would only slow them down, and that was assuming they were lucky. "Your highness, please give me a minute to explain. If I've delayed Kai's return to assure his family that he was well and safe, then I apologize."

For a moment he was still, then he moved in a blur of speed, his hand going for her throat. Kai caught his wrist, and the two of them stood poised, straining against each other, flickers of blue and red respectively tracing their way across their skins like veins in marble.

"Are you disobeying me?" The word *disobeying* had a particular charge as Shan Yuan spoke it—more than his previous references to insolence or failure in duty.

"Your action would shame you—and our father. I have an obligation to protect you from yourself." Kai had finally settled some private argument with himself; he was calm now, almost as though he was being patient with a child. "I won't let you hurt her."

The guttural noise that came from Shan Yuan—insulted by his *younger* brother—was a dragon's roar of fury filtered through human lips. He pivoted to draw Kai out of line, and struck with his free hand in a straight punch at Kai's chest, hard enough to break ribs if it had connected. Kai had to release his grip on Shan Yuan's wrist and draw back to avoid it, his footwork smooth and precise.

"You know what to do, Irene," Kai said without looking at her, and then dived forward to catch Shan Yuan in a grasp around the waist. The two of them crashed into the balcony rail, and it broke; they fell together, out into the room.

Irene bit back a scream and ran toward the rail, every movement seeming to be in slow motion. A fall could kill a dragon just as much as it could a human, and even though her mouth was opening and she was searching for words, she'd never be able to speak them before the two princes hit the floor . . .

Light flashed around the two falling figures—and then two dragons filled the center of the room, twined around each other in a writhing knot of ruby and sapphire, their lashing tails and wings knocking tables and desks across the floor. Visitors and librarians alike screamed and fled.

Irene could guess what Kai had *wanted* her to do: take the information they'd gained and use the fact they were in a library to force a connection to *the* Library, dragging Vale along for the ride. He trusted her to leave *him* here to be mauled and punished by his brother—noticeably larger than Kai now that they were in their true forms, with all the weight of muscle and brotherly authority to use against him. She was supposed to accept his self-sacrifice and do what must be done.

Well, sod that.

She couldn't turn the fire extinguishers on Shan Yuan, or throw furniture at him—there was too much chance of hitting Kai as well. She needed a more precise alternative. Taking a deep breath, she shouted at the top of her voice to make sure it carried over the crashing and screams: **"Floor, hold Shan Yuan!"**

The lovely marble floor, already chipped and scarred by the impact of the two dragons, rippled beneath them as Shan Yuan sank into it. His struggles increased, goaded to berserk ferocity, and Irene was absolutely sure that if he'd had the leisure to say anything at that point he'd have accused her of cheating.

But abruptly there were other presences in the library. Shadows rose from the ground, growing with every second, shrouding the white walls and painted ceiling in a swelling darkness. A fierce pressure ground down on Irene, forcing her to her knees, and she felt her ears pop and her head ache as though she were deep underwater. Presences closed in on her, invisible and unheard, but still perceptible; it was as though sharks were closing in on her, sniffing for the scent of her blood.

Fingers trailed through her hair, becoming more solid by the second as they sought for a grip, and she felt the ghost of an edge solidifying against her throat. She threw herself to the side, rolling to distance herself from the tentative grasp.

The building was creaking now, shuddering and trembling; flakes of dust and paint from the frescoes polluted the air. Shelves strained and groaned under their weight of books and gave way, letting their volumes topple to the ground in a thunder of abused literature.

Irene crawled sideways along the floor, groping for Vale's body. She couldn't see Kai or Shan Yuan in the darkness, though she could still hear them struggling. Terror made the jump before logic could: this was the result of her using the Language inside a library. Something or someone was looking for her and had managed to find her— and that something or someone wanted her dead.

She needed to get out of this library *now*. Even more importantly, she needed to get off the second floor before it gave way. Kai might be able to cope with a two-story fall; Irene would be lucky to stagger away without breaking something or killing herself.

Her hand hit a familiar shoulder, and she squeezed it. To her great relief, Vale made a muffled noise of semi-awareness. She shook him hard. "Come on, wake up—we need to get out of here before this place comes down on top of us."

"What have you done this time, Winters?" he mumbled.

"I'm far from the only person responsible. Can you walk?"

And then the roof cracked open with a great rending crash which drowned out even the noise of the fighting dragons. Light filtered in, dim and pale through the pulsing darkness which filled the library like water, but still *light*.

"Ah. I'm *not* blind after all." Vale shook his head and grunted in pain.

Irene gave up on explanations, put her shoulder under his, and helped him to his feet. Clearly Shan Yuan hadn't pulled any punches; Vale might be conscious, but he was only barely ambulatory. Together they staggered toward the stairwell.

Darkness filled the curve of the stairs and brooded between the walls, unpierced by the daylight slanting down from above. Darkness had a form, and it was coming toward them: a black-and-white montage of half-seen images, a jolting sleepwalker's dream of an old woman with flowing hair like a gray banner and a knife in her hand.

If she's solid enough to hurt me, she's solid enough to be hit . . . Irene abandoned Vale to sway, and grabbed one of the heavier books which had fallen to the ground, slinging it straight at the oncoming shadow. It flickered as the book passed through it, fading to half-visible before beginning to recoalesce.

Without pausing for even the briefest and most desperate of prayers, Irene grabbed Vale again and charged through the image. She felt those half-solid fingers clutch at her throat, a flicker of cold air against her skin as the knife sliced through her coat and only just missed her flesh, but then they were through it and stumbling down the stairs. The steps trembled under their feet as if they were in an earthquake, forcing them to grab at the walls for support.

Then they came out onto the ground level, and it was even worse.

A greater shadow had formed above both Kai and Shan Yuan—a dragon, like them, but so huge he filled the hall and rose to shatter the roof, his coils collapsing the balconies when they brushed against them. The two younger dragons weren't fighting each other any more; they were desperately trying to get out from underneath this dark paragon of their kind who crushed them beneath his weight.

The light pierced the shadows, but it wasn't enough. There had to be some way to get out of here, to get *everyone* out, to break the connection between here and whatever was coming through as darkness and nightmares . . .

Memory stirred, and Irene knew what to do.

"Be ready to drag me out of here," she told Vale, and looked around for a suitable implement. There—a fragment of broken stone tile from the flooring, sharp-edged enough for what she wanted. She darted forward to pick it up, then retreated to one of the plaster-coated pillars. Another memory spurred her to shrug off her jacket and wind it round her hands to protect them.

"Be quick, Winters," Vale warned her. Irene glanced behind her and saw the shadow of the old woman solidifying again. Her face was clearer now, in sharper definition; Irene could fully make out her expression and the glare in her eyes. It wasn't hatred, or bitterness; it was something that Irene recognized from her own mirror, a determination that could cut through mountains.

With an effort she turned back to her task, ignoring shadows and catastrophe alike. Her Library brand throbbed with her heartbeat. She set her jaw and carved into the pillar in the Language, using the very specific characters which referred to the Library in particular, rather than all libraries in the generic: **THIS IS NOT THE LIBRARY.**

The concussion blew her backward and ripped the makeshift tool from her hands, shredding her jacket. She lay there on her back with her head spinning, staring at the great shadowy dragon, watching it billow and writhe like storm clouds. Even if the woman-shadow had put the knife to her throat again, she couldn't have moved. Strength unwound from her like a cord attached to her breastbone, with every heartbeat taking more and more effort, every breath more difficult to draw. The Language and the Library were fighting against themselves—what else could one call it when she tried to separate this library from *the* Library and use the Library's own tools to do it?—and all the strength she had was going into making it happen, banishing this manifestation.

Slowly, too slowly, the shadows dissolved, and silence fell. She could hear tortured shelves creaking, people gasping, someone crying. She could hear the buzzing in her own head.

Louder than it all, she could hear her own voice in her head: *They came because you used the Language inside a library. They're after you. They're after all of you now. They know you know.*

"Winters." Vale was kneeling next to her. He offered her a handkerchief. "Your nose is bleeding."

In her dazed state, it somehow seemed entirely appropriate that her nose should be bleeding. If he'd told her that her head was dissolving into the floor, she'd have agreed with that too. She let him help her up to a sitting position and held his spotless white handkerchief against her face, the old tag about putting a cold iron key down someone's back to stop nosebleeds dancing uselessly in her mind.

Then reality began to pierce through the comforting clouds of shock. "What are Kai and Shan Yuan doing?" she asked.

Vale looked across. "Complaining," he diagnosed.

"Right." Her head was still spinning, but she needed to say a few words before the two dragons started fighting again. "Please help me up."

Vale sighed in exasperation, but assisted Irene to her feet. With his help, she made her way toward the two dragon princes, who had both returned to their human form. Their attention was entirely on each other, and they didn't even notice her and Vale approaching. Both of them looked significantly shaken. Kai was white to the lips, and Shan Yuan's hands were trembling.

"Excuse me," Irene said, jumping into a temporary gap in their argument. They turned to face her, and she pointed a finger at Shan Yuan. "Your highness, I have something very important to say to you and I think you'll want to hear it, but please allow me a moment to shout at your brother first."

As Shan Yuan opened and shut his mouth, doing a better impersonation of a frog than a dragon, she turned to Kai. She ached to fuss over his bruises and cuts, to ask him to sit down and rest—but there was something she had to make him understand first. "Listen to me very carefully," she said. "I would not ask you to sacrifice yourself for me. I don't want you to sacrifice yourself for me. God knows I love you, and—"

"You love me?" he said, stunned, his face suddenly a hundred times more handsome, his eyes like dark sapphires. That was a word they didn't allow themselves. There were too many forces that could come between them and separate them. Understanding it had always been good enough. Why did one need to say words out loud when actions spoke louder?

Except, perhaps, sometimes one had to say them to make one's point.

"I love you," Irene said. She managed to stand free of Vale, and put one hand on Kai's chest. "That means I value your life. Do you have any idea how I'd spend the rest of my life if you sacrificed yourself and I had to live with that? Your brother had the right idea about that, at least. Your father would feel *pain* if he lost you. Shan Yuan himself came all the way here to have a screaming fit at you because he thought you'd got yourself killed, and that *hurt* him." She ignored the ominous rumble from Shan Yuan's direction. "If you ever go and heroically self-sacrifice yourself again and expect me to run off and leave you . . ."

His hands moved to her shoulders. "And how do you think *I* feel, every time you put yourself at risk for the Library? You're human. You're a hundred times more fragile than I am. You recklessly throw yourself into danger and you won't let me stand in the way. Don't you realize how much it hurts me when you do this? How am I supposed to think of a life without you?"

Irene felt something twist deep inside her as she confronted a truth that they'd been avoiding for years. "It's going to happen, Kai. You're a dragon. I'm a Librarian. Either I live outside the Library to spend time with you, and I age and die, or I stay inside the Library and time doesn't pass for me, but then I don't have *you*."

"I could . . ." he began, then trailed off.

"You couldn't give up your family and your duties for me," Irene said quietly, "and I wouldn't ask you to. We get a human lifetime. That's all we'll get."

"Then take her away from this!" Shan Yuan broke in. "Kai, if your desire is to keep her safe, and if you really have this true and genuine affection for each other, find some quieter place to live and stop putting yourselves in danger. I'm prepared to admit I may have been hasty—"

Kai silenced him with a gesture. "I didn't fall in love with Irene the human," he said. "I fell in love with Irene the Librarian who doesn't abandon *her* duty. It's not your body, Irene. It's your soul. Your heart."

Irene had to blink hard to stop the tears coming to her eyes. "Just . . . don't try to sacrifice yourself for me again. I don't want to have to live knowing that you died for me."

"I wouldn't have killed him," Shan Yuan muttered.

"Then promise me that you'll try to live through this." Kai folded her in his arms. "Find a way out of this that doesn't get you killed. We may only have one lifetime, but I *want* that lifetime."

Shan Yuan managed about five seconds of patience before he tapped Irene hard on the shoulder. To her relief, his flesh was currently normal human temperature rather than superheated. "You said that you had something very important to say to me."

Irene regretfully removed herself from Kai's embrace. She had to admit she'd misjudged Shan Yuan. He might want Kai's job, but his desire to keep his brother safe was genuine. Just like hers. "Yes. Your highness—was that your grandfather just now?"

"My grandfather is dead!" Shan Yuan protested, a little too fast. "And even if he wasn't, why should he show up as some shadowy abomination in a second-rate library in a world so placid that it doesn't even need my family's attention?"

"Right." Irene staunched her nosebleed with Vale's handkerchief again. "The facts: there's something very badly wrong, which may involve your grandfather and may involve the worlds which have been disappearing." She saw his reluctant nod. He was aware of the situation. "It's possible that there's a malign force concealed somewhere in the Library which is doing this. Alberich is dead, but he gave us some information which led us here and we found a story about it."

"A story?" Shan Yuan scoffed. "History would be more useful."

"It would, but who'd know the truth of something so long ago? Perhaps his majesty Ao Guang knows something about it, or the other dragon monarchs. But all I have at the moment is stories. And I have stories from human records, and from Fae storytellers, which are all pointing at the same thing. I may be wrong. I don't know. But I *do* know that something just tried to kill all of us, and it turned up here the moment I used the Language in a library. Something is chasing us, your highness, and if I'm right about what I suspect, then Librarians and worlds across the universe are in danger!"

Kai looked at her—a long, desperate look—then took a deep breath. "Elder brother, I believe that this is something we can't ignore. I know that you want my position as treaty representative." His arm tightened round Irene, the grasp of a man who knows he's about to lose a treasured possession. "It's yours. I resign it to you and will say so before our lord father. You'll find my documents at our lodgings in Vale's world. I ask you to carry out the duties of that position and to see that it is done well. Here and now, I have to help Irene. She's right: the possibilities of what may be happening are too dire to ignore." He met Shan Yuan's eyes. "We both know who we just saw."

"I . . ." Shan Yuan was taken aback. "What are you going to do, then? Go to Lord Shang Yi?"

"Go to the root," Irene said. "I know who we need to ask for answers now. The Library will probably be appointing a new treaty representative soon. I hope that they'll work well with you, your highness. Vale, are you with us?"

"Do you really need to ask, Winters?"

Irene nodded. She leaned over to brush her lips against Kai's cheek. She knew what he'd said, and what he'd just given up. The future was in flux. If their suspicions were true, they were in deadly danger; if not, she and Kai had just burned their boats and might never have permission from their superiors to work together again. *I love you*, her kiss said, and *Thank you*.

"I'll tell our lord father that you aren't dead, Kai," Shan Yuan said. "I . . ." He hesitated again. "It may be days before he sends for you to account for yourself."

It wasn't quite an olive branch, but it was probably the best they were going to get. Kai inclined his head. "Thank you, elder brother. Irene—shall we?"

The three of them walked out of the ruined library together, leaving Shan Yuan standing there, uncertainty written on his face. He'd got what he said he wanted—but he didn't look happy about it at all.

CHAPTER 21

Night hung over London, thick and close; there were no winds to stir the spring fogs that shrouded the streetlights and veiled the surrounding houses. Irene waited in a back alley with Kai and passed the time by eyeing nearby windows with a view to burglary. Not that she had any immediate intentions, of course—but it never hurt to keep in practice.

Kai checked his watch. He didn't say anything, but both of them knew that Vale was running late. They'd all agreed it had made sense for him to undertake this part of the mission alone, but if something went wrong . . .

The sound of running feet broke the silence. Two people, coming fast. Irene and Kai exchanged glances, and Irene took a breath, ready to use the Language if necessary.

Then the two runners turned the corner into the alley, coming into sight, and Irene relaxed. It was Vale—and Catherine.

"Any problems?" Kai asked, as Vale slowed to a walk and led Catherine toward them.

"It all went quite smoothly. Madame Sterrington's servants weren't expecting any infiltration. Outright assault, possibly, but not infiltration."

"Well, you're the expert," Irene said. "Hello, Catherine. The good news is, we aren't dead—"

She broke off to catch Catherine's hand as the young Fae tried to slap her. "Not good news?"

"I didn't become your apprentice to play this sort of stupid *game* with you!" Catherine spat. In the light of the streetlamp her eyes were reddened and weary. "I trusted you—I told you my name—and then you let me think you were dead . . ."

"We have no time for this," Vale interrupted. "Young woman, control your emotions. If you want to be part of this operation, we require your cooperation rather than your tantrums."

Catherine looked round at all three of them. "Right. Yes. I can see it now. You're absolutely the sort of person who'd pretend to jump off cliffs and then leave your friends worried about it for *years*. I shouldn't have expected any better."

Irene still had hold of her wrist. "Catherine, first things first—I apologize. I'm sorry. But we have to hurry. I'll explain in the cab, but there's no time to waste. I need your help. It's going to be dangerous, but—"

"If you think I'm letting you run away again *now*, you've got another think coming," Catherine growled. "You aren't doing that to me again. Where's the cab?" She looked around as though she expected to find it hiding behind the lamp post.

"This way," Vale said. "Follow me."

"Next time, stamp on her foot while she has hold of your wrist," Kai advised Catherine helpfully. "Or play on her sense of guilt. It works better than an outright assault."

"You're not helping, Kai," Irene muttered.

Catherine waited until they were in the cab—stationed a couple of streets away—before fixing Irene with a gimlet eye. "Talk," she ordered.

"It's usually, 'You perceive that you want to tell me everything,'" Kai suggested, sitting back next to Vale as the cab jolted into motion. "That one can get almost embarrassing."

"Is this really necessary, Kai?" Irene asked wearily.

"It's doing wonders for my own conscience. I'm relieved to know I'm not the only person who had someone that worried about them."

"Mm. Point. All right, Catherine—the situation is that Alberich is dead, but that we've uncovered evidence of something else dubious going on, which is why we hadn't revealed that we were still alive. What were you told?"

"A couple of Librarians showed up and said that something had gone wrong and the entire world was destroyed," Catherine replied. "They said that Alberich had betrayed the deal and that the resulting blowback from the broken agreement with the Library killed him— and you. And the world. They wanted me to go back to the Library with them."

"Why didn't you?" Kai asked curiously.

"There was, um, a bit of a custody dispute. Sterrington wanted proof that they were genuine—so they did something with the Language. Then she wanted proof that they were the *right* people to hand me over to, given that you'd left me under her roof, and she was saying perhaps she should give me back to my uncle instead."

Irene had never thought she'd be so grateful for Sterrington's urge to grab any political advantage available. Yet a thought nagged at her. "We both know you could have made a run for it if you'd really wanted to go with these Librarians and leave Sterrington. Why didn't you?"

Catherine stared at her knees. "Two things. One is that I didn't want to give them my name. I know it would have let them get me back into the Library—but I didn't really trust them. Not like I trust you. So I kept my head down and let Sterrington do the talking."

Irene couldn't blame Catherine for that. A Fae's true name held immense power over them. She could understand why Catherine didn't want to give that sort of control over herself to any passing Librarian. "And the other reason?"

"Sterrington talked to me in private. She was sure there was something going on behind the scenes. She suggested that I let her make a public fuss so that I didn't have to come to any final decisions yet." Catherine looked at Irene. "She said that it was all just a bit too tidy to be true—even if you heroically sacrificing yourself made for a good story, *she* didn't believe it. And it all fitted with earlier, when I came back here from the Library and what I told you then. There *is* something going on—and if it had got you killed, then I wanted them to *pay*."

The protective anger in her voice made Irene's heart clench. *I don't deserve this. I don't deserve Kai's affection, or Catherine's loyalty, I don't know why I have them, but I don't want to give them up . . .*

Irene took a deep breath. "We may both owe Sterrington a favor. I'll be frank. I'm asking you to come with us because I suspect there's something wrong at the heart of the Library, and we may need both a Fae and a dragon in our group to reach it. This is absolutely not safe. It's extremely dangerous. You're within your rights to refuse."

"Then why are you starting this conversation by saying that you need me?" Catherine asked. "You usually disapprove of emotional blackmail."

Irene had already been through this discussion with Kai and Vale. Vale thought Catherine was too young, but Kai felt Catherine had a right to be involved, leaving Irene with the deciding vote. "Because if I'm *right* about what's going on, your life and freedom are at stake along with the rest of us. Under those circumstances, I feel less guilty about press-ganging you." The guilt was still there; if there had been any other Fae she could have dragged along, someone older, more mature, or less innocent, then she'd have taken that option. But no other Fae would give Irene their true name—and she needed that to get them into the Library.

Catherine frowned, her brows knotting together. "And what do you think is going on?" she asked.

Irene began to explain.

By the time they'd reached their destination—a small theological library near Baker Street, closed at this time of night—she hadn't fully convinced Catherine, but she'd managed to make her seriously worried. The younger woman was looking over her shoulder nervously as they clambered out of the cab and Kai paid the driver off.

Vale moved to the library door and began picking the lock.

"Can't you . . ." Catherine looked at Irene and waggled her fingers in a way meant to suggest supernatural powers.

"I think that the reason we were attacked in Helsinki is *because* I used the Language inside a library," Irene said quietly. "I'm going to have to use the Language to get us into the Library itself, and I have to assume we'll be noticed at that point. I don't know what's going to happen. There might be some sort of manifestation, or maybe the Library itself will try to attack us."

"Wonderful," Catherine muttered.

Irene patted her shoulder reassuringly. "We need to find a transfer shift cabinet as fast as possible. I have a . . . contingency, shall we say." She felt the need to ask again, to give Catherine a last chance to refuse. "Are you sure you want to do this?"

Catherine met her gaze, eyes furious. "Are you joking? I don't *want* to do this—but I'm *going* to do this. If you're wrong, there's no issue and everything's fine and this isn't a problem. But if you're right, then this goes against the whole of what being a librarian means to me. I'm not in this to be someone's pawn. Besides, if you're right, if they can hear anything that happens inside a library, then they have my true name. That makes it my fight too."

"All right," Irene said, accepting her decision. *And may God have mercy on my soul for dragging her and Kai and Vale into this.* "Vale, are you ready?"

"The door is open, Winters—and has been for over a minute now."

Irene nodded and glanced round the group. "Ready to go, then. Remember—stay with me and keep together."

Kai flicked a lazy salute in her direction. "Let's do it," he said, tense with excitement.

The theological library was dark and claustrophobic, with a narrow corridor leading to the main room. Irene put her hand on the door handle and took a deep breath. *Showtime.*

"Open to the Library," she commanded, and dragged the door open.

Light, clear and blinding, streamed through the open door from the Library room beyond. Kai was first through, shielding his eyes with one hand, with Vale a couple of steps behind him.

A deeper darkness gathered in the outer library where Irene and Catherine were still standing—a thick swirling mass of pure night at the end of the corridor, forming into shape and substance as the echo of Irene's words faded.

Irene leaped over the threshold, dragging Catherine with her; the words to bring Catherine through spilled from her mouth as she tugged on the Fae's hand, rattled out with desperate speed. Catherine practically threw herself through the doorway, eyes wide at the pursuing shadows. If she hadn't believed before, she did now.

The darkness came rushing down the corridor like an express

train filling a tunnel. There were wings in it, Irene could see that; and eyes, and teeth.

She slammed the door shut in its face.

Abruptly everything was normal again. They were in a large rectangular barn of a room, well lit and drafty, with rows of free standing metal-and-wire bookcases marching down its length. Catherine plucked down a brightly colored hardback to examine it. "Tolkien," she reported, her hands lingering on the book. "*The Tale of Alatar and Pallando.*"

Irene firmly took it from her and replaced it on the shelf. "Follow me, everyone," she directed. While she would like to believe they were a well-drilled squad who'd stay together through mortal peril, honesty compelled her to admit that they'd all be distracted—herself included—by any interesting discovery. And the Library was *full* of interesting discoveries.

There were no immediate signs of peril—no threatening shadows, no attempts by the walls to crush them or the ceiling to fall on them, or the books to assault them en masse—but Irene still had a growing sense of danger. The air had the prickle of an oncoming thunderstorm, and her back . . . her Library brand felt as if someone was trying to touch it, run their fingers over it, as though they were groping for something delicate and fragile, being careful for fear of breaking it, but once they had a firm hold on it . . .

The corridors outside were painted azure blue, lit with perfect clarity by golden lamps, but Irene found herself scrutinizing every corner and turning for hints of coalescing shadow. Each passing second was a risk. She found herself trembling with suppressed tension, knowing that *she* was the one being tracked. She had to remind herself that telling the others to go ahead without her would be simply *stupid*, since they had no way to use a transfer shift cabinet without her.

And still the temptation danced in her head, almost as if someone were whispering it in her ear . . .

Then she turned a corner, the others at her back—and practically bumped into another Librarian. He'd been walking as silently as them on the thick carpet, preoccupied with his own business, and was just as surprised as Irene. Their mutual yelp of shock had Kai reflexively tensing and Vale's hand tightening on his sword-stick.

"Sorry," the other Librarian said, raising his hands in apology, "so very sorry, I had no notion you were there . . ." He was a middle-aged man, balding, in a brown robe that would have suited a monk, with a plain linen shirt showing at the neck, but his sandals were luxury models designed for comfort, and his feet looked more pedicured than any monastic order would have approved.

"Not a problem," Irene said quickly. "Sorry, but we're in a hurry . . ."

"Of course, me too." He gave a little wave, on the point of turning away—but then he paused. His eyes darkened as though ink was leaking into them and spreading outward across the irises and whites, leaving pools of shadow like the eyeholes of a skull.

"Irene?" he said, his voice vibrating as though multiple people were speaking at once. "At last you have returned to us."

Irene felt a shiver of horror crawl down her spine. This was . . . just *wrong*. Librarians agreed to serve the Library, but they were never supposed to be its puppets. "Why did you try to kill me?" she asked.

"We were mistaken." This time a new voice seemed to be coming to the fore—a persuasive, understanding one, the sort of voice which could tell a thousand stories and have them believed. "The betrayer put his mark on you and deceived us. But you were spared. Your Library mark can be restored—and now you've earned the right to hear the *true* story of Alberich."

One thing Irene knew for certain was that when an adversary offers you exactly what you want to hear, you should be extremely suspicious. Also, if this hapless Librarian had pinpointed her position in the Library, other Librarians—or shadows—might be closing in on them. She might be able to duel with one Librarian with the Language; she couldn't handle multiple opponents.

She let her eyes widen in gratitude, moving sideways as she spoke so that the puppeted Librarian had to turn to focus on her. "Thank you," she said, her tone absolutely sincere. "You have no idea how much I needed to know that—"

Vale swung his sword-stick round casually and tapped it against the poor fellow's arm, triggering the electrification function. He screamed and collapsed.

"You were correct in your hypothesis, Winters," he said in the ensuing silence. "It seems that in the same way that Madame Bradamant was controlled, any Librarian can be used as a conduit for these . . . presences. Though if you are wrong about our situation, you may have to make a number of apologies."

"I'll do whatever penance is necessary, if . . ." Irene broke off.

The collapsed Librarian was moving, body spasming as though the muscles were having to remember how to work. He raised himself half-upright, pushing off the floor with knotted fists, and when he looked at them the darkness was spreading across his face like oil.

"Robe, gag and bind your wearer!" Irene ordered.

Folds of cloth layered themselves over the man's face as his sleeves tangled themselves around each other and immobilized his hands. He struggled with the bindings, confirming what Irene had hoped— while their enemy was possessing a Librarian, they had to *speak* to use the Language.

"Run!" Irene led the way, sprinting down the corridor. She *refused* to kill or maim a fellow Librarian, but apparently nothing less would stop him. Perhaps if Alberich had been there and able to conduct impromptu surgery on his brand—but that would mean Alberich being there, which would be a whole new order of complete and absolute disaster.

Like divine providence, a transfer shift cabinet came into view. It was battered, old, and barely large enough to hold two Librarians and a stack of books—but it would have to do. Irene indicated it. "There—get in!"

She could hear running feet in the distance now, heading in their direction. Her imagination painted a three-dimensional map of the Library with glowing dots triangulating on a position and moving to surround it. With the urgency of panic she shoved Catherine into the cabinet, crowded against Kai and Vale—doing his best to be a gentleman under the circumstances, which weren't in favor of personal space—and wriggled in herself, tugging at the door as she tried to close it on the four of them.

"This isn't going to work," Catherine gasped.

"Breathe in and shut up," Irene snarled. As the door finally touched the frame, she gasped, **"History!"**

For a moment she didn't think it *was* going to work. The cabinet didn't move. Not only were they going to be caught by their pursuers, they were going to be caught looking utterly ridiculous.

Then the streaks of light round the edge of the door vanished and the box they were standing in dropped like a stone. There was no room for them to be shaken around like dice, as usually happened; they were a solid mass of miserable compressed people, slammed into one wall and then the opposite one as the cabinet threaded its course through the Library. Someone trod on Irene's foot. She couldn't see who. Someone else—she suspected Kai, it felt like his elbow—prodded her in the stomach. But worst of all was the fear that the forces hunting them might be able to control this cabinet's movement and they might end up dumped out in front of their enemies, rather than in any sort of comparative safety.

When their ride finally came to a stop, there were no thoughts of taking stock of the situation or discussing what to do next. Irene flung the door open and staggered out, the others surging behind her.

She came to a sudden stop as she saw the gun pointed at her.

Melusine was facing the transfer shift cabinet square on, and she looked *tired*—the weariness in her red-rimmed eyes suggested that she hadn't slept for days, and a mountain range of used coffee cups was stacked across her desk. But her hands didn't shake, and her aim was steady. "Don't move," she said. "Don't say anything. Raise your hands."

Irene obeyed mutely. She was conscious that she was keeping the others bottled up, but there was nothing she could do about it. She didn't for a second doubt Melusine's sincerity.

"Four of you. All four. Yes, that fits. Nobody try anything. I *will* shoot."

Irene nodded. If she'd had free use of her hands and they hadn't been in the air, she'd have signaled Kai and the others to comply. She recognized the tones of someone under desperately high stress—and also the vocal patterns of a Librarian who might need to use the Language at any moment, and was deliberately keeping her sentences short.

"What's going on?" Catherine protested from the back of the cabinet, her view blocked by the taller Vale and Kai.

"Verification. All right, Irene. In the Language, so I know it's true. Are you working for Alberich?"

"I am not working for Alberich," Irene said clearly. That explained the situation; Melusine was afraid that Alberich had compromised or outright turned Irene. A worm of guilt nagged at her, since she *was* currently investigating a trail which Alberich had set her on, but she squashed it. That wasn't the same thing as working *for* Alberich.

Melusine didn't lower the gun yet. "Are you still loyal to the Library?"

"I'm still loyal to the Library," Irene answered obediently. *To my Library, at least*, she thought. *To the Library that I swore my oaths to, that I've served all these years. But not necessarily loyal to the shadows which seem to have infested us.*

"And why are you here?" The gun's muzzle seemed very large. The room wasn't hot, but a drop of sweat trickled down Melusine's temple.

"To ask for information and help," Irene replied. She took a deep breath, and made what wasn't a deduction, but was, she thought, a reasonable guess. "Margaret."

Melusine's hands shook, and she lowered the gun into her lap. "Fuck," she said, the first time Irene had heard her swear. "You know too much."

Now that the gun was down, Irene took a few cautious paces into the room, letting the others out of the cabinet behind her.

How did one deal with this sort of situation? In stories it was easy; meetings between long-lost children and their parents were usually the climax of the tale and ended in happy tears. This wasn't so easy and it certainly wasn't the end of the narrative. "I don't see that it has to change anything between us," she said cautiously. "I'm a woman myself. I can understand how it would feel to have a child forced on me, and why it might be preferable to give that child to parents who'd love and raise her as their own."

Melusine's laugh was a hollow groan. "Then you're doing a lot better than some of the other female Librarians who knew about it."

"How many did know?"

"Barely a dozen, and most of them are dead now. Kostchei is the only one left."

But Coppelia had known . . . Irene realized what Melusine's words must mean, and briefly shut her eyes in wrenching grief. She'd asked the older woman to wait. She'd *asked* her. But Coppelia hadn't listened—or hadn't been able to.

"Sorry," Melusine said. She sighed. "Let's get down to business. I'll explain the current situation, and you can tell me what you want. We may be able to sort this out without further mess."

"There's something I need to ask first," Irene said, pulling herself together. "Has anything odd been going on?"

Melusine rolled her eyes. "Define *odd*."

"More worlds going missing. Strange manifestations in the Library. Librarians behaving oddly."

"Yes," Melusine said. "All of the above. Just a moment . . ." She reached over to touch a button under her desk's lip. "That's the shut-off. People won't be able to get down here by the lifts until I open it again."

"That's convenient," Kai said.

"The one next to it is the self-destruct in case I decide you all need to be taken out by whatever means are necessary." Her smile was humorless. "So what's going on? Well, they think you're all dead—but that's partly because I told them so. I've been shielding you, Irene, and I hope that I'm right to have done that. Because you may be my child, but you're Alberich's child as well."

CHAPTER 22

"I consider myself the child of my *parents*," Irene said sharply. "Those are the people who raised me, Raziel and Liu Xiang. Speaking of whom—*please* tell me they aren't currently in the Library."

"They're not. I agree with you, that's a very good thing." Melusine touched her wheelchair, and it whirred back round her desk until she was behind it again—a barrier between her and the rest of the room. The gun had vanished somewhere under the blanket which covered her legs. "I hope we can get this sorted out before anyone tells them the bad news."

Irene had sympathized with Shan Yuan's feelings over Kai, and Catherine's anger at losing Irene—but the thought of her parents being told that she was dead slid a knife into her heart and twisted it as she imagined their reaction. She'd only considered how they might be used as hostages or tools against her. She'd avoided thinking about their feelings on hearing their daughter had died. "Yes," she said tonelessly, "that would be an excellent idea."

Melusine nodded. "You've been down here before," she said, gesturing at the cave-like cellar, the network of computers on the desk which vied with the coffee cups for space, and the thick leatherbound volumes which lined the walls. "You know that I can check individual books for Librarian transit to and from the specific worlds that the books are linked to."

Irene nodded, remembering. "But that shows travel through libraries, doesn't it? Not dragon or Fae transport."

"Right. Don't touch anything, Mr. Vale," she said, her level tone not changing. "There are all kinds of hideous lethal traps built in down here for anyone who isn't me."

"Very inefficient," Vale remarked, folding his hands behind his back. "Surely you can't do all the work yourself?"

"A woman must keep busy." Melusine opened one of her desk drawers and brought out a charred wreck of a book, like the ones shelved on the walls but reduced to near-charcoal and smeared with traces of fire-extinguisher foam. "Now, *this* is the book corresponding to the world where you were. I had it out on my desk while the meeting was going on."

"It looks damaged, madam," Kai said. Irene couldn't help noticing his sudden use of a respectful title. *Because she's admitted to being my birth mother?*

"It went up in flames."

There was silence for a moment. "Do books normally do that when the linked world is destroyed?" Irene asked. It seemed so casual a way to talk about *worlds being destroyed*. Such a huge concept shouldn't be easily expressed in words.

"Given that worlds usually *aren't* destroyed, I lack evidence," Melusine said sourly. "I can't even compare it to the worlds which have gone missing. Those disappeared from my shelves—the books, that is."

"Were any Librarians assigned to those worlds when they vanished?" Irene asked. A nasty thought was formulating itself in her mind.

"Yes. That's mostly *why* we know those worlds aren't there now—no report from the Librarian in question, investigation, door from Library not opening to that world, book in my archives gone. Why?" Melusine leaned forward sharply. "You know something?"

"I suspect that there is a force which acted *through* those Librarians to affect those worlds," Irene said carefully. "I suspect that force is the one which triggered Bradamant to set off a reaction which destroyed the world where the meeting was. That's what happened. Kai and Vale can confirm it." She nodded to the charred book on the table. "Alberich destroyed himself getting us out of there."

"What else did Alberich do?" That stressed danger was back in Melusine's eyes, and one hand had moved beneath the blanket that covered her lap—and her gun.

"He modified my Library brand," Irene admitted. "He said it would stop that force from controlling me as it had controlled Bradamant. I think he was telling the truth about that. I felt something trying to control me, to use me . . . I honestly can't find any good verbs for the subject, Catherine, so stop smirking. It wasn't funny at all."

Melusine relaxed. "It's a good thing you told me that. I'd have had to assume you were unreliable otherwise."

"He said that he'd done the same thing to you," Irene added. It was how she'd known that it would be safe to appeal to Melusine for help.

"Yes." She glanced at Kai and Vale. "For your information, we keep records here of all Library brands. When I saw that Irene's had been *changed*, in the same way that Alberich's was, and that mine was—well, you'll understand why I took precautions."

"And yet you let me come down here," Irene said softly.

Melusine looked away as though embarrassed. "I felt I owed you the chance."

"And now?"

"This story of yours about a mysterious force inside the Library is paranoid in the extreme," Melusine said curtly. "It's the sort of thing that Alberich talked about. Don't expect me to have any sympathy for his mad theories—or for him."

"The specific details are uncertain, but there's *something* at work," Irene argued. "We've got evidence from multiple different worlds and cultures in their literature about a group of people gathering to form the Library—three sources so far, and there may be more out there. A dragon, a Fae, a human collaborating, possibly for good reasons at first, possibly for personal power—"

"As I said, you're repeating Alberich's stories. And that's all they are—stories. Irene, you should know better than this. Stories in literature are not the same thing as actual history or recorded facts." Melusine gestured at the computers in front of her, the heavy books which filled the shelves. "These are *facts*. They're real things which have happened, which were observed or attested by reliable witnesses, which can be proved. The Library collects stories—but that doesn't mean we *believe* stories."

"It's a *fact* that we encountered something which I believe was a corrupted projection of my grandfather," Kai retorted. "No, I never met him, but I've seen pictures of him, and I recognize the family"—he looked for words—"essence, if you like. My brother knew him too. We've seen active influence from the Storyteller—the Fae who was involved—when he tried to kill someone to stop them telling us the story. If this is all paranoia, then what destroyed those worlds? What's chasing us?"

Melusine spread her hands. "I'll concede there may be dragon involvement. Or Fae involvement. I'll even accept that there may be a conspiracy. That's not the same thing as some sort of corruption at the heart of the Library."

"There has, however, been change." Vale turned from where he'd been inspecting the books on the walls, stalking forward like a predator who'd spotted his lunch. "When I first met Winters, her priorities were stealing books and preserving the stability of worlds. Over the last few months, I have watched her throw her energies into diplomacy instead—and never once question it. When I've met other Librarians, at least half of them have been preoccupied with diplomatic missions between the Library and the dragons or Fae. Bradamant confirmed a few days ago that the task of collecting books has been positively *neglected*. Since when have you Librarians become errand-runners and messengers? When did you become proactive diplomats? Is this the mission that you chose?"

They'd discussed this point earlier, but Irene still didn't feel he'd proved it was an issue. "Vale, if it's in order to serve a greater balance . . ."

He turned to Irene and tapped her forehead with a long bony finger. "Winters, the most frightening thing about this is that you haven't noticed. You continually make excuses for it whenever it's raised. You forget about my arguments a few seconds later. Strongrock and I have observed it. Isn't that so?"

"It's true that your perspective has shifted," Kai said reluctantly. "I'd accepted what you said about serving a greater duty, but in view of everything else that's going on—Irene, are you really sure something isn't influencing you?"

"Yes!" Catherine broke in unexpectedly. "Some of the other trainees were talking about it when I was here. They were talking about how the classes were focusing on courtesy and manners and not books any more. This wasn't what I wanted when I came here."

"You're all exaggerating," Irene said firmly. "Our primary mission is to preserve the worlds from the extremes of order and chaos. If it takes a bit of diplomacy to get it done, then we'll just have to be diplomats for that part of our job. I know my own mind."

She did—didn't she? An unhelpful memory surfaced of the first time she'd had the "you perceive" trick explained to her, about how the listener subconsciously justified what they'd heard so that it would make sense to them . . .

"I will be fair and reasonable to the whole boiling lot of you," Melusine said through gritted teeth, slipping into some personal idiom. "Yes, it's true that there's been more diplomacy recently. The whole situation has changed over the last couple of years. We have a treaty. We have arrangements. We have *deals*. We can't expect to go on the way we did previously."

"And who precisely decides your course of action?" Vale slid the question in deftly.

"Senior Librarians," Melusine parried. "Of which I'm one."

"And who gives *them* their orders? Who chooses which books are to be retrieved—or which messages are to be carried? You're the one who was talking about *facts* earlier, madam. What is the Library's history? Who is in charge?"

"Do you think I don't wonder that myself?" Melusine snapped at him. "I've been through the records, and they go back thousands of years, but there isn't anything definite about how this place was founded. Do you think I haven't checked? After what Alberich claimed, and what he did to me?"

Vale's jaw tensed and he fell silent. *Caught between the urge to question her further and Victorian propriety*, Irene diagnosed. But he'd given her an opening. "Can we agree that there is a problem?" she asked. "Even if we can't fully define its scope yet. Even if we aren't agreed on what its ultimate cause may be. Worlds have disappeared.

Bradamant *died* because someone or something used her to destroy that world. Was that you?"

"No," Melusine said slowly. "I don't deny that I might have tried something if I could have been sure it'd kill Alberich in the process— but no. The text in our agreement was too precise. It stopped any Librarian trying anything like that."

"Then who *did*?" Irene argued. "Please consider this—if it's some- one from *outside* the Library, then they have a way to influence the Library's inner workings. That makes it doubly urgent for us to stop them."

"You're right." Melusine seemed to come to a decision. There was a new set to her shoulders, a firmness to her gaze. "I owe you all an apology. I'm the person who's in charge of security—I shouldn't have needed you to find this out. There's an issue here, and we need to identify the best way to tackle it. I already have an idea of what's caus- ing it and why you're being chased: it's due to some bargain Alberich made with dangerous entities. He marked you, Irene, and now they're tracking you. See? No need for paranoid historical suppositions at all. Facts are a great deal more reliable."

"What you're saying makes a great deal of sense," Irene agreed cautiously, not wanting to contradict the older Librarian. Except . . . it didn't make sense. It didn't explain Bradamant's death and what- ever had used her to destroy that world. Melusine should have *known* that.

A thought crossed Irene's mind, clarifying itself in the same lan- guid, gut-churning way that an image in a horror movie would slowly become clear to a viewer. *This has all been too easy. We're chased into the Library, and then we encounter a possessed Librarian who's just enough of a challenge to make us panic and hurry to Melusine. At which point we tell her everything we know, and she gives us a convenient expla- nation that will lull our suspicions for long enough . . .*

We have walked into a trap.

"So," Irene said, keeping her tone casual, "when Alberich damaged your brand, how easy was it to get it fixed properly again?"

Perhaps her voice gave something away, or perhaps no question could ever have been innocent enough, for Melusine's eyes narrowed as they focused on her. "I had it done a few days after I returned," she said. "Why . . ."

She blinked. Darkness was spreading out into her eyes; it was like ink leaking from the pupils out into the hazel irises and surrounding whites. "Ah," she said, and her voice was different now, overshadowed by a stranger's tones and pattern of speech. "Once more we repeat this dance. Greetings, Irene, Librarian; greetings, my . . . grandson? I have forgotten too much, but I believe you are of my blood. Be welcome here as guests, little Fae, human detective."

The four of them drew together like frightened children. Kai's long intake of breath was more serpentine than usual. "Grandfather?" he said, uncertain, almost begging to be contradicted.

"You have done an excellent job of research." Melusine sat back in her wheelchair as though it was a throne and they were supplicants. "You will be valued agents in the future."

"I beg to differ," Vale said coldly. "I choose my clients; they do not choose me."

Melusine's small flick of her hand dismissed his comment, but it was nothing like her previous body language; she had the confidence of someone completely unassailable. "I'm sure that once you have access to all the Library's resources and the Language, you will feel differently."

"And when I'm carrying your brand, no doubt." Vale looked down at the seated Librarian with condescension; evidently her possession meant that he was now at liberty to be as rude as he wished. "I think not."

Catherine had inched forward and was plucking at Irene's sleeve.

"I thought that the Library brand had to be deliberately chosen," she said, attempting firmness and almost achieving it. "I can always say no to all this. I'm not going to have it forced on me."

"Resign?" Melusine's lips smiled. "Come, little one, we couldn't possibly think of it. You will be the first of a new generation of Fae who will serve the Library. We have been waiting for you to lead the way. Consent . . . can be retroactive, after all."

Irene's heart sank as she realized just how badly she'd led them all amiss. "You can't do this," she vowed. "I will not let you do this."

"You are currently locked in the Security suite at the bottom of the Library," the voice speaking through Melusine said. "Very shortly, a group of Librarians will arrive by the lift to take you into custody. They won't harm you any more than necessary. We recognize good material; we have no desire to waste it. Once your brand is restored, Irene, you will feel as you should do. You will think as the Library wishes."

"As *you* wish."

"We are one and the same."

But are you? Irene wondered. *Who set Alberich on his path, and gave me the tools to read Finnish? Why do these stories keep escaping into the alternate worlds where they can be found?* "But why?" she demanded. There had to be a way to appeal to this person—no, these people. If they were who Irene believed they were, there was one way that would have a chance of working, and one of the three who'd be unable to resist answering. The grandfather dragon might assert royal privilege, and the human of the group might keep her mouth shut, but the Fae who was the original Storyteller . . . "What's the story behind this?"

The expression on Melusine's face changed, though those black eyes stayed the same—holes in her face, unsettling and abominable. In a stranger they were bad enough, but in the face of someone Irene knew, they were . . . disgusting.

She shifted position, leaning forward in her chair. "Once upon a time, three people came together, and for excellent reasons they resolved to combine their powers to create a structure outside time and space. This would be a living thing, the center of a web that connected the worlds and prevented them from falling to either the calcification of order or the seas of chaos. All things would be preserved there and would not pass away or be lost. The construct worked as they had designed, indicating stories which must be collected and preserving its contents—and them. But as time passed, these three looked out at the folly of their descendants and resolved that they would do whatever was necessary. If their descendants would not govern themselves, then they must do it for them. They must protect them from their own willfulness. And so it came to pass . . ."

Melusine's face shifted, and the elder dragon's expression was visible once again. "And so it shall come to pass," he said, and the books on the shelves trembled at the force lying behind his words. "We have already removed worlds where the worst malcontents dwelled. Now we shall take positive action. You wanted peace; you have given your life to a worthy cause, and we shall use it well."

"I didn't give my life to *you*," Irene argued, working to control her temper—and her fear. "I gave it to the Library."

"These petty distinctions will not worry you in a little while," Melusine said comfortingly. Her black eyes moved between Irene and Kai. "Fear not; I will not part you two. You shall have your years together and be happy."

Seldom had Irene been less enthusiastic about approval from one of Kai's family. Kai himself was looking less and less convinced about the situation. "Grandfather," he said, "this is . . . not what I expected from you."

"No doubt my manner troubles you," Melusine said. "I admit the close proximity of a Fae and a human for a long period of time may have caused me to forget court protocol. Have no fear, grandson; all shall be set right. When you go from here, it will be to your father's court to bring him the good news."

Irene's mind slammed into a whole new vista of disasters. Bad enough that she and the others were to be turned into "loyal" servants of these hidden masters and sent out to play politics for them. But how much worse would it be when Kai informed the dragon monarchs that they were expected to roll over and be subservient? Probably about as bad as it would be when Catherine tried to present similar news to the most powerful Fae. They wouldn't just obey—they'd strike back. At which point more worlds might "vanish," or even worse . . .

Sweat was beading Melusine's forehead, and there was a faint tremor in her hands. This possession must be difficult for the Librarian's body to sustain—not that it was her choice, anyhow. Would the shadow stay in her until the reinforcements showed up, or would it simply depart and leave them here?

"How long have you been possessing my mother?" Irene demanded. It was a genuine question, but the more emotional they thought her, the better. They'd never believe it if she feigned submission; they would believe anger. "How much of what she said to me was real?"

Melusine didn't answer straight away. Finally she shrugged. "Her answers on the subject between the two of you were her own. We can look through the eyes of any Librarian—but we saw no reason to intervene with that. After all, you were telling us everything we needed to know."

Irene let go of her self-restraint and tapped into her inner fury. "You're liars and deceivers!" She stalked forward and slammed her hands down on the edge of Melusine's desk. "I gave myself to an ideal, and this isn't it. I didn't swear loyalty to some sort of tripartite consciousness that wants to use me to play chess to rule the universe!"

"Then you should have been more careful who you swore loyalty to, granddaughter, shouldn't you?" That wasn't the elder dragon or the Storyteller. That was a third person, a third vocal pattern. "Always a mistake to sign a contract without being absolutely sure what's in it."

Vale coughed meaningfully from behind Irene, no doubt remembering several occasions on which he'd questioned her about exactly who was managing the Library. Questions which she'd ignored, at the time—or had been encouraged to ignore.

"Contracts can be dissolved—"

"By mutual agreement." There was a hint of nasty amusement to Melusine's voice. "And if you think I'm going to let anything I own go, then think again. You're mine." Her gaze swept over the others in the room. "You're all mine. Ours. Our stories, our books—our servants. *Nothing* leaves the Library."

Something at the back of Irene's mind clicked in recognition, but she pushed it aside for later. "You don't really think of yourself as the Library," she said. "If you did, you couldn't have broken the truce offer. You killed Bradamant by doing it through her."

"We aren't the Library," Melusine replied. "We control the Library. There's a difference."

"Yes." Irene let her lips curl in a vicious smile. "If you think I'm going to accept this, think again. I'm going to force you out of my mother, whatever it takes—"

"Irene!" Kai protested.

She ignored Kai. "I'll find a way to expel you from her and all the other Librarians. You know what I've done before, what I'm capable of. You will *not* harm my friends. I won't tolerate this!"

Melusine laughed, a regal chuckle of condescending amusement. "Your spirit does you credit. However, we do not wish you to harm this servant. We will leave you here—to await collection."

Melusine's eyes rolled up, and she collapsed in her chair with the limpness of unconsciousness. Irene leaned forward to take her pulse—slow and ragged, but present. *Thank any gods that exist. And for my next request . . .*

"Vale," she said, her tone level again as she turned toward him, "find the secret door."

Vale's eyes widened at her request—and then he nodded in sudden comprehension, quickly scanning along the shelves.

"I realize I'm only the apprentice and the most junior person here," Catherine said, "but would you mind explaining?"

"No problem. But quickly—Kai, please cut me a very thin strip of Melusine's quilt. I know you have a knife on you."

"Certainly," Kai said, suiting action to word. He was clearly still shaken from the manifestation of his grandfather, but the fact that Irene seemed to have a plan was reassuring him.

"Point one—I wanted to get them out of here, out of Melusine. Those things"—Irene made a vague gesture intended to convey *possessing spirits from the dawn of time*—"with luck, we'll notice if they come back."

"Yes, all right, but secret passage? They said we were trapped here!"

"They may have thought so," Irene said, "but the Librarian unconscious here beside me is paranoid by nature and by job function. Are you seriously going to tell me that she has a center of operations in a cellar at the very bottom of the Library, with only one entrance—but *without* an escape route? I've asked Vale to find it because the other option is for me to shout at the top of my voice in the Language for all doors and escape routes to open, and that could have unintended consequences."

"I trust I can do so without triggering any unpleasant traps," Vale noted, not looking up from his work of checking the walls.

"Could it be a trapdoor?" Catherine asked. "Or in the ceiling . . . no, wait, wheelchair, sorry, I wasn't thinking."

"Well, she *could* make a wheelchair rise in the air with the Language, so it's not impossible, but I'm assuming that an escape route needs to be easy to use," Irene replied. She had one ear cocked for any signs of other Librarians arising. Unfortunately she didn't know how to turn on the defenses which Melusine had demonstrated to her once before—or, more precisely, wasn't sure how to turn them on without getting herself and the others targeted too.

"I have it," Vale said with satisfaction. "This panel in the wall, I believe. Winters, if you would?"

Irene quickly touched the set of shelves he'd indicated. They showed no sign of being any different from the other shelves, but she trusted Vale's observation. **"Area which I am touching, traps deactivate; unlock and open."**

There was a ripple of tiny clicks from the wall, and then it swung away from her, opening into a passageway. It wasn't the disused tunnel sort of escape route; it was well lit, smooth-floored, and wide enough for a wheelchair. "Right," she said. "Now just one more thing while we're still here. I need to ask you a question, Kai. What are your intentions regarding your grandfather?"

Kai had a stubborn, mulish set to his jaw. "We have encountered an entity who *claims* to be my grandfather. I have no definite proof."

"You presented quite a different argument to Melusine," Vale noted.

"Yes, well . . . I could have been mistaken."

That was a very specious argument. Still, it was better than *My loyalty is to my grandfather and I'll stand by him in any confrontation.* "All right. Now for my next trick, I need this pencil from my pocket, that strip of fabric you cut, Kai, your knife, and a finger you aren't using." She paused. "No, just the tip of the finger, not the whole thing, though I appreciate the gesture."

While Irene was talking, she was bringing up a current map of the Library on Melusine's computer. "Hopefully nobody's checking for my login—"

"We must assume the worst," Vale interrupted.

"But if they are, I was *going* to say, this won't take long and it'll only show that we were here, which they knew anyhow, and which is also why I'm going to use the Language here before we run for it. Sorry about this, Kai." She pricked his finger with the knife, then dabbed a few drops of blood on the end of the pencil, before knotting the fabric around the pencil so it dangled loosely.

It did worry her a bit that he would apparently have let her cut his finger off. She didn't *want* that sort of absolute devotion.

"Ah," Kai said in tones of understanding, sucking his finger.

"Enlighten your apprentice?" Catherine said hopefully. "Without cutting her?"

"If I ever cut you, you'll know about it," Irene said. She dangled the pencil in front of the huge map which spread across the screen. **"Trace of dragon blood, indicate on the map the location of your grandfather."**

"You're *dowsing*, Winters," Vale said in tones of disdain. "Of all the psychometric rubbish . . ."

"We have an established connection confirmed by the suspect himself, and the Language can be used in a metaphorical sense as well as a factual one," Irene said, watching the pencil oscillate. Abruptly it turned so that the point was facing the screen, and tapped against part of it. "All right, let me enlarge the map . . ."

The pencil kept rapping at a particular point on the computer screen as Irene moved the slider up to maximum size. She frowned.

"That's down in Dictionaries and Grammars. Right at the bottom. Sumerian."

"Is that lower in the Library geography than here?" Vale asked.

"Well, Security isn't featured on any of the standard maps. But judging by the fact that we're *here* on the map"—she pointed—"we're actually at about the same level as where D&G—Dictionaries and Grammars—starts. It goes a long way down and they're constantly having to expand it."

After all, what was the use of collecting stories if one didn't have the knowledge of languages to read them?

"Right." Irene turned off the computer. She glanced at the unconscious Melusine—but the safest thing for her birth mother was to leave her here, unconscious and uninvolved. "We're evacuating now. Follow me."

The others quickly followed her into the tunnel, and Irene closed the door behind them before leading the way along it, every sense on the alert. She didn't *think* their enemies could have predicted this; if they knew absolutely everything that all Librarians knew, then Alberich would never have been able to go rogue in the first place. But still . . .

"What's the next step of the plan?" Kai asked, joining her at the front. "And where do you think this goes?"

"Well, if it had been me organizing an escape route, I'd have made sure it led directly to a current information source and transport . . ." The tunnel opened ahead of them into one of the Library's standard meeting rooms, complete with a computer on the central table. "Bingo."

"And beyond that?"

Irene turned to face the others. "This is where we're going to have an awkward conversation, aren't we? Because we all know that the sensible thing to do is to go and warn other people—for their sake, and for our own."

She looked between the three of them. Kai, as beautiful as a statue and as immovable as one once his will was set, as stubborn and un-stoppable as his native element of water. Vale, focused on his trail like a hawk or a hound, bringing the full power of his intellect to the prob-lems that he chose and ferociously unwilling to let them go or to tol-erate injustice. And Catherine, the one she knew least, but in a way felt the most sympathy with—someone who loved books just as Irene did, and who'd just had the truth behind the Library dashed in her face like a pail of sewage.

"We have very little time," she said. "I don't think we can trust any other Librarians. The place we're going to is the heart of our oppo-nents' power. And once they realize we know where to look for them . . . they'll probably stop trying to take us alive." Her heart sank as she realized what she was about to say. *Someone who was truly ethi-cal would tell them to go; to get out of here and warn others.* "If I had any regard for your safety, I'd be sending you away, but as matters stand— I'm desperate and I need your help."

Kai nodded judiciously. "It's a good thing you understand we're going to be 'awkward' about this, because I haven't the first intention of letting you go alone."

"Indeed," Vale agreed. "You must surely know by now, Winters, that a leader's authority is limited to giving her followers orders that they will actually *obey*."

"I came here to be a Librarian," Catherine said, folding her arms and thrusting her chin forward. If she was afraid, it was subsumed in the anger which marked every line of her body. "I have the right to fight for that. Are you really going to send me away when you might need my help? Do you want to take that chance?"

Catherine was the youngest of them, and Irene was responsible for her in a way that she wasn't for the others. She could have said, *I have your name and you'll do what I say.* She could have forced Catherine to be safe.

She could. She didn't.

"All right," she said, guilt warring with a strange lightness at this loyalty. "Sumerian. This way."

"Besides," Catherine said as she followed, "we're probably all doomed anyhow, so I might as well get the full story directly from the Storyteller."

Irene had *known* she and Catherine had a lot in common.

CHAPTER 23

❦

The metal stairways leading off the long walkway spiraled down into darkness. Each one was enclosed by a cylinder of shelves, a wall of books, with gaps at each new walkway level. The ceiling high above twinkled with distant lamps that flickered and faded like inconstant stars.

It was always cold in this room, Irene remembered. There was enough open space between the walkways and spiral staircases for drafts to develop into winds, and many sheets of notes had gone spiraling from unwary hands into the darkness, to flutter down and land somewhere on the distant floor.

"You failed to mention this part of the Library on our previous visits, Winters," Vale commented.

"I'm sure I showed it to you on the maps—no? Sorry." Irene closed the door behind them and ushered the group along the walkway. "This area is a big exception to us only keeping stories here in the Library. We need to be able to *read* those stories, hence we need grammars, dictionaries, linguistic guides, and so on. You'd have been getting books for study from here once you started training, Catherine."

"*When* I start training," Catherine said firmly. "After you've fixed all this."

Irene could only hope that the Fae was correct. They'd managed to avoid other Librarians on their way here, which should mean their enemies didn't know where they were. If their knowledge came from watching through the eyes of branded Librarians, they were restricted to what their servants could see—and ignorant of what those servants didn't perceive. Her main reason for believing this was the case was the fact that they *were* still alive and at liberty. If their enemies could visualize them scuttling through the Library corridors and animate those corridors to stop them—well, then they'd already be imprisoned or dead.

Irene was still trying to figure out what to do. Outright confrontation had already proved useless. Alerting other Librarians would simply let their enemies locate them. Appealing to exterior powers, the dragon monarchs or the most powerful Fae . . . would be admitting the Library was weak at best, and a dangerous threat at worst. And even if they did try to leave the Library, their enemies might be able to sense *that*—or could simply read the evidence in Melusine's records. Even in a best-case scenario, if she could shove the others through and they escaped, she'd still be caught.

Their best hope was more information, and that lay somewhere below.

The Language works on real things, but it also works through symbols. If I can find the right symbol to stop them . . .

"I've only been here a few times," Kai said, looking around curiously. "I thought Security was at the bottom of the Library—but this seems to go down even deeper."

"I always thought Security was," Irene confessed. Now she found herself wondering just why she'd been so certain. Had this been one more thought that her Librarian brand had enforced on her?

"And so instead we plow into the depths of grammar—or gramarye," Vale mused. "I've seen that used as a term for magic in some traditions."

"Language is power, power is magic, language is magic," Catherine said briskly. "It's all in the translation."

"Language isolates are on this stair," Irene said, coming to a halt. "Ainu, Basque . . . Sumerian down at the bottom."

"What is a language isolate?" Vale asked. However quietly they tried to walk, their footsteps rang on the iron stairs of the spiral staircase.

"In standard terms, it's a natural language that doesn't have any links with others—it's not part of any language family in the way that Spanish and Italian and French are all related to each other. Of course, languages that are language isolates in some alternate worlds are part of language families in others—but that's why we have the connected stairs off this one. There aren't many of them."

Vale nodded, and Irene knew he was filing the information in the part of his brain that handled *data not currently related to crimes*.

"I'm still wondering about the timing of all this," Kai said softly. "Why should they choose now to make their move?"

Irene had been thinking about that herself. "One thing that comes to mind is that it has something to do with us getting Catherine into the Library. We established that it could be done. They said through Melusine that Catherine was to be the first of their Fae agents . . ."

"You mean me entering the Library may have destroyed the universe?" Catherine asked.

"You don't need to sound quite so impressed by it," Irene chided. "It's not something you want on your yearly performance review."

Whistling in graveyards, she thought. *We're making stupid jokes because we're walking down into the metaphorical Pit and we have no idea exactly what's down there, or how to deal with it, or even how to survive the next hour . . .*

Something shifted deep inside her, like a single domino beginning its fall.

I'm tired of being afraid.

I'm tired of feeling guilty for being afraid.

I'm tired of feeling guilty because I believed in the Library and I was betrayed.

I wasn't the one who did something wrong.

If they were . . . then I'm going to find a way to fix things.

The whole area had a constant underpinning of noise, as the wind sighed through and round the staircases and walkways, stirring loose pages and carrying whispers, and the metal infrastructure itself groaned and creaked. It was pure luck that Kai caught a sound coming from the next walkway down, and raised his hand for them to pause.

Perhaps it was their sudden halt that caught the stranger's attention. She called out, voice a little panicky, "Is someone there?"

They'd be in full view once they turned the next spiral of the stairs and reached the point where their staircase touched the walkway. Staying quiet wouldn't work. "Yes," Irene called back, modulating her voice to be hopefully unrecognizable and picking the name of another Librarian she vaguely knew. "It's Ianthe. Who's that?"

"Makeda. What are you doing down here?"

"Fetching and carrying because someone wants a couple of Elamite dictionaries," Irene said with a put-upon sigh. "Got some probationers with me to show them the area." She let herself advance down the stairs, wanting to catch sight of the other woman. "Same as you, I guess, or similar? Or is it your own work?"

"No, you're right."

Irene could see the other woman now. She was in a comfortable trouser suit, carrying a list in one hand.

"I got sent down here half an hour ago by Esseintes to pick up some books for him, but I can't find half the stuff he wants. But I'm not supposed to go back without them, so . . ." She shrugged.

This smelled like a trap—or at least a precaution by their enemies. In case Irene and her people came down here, they'd positioned a Librarian on their route to sound the alert if they passed. Irene glanced along the lines of walkways and stairways, and made a quick calculation. One *had* to go down this stairwell to reach the Sumerian depths; this was the last walkway where one could reach it from a different direction. It was the perfect chokepoint.

She quickly glanced to the others. Kai shrugged. Vale spread his hands in recognition of their lack of options. Catherine bit her lip.

They'd have to chance it.

Irene plucked a book from one of the shelves, winced at what she was about to do, and tossed it down the stairwell. She heard it bounce below her. "Oh damn! No!" she shouted, doing her best imperson-ation of someone shocked to the core of her being, and ran down the stairs after it, hoping that the other Librarian wouldn't do more than glance at her. It was a perfectly normal reaction, after all . . .

It was a lovely plan, and it was really a great pity that it didn't work. The other woman's eyes widened in shock. "Wait a second—"

How Irene *hated* hearing those words. But what she hated even more was the way that the other woman's voice abruptly cut off, as though choked in her throat by some greater power. Their enemies were here.

The metal framework trembled and the stairs rocked beneath her feet as something heavy—something very heavy—took form and weighed down the walkway above.

Irene kept on running down the stairs, the others behind her, but it was growing darker. She spared a moment to glance up at the ceiling. Overhead, without any fuss, the lamps were going out; one by one they vanished, and a growing patch of darkness spread across the roof of the huge cavern. The gloom increased with every breath, until it was barely possible to read the titles on the books and scrolls they passed.

She could see what else had joined them, though. Above, where they'd left the Librarian, a great shadowy dragon coiled along the walkway, turning its huge head as it searched for them. It spread its wings, and the whole structure shook as it took to the air, weaving between the staircases and walkways with a dreadful silence, a living wave of shadow and imminent death.

Kai caught Irene's arm. "This time there isn't a choice," he said. His eyes were gleaming red, and she felt the prick of his nails through her sleeve. "I'm the one he's least likely to kill. Go on."

Something clenched and tore in Irene's heart—the knowledge he was right, but also a fear that he was wrong and that a disobedient descendant was the *most* likely target for death at his grandfather's claws. But there was no time for argument, no time for objection, not even time for the most desperate of imagined kisses. Either she trusted him to do this—and everything else she'd always trusted him with—or she ordered him to stay with her.

She chose to trust him, and ran on, hearing Catherine and Vale's feet hammering on the stairs behind her like heartbeats. Behind her, a sudden blast of light cut through the darkness as Kai took on his dragon form, throwing himself out into the void in a briefly glimpsed flurry of sapphire scales and wings.

He's smaller, he has the advantage of speed and size in a place like this. The grandfather will have to catch him first . . .

But all the sensible reassurances in the world could do nothing to calm her inner panic. They merely gave her additional speed as she sprinted down the curving stairs. *The sooner I can finish this, the sooner he'll be safe . . .*

There was an almighty crash from above—impossible to see what, impossible to know anything except the horrendous noise of grinding metal and the way that the staircase was shaking. Irene caught hold of the rail and threw out an arm to one side to catch Catherine as she fell, steadying her.

They were at a walkway intersection. Someone was walking toward them—an indistinct figure, barely visible in the darkness, robes and headscarf rippling in the rising wind. But their voice was perfectly clear, a compelling low tone that could have been a man's voice or a woman's, and it ran in Irene's bones, holding her still.

"A very long time ago," the figure said, "a young woman went out seeking the roots of the Library which had raised her. Now this was a long journey, for the following reasons: it led through many worlds and many languages and many stories. And the first part of the story was this . . ."

They paused. Irene should have kept on going down as fast as her legs would take her, but the voice was like a chain round her heart. She had to keep on listening. She had to know the rest of the story. Part of her realized that this must be the Storyteller, and like any Fae who had a title of that sort they'd be a paragon of their art, capable of spinning a tale that'd hold anyone's attention, and that this was being used against her—but none of it made any difference. She *had* to know what happened next.

"Excuse me." Vale stepped forward, suddenly incisive and focused as any Fae, but purely human, simply who he was. "I fear you have not given me the full details. Who was this young woman? What is this

Library? Why should it be considered a long journey, and how do you define long? I require answers, not merely a fable. I require *facts*."

The force that was holding Irene in place and keeping her attention on the Storyteller frayed for a moment as they turned to answer Vale's questions—so inconvenient, so antithetical to the smooth flow of a narrative. With a gasp, Irene threw herself forward, nearly tripping over her own feet in her desperation to get away from that smooth, beguiling, utterly enchanting voice.

A roar hammered through the darkness, louder than Kai's had ever been, and laden with additional surprise and fury. *Grandfather didn't expect Kai to fight back.* Irene would have covered her ears, but she needed one hand to grip the rail, to stop herself from falling in the near darkness. The sheer force and fury of the sound made her stagger as she struggled onward. She knew she'd left Vale behind. There was only her and Catherine now, on a downward stair that felt as if it would go on forever, lost in the darkness . . .

The figure at the bottom of the stairs was barely perceptible, just one more shadow among shadows—but her eyes were clear and harsh, uncompromising and vicious. "Where do you think you're going?" she demanded.

"Past you," Irene answered. She wasn't entirely sure if she could shove past this woman, or how safe it would be to do so—but she was going to try.

"You've been looking for answers, granddaughter." She must have seen Irene twitch at the word, for she laughed—a thin rattle of noise, as though she was out of practice at breathing, let alone laughter. "Don't you like that word?"

"I question your right to claim the relationship." Irene could feel Catherine behind her, pressed against her, vibrating with nervousness.

"Can't I call all Librarians my descendants? I was here first. These books are mine. All of them are *mine*." There was a sudden harsh possessiveness to her voice. "You belong to me as well. I won't see anyone hurting you—but you have to stop fighting me, granddaughter."

Perhaps this one—the only human of the trio—could be reasoned with. "But is this what you wanted?" Irene tried. "We're still collecting books, preserving them, *saving* them. We shouldn't be playing politics. We should be focusing on what's important. If you try to use Librarians as your agents in some sort of power play, you're going to turn everyone from both sides against us. We're supposed to be keeping the balance between worlds, not controlling them—"

"Granddaughter," the woman interrupted her, "the only way to keep a balance is to *enforce* it. Nobody else understands. They're all biased toward their own side. They don't appreciate what we're doing—for them, for everyone. We're the ones in the middle, doing what's best. We have to—for *their* sakes."

Her eyes glittered in the darkness. Here on the floor of the vast cave, surrounded by bookcases, they were away from the winds that cut through the air above, driven by the wings of the two dragons, making the metal walkways and stairs creak and tremble. It was like being in a small room together with an older relative, Irene thought drowsily, her back warm with the comforting heat of her Library brand: someone who really *understood* you.

"You tried to cut my throat," she objected, clinging to something she remembered very clearly. "You want me dead."

"I thought you were someone else." The old woman came closer, almost drifting along the paved stone floor. "Think about it sensibly, granddaughter. We have to keep the books safe, the stories safe, and the only way to do it—the *best* way to do it—is to keep them here, where nobody else can touch them, nobody can endanger or lose them. We've gone to all this trouble. We deserve them. This is how the rest of eternity will be—down here in the darkness, with the books, *all* the books, keeping them safe, owning them, reading them. You're a Librarian. You understand that. You're my granddaughter, as all the Librarians have been my children. You'll join me, now that you understand what's important, what really matters. The books are ours and we will keep them here."

Irene shook her head. There was a counterargument to this, she knew it, she was sure of it, but she couldn't find it . . .

"That's not being a librarian." Catherine's voice shook, but gained certainty as she went on speaking, moving from behind Irene to confront the woman. "That's being a hoarder. You might be an archivist, but you aren't a real librarian."

"Child, you don't understand."

"You aren't using my name. You don't even call Irene by her name!" Catherine stumped forward, shoulders hunched and tense with anger, her fists knotted at her sides. "Irene shares her books. The Library sends copies of books back to where they came from and to other worlds. But you—you'd just keep them to yourself. You'd never let anyone new in to see the books, never let any of the books out. *That isn't being a Librarian!*" Her voice cracked with real fury. "You must have wanted more than this when you began. Because otherwise you're nothing but a hoarder. Irene's more of a librarian than you are. *I'm* more of a librarian than you. You're just . . . something that hides in the darkness."

The dizzy haze that had swamped Irene broke and split apart like broken wax. She grabbed Catherine's shoulder and dragged her out of the way as the woman lunged for her, a knife suddenly sharp and vicious in her hand. "Thanks for clarifying the situation," she said, balancing on the balls of her feet and ready to dodge again. "Care to tell me again how I'm your granddaughter and how you just want me to behave?"

"You'll be mine, one way or another. Humans are the sum of their stories, and I'll never let them go." She thrust at Irene, the knife a moving point of light in the shadows, and the tip of the blade kissed Irene's forearm, cutting through her jacket to leave a thin line of blood along her arm.

Irene had been waiting for the move and took advantage of it, stepping in to grab the older woman at wrist and forearm—she might not be good with a knife, but she knew her disarms. To her dismay, her hands simply passed through the old woman as though she was no more solid than the shadows surrounding her.

She can cut me—but I can't touch her. This isn't good.

Another thundering crash from above; books came raining down from shattered bookcases to scatter on the floor below, and the old woman yelled out in rage at the profanation of precious literature, shaking her hands at the sky. Catherine also cried out as Irene dragged her into the shelter of one of the bookcases, wincing in sympathetic pain as the books hit the paving stones.

Irene shared that distress—but it made her reconsider her priorities. *I'm not here to fight this woman. I'm here to get past her and find their lair. And if the entrance to their lair is down here, then I need to open it . . .*

This was the floor of the cavern; there weren't any doors or passages down here. The only entrances to the cavern were far above, on the high walkways, beyond the sound of Irene's voice. *If there's something down here which I can open, a door or a passage or a way in,* she thought with the logic of desperation, *then it has to be the entrance I want.*

She took a deep breath, and shouted at the top of her voice, **"Unlock! Open!"**

The Language rang in the echoing cavern like hammered iron,

and Irene felt it latch onto reality and *work*. Over to her right, perhaps twenty yards away, there was a sudden thud and a blaze of light from the floor—pale moonlight, but harshly visible in this great darkness. It had barely been an effort. It was as if the door had wanted to open for her . . .

The old woman hissed and lunged for the two of them with vicious speed, striking Catherine aside; the young Fae girl slammed into the bookcase, cracking her head against it, and went limp, slumping to the ground.

Irene ran. She bolted like a hare, racing for the column of light that shone upward like a signpost, conscious of whispering steps closing in behind her. There was something there—and, most importantly, the old woman didn't want Irene to find it. That was all the reason Irene needed to head for it.

The trapdoor which had sealed the opening was now wide open. As Irene approached, she saw there were no stairs, no convenient ladder; just the hole in the floor, and the light which came from it, and now that she was closer, the sound of running water.

More books came cascading down, one dictionary clipping Irene's shoulder and making her gasp in pain. The walkways above shuddered under the weight of the grandfather dragon, and his shadow deepened the darkness round her. *He's seen the light. He wants to stop me too. This is definitely the right way to go, I just have to reach it . . .*

The old woman appeared in front of Irene, no longer bothering with any appearance of maintaining physical laws. "Run onto my blade if you will, granddaughter, but don't think you can run through me!"

Without slackening her pace, Irene spoke a word in the Language that was noun and invocation and prayer all in one. **"Light!"**

For a moment the rising pale moonlight thickened, coalesced, and blazed as brilliantly as a star, fading the surrounding shadows to blurred ink outlines that were barely visible and barely present.

In that moment Irene took a deep breath, and jumped into the hole.

And she fell.

CHAPTER 24

Irene seemed to be falling forever; seconds stretched out until they felt like minutes, and the rushing air filled her ears so she couldn't hear any more than she could see.

Then she hit water and sank.

It wasn't a graceful dive, or even a controlled jump; it was a downright crash, unexpected and painful. She barely managed to keep her mouth shut, flailing in the water as she tried to reach the surface as though she'd never been taught how to swim. A current was dragging her downstream, and she had a moment of gratitude that she was still in a trouser suit from Helsinki rather than the long and cumbersome skirts of Vale's world.

Her head broke the surface and she gasped for air, shaking her head to try to get the water out of her eyes. The water tasted salt on her lips, like the ocean, and briefly the thought crossed her mind, *Kai should be here, he'd enjoy it . . .*

She could only pray that Kai was still alive.

A roar filled her waterlogged ears. Her first thought—*dragon*—

was quickly invalidated by the fact that it went on and on, grinding into her bones, like an earthquake or a . . .

Oh dear gods. She was in a river leading to a waterfall and she was being carried right toward it!

Survival instincts kicked in. Irene looked around frantically for the nearest solid ground. She was in a river with dark rocky ravine walls rising on either side—not a particularly wide one, making her wonder briefly how she'd managed to fall into the river rather than onto the rocks. Perhaps she was due a bit of luck. There were no obvious landmarks, no vegetation or buildings—and no hole in the sky which she might have fallen through. A cool illumination like starlight made it possible to see, although there were no visible lights; if there was a ceiling, it was so high above that it was indistinguishable from sky. No moon. No stars. No Irene, unless she got out of the water right this minute.

Mustering her courage in the face of sheer panic, she kicked out toward the nearer bank, feeling the river dragging her a dozen yards downstream for every horizontal yard she managed to win. She didn't even try looking downstream to see how far ahead the waterfall was. There was no Kai here to save her from the water, no way to use the Language to save herself—if she couldn't get to solid land before she went over the edge, then it would be a fall she wouldn't survive.

Her fingers closed over an angular bit of rock, and she clung to it. The current vengefully slammed her into the rocky bank, dragging her parallel to it as it tried to suck her farther downstream. Stone protrusions rammed into her hard enough that her ribs ached with the impact. Irene clung to the stone with the sort of death grip that she normally reserved only for books, desperately trying to get her head above the water so that she could breathe.

The water seemed to be trying to suck her back down, to deliberately drag her back toward the waterfall. Her mouth was full of the taste of salt and iron. She spat out water and dragged herself inch by inch up onto the bank, as bedraggled as any rat who'd fled a sinking ship and miscalculated their life raft.

Irene could see the waterfall now—or rather, she could see where the water went over the edge, foaming white in the dim starlight and choppy enough to suggest any number of rocks. She couldn't see how far down it went, and right now she wasn't sure she wanted to know.

She needed to get a grip on where she *was*.

The Library didn't have any sort of underwater system. It wasn't like the Paris Opera House; no secret lakes, no hidden stocks of gunpowder. It just . . .

Irene realized her subconscious was trying to convince her that everything was somehow normal. *Vale was right. We're encouraged not to think about the underpinnings of the world we live in.* Every Librarian from time to time had seen an empty world outside the occasional Library window, but trying to go out there was . . . unpopular. People who tried vanished, or were found wandering in other parts of the Library with strange lapses of memory. Even the most carefully planned expeditions with rope and multiple participants somehow went wrong. It was all written off as one of the mysteries of the Library, a charming background detail which was unconnected to their real job of stealing books. Unimportant. Not worth spending time on.

She'd have liked to scream at herself for never actually *thinking* about any of it—but that would be wasting valuable time. Kai and Vale and Catherine had bought her that time. In her theology, it would be a mortal sin to waste it.

Irene dragged a hand across her face—saltwater, it was nothing but the saltwater she'd just crawled out of—and pushed herself to her feet. She needed a direction. The ravine walls were too high to climb at this point—she'd have to go upstream or downstream. Reluctantly, she took out the pencil stained with Kai's blood, hoping that the water hadn't ruined it, and that nothing would immediately jump on her for using the Language . . .

A fragmentary silver sparkle condensed in the air, drifting toward her like a floating cobweb, assuming more definition as it grew closer. It seemed to unfold with every imagined step until it was human in size and form, but too blurred to be recognizable.

If it's interested in the pencil—does it want blood? Vaguely remembered bits of Greek and other mythologies flickered through Irene's mind, stories of ghosts who had to be fed blood in order to regain memories and volition. Unwillingly she found her knife, setting it to her wrist.

"I absolutely forbid you!" With an almost audible crack of air, the figure snapped into a fully recognizable form. It was Coppelia, but not bed-bound or weary as she'd been when Irene last saw her; instead she was bristling with annoyance. "I know you're prone to taking stupid risks, Irene, but at least check your folklore before you begin self-harming. Don't you realize you have a responsibility to other people to look after yourself?"

Irene closed her mouth from fly-catching position with an effort. *Well, there you go. I'm clearly dead. We all are.* "You're a fine one to talk," she retorted, her throat burning and eyes hot with unshed tears. "Going round catching pneumonia and then giving up on us all because you're *tired*."

"Well, I'm not so tired now, and I refuse to see you doing even more damage to yourself than usual." Coppelia propped her hands on her hips—both the natural hand and the wooden one. She was moving with an ease that Irene hadn't seen her display for years. "You need to learn that there are sensible limits to self-sacrifice."

"There are no limits to self-sacrifice when we're doing our jobs," Irene said wearily. "You taught me that. But it's a bit late now, given that we're both dead."

"I'm dead," Coppelia agreed. "You're not. I'm a sparkly mass of coherent thought and memories. You're a physical body who needs coffee and a few months of vacation. Observe the difference."

"I can't deny I've got physical bruises," Irene admitted.

"I have to admit I'm feeling a lot more focused than usual." Coppelia frowned. "It must be annoyance. I'm suffering from a strong urge to scold you—"

"Which you're fully indulging."

"Yes, well, seeing my favorite protégé about to slice her wrist open has provoked a perfectly natural irritation. If I wasn't restraining myself, I'd say a great deal more."

Strong emotions had worked where blood would have failed. Irene made a mental note to claim she'd done it deliberately rather than by accident if she ever survived to tell this story. "Are there other Librarian ghosts here?" she asked.

"Ghosts? Yes, I suppose that's the best word for it. Collections of memories, maybe. We are all the sum of our memories, after all." Coppelia looked briefly distracted, the shadows deepening on her face until it was almost a skull. "Yes. There are passages elsewhere here full of books, thousands, millions of them. We . . . wander. We read. We don't remember much. I think seeing you was the first really coherent thought I've had since I came here. This isn't what I expected." Anger sparkled in her eyes, crackled in her voice. "This isn't what I *wanted*. It's nothing but a waking dream. It's not a real existence; it's just being a memory of the person I once was. I had something rather better in mind. I think I need to present my complaints to the management."

"But where *is* here?"

"I don't know exactly where *here* is. My best guess is that it's some sort of liminal space—a boundary of the Library defined in metaphysical terms rather than physical ones. Maybe it's like one of those little sieves one puts to catch the tea leaves while making tea, and we Librarians are the detritus. Or maybe it's more like the garbage-catcher one puts in the kitchen sink to stop the drain becoming blocked up."

"Neither of those images is really how I want to spend my after-life." Yet how much time did she have to spend? Irene knew that look-ing over her shoulder for approaching shadows wouldn't help—but a reflexive part of her still wanted to do it. "Look . . . does this place have a center? A nexus? Are there three really powerful beings here, one of whom looks like a dragon?"

Coppelia pursed her lips thoughtfully. "There might be. I realize that's not much of an answer, and I apologize. The problem is that I only really relate to things I already know about—like you, or books, or some of the other Librarians I've vaguely recognized. I suppose you could say that I have no context for anything new. But there are things . . . people . . ." She seemed to grow more present, more *real*, as she actively struggled to think and remember. "They move through here like sharks in deep water. The landscape shifts around them to make way for them. Their presence—it's like a thunderstorm in the air. They don't talk to us."

"Us?"

"You asked about other Librarian ghosts? Just look."

Irene followed her gesture and saw the crowd of semi-transparent figures slowly drifting toward them. They moved slowly, mistily, like sticks caught in a light current rather than with the rush of iron fil-ings drawn to a magnet, but they *were* approaching—and focusing on her. She wasn't sure if this was good or bad. "Can they help?" she de-manded. Simple desperation, sheer helplessness, brought an edge to her voice. She'd come all this way, her friends had sacrificed them-selves, and now here she was in some sort of afterlife where nobody even knew what she was talking about. Coppelia, her teacher, one of her oldest friends, the person whom in her heart of hearts she trusted to be able to *fix* things . . . couldn't. She was alone. And she'd let her closest friends die—for nothing. For a moment she really did want to slit her wrists and give up. "Can *any* of you help?"

Coppelia reached out to touch her, but her glowing hand passed through Irene's wrist. "Tell us what's going on, Irene. Explain. Perhaps we can affect things here if we truly want to. Give us a reason to try."

"Yes. Explain." Another of the figures became coherent, recognizable: it was Bradamant, elegant and furious, so cleanly drawn and so driven by her anger that she seemed a hole of light in the darkness. "I died. What happened—and what are you doing here?"

"She has come for judgment."

The voice came from behind Irene, heavy in the air, a pronouncement—a judge's sentence. She turned to recognize the Storyteller. They were still a figure of genderless and unidentifiable shadows, rather than translucent light like all the ghosts, but here they seemed as solid as Irene herself. "Irene, Librarian, daughter, and possession of the Library. You will accompany me to answer for yourself before your judges."

"Who are you to judge me?" Irene demanded, fear and anger warring in her.

"Who but the founders of the Library?"

That brought a ripple of attention from the surrounding ghosts. Some of them coalesced into better-defined shapes, caught by their curiosity.

The Storyteller, attention focused on Irene, magnificently ignored the ghosts. "Why do you hesitate? What brought you here, if not the desire to see us face to face? Your friends are already our prisoners. Submit and save them."

They're still alive. A small flame lit in her heart; she hadn't got them all killed. They'd never forgive her if she gave up now. She had to keep fighting: to save them, to save herself, to save the Library.

"What is this place?" she demanded.

"Liminal," the Storyteller replied. "A place of story and memory."

"Then how am I real here?"

"Are you certain that you are?"

Irene generally disliked debating philosophy or being told that answers were true "from a certain point of view." Unfortunately, the ordinary vocabularies of fact and reality seemed to be useless here. She was going to have to find an answer to the question, "What is truth?" or make one up for herself.

"What's *your* story?" she finally said. "I've asked you about the story of the Library's founding, but I never asked you about your own motivations. Maybe the dragon king wanted to stabilize the worlds to save his children, and the human woman wanted to keep her books safe—but what did you want? What *do* you want?"

There was no wind. The Librarian ghosts said nothing. There was only the ceaseless drumming roar of the waterfall, and the dark landscape, and the empty sky.

"Nobody ever asks a storyteller about their *own* story because of an *interest* in them," the Storyteller said slowly. "It is always because the hearer wants to be moved, or amused, or carried away to a world far beyond this one. My words are keys to a thousand doors, to a thousand souls, and yet nobody would remember my name. Nobody knows *my* story. It is the price I have paid to become what I am."

"But I found part of your story," Irene objected. "In myths, in legends—Egyptian manuscripts, Finnish folklore . . . but none of it agrees. What did you actually want? What was your desire?"

A coldness seized the air and seemed to weigh down on Irene. All the ghosts drifted away, even Coppelia and Bradamant, moved to fear by the crushing pressure of the Fae's will. The Storyteller's eyes were filled with a bitterness past Irene's comprehension, centuries old—no, millennia. It was like seeing into cold wet caves lost somewhere far underground, where light never came, and where things bred and ate themselves and died. "I cannot remember," the Storyteller said, and the despair in their voice was absolute.

Irene had no words to answer that.

"Now come." The Storyteller reached out and caught her wrist, their sleeve fluttering so that she couldn't even see their hand, only feel its cold pressure against her flesh—like an insect's claw or fish-bones. The ancient Fae began to walk, drawing her along with a pressure that Irene couldn't resist, and the world blurred around them as though each stumbling step was a dozen or more.

"Coppelia! Bradamant! All of you—follow me!" Irene called over her shoulder.

"Do you seek an audience for your trial?" the Storyteller demanded. "We have no time for juries here. There are three judges whom you must satisfy, and that is all."

Irene tried to slow her pace, but her efforts were futile; the landscape streamed around them as though they were beneath the water and she was caught in a new undertow. This wasn't just a story she was caught in; it was a full-blown myth. "I want them to know the story," she argued stubbornly. "That's all." *Well, and perhaps a little bit more . . .* She turned, looking for any sign of being followed, and thought that perhaps she saw a distant light in the darkness.

"We are here." The Storyteller released her, and moved away to where three dark thrones stood, taking their place on one of them. The other two were already filled; one by the old woman who'd spoken to Irene at the bottom of the stairs, and the other by a dragon king in what Irene recognized as part-human form, dark scales glittering on his shadowy skin, long nails like claws, and horns on his brow.

Before the thrones lay the motionless bodies of Kai, Vale, and Catherine—as real as she was in this land of shadows and light, as physical and as fragile. Irene didn't ask for permission; she fell to her knees beside them, checking their pulse, looking for some sign of life. They all breathed; in response her heart jumped, grateful beyond measure for this small mercy. *The Storyteller wasn't lying. They're alive—for the moment.*

They were still beside the river, upstream from where Irene had been earlier, but the flow of water was milder here, quieter; it was a gently rippling flow, a murmur in the background, and the banks had receded to either side to leave a wide valley perhaps fifty yards across. The ground was black rock, no grass, no soil; nothing grew here. Beside the three thrones was a cage of shadows, and light flickered inside it, harsh, uncoordinated, ill-defined.

"You do well to kneel," the old woman at the center said, her voice harsh compared to the Storyteller's mellifluous flowing tones. "You have much to answer for."

Irene bowed her head in apparent contrition and took the opportunity to glance behind her. A glimmer of light caught her eye, then another. The ghosts she'd summoned were following her. But she needed more of them—she needed time. She had one last gamble to try, here at the bottom of the Library, on the edge of darkness.

"This isn't what I expected," she said, looking up at the three enthroned figures. "And I don't even know how to address you. Should I call you 'your majesties,' or should I name you 'fellow Librarians'?"

"'Your majesty' will do," the dragon king on the right said. She'd have thought he'd have chosen the central throne, but perhaps he and the Storyteller preferred having a human buffer in between them. Maybe they still automatically detested each other's presence as much as any powerful dragon and Fae would, by their nature—which made their thousands of years here in the shadows even more of a sacrifice, and almost pitiable.

"Call me by my title," the Storyteller said. "I'm no Librarian. Storytellers and librarians are two quite different things."

"Address me as 'grandmother,'" the old woman said. "After all, I am your metaphorical ancestress, even if I'm not a Librarian like you. I don't *serve* in this place." Irene could almost hear the unspoken *I own it* at the end of the sentence—but perhaps the woman considered that tactless in the presence of her colleagues.

"And who or what is that?" Irene asked, indicating the man-sized cage.

"His name was Alberich." It was the dragon king who spoke. "Like all property of the Library, all books, all souls, he has come here now that his mortal life is over. He too waits on our judgment. While you have not rebelled against the Library to the extent that he did, you have still disobeyed us. Speak now, Irene, in your own defense, and accept your punishment—or be cast out."

His words were like thunder in the air, backed with unquestionable authority and power. Irene felt the urge to stay on her knees and beg for mercy. Perhaps that way she could save the others who'd been condemned on her account because they had helped her. Perhaps they'd let her stay a Librarian.

She watched her hands curl into fists as though they belonged to someone else, feeling the tracks of old scars across her palms, wounds taken in the line of duty. *I've never been good at admitting my feelings. I've never been good at sharing my secrets. But most of all—I've never been good at losing.*

Slowly she pushed herself to her feet. "Your majesty, Storyteller, grandmother," she said. "Forgive me for not knowing who to address first. Please believe that I hold you all in equal reverence." She took a deep breath. "Allow me to tell you a story."

CHAPTER 25

❧

"Long ago in the distant past," Irene began, "so many years ago that even the ghosts of the oldest Librarians here had not yet been born ..."

She sneaked a glance over her shoulder. More of the ghosts were gathering. It seemed that tonight Irene and her story held their focus more than any memories or books.

"Three great and powerful beings came together," she went on, deciding that a spoonful of sugar might help the medicine go down. "One of them was a dragon king, the father of the current dragon monarchs who rule the realms of order. One of them was a mighty Fae, named 'the Storyteller' by their peers." She still wasn't sure whether the Storyteller identified as male or female—or, indeed, whether they bothered to identify at all. It wasn't a gender-linked archetype. "And one of them was human, a collector and preserver of books known for her wisdom—and her hospitality."

The old woman at the center was frowning but hadn't stopped Irene yet. Maybe the flattery had helped.

"Together they agreed to combine their strengths," Irene went on. "They would create a Library which would stand between worlds—not part of any single world, but separate from all of them. This Library would be linked to as many worlds as possible, by removing unique books from those worlds. I don't pretend to understand the metaphysics behind it, but it worked. The Library was alive—is alive—and had its agents constantly collect new books."

She took a breath. "But why was this necessary, you may ask? It's because the forces of ultimate order and ultimate chaos are both ruinous. Human beings who are caught in the forces of chaos either become Fae or become mindless—and as the levels of chaos increase, the Fae are subsumed into their worlds and lose all humanity. Equally, at the far end of the scale, worlds which are too high-order cause human beings to evolve into dragons—and then the dragons themselves become mindless forces of nature, losing their individual wills and personalities."

The dragon king spoke, leaning forward, and his shadow overcast Irene and her unconscious friends. "It seems to me that you know too much, Irene Winters."

"Your majesty," Irene answered, "I have only spoken my conclusions to the people here, within this *liminal space* with me. You—and these ghosts." She turned to gesture to the Librarian ghosts, who were still gathering. She was rewarded by the sight of more and more of them becoming recognizable as people, rather than outlines of light. They were interested in what she had to say.

"Let her finish," the Storyteller argued. "Her tale is not yet fully told."

It wasn't exactly a promise of safety for when she'd finished her story, but the dragon king nodded and sat back. "Go on," he ordered.

Irene inclined her head. "Besides this double threat from both ends of creation, there was also the hostility between the dragons and the Fae themselves. They were antithetical by nature—and also conquerors, both sides seeing themselves as the natural rulers of the worlds they could travel between."

"Do you dispute this?" the dragon king asked.

Irene shrugged. "Your majesty, I'm unlikely to argue that as a human I'm naturally inferior and should be ruled over by my betters. Equally, I can sympathize with others wanting to ... expand ... to the natural limit of their powers. I've been accused by my own friends of setting myself apart from 'normal humans' because I'm a Librarian. How can I criticize others for doing the same when they're born with such powers?"

She glanced down at Vale, and her heart jumped as she saw his eyelid flicker in a barely perceptible wink. He was awake—though still feigning unconsciousness.

"A politician's answer," the old woman said.

"But not a foolish one," the Storyteller answered.

Was the Fae on her side? Irene wasn't sure. Maybe they just wanted to hear her finish the story. Well, she was going to do her best to oblige.

"And so these three created the Library," she went on, "to bring stability to creation and hold back the destructive forces of both ends of the universe. But also, I like to think, they wanted peace between their kindred. They envisaged a world where a truce was possible— where both sides could live in relative peace and create something greater together than they could on their own. They dreamed—"

The old woman hawked and spat. "Less of the idealism, if you please. I'm a pragmatist, granddaughter."

"The Library itself is an example of what I'm talking about," Irene argued. "Neither side could have created it alone. It's real, but it's built on stories—and it's alive."

All three of her judges stiffened at her final words. "No," the old woman said. "It's a construction. It runs—what's the word?—automatically. It follows orders. There's no more to it than that."

"Then who is it that tells us which books we should collect from all the separate worlds? Who or what sent me on specific missions so that I'd find out what was going on? Who is it that's now crying out for help in collecting books and keeping the balance, since the Librarians are all off playing politics? Because that wasn't *you*. The Library is a web that binds the worlds together—but all webs have a spider which maintains them. If it's not you, then who or what is it?"

"Finish your tale," the dragon king commanded, and there was thunder in his voice that rolled across the valley and made the water shudder. The force of his command knocked Irene to her knees. She struggled to rise, and for a moment she didn't think she had the strength to get up.

"It seems she's done," the old woman commented. "Time to pass sentence."

But Irene saw Kai's hand move, very slightly—a gesture of encouragement, a beckoning for her to continue—and she forced herself, swaying, to her feet. "I'm not finished!" she protested. "This isn't over—because *none* of this is over. Have you ever heard the saying that she who controls the present controls the past, and she who controls the past controls the future?"

They exchanged glances—Storyteller, dragon king, human. "The phrasing's familiar," the dragon king finally said, "but I fail to see the point."

Irene swallowed. Her throat was dry. "I have read or heard three different versions of this story so far, and there are doubtless other ones out there—and they all differ on the *reasons* why you did this. One story says that your intention was to restore stability. Another story told me that you were going to create the ultimate tool to maintain your power over both sides. A third version had it that you were all seeking peace and safety for your children, but that over the years you thought you were forgotten and decided to seek vengeance. And you've told me yourselves that you resolved to force peace on both dragons and Fae because they couldn't be trusted to do it themselves. Are there other versions too? Which one is the right one?"

"We were forgotten," the old woman said, her voice like rusting blades. "That much is true."

"It's rather unfair to blame the rest of the world for forgetting you," Irene said mildly, "when you've gone so far to conceal yourselves."

"Yet if this is the past, and we stand in the present, what of the future?" the Storyteller asked. There was something desperate about the way they leaned forward, reminding Irene of Vale at his most urgent for a new case—or for a dose of cocaine. *He wants a story that will include him. His archetype's on my side as long as I give him a role to play . . .*

"You've said that you intend to take control." Irene waited for the dragon king's nod before she continued. "You'll impose peace on both the dragons and the Fae, using the Librarians as servants and destroying any worlds that disagree. You've already made some of the more rebellious worlds vanish."

"You're describing it in an unnecessarily aggressive manner, granddaughter," the old woman said.

Irene shrugged. "The person telling the story gets to choose their adjectives." The glow of the Librarian ghosts behind her had become stronger; she could see her own shadow cast on the ground in front of her. "But my point is that here in the present, *you* have the ability to tell me what the past was—and what the future will be as a result. Your majesty, Storyteller, grandmother, I appeal to you—I *beg* you— let this be a story where your intentions were good. Look at the world as it *is*. I stand before you together with a dragon, and a Fae, and a human being. We're living proof that we *can* all work together, that we *are* all working together. You succeeded. You *won*."

She was absolutely, utterly sincere; she could hear the desperation in her own voice. She meant every word. This wasn't a fight against someone who was trying to kill her because of hatred, or malice, or a lust for universal domination. If one chose the charitable interpretation of this story—and Irene wanted to—then it was a fight against people who'd done the right thing and sacrificed themselves thousands of years ago but had lost all perspective after millennia of isolation here in the shadows, and were now just trying to save all their "children." "You don't need to take this any further. Release the Librarians you've controlled. Let us get on with the business of living together. We Librarians didn't take the job to become enforcers—we're preservers, enablers, people who collect books and share them, who provide stability to all the worlds. Let us be what you first dreamed that we could be."

The dragon king tilted his head. "Is that what you think we dreamed?"

"I'd like to hope so," Irene answered.

"And are you threatening to destroy us and the Library otherwise—as your father attempted?"

Irene looked at the silent screaming pattern of light, trapped in the cage of shadows beside the dark thrones. "My father did the wrong thing for what he thought were the right reasons. I, on the other hand, did the right thing for the wrong reasons."

"Explain."

"My father . . . arranged for me to be born . . . because he thought that only someone with Librarians as parents could strike back against you. But it was being *raised* by two Librarians that helped form my character, that gave me the strength and the will to stand here today and make my case. Blood had nothing to do with it."

"And yet you seem to be repeating his mistakes. Blood will tell."

"Perhaps it will," Irene said reluctantly. "But this story isn't over yet. Consider this, please. I asked my friends to come with me—I manipulated them, I used their feelings of friendship—because I thought that it would need a union of three people to enter here. A human Librarian, a dragon, and a Fae. But those were the wrong reasons. It wasn't *what* they were that got me here. It was *who* they were. I'm here because of Kai's determination and willingness to fight, Vale's logic and intelligence and ability to question, and Catherine's wish to be a true librarian, to gather knowledge and to share it, and because she reminded me what it really means." She turned to face the crowd of glowing specters. "That was the root of what brought me to this place. That's what being a Librarian *is*. Do *you* remember?"

"Oh, we remember," Coppelia said, and her words were repeated in a susurrus of whispers that echoed through the valley.

"Silence." The dragon king raised his hand, and an oppressive hush fell, blotting out all speech or sounds. His eyes might have been kind, but it was the kindness of someone who considered himself far beyond her pitiful comprehension; condescension delivered in a staggering landslide that buried her words and opinions far beneath it. "Child, I will be merciful to you because you speak from naivety and honesty rather than malice. We have watched as the years went by, and we have seen that our descendants cannot be trusted. My own son betrayed his siblings and tried to stop the peace treaty from being signed. The Fae fight against each other, and there are as many who'd turn to violence as those who'd make peace. The risks are too great. We will not permit the worlds the chance of making any further mistakes."

Congratulations, Ao Ji, you may just have destroyed the universe, Irene thought. She had to keep on trying. "But what if your orders aren't obeyed? What if both sides turn against the Library? Are you simply going to send Librarians to destroy any worlds that dare rebel against you? The two sides are already starting to panic because of the vanishing worlds—it won't take much to drive them into war again. Paranoia will do it. Fear will do it—and you're going to be using fear as your weapon. You're going to make things worse."

"Control is necessary," the old woman said. "My lord speaks the truth. For the greater good, we must take action."

I wonder how often you call him "my lord" when you want to persuade him to your point of view? "Please *listen* to me!" Irene's voice cracked with emotion as she tried to put her will into it, to convince them somehow—without the Language or any supernatural powers—that they were *wrong*. "Storyteller . . ." She turned to the enthroned Fae. "Don't make this a story about tyrants imposing rule. Make this a story about freedom—about growth, about adults forging a new compromise. Let this be a story about how we're grateful for what you did for us—rather than a story about how you turned us into *slaves*."

For a moment she thought she saw uncertainty in the Storyteller's posture. But then the old woman leaned to their side and murmured, the words carrying loud enough that Irene could hear them, "A story is only told after it is done, Storyteller. We are the preservers of stories here, the keepers of tales. When this is finished, it'll be *our* story—one of how we brought peace to creation."

Irene's heart sank as she saw the Storyteller nod in response. "That is fair," they said. "The narrative will be ours. It will be a clear path from a hopeful beginning to a glorious ending. I accept that."

"Judgment, then?" the old woman said, and the two on either side of her nodded.

"Irene, granddaughter, child of the Library," the old woman said. The sky was still clear, but now it was the darkness of eternal space rather than the cool gloom of a starless evening sky. "We do not wish to be harsh, but we must be firm. You speak as a child and you understand as a child—and you must be treated like a child. For the sake of the Library and the future of creation, we cast you out. You are no longer a Librarian."

All three of them raised their hands, and the shadows rose to surround Irene, blotting out the outside world and trapping her inside a pillar of darkness. Panic seized her, and she bit her tongue so as not to cry out.

Then the pain hit, and she did scream. It was like liquid nitrogen tracing across her back, unwriting words she couldn't see and sentences she didn't understand, unraveling something which was part of her—but which was so closely interwoven with her soul that she'd never before recognized it as something separate.

She was so cold.

She was so *alone*.

It could have been only seconds, or it could have been hours—there was no space for rational measuring of time in the darkness, no way to count heartbeats.

When the void faded and dissolved she fell to her knees. She had no strength left, no ability to stand. She knew her Library brand was gone. The Language had left her; her voice was no more than a normal human's. She'd been brought down to common mortality, helpless and bedraggled, on her knees before the people who had taken her power away from her.

"Irene?" Kai's voice; he was on her right, trying to help her to stand. She could hear Vale and Catherine too, background noises behind the hammering of her own pulse in her ears. They must have given up the pretense of unconsciousness. And why not? There was nothing left to do, no hope of success, no chance to avert disaster. "How could you do this to her!" he shouted at his ancestor, stepping away from Irene to glare at the dragon king.

"Are you defying me, grandson? I thought you'd learned better by now. I would have thought you'd *know* better. Were you so badly taught?"

"I was very well taught," Kai retorted, "and what I know and have learned is that part of my service is to tell you when you are in error. My lord uncle, my lord father even, and you most of all. If I do less than that, then I am betraying you. I may die in doing so, but it is my duty to tell you that this is an improper and *incorrect* course of action!"

Irene knew how much that cost him. Her heart ached with the knowledge that she'd brought him and the others here, where the only alternatives were death or servitude, and—worse in a way—that he'd never blame her for it. *I love him and yet I've done this to him. He is far more than I deserve. I'm a manipulator and a liar, like my blood father, like all other Librarians . . . yet even we have our lines beyond which we will not pass.*

Irene was angry, yes, but beneath the anger was a bedrock of stubbornness. Like Catherine's hunched shoulders when she was most determined, or Vale's willingness to press himself past human limits when he was on the trail of a case, she too had an inner core of inability to let go and admit to failure. *This is my final line. I will not give up. They will need to unmake me entirely before I let them win.*

She staggered to her feet again, Vale at one side and Catherine at the other, and coughed to clear her throat. "This isn't over," she said, her voice flat.

"Are you going to appeal to us again?" The old woman didn't even bother to hone her voice with spite; she could afford to be pitying now.

"No." Irene set her shoulders. "You aren't my only audience. You never have been. I'm speaking to my brothers and sisters now."

She turned to the Librarian ghosts who filled the valley—many faces whom she had never known, who had died long before her birth, but a few that she did know. "We are all in one service," she said, her voice no more than human. "We all gave our lives for the Library and bound ourselves to hunt down books and preserve the worlds. This may be all the afterlife we get. You've seen that they've taken away my brand. I have no doubt that they can destroy you as well. But all the same—are you going to let this happen? Is this what you want the Library to become?"

Curiosity had drawn the ghosts here; memories made them answer. A flood of shining figures came pushing forward, surging past her, sparked to anger and given the will to act.

CHAPTER 26

Shadows lashed out from the three enthroned figures, a reversed lightning which dissolved the figures of light when they touched them. It was individual, like a reaper needing to cut down a field of corn one stalk at a time. It was also final, terribly final. Irene knew without having to be told that each Librarian ghost that was struck was deleted from this appendix to the Library, this strange afterlife, this *liminal space*.

Irene had done this. She'd caused every single death, asking them to go out there and court destruction for her sake . . .

No. For the *Library's* sake. She had to remember that. This was not the time to indulge in guilt.

"You'd better have an idea, Irene," Bradamant said, appearing beside them. She moved with human speed and anger, rather than the graceful floating of some of the other ghosts. Then her gaze moved to Irene's back, and somewhere between pity and fury, she said, "Not that you could do anything about it if you had."

"Can you do something?" Catherine demanded. "Irene may not be a Librarian now, but you are, aren't you?"

Bradamant spread her glowing hands helplessly. "I'm dead. The Language doesn't work any longer—I tried."

"There's more to power than the Language," Irene said through gritted teeth. "I *am* still a Librarian. I'm just suffering from a lack of Library brand—"

"And power, and Language, and anything useful," Bradamant interrupted. "I'm hoping you actually had something *useful* in mind, and that's why you told everyone to go and commit suicide."

"I do," Irene said. "There's no time to waste. Kai, I need you to get me upstream. Vale, Catherine, please try and slow them down if they ask any questions." A jerk of her head toward the silent fury around the thrones made it clear who the *them* was. "Bradamant, can you come with us?"

Baffled fury gleamed in Bradamant's eyes. "I can't enter the river. I can follow you above it . . ."

"At which point you would become a floating marker to anyone watching," Vale cut in. "Inadvisable. Winters, are you sure about this?"

"I'm going with the Finnish version," Irene said, "and it has to be now." No time for apologies, no time for instructions, no time for anything—her fellow Librarians were buying every second with their lives, and she couldn't waste that. "Kai?"

"I've got you," he said, catching her by one hand, and together they ran for the stream and plunged into it.

The water bent itself around their bodies. Kai flowed upstream like a salmon, graceful and elegant and utterly in tune with the river's music, holding her against his body with one arm. Irene bent her head against his chest as the flow pounded against them, trying to make herself as small a target for the oncoming rush of water as she could. In his embrace she didn't feel the need to breathe. She could only hope that their absence would go unnoticed, and that their passage upriver beneath the surface would be equally invisible.

"Why did you say the Finnish version?" Kai asked, his voice somehow audible in spite of their surroundings. There was a rasping, pained undertone to his breathing; she tried not to think about what damage his grandfather might have done to him while capturing him.

"It's been the most accurate so far," Irene explained. "I can absolutely believe that old woman's behind the worst of what's happening."

"Yes, but why upriver?"

"Kai, remember what it said? 'The rock on which they'd marked their charter wept bitter tears.' And this river we're heading up is *salt*. And the rock's still there—the manuscript said so."

"That's . . . plausible. It doesn't feel like a sea ahead of us at all."

"What does it feel like?"

"Like nothing I've ever sensed before." She felt rather than saw his jaw set, his face tensing in lines of strain. "Hold on. This is getting difficult."

Irene could feel the increased weight of the water pressing against them, pushing them back with an almost deliberate intent. It was like trying to make one's way into an oncoming gale. There were no fish in this river, no plants, nothing but the icy swell of the water and the jagged dark banks. The driving force of the water made it impossible to look ahead, so instead she looked back, and saw a dancing light gleaming somewhere above the surface of the river, pursuing them. "I think Bradamant's following us," she reported. "At least, I hope it's her."

"Whoever it is, let's hope none of *them* are watching." Kai's body was trembling with effort, and a trickle of blood seeped from the corner of his mouth, carried away in a moment by the rush of the river.

Irene knew that part of his struggle must be in maintaining the gentleness of his grip and the force of his will. If he were to relax his protection, the current would simply tear her out of his arms and drag her downstream and against the rocks.

The river channel was growing shallower. Kai tilted his head to look forward; the water tore at his hair so that it streamed back from his face. "I'm going to have to surface—we're running out of depth to stay submerged."

He didn't waste time waiting for her agreement, but instead rose to the surface of the water, dragging her with him. The landscape had changed drastically while they were underwater; instead of a mild valley surrounding a river, they were in a narrow ravine split by a single fierce rivulet. Ahead of them, the stream narrowed to a thin runnel of water which sprang from the dark mouth of a cave. The sky above them was split and furrowed with waves of light and darkness like the aurora borealis, a constant ripple of movement which threw them alternately into pale burning brightness and swallowing shadows.

Kai boosted Irene out onto the bank, then swung up himself, and the two of them ran for the cave mouth together. It was an obvious destination—too obvious, maybe?—but perhaps when one was grappling with mythic narratives, obvious was the only way to go. Irene knew how much of a gamble she was taking. Vale would have scoffed at her lack of evidence, and justifiably so. But it *felt* right in a way that nothing else did.

Kai glanced back over his shoulder, briefly slowing down. "We're still being followed," he reported.

"Don't do anything stupid like stopping to hold them off," Irene gasped. "We're in this together."

The mulish set of Kai's jaw suggested that he was quite prepared to stay behind and hold off any number of pursuers, however suicidal it was. But they were almost at the cave mouth now . . .

. . . and as they reached it, it began to close, jagged edges sliding together like jaws.

Irene was a step ahead of Kai, not having paused to look back. Without taking even a second for thought or to consider all the mental images of being squeezed like a worm in a mincer, she flung herself forward in a dive through the closing edges of the cave mouth, rolling as she landed.

The stone snapped shut behind her. As she came to her feet, she saw a faint light gleaming at the end of the bare stone passageway in which she stood. A narrow channel ran down the center of the floor, filled with a trickle of water which would become the river outside.

Every desperate instinct of affection, of love, screamed for her to turn back and try to open the passageway again so that Kai could follow her. Yet the part of her which was more cold-blooded than any snake told her to keep on moving. *There's nothing you can do to make the rock open. No powers, remember? No Language.*

Irene tasted the full bitterness of self-loathing as she abandoned Kai and ran down the passage, looking for what she could only pray would be here and would justify everything and everyone she'd sacrificed to get this far. However much she told herself that they were hunting *her* and not Kai, that he'd probably be safer without her, it still sounded hollow. *I brought him into this, I brought them all into this, and now I'm leaving them to die . . .*

Then she stumbled into the cave ahead of her and saw the source of the light.

The floor was suddenly smooth, as flat as if it had been planed and as dark as onyx, and it was covered with a circular design in the Language like a vast mandala. Lines of writing spread in all directions and knotted back on themselves, twining together like vines and blossoming into sentences and paragraphs which interconnected like a spider's web. The writing was stark white against the black floor, glowing with its own light, and the whole design was perhaps fifty yards across with no obvious beginning or ending. A narrow stream of water encircled the design in a constant whisper of sound, flowing out of the cave to form the river which Irene and Kai had ascended.

The sight took Irene's breath away. It wasn't just the complexity of the design, or sheer awe at the realization of what she was seeing; there was a constant throb of leashed power in the air. It was like being in the presence of a dragon monarch, only more so. No . . . it was like being at the eye of a hurricane.

She made herself step forward to read the closest sentences. Even though she'd lost her Library brand, anyone could read the Language; it merely appeared to be in the language they knew best. The part in front of her was a set of directions, or possibly a poem or a sonnet, in English—albeit English from the Middle Ages—and it seemed to be, as far as she could understand, about building chains between worlds.

A growing feeling of panic seized Irene as she understood the enormity of her problem. She'd been hoping—as much as she'd allowed herself to hope—for a nice small document, preferably with a set of signatures at the bottom. Names had power. Even without the Language, she'd have found some way to use them. Failing that, a conveniently legible charter with an obvious spot that she could have understood and somehow used or edited. But if she had to read this entire mandala of the Language, this whole design, assuming she could even *understand* it, she'd never finish before they caught up with her . . .

A thought teased at the back of her mind. She might not be *entirely* alone here.

"If anyone's listening," she said, her voice so loud in the hush that it seemed almost indecent, "if you can hear me, if the Library is conscious and trying to fulfill its function and set me and Alberich on this path to stop the three founders—then show me which part of this writing, this charter, I need to change to save you."

There was no reply, and her heart sank. It had been a desperate hope in the first place, but now it felt like the last fragment of a crumbling grip giving way under her fingers.

Then, slowly but definitely, a section of the writing began to gleam as though it had been struck by a ray of sunlight.

Irene sprinted toward it and fell to her knees beside it. It was a small section, barely half a sentence, but it was a nexus of meaning; lines of the Language spread out from it to tangle into other sentences and paragraphs, and from there across the mandala.

The wording was abstruse, but the meaning was clear. Everything that was brought into the Library and marked as part of the Library would be preserved—a parenthesis indicating this applied to both books and souls . . .

That was how the founders still existed. They'd created something which in turn preserved them. They might not be Librarians, but they were part of the Library, and as such it kept them alive—if *alive* was the right word.

A possibility suggested itself, so huge and so catastrophic that Irene hesitated. She'd already slipped her knife out of her jacket without thinking about it, but it lay unused in her hand. It was the classical editor's dilemma—did she dare take a knife to the text and risk destroying the universe? Or more specifically, destroying the part of the universe she in particular cared about?

"I would say go on," a voice broke her concentration, "but I don't think you're going to be able to do it."

Irene looked up. Alberich stood near the entrance, but it was only his voice that let her recognize him. His body was a jagged collection of angles and painful-looking twisted lines, a portrait by some artist who'd decided to go beyond all normal rules of art in depicting *The*

Human Spirit Deformed by Hatred. He was glaring at her; indeed, the deformity of his face made it impossible for him to do otherwise.

"How are you here?" she demanded.

"Oh, don't mind me. I just took advantage of the confusion to break free from that cage they put me in and follow you upstream. Where else would you be going? Your dragon lover is trying to break through the rock, but he won't manage it." His lips twisted. "Of course, I could pass through the rock perfectly well. Nothing solid is real to me here any longer."

"Then I suppose you can't touch this pattern," Irene said. She touched the point of her knife against an unwritten section of stone. It was as hard as stone would normally be. She might be able to scratch it, with a lot of effort and a bit of luck; she certainly couldn't cut through it. And she lacked the Language to tell her knife otherwise.

"If I could, I'd rip this whole design apart. But I *can't* touch it. I can't even step on it." There was an undertone to Alberich's voice that suggested crumbling foundations in ancient houses and cliffs about to give way. "You've seen it all now. You know the truth. You know how we've been used. Don't you agree with me?"

Wearily Irene stood, her knife still naked in her hand. "What I see is something that went wrong—but that was begun with noble intentions, and that's done a great deal of good. Even now I think that the founders believe they're acting for the best." She thought of the old woman's face again. "Well, mostly."

"How can you be so *blind*!" Alberich raised his hands in impotent rage, and Irene realized with what was almost sympathy that being here at the center of all his schemes, yet utterly powerless, must in a way be the ultimate torture for him. "Quick. Bleed on it. Perhaps it'll work."

"I'm not a Librarian any more," Irene reminded him. Gray despair was setting in. Half-formulated plans rattled round in her mind, but nothing would settle into a shape that would work. Then a thought came to her. "If you followed me, are they following too? The founders, that is?"

"Without a doubt." Alberich shrugged. "I suppose they could leave you here to suffocate or starve to death, but that would be untidy. I think they can perceive everything that happens in this world of shadows."

They'd certainly tried hard enough to stop her getting into this underworld. *If this didn't matter, they wouldn't bother. Therefore it matters. So what I need . . .*

"And their names are here, where they signed their charter," Irene said. She kept the tone deliberately casual, speaking to Alberich rather than playing to the galleries, but she suspected that she'd be heard. "Their original names. The dragon king, the Storyteller—I may not be a Librarian any longer, but if I gave you their names . . ."

Shadows thickened into shape, a cold wind sighed through the room, and the old woman was standing across the pattern on the opposite side from Alberich. Uncomfortably near to Irene, but nothing was ever perfect.

Bingo. Of course if there was a question of using someone's name against them, the Fae wouldn't want to come within earshot—and the physical setting was too confined for the dragon king to take his natural form here. The old woman, the *human*, was the natural person to come and finish her off.

Irene edged away from the old woman, raising her knife in self-defense. "Try and kill me," she threatened, "and I'll bleed on this."

"Bleed as much as you like; it'll do you no good." The old woman stepped across the stream and onto the edge of the writing. The pale lines of text were visible through the darkness of her foot. "You've run further than we expected, but all rabbit holes come to an end eventually."

"How did you find me? Are you omniscient here?"

"We saw you through your father's eyes," the old woman said, her smirk curling her lips. "Whatever else he likes to pretend, he's still a Librarian—still beholden to us, still *subject* to us."

"You've picked up some Fae bad habits," Irene noted. "Gloating. Excessive imagery. A tendency to refer to your opponent in a way that you hope will lower their morale."

An expression of annoyance drifted across her opponent's face. "If you want me to hurry up and finish you off, that can be arranged."

Irene flicked a glance sidelong at Alberich. "If she stabs me, do your best to distract her. Since there's nothing else you can do . . ."

"Not if, but when," the old woman said, and flickered across the writing toward Irene. She moved like a ghost caught on stop-motion camera; Irene couldn't see her passage clearly, only a trail of images that left out the movement in-between. That, and the gleam of her knife.

She was horrifyingly fast. If Irene hadn't expected her to take that distraction as a convenient opening to attack, she'd never have managed to dodge. She threw herself into a roll to one side and came to her feet again in the same motion.

Cold air touched her left side, and she cautiously lifted her fingers to touch her jacket. There was a slit in it. If the blade had been a fraction closer, or Irene a fraction slower . . .

"Tell me one thing," she said to the old woman, raising her knife in what would probably be a futile attempt to block. Her opponent's knife had to be solid at the moment of attack, but otherwise she could be as incorporeal as she liked. She could dance up and down in front of Irene, and Irene would never be able to touch her.

"Yes?"

"When was the last time you actually *read* a book?"

Sheer fury filled the old woman's eyes and twisted her face into a mask as poisonous as the expression Alberich wore. "You dare judge me? After everything I've done?"

"If you gave up everything you loved for a higher purpose, then I respect that," Irene said steadily. "I honor that. But I think that in the long term it's damaged you and the other two so much that there's nothing left . . ."

The old woman came at her again. This time Irene took a long slice along her left arm. Blood ran down to drip from her fingers and onto the writing. As the old woman had warned, it did no good, changed nothing.

She simply has to wait until I tire and she can finish me off . . . Fear cramped in Irene's guts. She might have a plan, but it was yet another gamble on top of a whole pile of them. No streak of luck lasted forever.

It's an unjust world, and virtue is triumphant only in theatrical performances . . . The quotation nearly made her smile.

The old woman saw the bitter quirk of her lips and misinterpreted it as smugness. "Do you realize how many of the Librarian ghosts have been destroyed? Because of you? They were fools to attack us—but you were the one who roused them. Now they're gone, past hope of recall by the Library. Their deaths are on *your* head. As for your friends—either they cooperate or they'll die too. All your efforts, this whole ridiculous escapade, has been nothing but an utter *waste* of lives—and all because of you. Even your father couldn't claim so much damage. You're his daughter; no question of it."

Her gaze flickered to Alberich, and Irene took advantage of that to adjust her own position and check where she was standing. "That's what I was thinking," she answered quietly, trying to bridle her rage at the old woman's words. "That's exactly what I was thinking. I'm guilty, and I'm going to take that to my grave."

"At least you admit it." The old woman shifted position, and Irene turned to face her.

"Yes," Irene said. "I'm guilty. We both are. But you know the difference between us, *grandmother*? I told them the truth. If my friends—my brothers and sisters—have sacrificed themselves, then it was their choice. You, on the other hand, have lied to us and kept us in the dark and *used* us. You're probably going to tell me that you did it for a higher cause, that you were just protecting us. But true higher causes don't have everyone deserting them when they find out the truth, grandmother. Genuine ethical purposes don't have everyone walking out once they know what's really going on. And causes that people care enough to die for . . ." The words were like ashes in her mouth, and she spat them out with the intent of hurting the old woman as much as possible. "All my brothers and sisters, all your grandchildren—they're quite clear which is the right side here, aren't they? How does it feel to see that in their faces? To know that they *reject* you?"

The old woman moved in a flash of darkness, closing the distance between them before Irene could dodge, and her blade went into Irene's side as she tried to twist away. "Then join them," she hissed.

It felt like a blow rather than a cut—like a punch, still painful, but not as much as one would have thought a stab to the guts would be. Irene went down on one knee, then collapsed to the floor, and the old woman followed her, keeping the knife firmly in place, trying to push it in further. She wasn't just trying to kill Irene now; she wanted to *hurt* her.

Irene's own knife dropped from her hand—and she gestured feebly at where Alberich was standing at the edge of the design. *Come on. For once, do the right thing . . .*

"Let go of my daughter!" Alberich's voice was furious, but it was like the distant crying of gulls, with no strength or life to give it force. "Stop it!"

For one moment the old woman looked up from Irene to smirk at him—and that was what Irene needed.

The old woman's knife, plunged in her side, was solid *while it was there* and sharp enough to cut anything. Irene had carefully judged her position; the area of text that she'd been shown was directly underneath her.

With all the strength she had left, Irene rolled to one side, supporting herself on her left arm, and locked her hand over the old woman's where it rested on the knife's hilt. As she did, the Language glowed beneath her once again, shining through the blood which was pooling on top of it and letting her read what she needed.

There.

She forced the knife down, slicing through her own flesh and into the stone below, cutting through blood and Language and rock until the knife was embedded in the **and souls**, editing it and slicing it out of the sentence.

The Library might preserve all the books that were brought into it and marked as its property, but not souls. Not any more.

And the Language was always true.

"You've killed every single one of your brothers and sisters!" the old woman shrieked at Irene. She pulled the knife free and brought it down in a slash at Irene's throat. Irene managed to get her right arm in the way, but the blow cut her to the bone in a screaming agony that was almost worse than the pain in her side. She collapsed back onto the rock, her strength gone, and saw the knife lift again, catching the light like the last star in creation.

But another hand caught the old woman's wrist. The Storyteller was standing behind her, still anonymous and faceless in their robes and veils. "It's enough," they said. "The story's over. The tale is done. We can't kill the only person who'd remember us."

"But what will she remember?" The dragon king was there as well. His darkness seemed to merge with the other two in a rising tide which blotted out the light.

But they were fading, all of them, receding into nothingness, no longer part of the Library's collection—free to pass on to whatever true afterlife there might be.

Irene wanted to point out that she'd be dead, which cut down on the possibility of remembering anything, let alone telling their story. Not only dead, but denied any possibility of returning as one of the Librarian ghosts. Was that a double suicide? She'd have laughed, but she no longer had the breath for it, and her vision had dimmed so much she couldn't see the shadows, or Alberich, or even the Language all around her. But she could feel it. The hurricane was still circling, the engine was still running, the power was still on, the Library was still there. That was the important thing.

It would be nice to think there was some sort of immortality of the soul which didn't depend on the Language or the Library, and that there really was something past death, something that wasn't a gray drifting through forgetfulness and stories, and that the other Librarians would be there, and that maybe after Kai and the others had lived long and happy lives—let them live, let them get past this, let them be *happy*—there might be a place where she would see them again.

Alberich might not believe in life after death.

But Irene wasn't her father.

She was so dreadfully cold.

She closed her eyes.

CHAPTER 27

The stars, Irene thought dreamily, were coming back on.

They flickered across the great arch of the night sky one by one, spreading out into unknown constellations, forming an astronomy she didn't know and an astrology she didn't believe in. They wrote words in the darkness in a language which she couldn't understand. They followed their paths without hesitation or pause, except when some black hole overshadowed them or a dark bridge or staircase interrupted her view . . .

Irene realized that her eyes were open and she was breathing. The shock of the realization made her gasp for air, then cough, as though her lungs were remembering how to work. Now that she was awake and thinking, she could feel that the cold stone beneath her was leaching the heat out of her. She sat upright.

Her head spun, and she clutched at her temples. It felt as if, rather than trying to add two plus two to get four, she was trying to subtract two from four and having problems with the resulting total. *I was dying. But now I'm alive. But . . .*

Then her eyes focused enough to see and recognize the three other bodies sprawled beside her, and she rejected all questions of metaphysics, or why her back was itching, to focus on the real and urgent question of whether they were alive too.

Vale's pulse was steady. So was Catherine's; she curled up as Irene released her wrist with a half-conscious murmur about time and the morning and killing people. And Kai . . .

Irene had been holding her breath. She released it in pure relief as his pulse throbbed steadily under her hand. His clothing was torn, and bruises stained his face and arms, but his breathing was steady and he was *alive*.

"Hello?" Irene identified the tentative voice as Makeda, the Librarian they'd passed earlier. "Are people down there?"

"Yes!" Irene called back. "One conscious, three unconscious. We need medical help, stretchers and assistance getting to the nearest lift or transfer shift cabinet."

"Speak for yourself, Winters," Vale mumbled, his voice blurred. He opened one hazy eye for an instant, then closed it again, his body relapsing into the limpness of unconsciousness.

"I'm a bit confused about what's going on . . ." Makeda called down, leaning over the edge of a walkway in an attempt to see what was happening.

Irene could sympathize with her curiosity, but this really wasn't the time. "Makeda, please, you can walk but I don't think I can, and this is urgent. Get help *now*—and contact Melusine in Security while you're on the job. We'll be right here."

She waited until Makeda had gone, her steps ringing on the iron stairs, then examined herself a bit more carefully. There were gashes in her clothing where the knife had cut her, but no corresponding wounds in her flesh—though the fabric was brown with dried blood.

It all raised very significant questions about how *real* their time in that liminal space had been: questions that she wasn't sure she wanted to think about too deeply. She was going to have to come up with some sort of explanation for her superiors in the Library—her genuine superiors, people like Kostchei and Melusine, not the three founders—and she had no idea what to say that wouldn't get her suspended from duty as unreliable or insane.

If I could use the Language, then I could at least swear to them that it was all true, but without my Library brand . . .

She stroked Kai's hair back from his face. "I would say that we need to stop diving into danger to rescue each other," she said softly, "but that isn't going to happen, is it? So perhaps we just need to jump together a bit more often."

Kai's eyes remained closed, but his hand moved, rising to clench around hers, tightly enough to hurt for a moment, then relaxing to a more normal grip, but with the implication that he didn't intend to let go. "Did you give him peace?" he asked.

Irene didn't have to ask whom he meant. "I think so," she answered. "I think they're . . . all gone from there. That *there* itself is gone."

"Then what happens when you die?"

"Nothing that I hadn't already expected." She clasped her free hand around his. "But I intend to live as long as I can . . . and in your company, for as long as possible."

His eyes opened and he smiled, and it changed his face from simply handsome to beautiful—far more beautiful than any icon of desire like Lord Silver. "Well, that spares me the trouble of arguing you into it."

"It's appallingly selfish of me," Irene confided. "But the fact of the matter is that I want you as part of my life."

He blinked as he looked up at her. "You've never actually said that before."

"We're in a liminal space here." She squeezed his hand again, trying to find the words—the *honesty*—to explain. "Which is why I'm going to say this. I thought that I was dying, and I was trying to come to terms with that, and wishing you a long and happy life . . . and I couldn't do it. When I closed my eyes, I was still wanting more years with you. More time with you. We'll spend it constructively—but I want us to spend it together."

"No holidays in Paris, then? Or Tokyo? Or Nairobi?" Kai's tone was gently mocking, but his eyes said far more than his voice could.

"Maybe a day or two if we're there on a job."

He paused. "What if you're not a Librarian, though?"

The itch on her back was proving persistent. Irene allowed herself to wonder, for the first time, just how permanent the removal of her brand had been. If she'd survived death, might other things have been temporary too?

If she tried this and failed, she wasn't sure that she could face the future—even with Kai. But if it worked . . .

"Just a moment," Irene said, and reached into her jacket pocket. The pencil she'd stained with Kai's blood was still there. She weighed it meditatively in her hand as she tried to remember the proper vocabulary—*and the words were there.* That gap in her mind was gone.

"**Pencil, rise,**" she said, for once not bothering about the precise details or boundaries in the Language.

It shot into the air like a tiny rocket. High up, afar, there was a distant clang as it collided with something.

"I thought you weren't a Librarian any longer," Kai said slowly, "and I've never been so *glad* to be proved wrong."

Tears stood in Irene's eyes. This wasn't just happiness; it was joy, something too large for her to explain, even to Kai. "Apparently the Library still thinks I am—and that's what counts."

Irene opened the door and came back into the room where Kai and the others were waiting, prudently taking a step to one side. An inkpot whizzed past her head from behind and shattered against the opposite wall, cascading to the floor in a mess of ink and antique pottery shards.

Kai sprang to his feet. "Are we under attack?"

Irene hastily closed the door. There was another crash from behind it. *Probably the desk lamp.* "No," she said. "No, quite the opposite. We're fine. Everything's fine. Things are completely under control."

"Indeed." Vale glanced meaningfully at the ruins of the inkpot, and raised an eyebrow.

"Well, they are for *me*. For us, rather." Just this once, she'd decided that her needs, and the needs of her apprentice and colleagues, were going to have equal weight with those of the Library—or more precisely, the Librarians in authority over her. "I—we—have full permission to return to your world, Vale, and to resume my duties, with Catherine as my apprentice."

Catherine smirked. "Did you blackmail them?"

"I'm shocked that you think I'd do any such thing," Irene answered. "Especially when presenting the truth was quite enough to settle the situation. But we should probably be on our way—"

The sound of raised voices filtered through the closed door behind her. While the exact language in question couldn't be identified, the words were quite clearly expletives.

Kai offered Irene his arm. "You can explain to us while we walk. I take it we aren't being offered a transfer shift this time?"

"No, and I'd rather not go back in there and ask."

Once they were safely out of the vicinity of the debriefing room, and on their way toward the exit to Vale's world, Irene decided she could explain. "The problem is the lack of physical proof. Between the four of us, we have a complete and coherent narrative of what took place—but we can't produce any *evidence*. I'm sure you can sympathize, Vale."

"The situation is not unknown," Vale admitted. "What did they suggest? That we were all hallucinating?"

"That was the main theory they had, yes. At least they knew better than to suggest outright that we were lying." The oak-walled corridor was wide enough that they could all four walk abreast. "I attested to my entire story *in the Language*. That put them in a difficult situation, since I couldn't be lying in that. So they proposed that Alberich had somehow trapped us all inside some sort of mutual nightmare and we'd wandered into the Library while we were off our heads, and injured ourselves in the process."

"I can see why they'd like that theory," Catherine commented. "It means that nobody's really at fault—apart from us for being careless."

Irene nodded. "However, there are a number of . . . oddities, shall we say? Certain Librarians have complete memory lapses, like Melusine, from when they were taken over by the founders. Others can't remember why they took certain actions. Quite major actions, in some cases—involving politics which they wouldn't have normally engaged in, and are now going to have to back away from. The whole blow-up-the-treaty-world-with-Alberich-on-it thing *wasn't* something the Library planned or actioned. They couldn't have written a peace treaty with him in the Language which then broke their own word." She thought about that sentence, and decided it wasn't worth trying to clarify the grammar. "You know what I mean. Then there's the fact that the Egyptian version of the Library's founding is a document here in the Library—and Lord Silver can bear witness to Aunt Isra's story if we call him in and ask him."

"Is my uncle a security risk?" Catherine asked, suddenly concerned.

"No," Irene reassured her. "The general agreement was that any threat to him might draw attention to the whole situation. Better to let sleeping dogs lie."

"And are *we* a security risk?" Vale asked. "It strikes me, Winters, that if the senior Librarians believe your story, they must be significantly concerned about being held to account for the actions of the founders. What about the worlds that have disappeared?"

Irene felt very tired. "It feels wrong to talk about them so casually. The founders destroyed them as though they were sacrificing pawns on a chessboard—and we can't do anything about it. Can't bring them back. Can't avenge them. The best we can do is what we did: make sure it doesn't happen again."

"Vale's right about the political implications, though," Kai said. "What's happening there?"

"I think," Irene said slowly, "that if you don't mind, I'll let that wait until we're back at our lodgings. It won't be long."

Perhaps the founders were gone, the last echoes of their memories or ghosts expunged from the Library—but it would be a while before Irene was entirely secure here, or before she stopped looking over her shoulder for shadows.

Nobody had blown up their lodgings in their absence. The worst that could be said was that quantities of mail had arrived. Irene began to sort through it at the study desk while Kai and Vale took advantage of the armchairs.

"Do I make tea or coffee?" Catherine asked resignedly. "Or do I pour everyone brandy?"

"You can sit down and listen to the rest of what I've got to tell you. It affects you as well." Irene flicked the letters into piles. "Advertisement, advertisement, bill, bill, personal letter for you, Kai . . ." She flicked it across to him. "Bill, tax demand, catalog, letter from Sterrington."

"Has she anything important to say?" Vale asked. Kai had ripped his letter open and was staring at the contents with a rather bemused expression.

"She refuses to take any responsibility for having lost track of Catherine, rather hopes it's our fault, and would like full details of what's happening." Irene put the letter down. "Alas, what she's going to get is the Library-agreed expurgated version."

"Which is?" Kai enquired, putting his letter down.

"What Vale said earlier is absolutely true. If the Library was connected with the worlds that have disappeared, it would be in a very awkward position. Excuses like 'our founders did it and then disappeared' tend not to work in politically vigorous situations. Actually, they tend not to work in any situation, but you take my point. There is a convenient scapegoat out there, though, who's currently unable to make any excuses."

Irene was never going to be entirely comfortable thinking about Alberich—or about the circumstances of her birth—but it was turning into the ache of an old bruise rather than the vicious pain of a current wound. He was gone. It made it that much easier to draw a line underneath the whole history and relegate it to the past. Of course it couldn't be quite *that* simple . . . but it was a place to start.

Vale pursed his lips disapprovingly. "Is this going to be a direct lie, then?"

"More a comment on the fact that he is definitely dead—witnessed by myself. Very definitely witnessed. Bradamant was responsible for taking him down." That had gone into the permanent records, at Irene's insistence. It was the only thing she could do for the other Librarian now. It wasn't enough—nothing could be enough—but it was something. "And if, once he is gone, the worlds stop vanishing—well, it's not the Library's fault if people assume a cause-and-effect relationship. His reputation will fill in a lot of the holes in the story."

"And what about us?" Catherine burst in, waving her hand at the rest of the group. She was perched on the edge of a footstool, hunching forward to keep her balance, her hair coming loose from its bun in a mass of curls. "Did you have to take the blame? Again?"

Irene found herself unable to meet anyone's eyes. "I'm afraid I may have been a little more aggressive than usual."

"You mean you threatened them," Catherine said happily. "I wish I'd been there to see it."

"It was a lot easier in the absence of witnesses," Irene said drily. "In our little discussion—which was *very definitely* off the record—I agreed that maybe it had all been a hallucination caused by Alberich, in which case we'd done our job and needed to get back to our regular positions with no further hindrances or penalties. Of any sort. Nice and straightforward."

"And if it hadn't been a hallucination?" Kai asked. He was visibly enjoying this.

"Well, in that case, all sorts of questions might need to be asked, and information might get out all over the place. Just to other Librarians to start with—but we all know how people talk. Even if nobody mentioned the vanishing worlds or connected it with the founding trio, it would mean a lot of people taking an interest in the Library. They might even try researching its history themselves; and when you have a thousand interested researchers, the odds of something damaging being found get dangerously high."

Vale leaned forward, his eyes intent. "But what about the genuine truth?"

"A full recording of my testimony has gone into the Library archives and will be preserved there. Melusine promised me that." Irene felt no urge to call the other Librarian *mother*: it wasn't something that either of them wanted. They had a good professional relationship, and that would be enough. Irene knew who her *real* mother and father were—the ones who'd raised her and who loved her. "In case future events make it . . . relevant."

"That seems reasonable." Vale relaxed back into his chair again, finally comfortable.

"Don't tell me you haven't suppressed the facts yourself in previous cases," Kai said.

"Oh, I have. I admit it. Sometimes a greater justice is served by silence. But with Winters here as the only Librarian who knew the complete truth—"

"There are the other ones she was telling earlier," Catherine put in.

"The only one who was interested in *preserving* the complete truth, then. We've had enough proof in the last few days that history shouldn't be lost."

"Assuming it was history." Kai's fingers toyed with the edge of his letter. "We had multiple different versions of the story, and even the founders seemed uncertain of the truth. Which was the real one?"

"Self-interest and power," Catherine said promptly. "Maybe enlightened self-interest, but that's still self-interest. They weren't altruists."

"Weren't they?" Vale questioned. "Self-interest is limited in what it's prepared to sacrifice. We saw quite clearly that they'd given up some of their essential nature to create the Library and stabilize the worlds. If their intentions had been solely to take power, they could have done that long ago."

"I'm biased," Kai said. "I believe my grandfather was acting for what he saw as the best—but I would never want to believe anything less of him. Irene, would you give a casting vote?"

"I think we'll never know," Irene said slowly, "and it'll have to go down in the records as undefined. But I'd like to *believe* that they were trying to do the right thing: that their sacrifice was greater than their self-interest."

She decided to change the subject. This next bit was going to be painful. "Kai, I know that you formally resigned your position as treaty representative, but—"

"He what?" Catherine gasped.

Irene stared at her until she subsided, then turned back to Kai. "How long do you think you have before they send someone else? I've given the Library warning that I may be resigning my position as well. That was partly why the inkpot. They weren't happy."

Kai's expression slowly blossomed into a smirk. "Actually, I may not have to do that. This letter . . ." He held it up. "It's from Shan Yuan."

Irene would have expected that to mean the worst, but it didn't fit with Kai's smile. "What has he written?"

"Oh, he said that it's possible he *may* have misjudged certain aspects of our relationship. He's been talking with our lord father— really talking—and I think it's changed his perspective a bit. He wants more information about what happened in Helsinki, but for the moment he's willing to put aside any claims on my position. He says that he's prepared to leave it be for, say, oh, the next few decades."

Irene's eyes widened. The span of a few decades was very little time to a dragon—but it might be all the time she and Kai would need. She could also see the possible danger. "What are you going to tell him about events?"

"I'll tell him and my lord father together." Kai gave her a very direct look. "I think that my lord father will agree with you and the Library that this information should be suitably buried."

And the fact that I and the Library know all about the dragon grandfather should be sufficient blackmail material to ensure that Kai isn't reassigned to Siberia somewhere and forgotten about for the next few centuries—or worse. Irene nodded, relieved.

"Well, I'm certainly not telling my uncle," Catherine said. "He wouldn't want to know, anyhow. It'd be too dangerous. He doesn't play in those circles."

Irene finally began to relax. They *were* going to get out of this in one piece—and still together. "Then I'm still treaty representative," she said, "and you're still my apprentice, Catherine. Though I suspect there will be a downturn in political activity. Which suits me. My business is books."

"And their acquisition," Vale added blandly.

"Oh, indeed. But first of all, their reading. I have those books my parents gave me which I haven't even *touched* yet. There are books in this house which I've been collecting for months and never had time to look at. I'm going to be doing some reprioritizing there. A Librarian who doesn't read her books isn't getting to grips with her job."

She rose to her feet and walked across to Kai, offering him her hand to rise. "And if you can wait a little while before contacting Shan Yuan, I have a suggestion—for all of us."

"Is that so?" Vale unfolded from his chair. "You have a case for me?"

"Not this time." She squeezed Kai's hand as he stood, exchanging smiles. There would be time for them to talk in private later, but they'd already said everything that they needed, back in the Library half a day ago. She knew he was there. She *had* him—and he had her.

"Bookshop?" Catherine said hopefully.

"Not that either." Irene could almost feel the world restarting around them with a new rhythm and tempo, clicking forward from spring toward summer. There were new possibilities everywhere, and she was going to look for them—and take advantage of them. "I have books to read. I have people to talk to. But first of all—I'd like to take you all out for lunch."

"Lead on," Kai said and smiled at her.

ACKNOWLEDGMENTS

As Sherlock Holmes remarked, when one has eliminated the impossible, whatever remains, however improbable, must be the truth. I will therefore note that it's not *impossible* that I've managed to write eight novels—it just seems highly improbable from the perspective of ten years ago. I'd like to hope I'll be saying something along these lines in another ten years' time . . . but with higher numbers.

For now, however, I would like to thank a lot of people for all their help, their support, their professionalism, their friendship, and everything they've done which turned this book from imagination to reality. My agent, Lucienne Diver; my editors, Bella Pagan and Jessica Wade; all the people at Pan Macmillan and Penguin Random House, Jessica Mangicaro, Alexis Nixon, Charlotte Wright, Georgia Summers, and everyone else; my beta-readers, Beth, Jeanne, Phyllis, Anne, Sharon, and others; and my coworkers who've so often put up with me explaining plot points over this last year, Sarah, Maureen, Naheeda, Hazel, and the rest. Thank you.

And to all the friends who've supported and encouraged me— thank you very much indeed.

It would be inaccurate to say that the story in this book was fully imagined and planned out eight books ago, and that I've been proceeding inexorably toward my intended destination with all the unstoppable might of a runaway Orient Express. Nice, but inaccurate. (I'm very vulnerable to "having a better idea" mid-writing.) However, elements in this book were planned from the beginning, and I hope that people who've been following from earlier episodes in Irene's turbulent career will find that some ongoing plot threads have come to conclusions.

Is this book the end of Irene and company? No. I think of it more as an end-of-season point; some plot threads are tied off, some characters are unlikely to appear again, and a reader can stop at the end and feel reasonably satisfied that the universe is in one piece—even if it's likely to need saving again tomorrow. I do have more ideas concerning Irene, and about the Library and its other inhabitants, and at some point they may get written. My next project is in a completely different area (involving vampires and the Scarlet Pimpernel and a hapless maidservant who'd rather be doing embroidery), but it's good to feel that I can come back to this universe later, and that there will be more stories to write, and people who will enjoy reading them.

Stories are like that. They'll wait for you until you can come back to them.

ABOUT THE AUTHOR

Genevieve Cogman is a freelance author who has written for several role-playing game companies. She currently works for the National Health Service in England as a clinical classifications specialist. She is the author of *The Invisible Library, The Masked City, The Burning Page, The Lost Plot, The Mortal Word, The Secret Chapter,* and *The Dark Archive.*